James H. Graff, George A. Lawrence

Maurice Dering

The quadrilateral - a novel

James H. Graff, George A. Lawrence

Maurice Dering
The quadrilateral - a novel

ISBN/EAN: 9783337349585

Printed in Europe, USA, Canada, Australia, Japan

Cover: Foto ©Andreas Hilbeck / pixelio.de

More available books at **www.hansebooks.com**

OR,

THE QUADRILATERAL.

A Novel.

BY

THE AUTHOR OF 'GUY LIVINGSTONE.'

New Edition.

LONDON:

TINSLEY BROTHERS, 18, CATHERINE ST., STRAND.

1869.

[The right of Translation is reserved.]

CONTENTS.

CONTENTS.

MAURICE DERING;

OR,

THE QUADRILATERAL.

CHAPTER I.

A FOUNDATION STONE.

At that shivered granite cross we seem to touch the point, where the collar-strain that has lasted for a long league shall cease. Our sturdy little team know it too, for they break of their own accord from the stubborn slouching jog that no yells or oaths could quicken, into a brisk imitation of a trot; a sharp swing round the hill-shoulder, and a couple of steep descents down which the diligence staggers, rolling like a ship with over-much deck-load, bring us right into the dreary, gray bourg of Broons, where we, who travel eastward from St Brieuc, must make our mid-day halt.

It is a real Finisterre day; glaring, yet gusty withal. No quiet outside under the swirling sign-bush, where ghastly beggars gather—clamorous or monotonously mournful; where half-a-dozen horse-keepers of both sexes are shouting intimidation at a refractory stallion, who is so evidently master of the position that he disdains to kick in earnest, and simply screams defiance. Not much of quiet in the

B

low murky *salle,* where a score of hungry diners have backed themselves against time for forty sous even, and seem to be winning all the way.

A dozen yards from the inn door there is the tiniest shop-of-all-trades that I ever remember to have seen ; just large enough to hold—besides its meek stock of wares— two ancient women, who sit there, I know, from dawn to twilight, prosing steadily on after the wont of Bretonne *commères;* softening down their pointless scandals with *Faut pas mentir,* and *Que sais-je, moi?* Emphasizing every other sentence with a nod of those stiff snowy coifs, that would make worse and grimier faces look honest and cozy and clean. Though it is so very diminutive, the nest of that pair of homely old owls looks comfortably quiet under the broad over-hang of tilework. I bethink me that my fusee box is match-less, and that I may as well, here, plenish it for the road; so entering I begin to chatter with the least rugged of the twain about the weather and the crops. These conversations are not dangerously interesting; you don't understand above one word in three, and what you do understand is not strictly remunerative; but the Breton means well, and departs with a placid consciousness of having amused or instructed the stranger.

While the dame was talking, I chanced to glance at a shelf whereon, evidently, the family ornaments were concentrated—a few coarse sea-shells, one or two candlesticks of polished brass, a savage saint in a black frame, and a little tinsel shrine. In the midst of these lay the fragment of a book, frayed, from constant use in horny hands, till the letter-press in places merged imperceptibly into the dusty margins,—dwindled from a fair volume into an emaciated pamphlet—a very waif and stray of literature.

The title-page had vanished long ago, but my first glance fell on a sentence—familiar, though I read it last a dozen years ago. I knew that I held in my hand the reliques of a romance once of world-wide fame, and not quite forgotten yet—the story of The Three Musketeers.

As an unit of a reading multitude, I claim a right to be amused or interested in any book whatsoever, provided it contains nothing subversive of morality or of common conventionalities; maintaining, that a critic is no more justified in quarrelling with my taste, or in insisting on the direction thereof, than he would be in dictating to the Object of my affections the fashion of her wreath at the next entertainment that she may adorn. So I am not ashamed to confess the fascination that held me when I first read that strange story.

Of course that it is wildly melodramatic, and full of 'situations' from end to end, serpentining always along the frontier line of the sublime and the ridiculous; the very title is a misnomer, and the slender thread of probability is often strained even to breaking; but, throughout, there are redeeming touches of natural feeling, and flashes, not unfrequent, of honest humour. The audacity of fancy has something refreshing in it; when the literary Briareus wrote, or helped to write, that book, I think his fluent imagination was at the turn of high-tide.

After all, Porthos is as good a sketch of the brave, boastful, blundering Plunger, as one could easily find. The criminal blonde is rather in fashion just now; but all the possible copies of Milady stand out faint and dim beside that terrible little creature,—with her slender murderous hands, and bright cruel eyes—her face always pure and virginal, though to the rosy lips she was steeped in all sin and shame—savouring so keenly all pleasures and passions, yet ever tremulously conscious of the evil Lily-flower graven on her soft shoulder long ago.

'It was a very beautiful history,' the old woman said. 'She had heard it read many times; and her nephew, who was *fourrier* in the 8th Chasseurs, swore it was all true.'

As the diligence lumbered on over the dull rolling champaign, I fell into a tobacco-reverie; trying to realize the awe and admiration of that auditory, who probably never travelled ten leagues away from their birth-place in the dull gray town, as they heard how Athos drank, and D'Artagnan schemed, and Porthos fought, and Aramis loved. So, still musing on, I began to recollect and connect certain sayings and doings that I wist of—no matter how—years and years ago, till there was built up before my mind's eye the vague framework that will be filled when this story is done.

Then and there I proposed, when time should serve, to tell to such as cared to hear it, the story of four men, the eldest of whom might now scarcely have passed middle-age, who did in certain points furnish no inapt parallel to those famous Musketeers.

Now, about the virtues or vices of these men, there was nothing colossal or superhuman. Speaking, and thinking, and acting in the tame modern groove, they never made the destinies of kingdoms or the fate of stricken fields change front at their sword's point; neither did they dazzle all beholders with the *outrecuidance* of their drink, their debts, or their duels. No fixed or definite purpose bound them together, and certainly they had been constrained by no romantic impulse 'suddenly to swear an eternal friendship;' neither could their association be accounted for by any identity of interests, community of pursuits, or even special similarity of tastes: indeed, in each of the four characters there was marked distinctive difference.

But, fighting the battle of life each after his own fashion, they found themselves after a while—unconsciously perhaps—knit into a brotherhood-in-arms, and kept the implied compact unbroken to the very end; acting independently as it seemed, they never lost sight of their unshaken motto—One for all: all for one.

You who read will judge, how far my parallel holds good.

CHAPTER II.

THE TABAKO PARLEMENT.

IF I wished thoroughly to confute or confuse one of these ingenious Gauls, who ceaso not to make mouths at our insular rigidity and reticence, I think I would induct the caricaturist into a well-organized smoking-room in any pleasant country house, about the hour of midnight. Then and there, placing my foreigner in the midst, I would say—

'Monsieur my friend, much of your trenchant satire is, unhappily, too true. We *do* beat our *blanche meess* occasionally with a thick staff. Those radiant creatures who left us a while ago, are always liable to sale in the public mart, with a cord of silk and gold about their swan-necks. Those loungers around you, in broidered raiment of many colours, *do* gorge themselves daily with the bleeding bit-

stek deluged with portare-beer—ask rather M. Victor Cas-
serole, our *chef* and your compatriot. I may not deny that
most of our notables—especially our Prime Ministers—die
early and miserably of the fatal spleen. Through the dull
winter months, every other leafless tree in our parks bears
the bitter fruit of a self-suspended aristocrat. All this—
casting upon my head these white ashes—I confess and
concede. But tarry here, I pray you, one short half-hour;
and then say if, in his own saturnine way, Milord is not
capable of a *causerie*.'

Truly the candid physiologist might be induced to tone
down his grotesque ideal; even as Jules Janin, the miso-
britannic, was somewhat moved to recantation, when, in
the Exhibition year, he stood astonied before 'the celestial
beauty of the officers of the 1st Life Guards.'

But by a well-organized smoking-room, I do not mean
a dreary chamber of refuge, at the extreme end of a chilling corridor, wherein, arriving the first—

> Herald of a mighty band,
> And a glorious train ensuing,

you find some ghastly faded lithographs on the bare walls
—the weather staring in through uncurtained windows—
a fresh-lighted fire struggling sullenly into existence, with
a guilty consciousness that it ought to consume its own
smoke—and a dozen gaunt chairs, exiles like yourself, that
have grown hardened and rugged in their shame. You
can smoke, and drink too—more's the pity—but a *causerie*,
to such as are cast out in these dreary places, is absolutely
unattainable. To a widely-different haven may favouring
Fates conduct me and mine, when our day's work, or play,
is done. Let it be a room, to begin with—not a peni-
tential cell—bearing tokens of constant human habitation;

neither gorgeous in ornament, nor exquisite in luxury, but with comforts enough to satisfy all those honest epicureans who delight in tho low-backed chair; a chamber wherein light reading and easy writing might be transacted, not incongruously; a sanctuary, in fine, wherein, if her court were *very* select, the Queen of hearts might linger for a brief space—

Sweetening the cobblers with smiles, and firing Havannahs with glances,

without grave impeachment of her gracious dignity.

It might have puzzled an ingenious Sybarite to suggest an improvement on the *tabagie* at Marston Lisle. It was, indeed, about the most attractive apartment in a very pleasant house, and the favourite resort of Philip Gascoigne's intimates at all hours of tho twenty-four. The first glance at the interior gives you an insight into the owner's tastes and character.

Evidently not a sportsman's den. Not one of the many objects around savours of the saddle or the gun-room. Those slight riding-canes are suggestive of canters in the Row, of lounges through shadowy glades under bright summer weather—of anything, in fact, rather than rough resolute cross-country work: the firelocks gleaming on the crimson wall, forgot to be deadly ten generations ago, and now only testify to the cunning of the craftsmen who damasqued or mounted them with silver and ivory and pearl: those lustrous flies—baits tempting enough to beguile the wiliest of salmonidæ,—were wrought by a Hand that has been in practice since the Creation-day. That carved book-case, filled with the creamy vellum of rare Elzevirs, would not be out of place in any scholarly retreat. But what has the earnest student to do with all theso delicate knick-knacks —jewelled, enamelled, and golden,—that would beseem

Belinda's boudoir; or with cabinet-pictures that might have troubled the sanctity of St Anthony's musings? That recess, half shaded by velvet curtains, might hold the bust of doctor, or divine, or poet, at the least. Wise Pallas protect us! It enshrines Pradier's latest sin in marble—a languid, lissom Leda.

No wonder that Philip Gascoigne seemed so thoroughly at home there.

Of a nature rather frail than frivolous, he would enter keenly into every fresh pursuit, and abandon it, not so much from weariness or disgust as from a moral incapacity to persevere beyond a certain point in any one path— that of duty excepted; variable as a weather-glass in his fancies, in his affections he could be firm and true as steel; Bolingbroke was not more delicately luxurious in his tastes, nor Sidney purer from the earthly taint of a voluptuary; a ruffled rose-leaf troubled him sorely, but he was capable of real self-denial and self-sacrifice, though in this way he had rarely been tried. His nerve was indifferent and his moral courage uncertain, but a Berserk was not freer from mere physical fear.

Altogether, it was a very lovable, if not a very admirable character; few *dilettanti* get through their social duties with more credit to themselves and satisfaction to their friends, than did gentle Philip Gascoigne.

Though this sketch may not be vividly like, you would pick him out at a glance from his companions, on this the first occasion of your meeting.

A slight figure, with a feminine roundness of joint and delicacy of the extremities; a fair, pale face, with small regular features, tapering off rather weakly below; black wavy hair; and great dark eyes, whose habitual look is

rather dreamy and vague: altogether a remarkable reproduction of his favourite family portrait—the lovely little
Provençal Countess, whom Aylmer Gascoigne brought here
a century ago, and could not keep alive through the fourth
winter, though he would have drained his own heart's blood,
drop by drop, to have saved her. The husband never
knew, till the young wife lay a-dying, how great love for
him was ever battling against her pining for the sunny
South, till the struggle, and her innocent remorse, had
killed her.

A stronger contrast, in all externals, to Philip you could
hardly find than in the man who is sitting nearest to him
now.

The face was handsome, certainly, but with no striking
peculiarity of beauty or intellect—bold, straight-cut
features, with a hearty frank expression, perfectly clear of
coarseness, of a type very common near the northern border,
such as you may see represented by the score at any parade
of the Household cavalry ;—a face that right seldom belies
itself, when it promises the *mens sana in corpore sano*. It
kept faith here, at all events. The first time Maurice Dering looked with his bright brown eyes full into yours, and
clasped your palm with his long sinewy fingers, you felt
that all that was in the man, be it much or little, was
thoroughly genuine and real ; you knew that he would say
what he meant and act as he meant, without favour or fear ;
an ally that a friend in bitter need might rest against, as
though his back were set to a rock.

The face was right well matched by the figure. There
were the long sinewy limbs, whose gripe might convince
the most obstinate refuser that honesty was the best
policy, even with a big 'double' to the fore ; and the

straight muscular arms, apt alike to the sway of racket or sabre; and the lissom wrist, that might send thirty yards of line skimming away with never a breath to aid it, or make a foil curl viperishly round an antagonist's blade; and the square deep chest, in which the lungs might play at their pleasure, against the breast of never so steep a brae.

Nevertheless, there was nothing gigantesque or Homeric about Maurice Dering. He was simply a fair specimen of a well-bred, athletic Englishman, in hard condition all the year round; one who would hold his own gallantly, without aspiring to supremacy, in fray, or field, or feast. Friend nor enemy could say more or less of him than this; —he *looked* at least his character, right well, of soldier, sportsman, and gentleman.

The third member of the conclave was not so pleasant to look upon as his companions. Dimly, through the drifting smoke-rack, you discern the outline of a spare figure; a pallid passionless face, scarcely lighted up by cold pale-blue eyes; a high, narrow forehead, from which the scanty hair is fast receding; a strong, shapely chin; and thin compressed lips, more apt to sneer than smile. It is altogether rather a negative than a positive face, bearing no traces of discontent, much less of melancholy, and it is rather indifferent than weary; you would say that, if Paul Chetwynde has been spared bitter disappointment or serious sorrow, he has had short measure of life's enjoyments, or lacked the power of appreciating them aright.

He was born with the slow, stubborn, phlegmatic temperament, out of which most philosophers have been made; and the indolent contemplative mood had grown on him, till the springs of strong emotion, or active exertion, seemed rusted utterly. It might have fared better with him if he had been forced to work for his bread; but tho great House, of which he was an off-shoot,—magnificent in nepotism,—forced Church or State to provide for its cadets even to the third and fourth generation. Paul Chetwynde had scarcely emerged from legal infancy, when he was inducted into one of those downy official chairs that modern upholsterers have ceased to manufacture, whose occupants are never troubled for their signature till their quarter's salary is due; and there he had lounged ever since,—morally and socially the most thorough-paced of sinecurists.

He would have been puzzled to count the half of his acquaintance, but he might very easily have reckoned up his friends. He was not at all proud or partial in the selection of his society. So long as the drama amused or interested him, he seemed to care little whether the curtain drew up in a saloon or a garret—whether the stage-players were Belgravian or Bohemian; he would patronize any theatre as a spectator, utterly declining in anywise to identify himself with the management. He would take his fair share of conversation—pleasantly or cynically—as it might happen; but the most simple-minded egotist never tried, a second time, to interest him in their hopes or fears, or joys or sorrows. It was understood that Paul Chetwynde was on visiting terms with the world in general, and that the intimacy was to go no further.

So it came to pass that, of the thousands with whom he interchanged salutes in the course of a season, very few liked, fewer still loved him: on the other hand, not a few disliked him intensely. Society objects naturally to vivisection exercised upon itself, especially when the experiments are conducted solely for the instruction or entertainment of the operator. Chetwynde's name had never been coupled with that of any woman, alive or dead, for honour or for dishonour; in his own rank of life he was free from suspicion of the briefest *liaison;* if he erred anonymously, his nearest friends were ignorant of the sin ; as for serious 'intentions,' he had never been troubled to deny them.

It was no wonder if the ranks of his feminine foes were recruited daily. The haughty Sultana chafed, unconsciously, in presence of the insolent barbarian, on whom her imperial smiles and frowns alike fell harmless ; the Fair Circassian (priced in the marriage-market at 100,000 tomauns) had not heart or patience to exhibit her little attractions and accomplishments before a guest hardly polite enough to applaud her; the brazen black-eyed Almè felt discouraged and constrained before the impassible Effendi, from whom, when all her songs and dances were done, she could hope to extract no more substantial recompense than a quiet half-contemptuous smile. Perhaps among the chaperones Paul's bitterest enemies were ranged. It was impossible to say how intensely some manœuvring mothers, exemplary Christians and good-natured women in the main, hated and dreaded those cold keen eyes of his; how they got fidgety, and hot, and nervous, under an uneasy sense of detection ; striving, all the while, to wrap up their pet ' plants ' and plans, just as a Romagnese peasant shields her baby from the *jettatura.*

Yet the conscious matron disquieted herself in vain ; a faint speculative curiosity was the only motive for Chetwynde's apparent vigilance ; interference one way or the other, to aid or to thwart, was utterly out of his line ; though he would not help in laying the toils, he would not trouble himself to warn any 'stag of ten' going blindly to his doom. Nevertheless, it is possible that certain intended victims, meeting by chance one of his searching glances or cynical smiles, may have been roused in time to a sense of their danger; even as sound sleepers toss uneasily and awake at last with a start, if you gaze down in their faces long and steadily.

I have given more space to this sketch of Paul Chetwynde than to those of his companions; because, in his nature, the contradictions were far more subtle and hard to understand; indeed, he would have been sorely puzzled himself, at times, to define his own motives.

The marked difference in the characters of the three men displayed itself, even in such a trivial accident as the manner in which they severally consumed tobacco.

Under Maurice Dering's thick chestnut moustache rested easily one of those strong, firm, smooth cheroots, that look so thoroughly business-like, hard to ignite, harder still to extinguish, that will waste away steadily to the very end in any ordinary wind or weather; a weed to solace a half-hour of expectancy, while the beaters are 'getting round' in an interminable cover, or while the hounds are drawing, painfully, 200 acres of tangled woodland, to find that staunch forest-fox that has beat them thrice already, and will beat them again to-day The *papelito*, redolent of priceless Latakia, that Philip Gascoigne's slender fingers renew with such swift lissom dexterity, seems made for those delicate lips, womanlike in the softness of their outline. That wonderful pipe of Chetwynde's might have aided the meditations of Whately—a pipe that would strike terror into the soul of the stoutest Fox that ever was initiated into Burschenschaft, especially if filled lip-high with the strong seductive mixture, the secret of which only Paul and his purveyor knew—admirable, if only as a masterpiece of Viennese art—the bowl, a huge urn, held up in the arms of a *bayadère* reclining along a carved tree-stem, her long lithe limbs tinged, as the living models might be, with a tender golden-brown.

The longer you looked, the more clearly some trifling peculiarity of voice, or gesture, or manner, brought out the distinctive characteristics of the three—soldier, *dilettante*, and philosopher.

No one would have suspected Philip Gascoigne of purposeless indolence or want of energy, if they had seen him that night for the first time. Evidently, for once, he was thoroughly in earnest, and bent on carrying his point in the argument, which—in rather a one-sided way—had been sustained for nearly half-an-hour. It had risen on Dering's avowal that his name was down for exchange into one of the cavalry regiments serving in India.

Maurice made the confession with a certain amount of diffidence and hesitation ; and, throughout the controversy that ensued, an odd conscious half-contrite look, such as few had ever seen there, clouded his frank, bold face—the look of a man who, having done rather a foolish thing which he is bound to abide by, finds himself, morally, so tied up, as to be unable even to explain his reasons. He was so utterly unpractised at evasion or excuse, even with strangers, that it was no wonder if he soon became miserably entangled in his talk, when, for the first time since their intimacy began, he seemed bound to exercise some reticence towards his friends.

He had hinted at first that there might be motives, prudent and pecuniary, for the step he had resolved on ; but when he saw the puzzled expression of Gascoigne's great black eyes change into reproach—the impatient shrug of Chetwynde's shoulders was equally significant in its way— he broke down in the middle of rather an involved sentence about—'York being very expensive quarters—hunting five days a-week all last winter—bad luck with horses,' &c.

'No; it isn't that. I swear, it's too bad to abuse the fine old city, that was so kind to us—to say nothing of the county. I wish I had hunted six days a-week instead of five; and The Moor is worth twice what I gave for him, even if he don't win the Cup. Phil, you needn't look so sad about it. Of course, I owe a little; but if I'd been really hard up, I would have told you before I told the Jews. But I think I ought to see India: the regiment's so low down on the roster, that it may not go out for the next ten years. One ought to have a year or two, at all events, where there's a chance of real work, if one really means soldiering. I've got my troop so lately, too, that I shall hardly lose a step. It's the right thing to do, I'm certain; though I know you wouldn't like it.'

'You did guess that?' Gascoigne retorted, with a very unusual inflection of sarcasm in his gentle voice. 'I wonder you troubled yourself to think about it at all. I don't a bit believe in all that military conscientiousness. But, if it's all as you say, you need not have made arrangements till you had done your duty—yes; I say, your duty,—by Geoff, and me. It was only yesterday, that Georgie was telling me, to be sure and book you for best-man directly you came here, unless his Reverence had been beforehand with us. There, you needn't flush so; it's no great compliment. I suppose she was afraid I should choose that dreary disagreeable old Paul—*pas si bête*—who sits there, smoking like a donkey-engine, never helping me out with a word.'

'Don't be fractious, Philip,' Chetwynde said ; 'and do remember that abuse is no argument, especially when it's levelled at an unoffending innocent like me. How could I help you ? I don't know which to admire most ; your elo-quence—a little querulous, perhaps, but *very* moving—or Maurice's newborn sense of duty. Bless you, *mon sabreur ;* I wish I could paint. There should be a pendant to the Awakening Conscience. But I do hope you won't leave this Paradise, where there's so much marrying and giving in marriage, before the Feast of Roses. Miss Verschoyle is thoroughly right. I've no sort of business to stand in the foreground of her wedding-picture : it would be a sin to spoil the blaze of bridesmaids. The other will be a much quieter affair. I suppose Geoff will charter me, and Ida won't object to my dreariness : she's used to it, you see.'

'How absurd you are, Paul,' Gascoigne said peevishly ; 'taking everything *au sérieux*. You'll be fancying next that Georgie dislikes you. Now, I know——'

'Don't flurry or worry yourself,' Chetwynde broke in, 'I choose not to fancy anything of the sort. It's a simple question of decoration. Miss Verschoyle has as much right to exercise her taste here, as in the setting of her jewels. I don't believe she has the shade of an unkind feeling towards me, or towards any one else in the world, for that matter.'

'She is a dear good little thing,'—Gascoigne assented, flushing up with pride and pleasure,—'I can't think how any one can have the heart to disappoint her. The most provoking part of it, after all, is, that I can't guess at the real reasons for this Indian fancy. It is unlike Maurice to make mysteries unnecessarily.'

'Don't you see that you are begging the question, you simple Philip? The necessity for his silence, is the very point that must puzzle you and me. If Maurice is in any scrape that won't bear talking about, I'm as sorry for it as you can be; but I'm not inclined to be plaintive, because he chooses to bear his burden alone. His shoulders are broader than ours, remember. Besides, there must be a limit to confidences somewhere. *Que diable*, we are men and not school-girls.'

In spite of Chetwynde's special pleading, there was more of the judge than the advocate in the keen cold glance that rested steadily, though not unkindly, on Dering's troubled face. Nevertheless, Maurice met it fairly; his mind had evidently been made up during that slight diversion of the talk; and, when he spoke, there was the old ring of truth in his firm decided tones.

'It serves one right for making excuses,' he said, with a short half-laugh. 'Paul, I do believe you fancied, a moment ago, that I had done something to be ashamed of. You villanous cynic! I wonder what you will doubt next. The fact is, I'm not in any scrape at present; and—I don't mean to be—that's why I'm down for India. I hate making mysteries; but I simply *can't* tell you any more now: some day, I dare say, you'll know all about it; till then you must take me on trust. And, Philip, I'll promise you not to start till I have seen you fairly wedded, unless the exchange absolutely obliges me. Won't you be satisfied with that?'

A harder heart and a sulkier temper than Gascoigne's might have melted and softened before the kind eagerness

of the honest handsome face : he wrung Dering's hand
with more strength that you would have thought lay in the
slender white fingers.

'I trust you to the very end, Maurice, through all and
in spite of all. I'm sorry, of course, that you must go ; but
I'm not childish enough to press for more than you promise. I'm certain you're right; and Paul thinks so too :
he never doubted you any more than I did; it's only a way
he has with his eyes.'

'Quite so,' Chetwynde said, shaking out the last ashes
of his pipe with a slight yawn. 'You put it very prettily,
Philip. There's an acidulation in your abuse which makes
it rather pleasant than otherwise. Now I'm going to bed ;
not that I'm sleepy, but I want to set you a good example :
you must train gradually into keeping better hours before
your bachelor-hood is done. I do believe, now, you consider natural sleep the very last resource of an intellectual
mind. *Ite : missa est.*'

And so, with few more words of no moment, the conclave
was broken up. It is certain that Paul Chetwynde spoke
truth when he said he was not sleepily inclined. Long
after his comrades had passed into dreamland, he sat in his
own room—his brow bent in grave perplexity—gazing
moodily into the embers of his decaying fire ; as if hoping
that some figures of the faint future might reveal themselves there.

CHAPTER III.

AUNTS AND COUSINS.

A CERTAIN out-look from the manor-house of Marston Lisle was one of the country wonders. The building was niched on a shelf—half artificial—of an abrupt shoulder of the chalk downs, just where the vale of the Lene opened out to its broadest; at one especial point the ground fell away so suddenly, that there was scarcely level space under the walls for a terrace and a heavy stone balustrade. Just at this angle jutted forth the huge eastern oriel of the dining-room; there was nothing in the foreground to break the view : so that, from thence, the eye could range right over the glistening river-reach below, and the soft green meadow-lands beyond it, into the thick beech-woods of the opposite hill-range, two long leagues away. A very fair landscape—with the peculiar charm of being thoroughly *homely* and English in the minutest detail.

In that same oriel, early in the afternoon following the night you have heard of, all the Marston party, with the exception of Paul Chetwynde, were gathered; lounging and chattering, as people will do, when luncheon is just over, and no important expedition is on hand. Two of the group you know already; two, at least, of the others deserve to be sketched, before we meddle further with their fortunes. Place and time considered—Gascoigne's bride-elect has a right to come first in order.

It is rather difficult, now-a-days, to define exactly what attributes are indispensable to the attainment of a place in the world's unprinted Book of Beauty.

There are some, of course, who took rank there, from
the first, by virtue of statuesque proportion of figure and
face, whose absolute perfection we cannot cavil at in our
bitterest moments of boredom; for the fairy tale comes
true in real life much too often for our comfort, and the
ugly princesses monopolize the family-wit remorselessly;
so that our adoration of the Fair Sister becomes more and
more distantly respectful, till we are content to exchange
glances through powerful lorgnons, and to admire, with
the width of an opera-house between.

Others, again,—fortunately they are few,—with scant
outward and visible claims to such distinction, seem to win
and hold their place by fear instead of favour. These are
the redoubtable *mauvaises langues;* the social gladiators
who are never out of training; whose weapons no novice
may hope to baffle or escape—from constant practice they
wield them so deftly—the sword of sarcasm, the trident of
ridicule, and the net of inuendo. We do not love them,
certainly; we may flatter ourselves that we do not fear
them: but, when brought in contact with such, we bear
ourselves discreetly and warily; rather careful to avoid
offence, and not too keen to remark a glove lying near our
feet; even as a stout legionary, bearing scars of many
wars on his breast, may have given the wall to a Mirmillo,
without sense of shame. So the usurpers sit in high places
without let or hindrance : nay—when they are plying their
vocation, and their opponent is writhing under a bitter
thrust sent home over the tardy guard—if we do not
openly applaud we look on complacently with folded hands,
and thumbs, perchance, downwards turned.

To neither of these classes of pseudo beauties did Miss
Verschoyle belong. In all her nature there was not a

grain of gall; and if she had felt vieious for once in her
life, she must have sulked in enforced silence: a prettily
pettish repartee about exhausted her powers of malice; if
she had invented or chanced upon a sarcasm, it would have
lost all sting in passing through those rosy pouting lips.
Her features, too, were anything but faultless; taken
singly and severally, perhaps not one came up to a moderate standard of perfeetion; but no ordinary mortal was
equal to the analysis, and the critic was yet in the future
who could quarrel seriously with the small face, set so be-
comingly in bands of gold-brown hair—with the tender
pink-pearl tint of the smooth round cheeks—with the long
lustrous eyes (no one knew if they were blue or gray) that
would change, swiftly as a kaleidoscope, as they became
pleading, or grateful, or loving, or piteous, or anything
you please—but severe.

Meeting or speaking with her, for the first time, you
were at once aware of a pleasant softness and harmony,
physical as well as moral; indeed, there were no more
angles about Georgie's character, than about her delicate
figure and limbs, moulded like a sculptor's dream. Add
to this, a half-shy, confidential manner—not the less subtle
because it seemed so perfectly natural—that always made
her companion for the moment fancy that there existed
some secret sympathy between them, of which the world
in general was not worthy; a smile more often conscious
than simply mirthful; and a voice perilously musical in its
low intonations. It is no wonder that Miss Verschoyle
became a celebrity very early in her presentation-season;
and had reigned ever since, with credit to herself and
satisfaction to her friends, in her own little principality.

Many knights, stalwart or skilful, and many barons of

name and fame, had broken figurative lances in her honour, since her first Drawing-room; and many strong, stubborn hearts had quivered and thrilled as she fluttered round them, before she folded her wings at last, and seemed to settle down contentedly on the loving, trustful breast of Philip Gascoigne. There must be love on both sides, people said; for, though her betrothed was wealthy and well-born, Georgie might have chosen from a dozen more brilliant alliances.

The truth must be told sooner or later. She was a coquette to the core of her nature, and had never let a fair chance of flirtation slip, from her cradle upwards until now. The exquisite arts and *finesses* of attraction, that other women acquire slowly and painfully by imitation or ex-perience, Georgie practised instinctively in early girlhood. She had made angry passion rise in many boyish breasts, and drawn tears of envy from many of her small rivals, long before she entered on her teens.

Indeed there was still something childish in her coquetry. She had a legion of friends of her own sex, and liked or loved them, as the case might be, honestly and unaffect-edly: nevertheless, she could never resist the temptation of detaching the admirer-in-chief of her most cherished in-timate; and triumphed, without a shade of remorse, in his temporary infidelity. It was admiration—not devotion—that she sought to engross; when a position became em-barrassingly earnest, she could extricate herself with a tact truly marvellous, without seriously offending the pursuer. Just at the critical moment, when victory seemed very near, the aspirant found himself standing alone, with empty outstretched arms, puzzled and baffled, as Ixion when he would have clasped his cloud-love.

With so many little sins on her sunny head, it was very remarkable that Georgie should have incurred so few animosities. So far she had been perilously fortunate;—'for all men (and women) spake well of her;' if she had any covert enemies, they kept their own counsel, and bided their time.

It would have been hard to show a prettier contrast to Miss Verschoyle than was found in her trusty and well-beloved friend and cousin, Ida Carew. Those two had been almost inseparable since their childhood, and Georgie's promotion had been somewhat ante-dated, that the pair might be presented at the same Drawing-room.

The contrast was not a foil; indeed, an impartial spectator might have given the palm of beauty, pure and simple, to Ida, as she sate there in the angle of the oriel —her face half turned aside, so that the small regular features came out in relief against the light—her clear dark eyes gazing out earnestly on the fair landscape, of which they saw not one detail. You could scarcely dream of anything more perfect, on such a very tiny scale : there was nothing *mesquin* or frail about her shapely, rounded figure, where every contour was admirably developed in miniature.

Those of the Fenella type usually have something elfish about them, and are apt to run wild, at least in their caprices. Miss Carew's nature, as far as the world knew, was provokingly quiet and serene; her manner was scarcely cold or sedate, but it was certainly indifferent. She was cleverer than her cousin, and ten times better read, and could talk well on most subjects when she chose to exert herself; but none seemed to interest her deeply, and she had no especially favourite pursuit. Many men,

attracted by the delicate figure and handsome thorough-
bred face, had tried their uttermost to inveigle Ida into a
flirtation; but very few were courageous or conceited
enough to persevere. Even compassion could not keep the
listless, absent look out of her wearying eyes, that seemed
to grow less brilliant as the *persiflage* proceeded; aversion
itself would have been easier to overcome than that courteous supine endurance. So, up to the hour of her engagement, Miss Carew was supposed to have kept herself fancy-
free. Geoffrey Luttrell had wooed her—no one knew why
—after his own bluff, straightforward fashion; and had
won her, no one—perhaps not even himself—knew how.

It is better not to waste time now in analyzing Ida:
some of her oldest friends would have told you that there
was no coil in her character worth the unravelling.

That comfortable matron, admirably dressed in the
quietest taste, sitting somewhat apart from the group,
seldom lifting her eyes from the chronic crochet, which is
part and parcel of her ante-prandial existence, is Mrs
Carew, mother of Ida, and acting chaperon to Georgie
Verschoyle, whose natural protectress is a helpless invalid,
flying southward yearly, a little before the swallows.
Though she seems so intent on her swift stitches, it is
evident that no word of the talk going on around escapes
her;—not that she is the least interested therein, but the
habit of covert attention has become natural and involuntary. There is a strong family likeness between mother
and daughter; though the former's features and figure
must have been cast originally in a larger and coarser
mould. Both have the same dark, bright, rather cold
eyes; but Ida's glances, even when most keenly searching,
are not cunning, like the elder dame's.

Mrs Carew's social work has been all against the collar, till now. In early life she had to fight the hard battle of the well-born poor. When money matters looked somewhat brighter, soon after her long widowhood began, she was delivered over, bound hand and foot, to the mercies of an awful trustee—no other than Paul Chetwynde's father —Dean of Torrcaster, and sternest of ascetics—before whose name Exeter Hall bowed itself in fearful reverence, and light-minded minor canons trembled. Conciliation and submission were the poor lady's only chance in those days of terror; she is emancipated now, for with Ida's legal infancy the Dean's guardianship ceased. But it will be long before she forgets the heart-sinking that overcame her, as, on each of the annual visits that she dared not omit, her carriage rolled under the dark echoing archway of the Close; and she knew that, for three long months, only letters from worldly sympathizers without could console her for involuntary austerities, disciplined dissimulation, and hourly enforcement to instancy in prayer.

The trouble and subjection lasted so long that it is not strange if, now in her late resting-time, the old nervous anxiety and timid craft hang about her still. If Mrs Carew had once held her head fairly above-water, she might have turned out a worthy, cleverish, managing woman; as it is, she will remain to her life's end a purposeless schemer—a sycophant, with nothing to gain. If anything could have disturbed Ida's haughty self-possession, it would have been the evidences of these maternal failings; but she ignored, or tolerated, or palliated them, with admirable tact and patience. Perchance she remembered on *whom* had fallen all the burden and heat of the long labouring day, and so, in justice,—if not in compassion,—was fain to forbear.

The sketch of Aunt Nellie ought not to have been left to the last. If in that room there were fairer faces, surely there is not one pleasanter to look upon than hers, as she lingers still in her place at the deserted table, coaxing and feeding her pet lory. Even Time could not help laying his hand lightly and lovingly on the gentle brow—smooth and white as an infant's still, though hard on half a century has fled since Nellie Gascoigne was 'chrissom child.' Her face must always have been lovely in its delicacy, without a claim to real beauty Perhaps it was never more attractive than at this moment; framed in the quiet cap, artistic in its modesty, and in the smooth bands of the soft abundant hair that changed before its time, and glistens now, silvery-gray.

In the lives of most old maids, I suppose, there is a secret; not a horrible skeleton, mouldering slowly away in the closet, that must be opened daily; but—let us hope in charity—a relic all the more precious and fondly cherished because there is a tinge of sadness—perhaps of deep-rooted sorrow—in the memories to which it is bound; a relic more powerful to drive away sullen lethargy and hot heart-fever than any that has been blessed in the Vatican; a relic, the sight and touch of which keeps life in hope rather than in despair,—one that a tender, patient Christian woman may hold close to her breast, without fear or shame, even when heaven's dawn is breaking, and the meeting is very near.

Of all the tears shed on this earth of ours, not the bitterest, surely, are those sprinkled on Dead Sea roses till the sere leaves bloom again.

Such a secret, Miss Gascoigne's gentle heart guarded in

its chamber beyond the veil. But the story was never told, even to Philip, the centre of all her hopes and fears —Philip, who had scarcely missed his dead mother, since he sobbed himself to sleep in Aunt Nellie's arms, an hour after he was left an orphan.

Exemplary matrons, immaculate in all respects as Cæsar's ideal wife, will, we are told, occasionally, over the midnight hearth, interest the trustiest of their cronies in certain romantic reminiscences, relating—not to the respected Head of the family, whose fitful snorings from the drawing-room below play quaint accompaniment to the whispered tale; but rather to a tomb toward which the good lady will travel back in thought at rare intervals, to hang a tiny wreath of *immortelles* there; though her lot has fallen in pleasant places since the burial-day, and she would thrust back the faintest repining not less severely than any other temptation to ungrateful sin. The memorial wealth of widowhood is proverbially vast, and lavishly dispensed. But the mature maiden—as I like to fancy her—is more shy and reticent in her confidences : many such, frank and open as the day on all other subjects, have lived and died, leaving their nearest and dearest in ignorance and doubt as to the *one* recollection to which they clung with a simple steady faith, knowing no variableness, neither shadow of turning.

We have lingered long over the *mise-en-scène*; but I hope you have nearly realized the group in and around the great oriel window, on that bright, breezy October afternoon.

Rather an animating discussion is in progress just now. By a rare chance, Miss Verschoyle seems not to have it all her own way; her fair cheek is slightly flushed in pretty provocation, and mutinous mischief glitters in her eyes; nor can the thick folds of the riding-habit always deaden the significant sound of a tiny boot-heel venting impatience on unoffending oak. It is very evident who are her opponents in the controversy; for there is a vexed, anxious look on Dering's face, and puzzled perplexity on Gascoigne's.

The case is simple enough. Miss Verschoyle has set her heart on riding Queen Mab, a recent addition to the Marston stable; Maurice has volunteered an opinion, that the experiment would be hazardous in the extreme. No wonder poor Philip was in a great strait; he had yet to learn the possibility of discussing any one of his wilful mistress's whims; but he had implicit confidence in his friend's knowledge of horseflesh, and, for years past, had been wont to consider his decisions final. It so happened that the mare in question had been purchased by the stud-groom, almost on his own authority, in Dering's absence; the latter, by the merest accident, had seen her out at exercise that morning; and the conclusions he then drew were confirmed by closer inspection

Never was human being less fitted for an arbitrator than Philip Gascoigne, especially when both the contending parties were very dear to him in their several ways; so there was a palpable timidity about his attempt to temporize.

'Georgie—would you mind waiting just a few hours longer, till we are quite sure the mare is fit for you? Maurice wouldn't disappoint you any more than I would, if he could help it, I know. He shall ride her himself to-morrow morning, and, if she is really gentle, you might mount her in the afternoon. I do feel nervous about a first experiment to-day ; especially as I can't look after you, for those terrible lawyers will be here direetly, and they'll hold me fast till dinner-time.'

The pout of Miss Verschoyle's plump, rosy lips seemed more confirmed; she threw back her pretty head in disdainful petulance, and the restless foot quickened its movement perceptibly.

' No, thank you, Philip, I don't care for half concessions. If 1 don't ride Queen Mab to-day, I will never mount her at all. It is too absurd : we saw her out twice last week, and she was going so beautifully. Perhaps I had better give up riding altogether for the present. I am quite tired of that steady, stupid old Caliph ; he is never thoroughly awake, except when he hears the hounds. I suppose he was dreaming of some famous run when he stumbled with me last Friday—he did, though you wouldn't allow it,— now, that really *was* dangerous. Yes, I'll stay at home this afternoon, and help Aunt Nellie to do the honours of Marston to Mr Rule and the other terrible lawyer. *I'm* not afraid of them.'

There was not a tinge of the virago in all Georgie's delicate nature ; but she certainly looked afraid of nothing just then ; only, more provokingly lovely than ever, in the assertion of her wayward self-will.

Philip turned to his ally with a glance and gesture of serio-comic despair.

' You see, and you hear,' he said. ' What can one say or do ? *C'est plus fort que moi.* Perhaps, if you rode very slowly and carefully ?—Certainly, Price did tell me, yesterday, that the Queen was perfectly safe.'

' Of course,' Maurice retorted, with something nearer a sneer than he had often indulged in--' I dare say he told

you, too, she was perfectly sound. I'll forfeit five times
her value if her hocks stand summer work, when the ground
is hard again. I saw this morning how she could catch
hold of her bit; and if there is not temper, or worse, in
that eye of hers, I'll never buy a horse on my own judgment again. When did you ever know a stud-groom allow
a fault in an animal that he had bought himself from an
intimate friend of his own ?   I warned you, from the first,
not to trust that man too far; there's too much of the
dealer, and not half enough of the sportsman in the place
he came from to you.   If Paice knew his own business, as
he pretends to do, your horses would be three weeks for-
warder in condition at this time of the year.   I'm not
quarrelling with ignorance, now; but with obstinacy.   If
Miss Verschoyle would only condescend to mount that
poor disgraced Caliph once more—he's the best hunter you
ever owned, Phil—and allow me to ride the Queen to-day,
I think she might alter her opinion.'

The spoilt child was more seriously angry than she had
often been in her light-minded life. This last malignment
of her favourite was quite too much for her equanimity;
she rather prided herself, too, on her judgment in horseflesh—on never being captivated by a showy head or tail;
when Queen Mab was brought up for her inspection and
'passed' with high approval, Mr Paice had condescended
to compliment her acute discrimination.   She liked Maurice
sincerely, and had always admired his physical prowess;
but all this—and more—was forgotten in the keen irritation of the moment.   As she answered, she swept a low
graceful curtsy, defiant as a swordsman's salute.

'Miss Verschoyle is infinitely obliged for the kind offer,
and deeply sensible of all this anxiety for her safety; she

would prefer dispensing with both. My poor Queen shall
not be so hardly tried : I could fancy *anything* being fretted
into a wicked temper, if it were subjected to Captain
Dering's science and powers of aggravation. If strong,
wise people would only let us weak, foolish ones alone—
how much nicer it would be! Philip—suppose this *is* a
whim of mine—it is the very first one you have ever refused
me. If you choose that Captain Dering shall be master of
the household as well as of the stable, and dismiss your
servants or your horses at his good pleasure, of course I
have not a word to say. Yes—just this one—it is quite
too soon for *me* to submit to his authority '

No such bitter or uncourteous speech had ever passed
her rosy lips since Georgie's nursery quarrels ended: before
it had been uttered five seconds, she felt heartily sorry and
ashamed of it.

Maurice started as if he had been sharply stung. He
bit his lip hard, and bent his brows involuntarily, as he
drew back into the corner of the oriel; nevertheless, there
was more of pain in his expression, than of anger or
offended pride. A very close observer might have noticed
a swift faint flush sweep across Ida Carew's pale cheek; a
slight curl of the scornful lip ; the briefest flash of the cold,
bright eyes that still looked musingly over the glistening
lowland. Gascoigne's face, ill-trained to suppress emotion,
told plainly enough his vexation and bewilderment. Nor
was Aunt Nellie's less eloquent in its sad surprise.

But, before any one else could speak, the honeyed
accents of the veteran chaperon, expert beyond her fellows
in all arts of conciliation, glided smoothly in ; that widow's
cruse was never void of its oily store, when troubled waters
were around her.

'My dearest Georgie, how can you be so thoughtless and ungrateful? What possible motive, but kindness, can Captain Dering have, in warning you? It is useless my interfering, I suppose; you never listen to me, now—you wicked, wilful puss! What should I do, if anything were to happen to you? I could never meet your dear mother again; and, as for poor Sir Archibald——'

Solvuntur risu tabulæ. Georgie's silver laugh rings in, merrily, here—cutting short the plaintive reproof, and enticing Philip and Aunt Nellie irresistibly to join her. The cloud breaks on Maurice Dering's brow; even Ida cannot repress a smile. The idea of Sir Archibald Verschoyle's paternal solicitude has vanquished the gravity of the entire party.

The august eyes of that great Indian magnate have not rested on his fair offspring since she was carried on board the 'Ganges' in her gorgeous *berceaunette*; he keeps a royal house, in the far upland district, where he rules in serene autocracy, that he will be loth to exchange anon for a seat in the Supreme Council; and has identified himself, if all tales are true, with more Eastern customs than one; indeed, he might adopt the Koran conscientiously, in most points save in abjuration of wine. His interests are all bound up in the land of his adoption; an important promotion in his own service affects him far more deeply than a change of ministry at home; though 'home' is a strange misnomer for one who has never cared to go on ship-board, since he sailed down Channel with the beard whose grizzled luxuriance might almost rival Charlemagne's, just sprouting on his chin. Sir Archibald Verschoyle is laudably regular, and chivalrously lavish, in all matters of finance; besides these fiscal communications, he writes, or causes to be written, a formal letter of inquiry, four times a year; but within these limits his notions of marital and paternal duty seem to be confined; and, otherwise, it may be doubted if he recognizes the existence of legitimate wife or child.

If ridicule kills romance, it certainly is fatal to worse things too; so it was proved now. The cunning meteorologist, wishing to avert the coming storm, could hardly have devised a more efficient lightning-conductor than that last unfinished sentence: if she used it by chance, those lucky instincts were not uncommon with her; if of aforethought, her look of puzzled reproach—as if she could not conceive what every one was amused at—was a creditable triumph.

Miss Verschoyle's face changed, rapidly as was its wont, from gay to grave, softening into the prettiest expression of timid penitence.

'You are quite right to scold me, Aunt Mary; only it was not Georgie that spoke just now, but some evil spirit in her likeness. But Captain Dering and I are too old friends to quarrel long about some stupid hasty words, which meant less than nothing; and, Philip, don't be deceitful—trying to look cross, when you know you've forgiven me already. You'll let me ride the Queen, after all, if it's only to see what care Captain Dering will take of me. You will do that, won't you—Maurice?'

It was the very first time she had ever called him by his Christian name, though she often spoke of him thus to others. The dangerous, subtle caress of her accent sent a thrill through Dering's whole frame that might have betrayed itself in his voice if he had answered in words; but he only bowed his head, and laid his lips lightly on the

D

little extended hand, with a knightly courtesy that became him well; sealing at once a truce and a promise. Gascoigne was too pleased at the turn matters had taken to press objection further, especially when he saw that his chief backer had evidently deserted him.

Ida Carew rose quickly from her seat; shaking her riding-skirt clear, with rather an impatient gesture.

'The horses must surely be ready by this time,' she said; 'it is a pity to waste more of this lovely day. What do you ride, Captain Dering? It will have to carry a heavy responsibility, besides yourself, remember.'

'The Moor, of course,' Maurice answered, gaily. 'One always mounts one's first charger, or—what comes to the same thing—one's best horse, for escort-duty. He has had a steady gallop this morning, too; so he ought to set an example to Queen Mab, if she needs one. But, after all, a gentle light hand works wonders, and I dare say she will give us no trouble. We can start as soon as that lazy Paul is ready.'

The person alluded to sauntered into the room, just as the last words were spoken; but if he heard them, he did not choose to take up the challenge: his sharp searching eyes roved over the faces round him: though all now looked cheerful and serene, by some strange instinct of discrimination, he guessed part of the truth at once. So, while the rest still lingered, talking about letters that ought to be written, or other trifles not worth recording, he drew Maurice aside, and questioned him in a whisper. When a dozen hurried sentences had told him all he wanted to know, the significant shrug of Chetwynde's shoulders, and lift of his marked eyebrows, were a better commentary on the absurdity of the whole discussion than any spoken sarcasm. *He*, at least, understood the futility of debating, at that time, the wildest whim expressed by the empress-elect of Marston Lisle.

Sweet Georgie Verschoyle had a natural talent in such cases that the astutest of female politicians might have envied: somehow or another she always contrived to turn the tables of right and wrong on her opponents, impressing them with a conscience-stricken sense of having oppressed her tyrannically. In spite of her charming contrition even now, you will observe she had her own way absolutely at the last.

* * *

CHAPTER IV

BEFORE THE START.

DERING was in the gravelled court before the great hall-door, where the horses were waiting, some minutes before the others joined him.

Mr Paice was there, on foot, of course. That dignitary condescended, for once, to assist at the ceremony of mounting, so that the riding party should start under the most favourable auspices.

The appearance of the great stud-groom was certainly not prepossessing. Sulky conceit was written in every line of his flat coarsely-hewn face, whose dogged expression could never be mistaken for blunt honesty: it was easy to guess how he would bully his subordinates, and resent any interference with his own province on the part of his superiors. To these last he would probably have brought himself to cringe, if he had not discovered that saturnine

self-assertion answered best; people were disposed to believe that a servant could not be so thoroughly disagreeable, unless he were conscious of being worth something to
his masters.   In truth, he was rather more ignorant and
idle than Dering had given him credit for; his last em-
ployer was a clever, unscrupulous, gentleman-coper, and
had given Mr Paice a gorgeous character, as the only way
of getting thoroughly and quickly rid of him.   He dressed
his assumed character, at least, to perfection; from the
crown of his low napless hat to the lowest wrinkle of his
trim gaiters, there really was not a fault to find; the fold
of his white diamond-shaped scarf was in itself a miracle
of study and practice.

He acknowledged Dering's presence with a sort of salute
under protest—his hand did not quite reach his forehead
in its careless upward move—and then resumed his inspection of the horses and their appointments; never ceasing to
revolve between his compressed lips the everlasting sprig
of myrtle.

Only two of the other animals are worth especial notice.

Few men in the army had owned better cattle, or ridden
them straighter, than Dering; but he only spoke the truth
when he said that The Moor was the luckiest purchase he
had ever made.   A dark-brown horse—with a tan muzzle,
and flecked in places with the same colour—so powerfully
and compactly built, that few guessed his height within two
inches till they stood close to his withers; broad flat legs,
clean in sinew as a Nedidje stallion's, with thrice the bone;
quarters massive, without being heavy; betraying vast pro-
pelling power in every line, though an equine artist might
perhaps quarrel with their symmetry; a small plainish
head, admirably set on a clean-carved throat and strong

neck, with the lean workmanlike look about it often seen
in the descendants of stout old Slane; his girth is enormous, and there is not a suspicion of lightness about the
after-ribs, though he carries little loose flesh just now; for
The Moor has been doing steady work this month past,
and is forward in preparation for the first big Military
Race, and other autumn engagements. A horse that a
brave heart might trust for life, if hard bestead as the
Cavalier, who rode straight down on the Northern Water
with the avengers of blood on his track.

Queen Mab was a very different stamp of animal. Certainly she looks picturesquely handsome just now; with
her long swan-neck arched aside, till the tapering nostrils
touched her near shoulder—her bright bay coat, relieved
by coal-black points, glistening under the soft autumn sun
—as she steps daintily along, coquettishly conscious of her
showy attractions. But she will not bear examination in
detail: that looseness of joints, narrowness of chest, and
lightness of barrel, must be fatal to stoutness or endurance;
there is far too much length below the knee, and decided
weakness about the slender pasterns; she is sure to have
a flashy turn of speed, and may be hard to beat for a mile;
but it is simply impossible that she can stay. Dering was
thoroughly right in distrusting the mare's temper; the
backward glance of her false glittering eye, always on the
watch for mischief, was a sufficient warning.

A believer in the transmigration of souls might have
easily indulged his fancy—looking at the pair. In The
Moor might be supposed to dwell the spirit of one of those
puissant ancient worthies—large of heart as of limb, somewhat rough and stubborn of mood, but always honest, and
kindly, and true—men who clave their way steadily on,

through good and evil report, to the accomplishment of the task set before them ; neither shrinking from danger nor repining at toil ; satisfied either with death in harness on a stricken field, or with brief, honourable rest in extreme old age—so that they fought a good fight, right on to the last. That showy carcase of Queen Mab's must surely have held the fretful soul of one of the wild, wicked beauties, who in all ages have arisen to serve the Tempter's ends ; luring sages, soldiers, or statesmen, to sin, and ruin, and shame.

No such romantic thoughts as these crossed Dering's mind as he stood there ; never noticing his own horse, but scanning the mare rather anxiously. His practised eye lighted instantly on something peculiar in the bridle, and he walked forward to examine it.

The bit turned out to be one of those evil inventions of second-rate saddlers that are supposed to insure safety to timid or unpractised riders ; but are more likely to bring a really good horseman to grief. This especial complication of leverage, and leather, and steel, was called the Lupo-Frænum (those ingenious patentees are ambitiously classical, but usually unhappy in their grammar) : it was quite enough to irritate a well-conditioned animal into sulkiness or rebellion.

Maurice looked up quickly, after a moment's inspection, with a frown on his brow, and a darker discontent on his face.

'Who, on earth, ordered you to put on such a thing as that ?' he asked the groom who led Queen Mab—touching the bit contemptuously with his finger.

The man hesitated ; but Mr Paice answered for him from behind Dering's shoulder.

' It was my horders, sir; and, Captin, I must beg you won't hinterfere with my men or my hosses. No man can't do his business if he's allus bein' hoverlooked and meddled with. I knows where I has to give satisfaction; so long as my hown master's pleased, it ain't no odds to any one. If hanything goes wrong, I'll hanswer it.'

Dering's conduct towards his inferiors was never imperious or overbearing : he exacted no undue deference; and was not apt to take offence at mere boorishness of manner : but, both as a soldier and civilian, he was used to being obeyed; and would no more have passed over impertinence from a subordinate than insult from an equal : at any other time the coarse insolence of Paice's tone would have chafed him sorely. But now, he had no time to think of himself; graver anxieties engrossed him too entirely to leave room for personal irritation. Perhaps he would have urged his point with ever so slight a chance of carrying it; but, just then, he caught a glimpse of a scarlet feather gleaming through the twilight of the vast dim hall within. He was not brave enough to risk a rupture of the peace, so lately signed and sealed; and drew quickly back, hating himself for feeling ashamed at having been nearly caught close to Queen Mab's side.

But as he turned he set his teeth savagely, and muttered —so low, that not even the threatened man caught a syllable :—

' Answer it? By G—d, you *shall* answer it—to the uttermost. And how will that help us?'

Gascoigne came out upon the steps with the rest, ever and anon whispering a fresh caution into the little pink ear, coyly revealed under the close golden braids, that never heeded if it heard. His last words to Dering were—

'Mind, I trust her entirely to you.'

The other answered only with a cheery, confident nod. Whatever his forebodings might have been, Georgie Verschoyle's bright face did not look happier than Maurice's, as he swung her dexterously to saddle, and settled the intricacies of her skirt like a practised hand.

Philip stood for some seconds alone under the huge gray porch, watching the party

As lightly they rode away.

There was always a subdued tinge of melancholy in his smile; but it was sadder than usual just now : he could not shake off a vague sense of impending evil. In very truth, his happiness was in more peril than he wist of; and the danger came in more shapes than one.

Mr Paice, too, looked after the receding figures till a turn in the avenue cut off the view. An ugly saturnine satisfaction was dawning on his face, that—but for a natural lack of intelligence—might have expanded into a sneer.

'D—— *his* impudence !' he muttered; 'I'm right glad I spoke out. I reckon he won't be so ready at shoving his oar in, next journey.'

Revolving these things in his mighty mind, Mr Paice retreated to his own dominions; grinding the gravel to powder under his heel as he walked, for his wrath was yet but half appeased; it was not till he had cursed several innocent helpers very freely, and 'quilted' the stable scape-goat—a silent, bullet-headed boy, off whose hardened hide the blows glanced like rain from a pent-house—that he was enabled thoroughly to relish his first afternoon cigar.

CHAPTER V

A RACE FOR TWO LIVES.

'WHAT's that new fancy of yours, Maurice?' Chetwynde asked, when they had ridden a little way. 'I never saw you ride The Moor with spurs before, when you had no cross-country work before you.'

Dering coloured slightly, as he turned his head to reply. He was riding slightly in advance of the other two, side by side with Miss Verschoyle:

'Well, I don't know; he's been showing temper, once or twice of late, since we began to train him, and I may want to remind him that we are all on our best behaviour. Miss Verschoyle, will you drop your hand a little, and feel the Queen's mouth only with the snaffle? They've tried a new bit on her to-day, and it may fret her till she's used to it.'

His words did vile injustice to the stanch old horse, who was good as he was game; but Maurice preferred calumniating his favourite, to the chance of shaking Georgie's nerve, by betraying his fear that steel might be bitterly needed before they got safe home again. Nevertheless, for the present, he really did thrust all such bodings aside.

It was no wonder. His fair charge had never seemed to him so marvellously attractive; he thought that quite half of her charms had been kept in reserve till now. She was evidently bent on making ample amends for the morning's ungraciousness and ingratitude. Her low, sweet voice changed its accent when she answered him—soften-

ing almost to tenderness; and in the deep gray eyes there
was a liquid lustre, that only a favoured few had ever seen
there, as they met his own with a shy invitation to exchange of confidences. So, as he rode on slowly through
the warm, breezy weather, close by Georgie Verschoyle's
bridle-rein, it must be confessed that stout Maurice Dering yielded, half wittingly, to a spell of fascination too
deliciously potent for sense of guilt to creep in. Conscience was silent for awhile, biding—as is her wont—in
stern serenity, her inevitable appointed time.

If, in so yielding, our poor hero was unpardonably weak—
nay, if he committed things worthy of death—which of us,
my comrades, shall avenge virtue with the first stone?

Wiser, surely, and purer, if not happier, than his fellows
is he who has not once in life, for never so brief a space,
lingered in some false paradise—hope, fear, and memory
all merged by the languid luxury of the hour—while

> Over him stood the weird ladye,
> In her charmed castle beyond the sea,
> Singing—'Lie thou still and dream.'

It is Rinaldo's story over and over again.

'True,' saith the knight; 'not so long ago we swore
fealty to the Red Cross, and enmity to the pale Paynim
symbol that gleams yonder through the shadows of the
Delightful Garden. Perchance, even now, the trumpets of
Godfrey and Bohemond are sounding; the Templars are
chanting their war-psalm; and our brethren-in-arms gather
for another escalade. Let be: the alarum may ring louder
yet, and wake no echo here. There is more music in your
song, O white-robed Syrens, than in the monotone of
Quare fremuerunt gentes; there are sickles sufficient for the

harvest of blood, though one reaper be resting from toil.
The winter campaign was long and dreary: some short
breathing-space has surely been earned. If for awhile we
forget our vow, the good hermit will assoilzie us, with light
penance done; and the lost time shall be honourably redeemed. Armida is passing fair, and there is wondrous
savour in her wine. So, fill up another beaker, sweet sorceress. Bow down—lower, lower yet—till your fragrant
breath stir the roses in our hair. It will be time enough,
to-morrow, to buckle on that heavy harness, and do our
devoir in the front of battle.'

To-morrow? Ah me! the minutes glide swiftly into
hours, and hours into days. If calm, cold Ubaldo comes
not soon, he comes too late. He will preach to deafer ears
than the serpent's, and taunts or prayers will be wasted in
vain.

Everything for the first half-hour went smoothly enough
with the riding-party. Queen Mab seemed determined to
justify her mistress's championship—contenting herself
with an occasional snap at the infernal machine between
her jaws, and a backward slope of her pointed quills of
ears, for which, perhaps, the teasing flies might be respon-
sible; the gait of those long, slender pasterns was smooth
and easy enough, certainly, if not very safe. So there was
nothing to distract the attention of Georgie or her cavalier
from each other—nothing to break the flow of their low,
pleasant talk, as they led the way slowly through the
winding grass-lanes.

Neither were the rearmost pair silent. Their converse
went on, with brief intervals of silence, after a quiet, sober
fashion; enlivened, however, by not unfrequent flashes of
irony, or a quick, sharp repartee, deftly parried. They

were fast friends, those two, though there had never been
a flutter of warmer feeling in either breast.

When Ida and her mother first visited the Deanery,
years ago, Chetwynde could not choose but admire the
cool, dauntless way in which the girl held her own against
the tyrannous asceticism to which the woman bowed so
meekly,—too wise to bring things to a crisis by overt rebellion, but too proud to surrender, utterly, reasonable
free agency or decent self-respect. That day was always
marked with a white stone in Ida's dreary Torrcaster
calendar, when she heard orders given for 'Mr Chetwynde's room to be got ready;' she felt, instinctively,
that succour was coming, though the alliance was tacit, and
simply defensive. Those rare glimpses of Paul—rarer and
rarer each year—often enabled her resources of patience or
endurance to hold out, when both were drained to the
lowest ebb; just as the accession of an influential sleeping
partner will help a tottering firm to tide over a perilous
crisis, when the commercial cables are sorely strained.

Others besides her had remarked that Paul's presence
was not eagerly insisted on at the Deanery, even if it was
not positively unwelcome to its master. If that austere
dignitary could ever be ill at ease, such certainly was the
case when, after delivering a bitter diatribe, a ponderous
dogma, or a pompous peroration, he met his son's cold, sar-
castic eyes. There had never been an actual quarrel or expressed hostility between the two; but some of the Dean's
fanatic adherents were wont to shake their heads, at times,
in solemn sympathy, lamenting that even such an eminent
saint should not be exempt from the thorn in the flesh of
hard family trials; for Paul's only sister (who will not ap-

pear on the face of this story) was a helpless cripple from a spine-complaint born with her.

So they wandered on, pleasantly enough, till a sharp turn in the lane brought them out on a main road, in view of the huge Norman gate-tower of Harlestone Park.

The great Earl who owned that fair demesne had visited it about a score of times in as many years. He was induced to preside at certain festivities given to celebrate his coming of age; and the recollections of his sufferings on that occasion had never been effaced, though he had travelled in many lands since then, and his age 'spoiled the fifty.' The Bankshire yeoman is a rough-and-ready customer at his politest time. The enthusiasm of the tenantry, replete with the mighty Harlestone ale, was quite too much for their languid lord; he had to undergo about the same amount of hand-shaking as a popular candidate on canvass, or a 'lion' at an American *levée;* and was oppressed by a great terror and exhaustion long before the time came for making the set oration, in which he utterly broke down. The Radicals of the neighbouring borough, of which the Earl of Tancarville possessed the fee-simple, were wont, at each succeeding election, to get up the hopeless mockery of an opposition, chiefly for the sake of airing their eloquence, in furious invectives against the omnipotent absentee, and frantic appeals to the Goddess of Liberty : 'bloated aristocrat' and 'hereditary tyrant' were among the favourite points that never failed to bring the pothouse down.

In very deed, he was a pale, slender man, rather weak in health, with a gentle, nervous manner; a remarkable talent at piquet; and a refined taste in pug-dogs and snuffboxes. He would no more have thought of deliberately oppressing an inferior than of beating his valet. The Harlestone tenantry sate at the same easy rent as their grandsires had done; the cottages on the estate were kept in just as perfect order as the hothouses; and the Earl's name headed the subscription-lists to all local charities, with an oblation that might have shamed his followers into liberality. In acting thus, Lord Tancarville neither sought for gratitude nor intended to avert obloquy; it seemed that he was equally indifferent to either. He had peculiar notions as to the obligations of nobility : an ultra-Conservative—simply because too lazy or too prejudiced to march with the times—he set his face with a placid obstinacy against any concession or conciliation that might lead to a fusion of orders.

Trianon itself was not more jealously guarded against the commonalty than the demesne and gardens of Harlestone; no relics of pic-nics mouldered round the roots of the vast shadowy beeches; the Lady's Walk, that wound for a long mile round the inlets of the lake, was innocent of the steps of lovers, unless they came to woo some keeper's or woodman's daughter; the picture-gallery, whose renown extended beyond the four seas, was a sealed paradise to all who could not produce a card bearing in its corner the Earl's small feminine initials. His agent was provided with a store of these, with injunctions, strict and stern, as to their dispensation. A favoured few of the county magnates had the privilege of riding in the park at their pleasure; and none were better known or trusted at the gates than the inmates of Marston Lisle.

When the party were once fairly launched on the smooth sound turf, a canter, of course, was inevitable. Queen

Mab went quietly enough, though she bore unpleasantly on her bit at times, in spite of all the humouring of Georgie's practised hand. The mare kept glancing sideways at the strong brown horse stealing along so steadily at her shoulder; it seemed as though she knew by instinct that it would not answer to play tricks till she could shake off that close, careful companionship. The last fifty yards of road, leading to the gate in the iron deer-fence, dividing the Home park from the outer Chase, had been freshly stoned; as ill-luck would have it, The Moor picked up an awkward flint, that, for a few minutes, puzzled the groom's picker. The other three walked slowly on, riding abreast now.

Miss Verschoyle chanced to turn her head, just as Dering was mounting again. The spirit of merry mischief woke suddenly within her, and, for the nonce, both contrition and prudence were forgotten. She thought she would take advantage of her momentary independence, to give her guardian just one tiny fright.

'One more canter,' she said, with a light laugh; as she shook her reins, and drew her slender whip smartly across Queen Mab's neck.

The others were off, not a second later; but Georgie had the advantage of the start, and drew ahead of her companions at once. The mare meant vice the instant she found herself alone; a rabbit bolting from one patch of fern to another, almost under her feet, gave her the shadow of an excuse that she wanted.

A savage snatch at the bit—a boring forward plunge, that almost dragged her rider from the saddle—and Queen Mab was away at a mad gallop, with the patent Lupo-frænum fairly between her teeth.

Of all manhood's sharp trials, surely that is the bitterest to bear, the most agonizing to remember—when we are forced to witness the mortal peril of a dear friend—powerless to help as if our feet and hands were bound; and amongst the terrors of ordinary life none is more appalling than the sight of a run-away horse, going over unknown or unsafe ground, with a woman in the saddle.

I pray, for the sake of common charity, that no word written down here may be misconstrued. If it be wrong, on a page like this, to allude, ever so vaguely, to a tragedy bitterly real, judgment—not feeling—is at fault. At this very moment, I swear, there is upon me such an awe and sadness as needs must affect us in presence of the innocent dead.

It was my evil fortune, many years ago, to witness a horror, that none who were brought near it will ever forget. I remember the fair girl's happy face, as she started for the gallop of which only God's eye saw quite the end. I remember it, too, as she lay in the death-stupor, a few minutes after they lifted her from the cruel stones that had no mercy on her beauty. That last face——The same shrinking shudder that unmanned me then, overcomes me now, whenever I feel that it will reveal itself soon, as I walk through some dark valley of Dreamland.

Chetwynde did not greatly admire Miss Verschoyle. With him, coaxing could not atone for her coquetry; he was apt to be more provoked than amused with her caprices; and not unseldom murmured within himself, that Philip had better have chosen a less light-minded mate. But these unfavourable impressions did not amount to dislike; and, had the feeling been positive instead of negative, it would have utterly vanished in his concern for Georgie's safety. In truth, Paul's cynicism was rather surface-deep; and he took thought for others much more, and much oftener, than the world was aware of. His fears, however, had hardly time to assume a distinct form; nor, when he instinctively increased his pace to a rapid gallop, had he any clear idea of how he could help or interfere. In another instant, a swifter, firmer hoof-beat drowned the trample of Paul's and Ida's horses; and Maurice Dering flew past—a haggard terror in his eyes—his white face set, like a corpse's three hours old. His clenched teeth parted for a second, just as he went by; but Chetwynde rather guessed at the meaning of the hoarse whisper, than caught the words—

'The chalk cliff!'

Those three syllables made Paul bound in his saddle, as if a bullet had struck him. He knew the place right well; so did every native or visitor within ten miles of Harlestone. It was the only sight on his broad domain from which the Earl could not debar the profane vulgar; for it was visible from many different points on the country-side that he could not control. Indeed, a clump of tall firs on the crest of the ridge had been a landmark for centuries.

It seemed as though nature had suddenly grown aweary of the monotony of long rolling downs gliding into valleys with slopes, often steep, but always smooth and unbroken. Here, for half a mile or more, the chalk went sheer down, in an irregular cliff from fifty to seventy feet high, to a shelf along which led a rough farm-road; from thence the ground fell abruptly, but not perpendicularly, to the narrow meadows that lay on the hither side of the Lene. There had been quarries there long ago, but some whim of a Lord of Tancarville had caused these to be discon-

E

tinued, and they had never since been reopened. The brushwood, growing dense wherever it could cling, made it hard, now, to distinguish God's handiwork from man's.

The chief wonder of the spot were some yews of fabulous age, whose roots had suited themselves, after the quaintest fashion, to the irregularities of soil and stone. A local poetess, of some repute, had once compared them to the rough, honest lover, who, in despite of coldness and caprice, clings ever to the side of his chosen 'white maid.' In one place a huge gnarled trunk shot out almost at right angles with the face of the cliff, where one would have thought a bush could scarcely have found foot-hold; but boys, who had ventured their necks that they might boast of having bestridden the King Yew, looked up at that famous tree when their eyes were growing dim with age, and knew that he was not an inch nearer his downfall, but might carry their children's children on his sturdy back.

A right pleasant place to look up at,—floating lazily below it, when May-flies are abroad and lilies are rife on the Lene. Pleasant, too, even in late autumn, when the woodland puts on its many-coloured raiment of green and purple, and golden-bronze. But a gruesome place to think of—sitting on a mad horse's back, with his head set straight for the upper verge.

No wonder if Chetwynde was moved, almost past self-control, at the thought that only a very few seconds lay between sweet Georgie Verschoyle and such a death. It was very characteristic of the man, that amidst all the pity and fear which possessed him, he should have found time to read aright the story of Dering's face: he never forgot it; no—not the secret it told.

A riddle harder to decipher — one that would have

puzzled even that acute physiognomist—might have been found in the countenance of the girl, galloping on swiftly and silently close by his bridle-rein.

The expression, indeed, was one of those nearly impossible to define accurately. When Ida Carew first became aware of her cousin's mortal peril, she felt a terror quite unfeigned, and the low cry that escaped her lips was the utterance of an emotion strong and sincere. But, five seconds later, Maurice Dering's white agonized face flashed past; perhaps it told her only what she knew before; but an evil change came instantly over her own, hardening and sharpening every line, as if wax had been turned into marble. There came into her eyes, a strange look of eager expectation and cruel contentment: with that same expression some fair patrician, habituated to Circensian excitement, may have watched from her gilded gallery the last scene of the bloody drama that the sword-players below had been acting since noon.

But of all this Paul saw nothing. He was too intent on following those flying figures in front, riding the terrible race for life.

'God help her!' the groom said, with a sob in his voice. 'It's all over in three minutes, if the Captain can't turn her. And so young, too!'

He had ranged up alongside of Chetwynde—mechanically, as men cling to each other in times of sharp peril; but was too wise to attempt a hopeless chase, or to make the mad mare wilder yet with the trample of more hoofs behind her.

'But he *will* turn her—he must,' Chetwynde said. 'Don't you know The Moor is far the fastest? He's gaining on her every stride. Can't you see that?'

E 2

He spoke hastily—almost angrily ; but in his glance, as
for an instant it met the other's, there was the earnestness of one pleading for a shadow of hope.

The groom shook his head despondingly.

'We know the old horse's pace, sir, and he'll last for
ever ; but we don't know much about the mare's. The
distance is so terrible short, too. But I do think the
Captain's drawing up, though I can't see very plain.'

No wonder those honest eyes were dim ; for his glove
was wet already with the drops dashed from their shaggy
lashes.

The Chase was rather a misnomer now ; there was less
of forest there than in most other parts of the demesne.
It was a vast tract of roughish pasture, dotted here and
there with small game-coverts and clumps of tall elms
or beeches ; the ground undulated everywhere, but in
one direction sloped steadily upwards, to where some
scattered firs and a low line of rails marked the brink of
the chalk cliff. Altogether, it would have been as safe a
place as could have been found for a run-away, if a
miserable fatality had not set the mare's head straight for
destruction, when she first broke away.

For a second or two, one of these clumps hid both
Georgie Verschoyle and her pursuer from the others.
When they shot into sight again, the latter's advantage
was more perceptible. The Moor evidently had the turn
of speed as well as of stoutness. But it is difficult to
calculate the dangerous power of man or horse, when
either is possessed with a mad devil, that, for the moment,
enables ferocity to hold its own against courage, and
makes flaccid muscles tense as iron. The chances of life
and death were still fearfully even.

Dering's object was to thrust himself between Queen Mab and the cliff's edge, so as to turn her head from it; for no human hand could have checked her career by direct strength, even if it had grasped her bridle. To do this, he was obliged to ride wide of her track on the right— closing in again if he could head her; thus he lost all the ground of the arc: every stride that brought him nearer to Georgie, brought them both nearer to the precipice. Maurice felt it would be a question of a few yards at last. He felt something more than this: without any deliberate purpose of suicide, even in the event of the worst, he had a dim foreknowledge of what the end would be; he knew that another life was swaying in the same scale with his own; that, one way or other, he was sure to escape the horror and shame of seeing—himself unhurt — those delicate limbs shattered and that bright beauty marred. But he could trust his nerve, even with that awful stake in abeyance. After the first agony of horror had passed, he never lost hope—no, nor faith; for, though his lips were rigid, his heart found time to utter one prayer —more acceptable, perhaps, in its simple earnestness than many a long liturgy—

'May God help me to save her, or have mercy on both our souls!'

When, some weeks later, at the Walmington Grand Military, Dering landed The Moor a clever winner, and disinterested turf authorities grew warm in praise of his science and judgment, he did not show one whit more of patient coolness, than he did that day in Harlestone Chase; and the last-named race was far the closer of the two.

We have left the poor little heroine of the brief melo-drama entirely to herself, all this long while—long, on paper only; for, Heaven knows, the sand flows swiftly enough, when it seems as if the hour-glass will never be turned again.

Georgie Verschoyle was really an accomplished *cavalière*. Her graceful figure was set firmly and easily in the saddle, and her hand was nearly perfect. She never attempted to emulate the feats of the professional huntress or 'horse-breaker;' but took any necessary fence with satisfaction to herself, and was not to be discomfited by ordinary kicks or plunges. She had far more nerve, too, in spite of her delicate organization and *mignonne* ways, than any one, at first sight, would have given her credit for. She was startled of course, and shaken too, by the first mad bolt, that almost dragged her from the saddle; but she soon settled herself again, and took a steady pull at Queen Mab's mouth. Poor child! She soon found that she might as well have dragged at an imbedded sheet-anchor as at the bit clenched in the vice of those savage teeth.

Then a cold faint feeling of fear, mingling with a vague repentance, began to oppress her. She wished—ah, how earnestly! — that she had listened to Maurice's kindly warning. More than all—why did she ever leave his side, where she would have been safe, in spite of her folly? If he were only near her now ;—but he was so far away, when she cast that last saucy look behind ; and Queen Mab was going so fast—surely, every second, faster and faster. Soon, too, she had to fight against physical, as well as moral, exhaustion. No one, except those who have ridden a thorough-bred at top-speed for the first time, knows how soon a novice's breath will fail. Yet she was very near the point of peril before she realized it. She flew past several familiar tree-clumps without recognizing them. All at once her eyes lighted on five firs, right in her front, standing up gauntly against the sky—all blank beyond.

She knew then that she was heading straight for the chalk cliff, at its highest point; with nothing between her and hideous death but—two furlongs or so of turf, and a slight rail, just high enough to mask the abyss, and tempt a run-away horse to fly it.

A brave man, used to grapple with all dangers of flood and field, might have shivered then, and owned it without shame: how could it fare with a delicate darling, petted from earliest infancy, in whose cheek a strong sensation-story would make the bright blood ebb and flow? The poor child closed her eyes involuntarily: for a second or two she felt so deathly faint, that she must have fallen if she had not grasped her pommel convulsively: then came the worst ' bitterness of death '— a dim sense of guilt—a consciousness, that the life had been wasted that seemed so near its ending. She was too bewildered, in her mortal fear, to think of any formal prayer; at last, there broke from the white lips a low smothered wail—

' For Philip's sake—poor Philip's—'

She was hardly conscious of the words; but it seemed as if they sprang from a vague hope, that Heaven might spare to crush that other true, tender, blameless heart, even if she herself were unworthy of its mercy.

When Georgie opened her eyes again, the firs were fearfully nearer; the wind whistled shriller past her ears, as if mocking her agony; and the mad brute under her tore on, faster and faster. All the face of the terrible cliff, just as she had seen it last from a shallop on the Lene, rose up before her—clear as though reflected in a camera. Any death

—surely, any—better than *that !* The greensward cannot
be so cruel as those gnarled roots and rugged stones.

So she began to disentangle her habit, half mechanically,
with weak trembling hands, and in another moment would
have cast herself from the saddle. The instancy of the
crisis brought back something of self-command; and her
heart went up to the Great Throne in one last pleading for
pity, before she sprang.

A human voice answered the unspoken prayer—a voice,
hoarse, and changed, and tremulous—but still recogniz-
able as Maurice Dering's: the cry came—*level*—from the
right—

'Georgie—love—in God's name sit fast!—only a second
longer!'

The blood that had frozen round the fluttering heart, till
its pulses were almost stilled, rushed back through the
tingling veins with a revulsion painfully sweet : more than
this—the girl remembered afterwards the strange thrill
that pervaded all her being, as the intense suppressed
passion of those tones smote upon her ear—a thrill such
as she had never known from any word or caress of Philip
Gascoigne's. The secret was out at last : in the same instant
that Georgie knew she was saved, she knew also that
Maurice loved her dearly.

I wonder, is there any moment, in life or death, when a
real woman is quite indifferent to a fresh evidence of her
power?

It is true that Miss Verschoyle could not, just then, enjoy, or even thoroughly realize, her new triumph; but, that
she was conscious of it, is equally certain.

Dering had never let The Moor's head go, and made his
effort with consummate judgment; when he ' came,' it was

with a vengeance; the game old horse had never known
what real punishment was till now : but he answered each
plunge of the cruel rowels without a flinch or swerve; running to the end as straight and staunch as steel. The cur-
rish, cowardly drop in Queen Mab's blood served them
well. Directly she saw, first the wide tawny nostril, then
the long lean head, then the mighty brown shoulders of
her antagonist closing in from the right, the devil seemed
to die in her; her tense muscles relaxed; her head went
up suddenly; and she began to go short, swerving to the
near side. So Maurice had little more to do; for he could
have borne Queen Mab round by sheer weight, when once
alongside. He had thrown his whip away long ago, to have
both hands free; and, as he ranged up, he laid his left
firmly on the mare's bridle, just above the bit; the wrench
which tore the Lupo-frænum from between her teeth, well
nigh dislocating her jaw, was rather an unnecessary violence,
though a most natural impulse under the circumstances.

They marked the spot, next day, where the hoof-tracks
turned, and measured the distance to the rails—eighty-five
yards to an inch : a narrow space for a finish, with the
winning-post set between Life and Death. A white marble
cross stands there now, bearing the date and the initials
of the riders : a suitable inscription will be added, so soon
as a scholar shall be found, able to satisfy Lord Tancarville's fastidious taste, in elegance of Latinity and polish
of epigram.

'They're nearly level, now. Why don't he close in?
Does he see where the rails are? They'll both go over :
it's too horrible. Ah!—did you see that rush ? Look up,
Ida : she's safe—quite safe. Hurra ! I knew it—I said
it. Maurice has won, by G—d.'

Those words were spoken just at the crisis of the race—
the first muttered under breath through grinding teeth—
the last in a cheery shout; and calm Paul Chetwynde,
tossing his hand aloft, waved it in a paroxysm of triumph:
he had not been so excited since he helped to win the
cricket-match that was the crowning glory of his school-
boy days. Then he glanced aside at his silent companion,
as they still galloped swiftly on.

Ida's gaze had followed every moment of the struggle
for life, and she needed no telling that it was over: well
over for others, but—how for her? For one second a look
deformed her features, such as would not easily be matched
on this side of Hell—a look of baffled malice, insatiate hate,
and savage despair. Then the pale face put on its beautiful mask again, and could defy scrutiny once more. The
mute gratitude, expressed by the lifted eyes and clasped
hands, was correct in execution to a shade; but, if any inward ejaculation accompanied the devotional gesture, I wot
less impious mockeries of thanksgiving have gone up from
The Brocken, when witches, and their Master, held Sabbath
there.

Paul did not notice anything suspicious in his companion's demeanour, nor wonder at her strange silence from
the first; neither did he speak again till they reached the
spot where the others stood—motionless now.

A good deal of talking is done on the stage, at such moments as we have been trying to describe; but wonderfully
little, when the melodrame is being acted in bitter earnest.
For a minute or so after Dering's grasp was laid on her
rein, Miss Verschoyle was physically incapable of uttering
a syllable—simply from weakness and want of breath: the
horses had stopped before she found her voice. Maurice,

too, kept silence while they were slackening speed; he could not trust himself thoroughly yet. Though he scarcely remembered what the words were, that broke from him a while ago in his agony, he had a vague guilty idea of having betrayed himself, and would not risk adding folly to folly, or sin to sin. It was well that he took time to rally all his powers of self-control, for in the next few minutes they were tried to the uttermost.

As they came slowly to a halt, Dering saw his charge sway helplessly in her saddle : he flung himself to the ground, just soon enough to catch the little drooping head on his shoulder, and to support the slender panting waist with the circle of his arm.

Had a cunning modeller of metals been present then, he might have achieved a wondrous triumph, by reproduction of that group of four.

The delicate, girlish figure, bowed down on the neck of the stalwart soldier—till golden tresses mingled with chestnut beard—in the mere helplessness of its abandonment inexpressibly lovely; and graceful withal as any tendril, that softens the outline of granite columns. The mare—a very picture of violence self-exhausted—as she rocks to and fro on shaking pasterns; panting painfully through nostrils overstrained; her wide fixed eyeballs staring wildly still—half in terror, half in rage. And the stately Moor, standing gravely by; recovering his wind after a sober and decorous fashion, as if disdaining to allow that his own bolt was nearly shot in the moment of victory; true—the mighty flanks are heaving, and the swollen flesh quivers painfully now and then where the sharp rowels lanced it most cruelly; but there is no malice—not even reproach—in the sidelong glance that the brave old horse casts ever and anon on his master: it seems as though he knew that of all the laurels they may struggle for together, the crowning wreath has been won to-day.

So, outwardly, all looked fair enough; but how, think you, during those brief minutes, did it go with Maurice Dering's heart?

He held the one creature he loved beyond all the world beside, almost in his embrace; her soft cheek rested against his own; her breath lifted his hair, as she murmured in his ear low broken syllables of sweet gratitude and sweeter repentance: he knew, by one of those instincts that speak to men, seldom falsely, in the orgasms of life, that he had only to complete an avowal already half made to secure the beautiful prize. It was so, too. One of those strange revulsions of feeling, that make women the chief of paradoxes, possessed Georgie Verschoyle just then. She had been so very near death, that, for the moment, she seemed to be beginning a new existence, on which the ties and memories of the former one had no hold. An hour ago she had loved Philip Gascoigne sincerely, after her own fashion; and now—she would have cast aside the one and clung to the other, without a remorse or regret.

Maurice knew all this, and yet—was strong to forbear; strong enough to crush the passion crying out fiercely within him, as one might strangle a snake in an iron gauntlet. He never pressed his advantage by word, or look, or gesture; his arm never belied the loyalty of support by a momentary tightening of its clasp. If honour and honesty had not kept him from stealing away his friend's treasure, he would still have been too proud to avail himself of a girl's romantic impulse—an outbreak of gratitude too reckless to count the cost, though it might have been a life-long repentance.

'He only did his duty.'

Of course. But, O saintly neighbour of mine—whose tithes of anise and cummin are paid to the hour; whose mites of conscience-money form a regular item in the Chancellor's balance-sheet; whose frown is a caution to sinners, when you walk abroad with your august lady, if her sweeping skirt chance to be brushed by the passing Pelagia; whose moral lightning-conductors and fire-insurances, so to speak, have been doubled, since the stranger came to dwell near your well-whitened gates—it might profit, perchance, even your immaculate self, some day, if you could recall a struggle and a victory like this.

As for me—speaking as one of the large, if not influential, constituency to which the Publican belonged,—which, in spite of you and yours, Heaven has not yet seen fit to disfranchise,—I never can think on these things without remembering the good Earl of Derby's words at that famous Scottish tournament, when the lance-shaft was dragged out through skull and helmet, and the Ramsay never shivered or moaned,—

'Lo! what stout hearts men may bear. God send me as fair an ending!'

'It is all over now, and well over, Miss Verschoyle. I'm sure you are too brave to faint; especially if you remember, that there's not a drop of water nearer than the Lene.'

The cold levity of Dering's tone seemed cruelly ill-timed just then; but the shock relaxed at once the tension of the girl's strained nerves: the little fluttering heart, after one painful throb, came back to a sense of its duties. Perhaps Georgie had never looked so dangerously bewitching, as when she raised her head, quickly, from its resting-place; her cheek flushed with excitement, and somewhat too with shame; surprise and reproach in her soft eyes—softer than ever now, as they glanced timidly through the veil of the long wet lashes.

So—with a bitterer jealousy gnawing at her heart—thought Ida Carew, who rode up at that instant. But with this there mingled a fierce thrill of pleasure, as she marked the contraction of Dering's brow and the expression of his face; an expression not of satisfaction or triumph, but rather of patient suffering and steady resolve; such a look as you may often see, standing by a wounded soldier's bed, a minute after the surgeon's knife has gone sheer through nerve and bone.

It was only that last sight that enabled Ida to play out her part of friend and cousin so admirably; she was sympathetic without being sentimental, just sufficiently coherent in congratulation; neither too expansive in her praise of Dering's prowess, nor too sharp in the tender reproaches levelled at Georgie's nearly fatal self-will.

What the others said and did, is hardly worth recording. The Caliph was out that day, ridden by the groom, and Miss Verschoyle had no shadow of objection to a change of saddles. Indeed, it was with a sensation of security, and relief, and rest, like that of one who has just left a tossing skiff for the deck of a stout vessel, that she found herself on the back of her old favourite pacing soberly homewards.

CHAPTER VI.

IDA CAREW'S PASSION.

Amongst the troubles to which wealth is heir, not the lightest, I think, are the pomp and ceremonial that needs must attend its alliances. The vagrant, whose purse is lighter than his heart, may add another versicle to the song of defiance that he chants in the face of peril or plunder; reflecting, that—whatever trials may await them hereafter—he can at least wed his Dorothea, so soon as the marriage licence is bought, without let or hindrance, or flourish of legal trumpets, or any other of the preliminaries, inevitable when one of the purple-clad mates with Dives's daughter. The post-nuptial paradise of such may well promise fairly; for the path leading to its entrance gate is very tedious and winding—more so than the issue, now-a-days.

For two mortal hours Philip Gascoigne had been paying head-tax for his great possessions; listening and assenting to endless details of settlements and dower-charges, till, at last, in spite of courtesy and real interest in the matter, his pleasant face settled down into a helpless weariness. True it is, that the effect was much enhanced by the character of the man with whom Philip had principally to deal—rather a remarkable person in his way.

Solicitors, as a rule, I fancy, are rather a genial and jovial race, out of office hours; much given to hospitality, and avid of amusement of all kinds. The stiff, cautious legalist, who has been exasperating you with technical objections, till you wish yourself an outlaw for the nonce,

will often surprise you with his rapidity of transformation,
if you wait till the ominous black 'oak' has fairly closed
behind him.

Mr Serocold, in this respect, differed widely from his
fellows. In his office he was disagreeable enough, certainly. Men of portly presence, well-to-do in the world,
and excellent fathers of families, had been known to enter
there, bearing themselves jauntily, with a comfortable self-
confidence; and to issue thence half-an-hour afterwards
with a dejected mien, and a guilty sense of having been
only just prevented by their severe adviser from wasting
their substance, and wronging their children. But Robert
Serocold seemed rather to stiffen than relax when business
was done.

He was unmarried, and lived always alone in a large
brick house, not less rigidly repulsive than himself, in a
Surrey suburb; where he ruled several parochial roasts, as
perpetual churchwarden and poor-law guardian. In the
latter capacity he had, of course, many opportunities of
grinding the faces of his inferiors, and never let one of
them slip; but he was not satisfied with these. He delighted in giving evening lectures, at the school-house, on
the Improvement of the Labouring Classes, and other like
subjects; which gave him an opening for indulging in
fierce invective against drunkenness, improvidence, and
worse vices yet: all of these he imputed freely to the
puzzled, frightened listeners, who sate shivering there, with
a faint hope that their stern task-master would remember
their faces on the next board-day. He was very great
upon the points of total abstinence from strong drinks,
and punctual attendance at all church-services. There

began and ended his ideas and suggestions for the improvement of the proletarian.

Mr Serocold was a warm admirer (if he could be warm about anything) of the Dean of Torrcaster; and followed—not over humbly—in the steps of that austere divine. The tenets of both belonged to the scarce dissembled Calvinism which lurks in the outermost frontier of Low Church; the acrid school of 'professors,' so liberal of threats and niggardly of promises; who would narrow the circle of the saved till they might be counted by thousands, and enlarge that of the lost till it became merged in infinity; the venomous fatalists, who, deeming their own salvation sure, would not spare to others one throb of Hell's agony; the preachers, who roll out the Commination with an unction as if they were cursing their mortal enemy; but who, when the round of duty brings them to Quinquagesima Sunday, read the Epistle under grim protest, striving to rob the gentle words of half their meaning, by the harshness and hardness of their tones; thinking all the while within themselves that there is a taint of unsoundness in the theology of St Paul. Truly, fitting followers of the gaunt Genevan, who, with a hateful smile on his thin lips, would have beheld Servetus' death-struggles in the fire.

It was no wonder, if Mr Serocold's name stood high in his profession, though he had bought—not inherited his practice; and of his parentage or antecedents nothing was known. People felt themselves perfectly secure in the hands of the pitiless pietist; trusting him far more implicitly than they would have done a more genial adviser: indeed, it may be, that some of a timorous or nervous disposition were uuconsciously trying to propitiate him, by an extra display of confidence.

F

When Gascoigne's old family lawyer died, Chetwynde recommended him to take Mr Serocold.

'He's so intensely disagreeable that he must be safe,' Paul said. 'If you wanted to ruin yourself he wouldn't let you do it, merely out of the spirit of contradiction. He's got a cool, long head, too, to give the devil his due. When that £5000 legacy of my uncle Randolph's fell in, I gave it to him, with *carte blanche* as to investment. I don't think I could tell you where it is exactly—he has power of attorney and all that sort of thing—but it pays six per cent. regularly.'

This was the man that sate, now, in the library of Marston Lisle; tall, grave, hard-featured, and pale; checking the current of his clients' liberality with staid objections and sharp reminders; fixing him, too, all the while with frozen gray eyes not a whit softened by a pair of blue steel spectacles; till poor Philip began to feel as if he were only tenant-at-will of his own property, and that will—Robert Serocold's.

Mr Rule, the other solicitor, and Miss Verschoyle's representative, was a meek-spirited man, who would in any case have been over-awed by his tremendous brother-in-the-law; but, in point of fact, he had little to do, but to assent admiringly to the magnificent settlements that Gascoigne proposed.

Mr Serocold—in despite of a harsh-grating voice, and ungraceful delivery—was rhetorically inclined, and rather proud of his periods: it was in the middle of one of his best-turned sentences that the door opened quickly, and Paul Chetwynde entered, with a hurried step, very different from the lounging, lazy gait habitual to him. There were traces, too, of past excitement, still fluttering about his mouth and eyes. Those quiet faces when once thoroughly moved take time to settle again; just as a sheltered tarn, ruffled by some caprice of the wind, is slower to subside than the open mere where breezes wander at will.

The first glance at that face was enough for Gascoigne; he sprang up, with a frightened eagerness on his own, asking,—

'What has happened?'

Paul answered in his old placid deliberate way,—

'Nothing has happened, but—the best race it has been my luck to witness. Miss Verschoyle can tell you all about it; and, Philip—if I were you, I should go and talk to her at once. She has this instant dismounted.'

You may guess how long Gascoigne lingered. As the door closed behind him, Mr Serocold spoke; since the sudden interruption the gravity of his expression had deepened into gloom, and his bushy brows were more markedly bent.

'You do not often act hastily, Mr Chetwynde. May I ask your reason for calling Mr Gascoigne away, when such important business is on hand, which must be transacted within a very limited time?'

The grand, austere manner, that had proved so useful with many of his weak-minded clients, only provoked a faint smile from the placid cynic, who stood, comfortably warming himself at the wood-fire.

'Ah, Serocold! how are you?' he said carelessly. 'I hadn't time to salute you, when I came in. Yes—of course, I had good reasons for calling Gascoigne away. In common courtesy—if not in kindness—he ought not to delay congratulating his affianced, on one of the most wonderful escapes on record. I shouldn't wonder if you were to call it a "special interposition!" Would you like to hear how nearly all those deeds became not worth the parchment they are written on? And Gascoigne—if I know him—would never have given you a chance of drawing out other marriage-settlements. Listen, then.'

So Paul, in a very few curt, graphic sentences, told them —what you know already.

Mr. Serocold lifted his eyes heavenward, and slightly raised his joined palms; much after the fashion of certain devotees when they ask a blessing before meat.

'The ways of Providence are indeed merciful and inscrutable!' he said. 'I trust Miss Verschoyle has already given thanks, where thanks are chiefly due. If not——'

But it may be as well not to follow the fanatic further. It was one of the strange declamations characteristic of his school — half blasphemous, even if all sincere — where preaching mingles with prayer, and warning with self-exaltation: you can fancy enough for yourself, if my sketch has at all enabled you to realize the man.

Paul Chetwynde heard it out, with a lip slightly curling, but not without a glimmer of approval in his eyes; just as he might have listened to any other performer who got through his part creditably.

'You are a most excellent lawyer, Serocold,' he said; 'but I've always thought you mistook your vocation. You would have been exceedingly powerful on the platform, and right hard to beat in the pulpit. I wish the Dean had heard those last few sentences; they're more in his line than mine; but—after my light—I applaud. I fear I must leave you now. If I may advise, you could show Mr Rule (you might as well have introduced us, before proceeding to improve the " occasion "), some of the beauties of Marston

before the sun goes down. I don't think you've a chance
of catching Philip again, before dinner: you'll have to
finish him in the evening. Are you sure I can do nothing
more for you? Till dinner, then.'

So Paul lounged slowly out of the library; as if he had
performed more than his share of vicarious hospitality, and
was rather exhausted with the exertion.

But a pair of icy gray eyes followed him venomously,
and something was muttered between two rigid thin lips,
which was scarcely a blessing; every syllable of that careless banter was treasured up in a memory that never forgot
or forgave; and, it may be, bore fruit in the after-time.

Men of approved hardihood have turned sick and faint
ere now, when it was revealed to them that they had
passed unconsciously along the verge of violent death,
though the peril was passed. So, it was not strange that
Philip Gascoigne's gentle heart stopped beating, when he
heard of the awful hazard that had threatened a life dearer
than his own. He was too utterly unsettled for the moment, to notice the odd constraint in Georgie Verschoyle's
manner, or the painful flush that often shot across her fair
cheek, as she faltered and hesitated through her brief recital. His first intelligible words were spoken—not to his
love—but to his friend.

'Ah, Maurice!—how thoroughly right I was to trust her
to you. Trust you? So I will always—in everything, and
in spite of everything—through life and through death!'

The kind brown eyes were so very dim just then, that
they never saw the dark trouble on Dering's face—no, nor
the effort it cost him to answer lightly.

'My dear Philip—don't overwhelm me! Your own
groom could have done as much as I, if he had been

mounted as well. If there is any loose laurel about, The Moor, only, ought to be crowned. Didn't I tell you, last night, he was the best purchase I ever made? Queen Mab won't trouble you for some time to come. I'm much mistaken if that hock comes out sound to-morrow. But, if I were you, I should say a word in season to Mr Paice before dinner. He deserves it.'

Perhaps it was as well that Aunt Nellie and Mr Carew came in so opportunely, to cover everybody's retreat with their demonstrative congratulations and tender solicitudes: Ida had stolen quietly away, long ago. Of course, the chief thing they insisted on was,—that 'Georgie should lie down till dinner-time.' Feminine physicians prescribing for any disease, mental or bodily, however they may differ about particular nostrums, are generally unanimous in first making their patient supine.

No one was present at Philip's interview with his head-groom; but that worthy was 'beheaded,' with short and sharp shrift.

The master of Marston Lisle was easy to a fault with his dependents; nevertheless he was not disposed to look over gross ignorance or obstinacy—especially when they affected others than himself. It is probable that the dismissal was made easier by Mr Paice's peculiar fashion of self-exculpation; for that agreeable person, when driven into a corner, had a rat-like habit of turning and snapping savagely.

Had these things happened beyond the Channel, Philip would certainly have saluted Maurice on both cheeks, after dinner, styling him his saviour and benefactor; and then have 'carried him in a toast.' But those who know how singularly undemonstrative is a well-regulated English household, both in its joys and its sorrows, will not wonder if the last hours of that eventful day passed very much like the ordinary evenings at Marston.

Miss Verschoyle did not seem at all nervous or depressed; but she was much more quiet and subdued than usual, and evidently not up to much conversation. So she nestled into the corner of a remote sofa; and there, half-reclining, gave herself up to the tender mercies of Aunt Nellie, whose talents in the potting line were always equal to the emergency.

Ida Carew established herself at the piano, and straightway won Mr Rule's heart—soft in its mature autumn—by allowing him to turn over the leaves for her, and complimenting him on his sleight-of-hand. The honest elder was a musical fanatic, and the embers of romance still smouldered within him; he felt, for the nonce, translated into the body of one of those curled darlings of fashion whom he had often distantly admired: it was good to see him casting side-glances at his awful colleague, whose social inferiority he could now afford to commiserate.

As the girl's sweet clear voice sank or swelled, there was not one strain or break in the melody, nor one false note in the sparkling fantasias or melting cadences, created by the caprice of her lissom fingers. Her cheek was, perhaps, a shade paler than its wont; but still inscrutable —ay—even to those keen eyes of Paul Chetwynde's, that watched her among the rest, over the pages of the *Revue* that served him as a partial ambuscade.

Gascoigne wandered from one group to another—he was ever the most courteous of hosts—with a kind or pleasant word for all; but he lingered oftenest and longest behind Dering's chair, who had been rash enough to match himself at piquet against Mrs Carew. Each time that Philip

leant over to look through the hand, or whisper a sugges-
tion as to the discard, his hand would fall on his friend's
shoulder, and rest there, in a mute but very meaning
caress.

Yet Maurice shrank more than once from the light
pressure of these gentle fingers, as if they had touched a
scarce-healed wound ; and at those times the same dark,
set look of suppressed pain would sweep across his face,
though it vanished again instantly. He fell into fits of abstraction too, that had nothing to do with the game, and it
is needless to say, utterly failed to make a fight of it
against his astute antagonist.

Mr Serocold—solemn and solitary—digested a copious
dinner after his own saturnine fashion; holding a 'Quarter-
ly' in his hand, and keeping up the appearance of reading
—as he did of every duty in life—most respectably. He
sate apart from the rest, and interested himself in nothing
going on around him ; yet, somehow, he seemed to radiate
gloom. With a grim satisfaction he saw the hour arrive,
when he could decently venture to carry off Philip to complete the business that had been left undone.

Mr Rule, of course, was compelled to follow : with a
plethoric sigh, the good man issued forth into his own arid
legal world again, and heard the gates of Fairyland close
softly behind him—never to be unlocked again for him; at
least, so far as this deponent knoweth.

The Tabako-Parlement did not sit late that night, nor is
the debate worth recording : nothing of importance could
be discussed ; for Mr Rule was present in the stranger's
gallery. Mr Serocold, when Philip, as a matter of
courtesy, asked him to join them, had declined with a look
of holy horror, which was in itself a Counter-blast. He

was a bitter anti-nicotian of course, and lost no chance of taking up his parable against the pernicious weed : had he been a clerk in the reign of the First James, he would certainly have attained a deanery ; perchance, that of Carlisle.

If darkness and sleep settled down soon on all other chambers in Marston, in one room the lights burnt late, and the watching was long—the room in which Ida Carew lay ; plotting and pondering ; her busy head resting on the little hand buried in her braided tresses.

The perfect mask that fell for one second, once before to-day, is quite laid aside now. The girl's features have settled down again into that same strange expression that utterly changes, if it does not mar, their beauty ; a look that, I believe, is right rarely seen on the face of English maidenhood ; but which may well have been worn by one of Catherine's fair wicked minions, as she sat musing, without ruth or remorse, on what the morrow would bring ; holding between her steady fingers *that* which must end at once her own mad jealousy and her rival's life—a pinch or two of shining gray powder, bought an hour ago at a hundred times its weight in gold—the latest devilry of René, the Queen's Poisoner.

Ida's lips kept moving perpetually ; but for some time only broken syllables escaped them ; indications of busy brain-work, just sufficient to prevent a cunning hunter of thoughts—had such been near—from quite losing the trail. But as she waxed more restless and impatient, some few connected words forced their way outwards.

'Georgie—darling Georgie—if you knew how I love you now ; how I have always loved you,—with your sweet baby-face, and soft eyes, and pretty coaxing ways ! The luck

has been yours since we were children; but the end is not
quite yet, and, perhaps——. The end—how very near it
came to-day. Just a few yards farther——. I know, I
know; she might have been lying now at the foot of the
chalk cliff, and I no nearer what I strive for. Yet I wish
—I wish——'

With all her cruel hardihood, and in despite of the bitter
passion that possessed her, Ida Carew dared not finish that
sentence aloud, or trust all her confession even to the
night. But the small white teeth were clenched sharply
and firmly, as the jaws of a steel-trap; and the viperine
light in the contracting pupils glittered yet more dangerously. After a minute or two, she began to mutter again;
then both her face and manner were softened; and a
certain plaintiveness in her voice told that the fountain of
her tears was not locked up for ever.

'No; I cannot hope. He would never think of love and
me together; if Georgie were dead, there would always be
another barrier. Geoffrey is as much his friend as Philip.
He would never be true to one and false to the other. He
was true, to-day—my own Maurice—I saw his face when
she lifted hers from his shoulder—it was so pale and pained; but always so honest and brave. I know he never
said one wrong word, though she tempted him—as she *can*
tempt. And he will go away—so far away—and die, perhaps, without ever guessing that I would follow him so
gladly, and take all the burden of the sin and shame; and
never grudge it, nor reproach him; no, not if he wearied
of me at the year's end. He shall not go away—so. I
will——And Geoffrey comes to-morrow. God help me!
What *shall* I do?'

God help her—To what?

Evil as she was by nature, it is probable that Ida would have shrunk from that ejaculation, if she had realized its hideous blasphemy. But she uttered it quite mechanically. There is nothing unnatural in this. Wo will not speak of those devotional assassins of Italy and Spain, who invariably attend mass when a grand *coup* is preparing; because they are benighted Papists, you know, and steeped in vain superstition to the lips. But have you never heard an enlightened Protestant indulge in similar petitions, while meditating or practising things, that, if Heaven forgave, no more could bo expected from its mercy? If not, you have been luckier than I.

However, with no other orison, Ida Carew laid down her tired head at last, and slept soundly till late in the morning.

O simple-minded sister of mine! You weary sometimes of the quiet monotony of maidenhood, and murmur in your innocent heart that the romance of life is long in coming. That sleeping girl might have forgotten already—and it would have been well for her—more than you are ever likely to know; yet, I think, you need not envy her her dreams.

CHAPTER VII.

PUNISHMENT PARADE.

MAURICE DERING rose on the following morning after restless, broken sleep, with a feverish sensation of discomfort and discontent, very foreign to his usual careless cheerfulness. Men of his habits and organization, when anything has gone wrong with body or mind, resort to active exercise as the first panacea, just as naturally as a wounded deer takes to 'soil.' He thought he would try the effect of a brush before breakfast through the fresh autumn weather, and see whether The Moor was at all stale after his strong gallop: he generally superintended the horse's exercise since the training had begun.

While The Moor and a hack were being saddled, Dering lounged through the stables till he came to the box where Queen Mab was standing. The first glance told him the state of things. The mare was resting her near hind-leg, and waving her head restlessly from side to side—evidently in pain, in spite of the wet bandages that swathed her hock from pastern to knee. The first real trial had told fearfully on her weak points; there she stood—dead lame; in all probability, not worth as many shillings as she had cost guineas.

'I thought how it would be.' As Maurice spoke these words half aloud—thinking himself alone—there mingled with the compassion that every true horseman must feel for an animal in pain, the faint satisfaction of a judge, whose opinion has been justified by the event.

'Yer thought so, did yer?' a hoarse thick voice said behind him. 'I hope yer satisfied, heveryway. I s'pose yer come to see me hoff the premises, now you've got me the sack?'

Maurice turned quickly on his heel, and there, close at his shoulder, was the bull-dog face of the discharged stud-groom—flushed with liquor even at that early hour—a glare of irrational fury in his blood-shot eyes.

'You had better take yourself off peaceably, before worse

comes of it. I should not discuss the question with you,
even if you were sober. I believe Mr Gascoigne wanted
no prompting to discharge you; if he had, I should have
advised him strongly to do so. There's no safety in any
stable—not even for life—where the head-servant is insolent, or ignorant, or dishonest, or a drunkard. One
doesn't often find the four faults together; but they would
all go into *your* character, if I had to give you one. Stand
out of the doorway; I wish to pass.'

If Mr Paice's morning draught had been a little less potent, he would have been warned by the gathering darkness
on Dering's brow, and by the compression of the lips—
braced till the heavy moustache almost hid them—that he
had gone to the very verge of safety. But he was nearly
blind with drink and rage, and deceived, too, by the
speaker's tone—exceedingly quiet and calm, though the
words were the reverse of conciliatory. The crimson of
his cheek deepened to purple, and the veins on his forehead swelled like whipcords, as he answered—

'Yer want to pass? Not afore I've given you another
bit of my mind. Whose fault do yer s'pose it is, as that
there mare's broke down? Why, a child might have
ridden her, if it knew how to ride. So I'm to look for
another place becos a young 'oman's got no hands.
D—n——'

At whom the intercepted curse was levelled, can only
be known to Mr Paice's own conscience; for all further
words were lost in a choking gurgle, as an iron grip closed
round his throat, forcing him backwards through the open
doorway. In the midst of his wrath, Dering remembered
stable discipline, and forebore to use his whip, till they
were fairly in the open yard. Once there—he shifted his

grasp from the delinquent's neck to his collar, and the punishment parade began.

Now there are diversities of chastisements.

There is the chastisement fantastic : when, after a light stroke or two, that the flesh can scarcely feel, however they may gall the spirit, the patient is requested to consider himself horsewhipped—an utter impossibility sometimes, unless he chance to be gifted with a vivid imagination. Again, there is the chastisement spasmodic : where the executioner loses his head after the first blow or two, and begins to hit wild ; in this case the flurry and flustration bear an inverse proportion to the real work done; when all is over it is often difficult to say which of the two parties concerned is the more thoroughly exhausted and blown; and the spectator is irresistibly reminded of the Satanic comment on the shearing of the swine. Thirdly and lastly, my brethren, there is the chastisement proper —or judicial; not erring on the side of mercy, nor yet degenerating into brutality; where every blow descends with the deliberate emphasis of scientific strength ; where the performer has sufficient self-control never to infringe on the two-score, if he has previously determined to administer forty stripes, save one.

Such a spectacle is not a pleasant one to witness, of course; but if the provocation has been intense, it may be —endured. The chiefs who gathered round Agamemnon, during that weary Decade of years, assisted, I fancy, at scenes more displeasing to their heroic minds, than the punishment of Thersites.

Should these pages ever travel so far East as the heart of the Indian hills, and fail to find an echo in all other breasts, I think they will strike a memorial chord in that

of a certain stalwart veteran, of whose prowess in this line
(also exercised *in corpore vili* of an insolent groom), I, who
write, retain a respectful recollection. O, fair-haired son
of Milesius! Mighty wielder of the strident scourge!
Wheresoever you may be—under roof, under canvas, or
under the stars—*Waes hael!* I drain this cup in your
honour, and—were it not superfluous—would wish 'more
power to your elbow!'

Mr Paice had had considerable active experience in the
punishment of boys and beasts; he soon discovered that
he was in a very false position, or—to use his own vernacular—'had got into a real bad thing.' He struggled—
almost silently at first, for the dogged devil within him
was not easily cowed—but he had no more chance of getting loose than if he had been lashed to the triangles; then
curses, mingled with uncouth prayers for mercy, gushed
out with the foam from his working lips; and then all
words were merged in hoarse howls of rage and pain.

Through curse, and prayer, and shriek, Maurice Dering
smote on—neither moved at all to relenting, nor yet stirred
to greater severity—till he thought the offence amply
atoned. Then he cast the victim away, with the full force
of his arm, flinging the whip after him, where he fell; and
spoke, just as quietly as before, without a quickened breath
or altered tone.

'Now, will you go? You might have known that as
soon as you left Mr Gascoigne's service, you were no safer
from me than any other drunken ruffian who might choose
to be insolent. You may take the whip with you, if you
like; I'll never use it on an honest horse again: that's all
the compensation you'll get from me, unless you choose to
go to law about it. You've got a fair five-pounds' worth,

I fancy.—Turn him out, some of you, if he's not outside
the gates in five minutes, and send his traps after him to
the Gascoigne Arms. And, Harris, take The Moor out for
walking exercise : I shall not ride this morning.'

So, turning on his heel, without another look at the
figure that lay rolling and writhing on the stones, Dering
walked slowly away.

Painfully, at last, the stud-groom gathered himself together and rose to his feet; he shook his fist once, in stealthy
menace, at the back of his chastiser; but spoke not a
syllable aloud. He was wise enough to remember that
every one of the stable-men who stood by, with triumph and
satisfaction on their faces, had more or less been forced to
endorse his brutal tyranny, and would like nothing better
than to find an excuse for taking a share in reprisal.

Foremost in the knot of spectators was the bullet-headed
boy afore-mentioned—every expression of his blunt features
merged into a superhuman grin. Narrating these things
to a village comrade, afterwards, said Jem—

' I got a many weltings from old Paice : that's sartain.
But the Capting giv 'em back to him—the Capting did—
all biled down into one.'

So the great stud-groom departed incontinently and
ingloriously, under cover of a derisive cheer from his late
subordinates. He did not go to law : this moderation was
easily accounted for when Philip examined his accounts
afterwards, from curiosity (he had been too idle to do this
at the time of the dismissal); they revealed a really remarkable system of comprehensive plunder, and a talent
for cooking figures that would have done credit to a Quar-
termaster-general, or any other of the splendidly fraudu-
lent officials who sit in the high places of Federaldom.

As Maurice Dering sauntered back to the house, which was at some distance from the stables, with a belt of high forest-trees between, he felt slightly contrite and ashamed of himself; not because he had yielded to a natural impulse of violence, but because the opening of the safety-valve had relieved him so intensely.

On the steps, before the great hall-door, stood Paul Chetwynde, bareheaded; drinking the fresh autumn air with evident relish : his eye ranged over the fair landscape with critical appreciation and tranquil approval, much as if he had been looking at a masterpiece of Turner or Claude Lorraine.

'Whence comes my Maurice, through the rosy dawn?' Paul quoted, as Dering drew near (it was close upon 10 A.M., but the speaker's habits were the reverse of matinal).

'I've been to the stables,' the other answered, 'meaning to see The Moor out before breakfast; but Paice upset my plans altogether.'

'What on earth had *he* got to do with it?' Chetwynde asked, opening his eyes rather wider. 'I thought he had ceased from troubling? Didn't Philip discharge him last night?'

'Certainly. But, you see, he wouldn't go quietly : he fancied I was the cause of his dismissal, and he had been drinking up to boiling-point besides. He was insolent— more insolent than you can imagine;—but I gave him a lesson he won't forget in a hurry. I never thrashed a man with a whip before; and I don't care to do it again : though Paice *did* deserve it.'

Paul contemplated the stalwart speaker with a lazy admiration.

6

'How I envy people of active habits,' he said. 'Now you'll have an appetite at breakfast, à faire fremir, while Philip and I are trifling with our dry toast and muffins. It would have refreshed me exceedingly to have seen Paice punished. I've had a personal animosity against that man since I first set eyes on him, though I don't think he ever spoke to me. You'll want a biographer soon, if you go on with these exploits. There's sure to be some fresh parsley at breakfast: shall the women weave you a little athletic crown?'

'Don't say a word to them about it,' Maurice broke in, anxiously. 'I'm half ashamed of myself, as it is; I got up in a devil of a temper this morning; and, I'm afraid, I was only too glad to find something to vent it on. Bad form that—all over. It's full time for me to get away. I'm doing no good here.'

Chetwynde gazed into his friend's eyes, wistfully, for several seconds, before he answered; and there came over his face a look of grave kindness, very different from its usual cynical indolence.

'So you still hold to your exchange?' he said. 'I swear, I like you better for it. This home-service is a simple waste of energies like yours. York, and Dublin, and Brighton are good quarters enough; but there are pleasant places—and pleasant faces too—in the far East: and, for some constitutions, there's nothing like a thorough change of air. Maurice—I think it will do *you* good.'

Then Dering knew that his secret was his own no longer. Perhaps he would have chosen Paul Chetwynde out of the world as his confidant. Nevertheless, a sharp throb of pain shot through his heart just then: his cheek flushed dark-red, and he bit his lower lip, unconsciously, till the blood sprang.

'So *you* can't trust me?' he said, sadly. 'I can't wonder at it, when I don't always trust myself. And yet——'

'How dare you say those words,' the other broke in. 'Trust you? I rely on your faith and honour, more than I do on my own. Maurice, I am not thinking of others, but of your own honest self, when I say—Go!'

The momentary flash of anger faded out of his keen blue eyes before Chetwynde had finished speaking, and they rested now with a loving earnestness on Dering's troubled face. For a minute or so, both were silent: then Maurice drew a deep breath, and spoke quite coolly and calmly.

'We won't talk about this any more. But, Paul, I'm so glad you know it all, and take it as you do. You must help me with Philip, you know. Poor old man! I think he'll miss me more than either you or Geoff. He would never get over it, if I went before the weddings came off. I must stay till after that, if possible. Don't you think so?'

'Decidedly,' Paul answered: and so they went in together, without more words.

Of all the trials that put passive hardihood to sore proof, the sharpest, I think, is, when we are compelled to stand by, and see the thing dearest to us on earth passing slowly into another's possession; being expected all the while not only to dissemble our own misery but to sympathize with the winner's happiness. It does not much mend the matter, if he happen to be 'our trusty and well-beloved cousin;' or if the rivalry be only known to our own conscience.

Now mark, I pray you, how it stood with these two men.

The one was deliberately condemning himself to another month or so of this bitter penance : the other approved and confirmed the resolution ; simply because, had their positions been inverted, he would have done precisely the same. The act of self-sacrifice for a comrade's sake, appeared to both perfectly natural—if not easy. Yet both were tough, practical men of the world, without a spark of sentimentalism ; not even endowed with peculiarly acute sensibilities : there were no more elements of a romantic hero in Maurice Dering's character, than might be found in that of most soldiers of gentle birth and breeding ; surely, if Paul Chetwynde's best friend were seeking for an example of impulsive generosity he would have looked for it otherwhere than in that hard, cold, sardonic materialist.

Is it worth while to analyze these ethical anomalies—to settle by the Stagyrite's rule the exact Attribute, that is the mainspring of the heart-machine, when it works eccentrically?

I think not. Life would be dull work without its little riddles—hard work, if we were bound to solve them all. Besides, every page of these sealed books will, perhaps, be laid open for us, if only we possess our souls in patience, until the dawning of a certain Day.

CHAPTER VIII.

THE SPORTING PARSON.

THE clouds that seemed gathering round Marston Lisle vanished with Mr Serocold, who made his adieux immediately after breakfast, with staid, freezing courtesy : not even then relaxing his tacit disapproval of the worldliness regnant there. As a matter of conscience, he declined to remunerate either the servant who had attended him, or the groom who drove them to the station; and punished his meek associate for paying double, by snubbing him at five-minute intervals all the way up to town.

When that grim Presence was once removed, every one appeared disposed to make the most of the bright October day. The womankind started about noon, to join the last croquet-party of the season, at a pleasant manor-house some ten miles off; and the men addressed themselves to the depopulation of certain small covers and plantations that lay temptingly near at hand.

Philip Gascoigne was certainly not made of sporting stuff. He met the hounds when they were within easy distance, and the weather looked promising : few places in the country boasted a larger herd of game than Marston : but he hunted and shot very much as he attended quarter-sessions—after a listless, languid fashion : not exactly bored; but still, evidently, discharging a duty of his social position. Of the other two, Chetwynde was an unvarying steady shot, Dering a very brilliant one; though he was hardly in his usual form that day.

The afternoon was far spent, and the hottest corner of several warm ones was nearly done. Maurice was standing alone, out in the open, about 50 yards from the edge of the belt (they let their birds rise fairly, and never butchered them at Marston) ; he was just drawing on a pheasant, almost out of distance, that was heading back up the cover, when a voice spoke close to his ear—

'A long shot—too long for clean killing. There—I told you so : that's a strong runner, for money.'

Dering's nerves were not easily startled : he pulled
trigger just as steadily as if he had been still alone ; and
if the old cock fluttered down, instead of dying in the air,
distance rather than change of aim was the cause. Then
he turned and greeted the new-comer, laughing merrily.

'Why, Geoff, you're three hours earlier than we expected.
I wouldn't say much about that cock, if I were you. Is
that a new Devon fashion—speaking to a man on his shot ?
See the jealousy of these sporting parsons ! They can't
bear to see any one else kill, even when they've no gun in
their hands. Take mine, old man ; I know your fingers are
itching for it ; and I've shot till I'm tired. I suppose you
found no one at home. The womankind are all croqueting
at Sele Abbey.'

While Geoffrey Luttrell takes the offered gun—not unwillingly—and stretches himself preparatory to keeling
over that brace of cocks that are coming up, high and
wide, let us scan him over for a minute or so.

A sturdy figure, below middle height, square of shoulder
and deep in chest, with brawny limbs, that are only kept
down from fleshiness by habits of temperance and strong
exercise. A healthy florid face, very pleasant to look
upon ; but too irregular in feature for any class of beauty,
despite the advantages of a ready smile, superb teeth, and
two broad blue eyes—not hard and cold like Paul Chetwynde's, but full of a warm genial light, though at times
they might flash irascibly : all this is framed in portentous
whiskers that only just escape the beard, of a redder brown
than the strong close-cut hair.

The voice matches the face and figure right well—full,
sonorous, and jovial ; with a slight West-country accent,
that brings back at once to the hearer memories of bare

moorlands, heathy hills, bosky combes, and clear rivulets racing seawards—all ripple and sparkle and foam.

Truth to say, his attire—a suit of the correctest dark-gray—is about the most clerical attribute of the reverend **man's** exterior. Yet, after his own fashion, Geoffrey Luttrell did his duty well : if other parish priests were more respected, few certainly were better loved. He had taken orders as a second son, and the family living; with no especial leaning to the profession, yet not sullenly, as by enforcement. When the death of his elder brother, child-less. made him Head of his House—the lands were not broad, but the Luttrells had owned them through five centuries—he shifted his quarters from the Rectory to the Court, and took an old college friend as his curate : these were about the only changes in the Clerk-Squire's manner of life.

He had always given play to his robust organization, by a liberal indulgence in athletics ; a slashing unscientific hitter and mercilessly swift bowler at cricket ; a thorough rough-weather fisherman, both by land and sea ; with an eye for a cock in thick uneven cover, renowned through-out North Devon. All these pursuits Geoffrey practised still ; but not a whit more strenuously than when he was a parson in sole charge, with very limited means.

Strangers, who have only hunted occasionally in those parts, will not be inclined to give our divine credit for much self-denial, in utterly abstaining from the hunting-field, though he subscribed liberally to the hounds. But for a native, even an unenclosed waste, with alternating perils of bog and boulder, has its attractions ; perhaps there is as much excitement in a quick forty minutes over Dartmoor as in a burst of half the length from Lilbourne.

It is fair to presume that Luttrell—a Devonian to the back-bone—would have enjoyed a gallop through the bracing moorland air not less than his fellows : so let us credit him with real scruples of conscience.

Though Geoffrey kept a curate now, he was by no means inclined to shirk his fair share of duty. The dwellings of the poor are widely scattered in those parts; but none, sick or needy, in that parish had long to wait, before the Rector came to help, not only with his purse but his prayers. He preached to his people once each Sunday, in strong simple words of his own ; never descending to the vernacular, but never soaring above plain Saxon-English ; he did not attempt to frighten or bewilder his hearers, nor to drive religion into them, as it were, with a sword's point; yet he could speak sharply when there was occasion; wilful sin or shame was more likely to find mercy in the eyes of the austerest divine in the country-side, than in those of the sporting parson of Minster Combe.

And this man was about to trust his happiness to the keeping of the pious young person, at whose evening medi-tations and devotions you partially assisted awhile ago.

A curious conjuncture—if it were not so often paralleled. For, of a truth, scarce a day passes wherein one might not quote—

> Sic visum Veneri : cui placet impares
> Mentes atque animos sub juga ænea
> Sævo mittere cum joco.

It was easy to guess which of the twain was destined to honour and obey. Indeed, that question was settled already, and the wifely homage of the marriage service could only be a mockery now. Those honest impulsive natures are just as helpless in the grasp of a clever unscrupulous woman, as a strong wolf-hound in the coils of a boa. It was so before history began : it will be so till futurity is fulfilled. The same spells that subdued the Demigod, the Assyrian, and the Jew are woven round many museular Christians in this our day; it matters little whether the name of the sorceress be Omphalè, or Semiramis, or Delilah, or Ida.

The most provoking part of it is, that the thrall gets no more credit for submission from the enslaver, than if he had been born in serfdom. Power, of course, is the thing that all these 'fair Mischiefs' love most dearly; but it by no means follows, that the love is extended to the most faithful of their subjects. Remember I am not speaking now of true women, too proud to scheme for sovereignty, too generous to abuse it when attained ; but of those, who will risk fame and fortune to gratify a passion or a whim, and accept the gift of a life's devotion with serene ingratitude. Clytemnestra will humble herself to the dust at the feet of the base-born Ægisthus, while she tramples under her own the faith and honour of Agamemnon.

When Ida Carew listened to Geoffrey Luttrell's wooing, it is probable that she fully calculated upon uncontrolled supremacy ; this came with conditions of a 'good match,' just as the social position of her suitor might do. But if her heart—such a heart as it was—could ever have gone with her hand, it would have been given to a man strong enough to put bit and bridle on her wild nature, and wise enough never to let the reins quite out of his grasp ; nor would she have liked him the less if he did, at times, draw the curb rather sharply.

As it was, she treated her betrothed very much as the Beauty of a family treats

The dozen tall Irish cousins,
Whom she loves in a sisterly way.

That is to say, she was always pleasant and good-natured and amusing, but objected to transports of any kind. Without being actually repulsed or repressed, Geoffrey soon learnt that he must refrain from many familiarities that are usually sanctioned in courtship; unlimited osculation, or promiscuous caresses, were by no means allowed.

But he was of that happy disposition that looks ever on the silver side of life, and is content to trust to time to set all things even: if there were moments when he felt discomfited or disappointed, he shook off the chill before it could fasten on him, laughing at himself in his own hearty, jovial way.

So the future of these two might well be calm and prosperous if not brilliantly happy.

Very calm, too, was the gray autumn morning when we stood on the North Devon coast; and, looking seaward, marvelled that the bread-winners of Clovelly, and Bucks, and Hartland should turn homewards so early. There was no sign or omen of storm, save a jagged rim of cloud climbing the western shoulder of Lundy, and a murmur—less menacing than mournful—of the dusky sea. But, before the sun went down, the moan had deepened into a savage roar; there was thunder and rattle on Northam pebble-beach; and far away—white under the lowering rack—a broad, waved belt of foam showed where the surf-strife was raging on Bideford Bar.

CHAPTER IX.

A LOSING HAZARD.

You may suppose the greeting that ensued, when Chet-wynde and Gascoigne joined the others. It was good to see the twinkle in the Parson's broad blue eyes—though he shook his head once, as a matter of form—when they made Maurice, very reluctantly, repeat the details of the morning's execution.

Truth to say, before he became a professional man of peace, Geoffrey himself had been a noted artist with the gloves. There was never in his big tender heart a grain of malice against any living creature; but, in his under-graduate days, that square, sturdy figure was always to be found in the front rank of the roysterers on the Ides of November. On one special night—a night that many now living well remember—when the Gown, heavily over-matched, was giving ground in the Turl, till the flank of the enemy was fairly turned by the column debouching from Brasenose Lane—Luttrell had dined with the 'Phœnix;' and fought shoulder to shoulder with the valiant Cyclops who led that famous charge.

So, at last, you see the Quadrilateral complete.

Whatever these four men might be—taken singly—it is certain that, standing together, back to back, they made up a formidable rallying-square.

The meeting of the betrothed would, probably, have been a very quiet affair, even if no one had been by to witness it. As it took place in public—the womenkind were loitering about the Terrace when their cavaliers re-

turned—neither party could claim much credit for their
undemonstrative manner. Yet Ida drew back, rather
more quickly than usual, from the light brow-kiss, though
it was almost a formal salute; and her cheek flushed
angrily, when, a second afterwards, her eyes met Maurice
Dering's.

Neither could she, with all her self-control, prevent her
glances from straying furtively in that same direction
during the brief *tête-à-tête* with which she indulged her
lover in the course of the evening. She listened to all that
he had to tell with her wonted show of good-natured
interest; but sometimes answered at random. A keener
observer than poor Geoffrey would soon have seen, that
her thoughts, as well as her eyes, were wandering. Yet
when that great honest heart was beating closest to her
own, Ida never flinched or faltered in her set purpose.

What that purpose was, you will know very soon, if you
have not guessed it already.

For the next three days things went pleasantly and
smoothly as usual. Between Miss Verschoyle and Dering
there might still have been a shade of awkward consciousness that would have caused either to avoid an interview
en champ clos; but it was not grave enough to make the
position painfully embarrassing.

On the fourth morning, Gascoigne was obliged to go to
the neighbouring county-town on sessions business; the
other three men were to shoot some small belts and clumps
in the park. Soon after luncheon the two girls walked
out to join them, and stayed chatting and looking at the
shooting (at a decent distance) till late in the afternoon.
When the last clump was cleared, there was still some
daylight left: several snipe had been seen lately about the

low grounds and river-meadows; his Reverence, still insatiate of sport, would not consent to leave the poor passage-birds in peace; so — with a slight apology, which was easily accepted—he set off with the head-keeper to try his luck; leaving his friends to escort the damsels home.

The *quartette* seemed to pair off by tacit consent: if there was any pre-arranged plan, it was certain that the contriver had kept it to herself, and that the others were quite innocent of connivance. Yet it so befell, that, after a little, Dering and Miss Carew found themselves considerably in the rear of the other two.

The walk home went winding through brush-wood and fern, along the edge of the steep upland; they had just reached a point where a sharp turn and some thick shrubs hid the foremost pair from sight, when Ida halted—saying, in her usual quiet tones—

' Is not *that* worth looking at ?'

It was of the landscape she spoke, which indeed did deserve more than a passing glance. The sun wanted yet a full hour of setting, but it had gone down behind a heavy bank of cloud, through the rifts of which pierced gleams and gushes of sombre, unearthly flame—wherein purple, and crimson, and orange, and many another prismatic tint beside—were mingled, like the strange radiance that struggles to the surface of fire-marble, or Labrador stone. The fair valley of the Lone was looking its loveliest just then; for the gorgeous autumn colouring was heightened everywhere, in fore and back-ground, by the marvellous effects of light and shade.

Dering stood silent for a minute or so—slightly in advance of his companion—gazing on the scene with a

genuine admiration; his left arm resting on the muzzle of
his empty gun, his right hanging listlessly by his side.

Suddenly, slender fingers stole round that right wrist,
lightly, at first, as thistle-down, but always tightening
their clasp; and a voice, low and sweet, though tremulous
with unutterable passion, murmured in Maurice's ear one
word—his own Christian name.

Only one word. What of that? Have we not known
orations, funereal or valedictory, that took days in the
composing, hours in the declaiming, and yet were not half
so eloquent as Astarte's farewell?

That little lissome hand, in despite of the fiery blood
that was leaping through its blue veins, was soft and cool
as white velvet; but under its touch the strong soldier
shrank and shivered, as the Baron of Smaylhome's false
wife may have done, when the dead adulterer's grasp
scorched her to the bone.

After that, he stood still in his place, as if under some
mesmeric spell; never turning his head, nor diverting his
eyes from their fixed gaze, though surely they realized no
one object, far or near. He did not hear the half of the
broken syllables that followed that first word which told
him all. For Ida would not leave her self-abasement incomplete.

Not one of those syllables shall be written down here.
It was necessary that the scene should be partially pro-
duced, because it is one of the main hinges of this story.
But—in spite of all imputations to the contrary, past, present, and to come—I *can* say, in simple truth, that I would
not wittingly linger over any ensample, real or imaginary,
of woman's degradation or dishonour.

Do not suppose that while Dering stood thus, silent and

still, he was struggling with any temptation whatsoever. If his heart had not been already filled with his hopeless love for another; nay, if she herself had not been contracted to his dear friend, there never would have been a corner in it for Ida Carew.

Maurice was not suspicious by nature, neither was he a particularly acute observer: he had not of course penetrated far below the surface of the dark tortuous character which had foiled even Paul Chetwynde: but he would never have been lulled into security like poor Geoffrey Luttrell. Though the girl's manner was so haughtily indifferent, her temper seemingly so perfect, her affections so admirably distributed and controlled, the cold bright eye had said to Maurice, often and often ere this—

> Yet is there something dangerous within me,
> Which let thy wisdom fear.

So it was easy for him now to close his ears to the voice of the charmer. Indeed, he scarcely thought about Ida at all. For a few seconds there was upon him a horror, hard to describe; an awful apprehension of treachery and danger gathering under the feet of those whom he loved best on earth; mingling with a consciousness of having himself—wittingly or unwittingly—much to do with the laying of the mine.

It is only justice to him to say, that he felt not one thrill of gratified vanity at Ida's avowal. In some things he was wonderfully simple and single-minded. Indeed in these respects he rather resembled a certain honest friend of mine own—gifted with remarkable personal attractions—who is perpetually achieving small conquests at first sight, and invariably declining to follow up the advantage. I remember well the meek reply, that once disarmed those who were bantering *ce bon Arthur* on such supineness—

'Well—I dare say you're quite right. Only—you see, I don't go for "killing."' He meant 'lady-killing.'

When Dering turned, at Ida's last passionate appeal— 'at least to answer her—only one word,'—his frank face had grown strangely dark; darker than when, four days ago, he began to chastise the insolent groom. But he used no more force than was necessary, to draw his wrist gently out of her clasp; and his voice was rather sad than stern. Indeed, he was speaking rather to himself than to Ida:—

'If Geoffrey knew this, I believe it would kill him.'

In good sooth she *was* answered. If one little flame of hope still flickered in the girl's breast, it was quenched then utterly, for ever.

One night, some forty years ago (an eye-witness told me all this), in the card-room of a certain club, a ring of lookers-on were gathered round the table, where a match at piquet was proceeding, for stakes exceptionally high even in those days when giants gambled. Fortune was steady against one of the players; a tall handsome man, with a fine thorough-bred face terribly worn by hard living and late vigils. There was one small red stain on his elaborate *jabot* (our grandsires, you know, were gorgeous in fine linen), where a drop of blood from his lower lip had fallen. That was the single sign of annoyance he betrayed from first to last of the long sitting. Indeed, his manner was far more gay and careless than that of his opponent; and his occasional laugh at some extraordinary phase of ill-luck did not seem forced or unnatural. Yet, with every deal of the cards, the Shadow was closing round

that man, faster and nearer; the letters were lying at
home, directed and sealed, that told those who cared to
hear, how he had gone out that night determined, one way
or another, to settle accounts with the world; and, four
hours after, as the gray March morning was breaking,
they drew him out of the mud of the Serpentine, dead and
cold.

Somewhat similar was Ida's case. She had resolved on
the venture, not without counting the cost; she knew that,
on the one side was a desperate chance of winning—on the
other, fruitless humiliation—a very suicide of honour. So,
now that the game was lost, she stood prepared to pay that
which was owing to the uttermost; asking no favour, attempting no evasion. Before Dering had finished speaking,
she was far calmer than he.

'I must have more sins on my soul than I knew of,'
Maurice went on—'or these trials would not be sent. How
am I to answer you? I would not say one harsh or cruel
word; but it must be best, not to lie. I must tell you,
that if there had been nothing binding you to Geoffrey—
nothing that makes it baseness in me to listen to any such
words as you have spoken—there could never have been
any link stronger than friendship between you and me. I
cannot tell why—but I feel it is so. You have power
enough over men, to bear hearing the truth, for once.
And I cannot thank you, either. God forgive you'—there
was a sob in his strong clear voice. 'Do you know what
you have done? Do you know how long it will be before
I shall look Geoffrey Luttrell in the face, without shrinking
like a traitor? You are no true woman, or, in pity, you
would have spared me this.'

He wronged her there. With all her sinfulness upon

H

her, it *was* a true woman that answered Maurice then, with
a voice and eyes far steadier than his own. A true woman
—because, when shame or sorrow hung over the man she
loved, her first impulse was to bear her share of the burden
—and more.

'How can you speak so?' Ida broke in. 'You a traitor—you, who have never by look or word encouraged my
madness—who have been brave enough to speak the hard,
honest truth, even now? What could Geoffrey blame *you*
for, if he knew all? The treachery and shame is mine—
all mine. I feel neither now, whatever I may feel in after-
time. Maurice, I will never repent having spoken to-day.
I would rather that you trod my love under your feet, than
that you should go away and never know it was yours. But
I will never speak again, till I die. Ah, don't turn your
head away again, without saying that you will forgive and
forget.'

Perhaps, in all her life, Ida Carew had never looked so
lovely as she did at that moment; before the passionate
flush had quite faded on her cheek, or the eager fire in her
eyes. Not one spark of admiration was kindled in Dering's
heart; nevertheless it melted marvellously, as she gazed
up into his face with a faint, timid smile, more piteous
than tears.

'I spoke far too harshly,' he said; 'and selfishly, too.
What am I, that I should judge you? Nay, I will not
have you judge yourself too hardly. Perhaps no real harm
need happen after all. You are very young, and we all
know the fate of most girlish fancies. Years hence, when
you are a steady chaperon, and I a battered veteran on
half-pay, we may laugh over this one.'

Ida saw the effort it cost him to speak thus lightly, and

seconded it bravely: it was not all bad in her, you see.
She cast her eyes down, lest ho should see in them reproach or denial; knowing all tho while how long it
would be before *she* would smile, remembering that 'girlish fancy'

'I dare say you are right,' she said, softly. 'At any rate,
be sure Geoffrey shall not suffer. I will do my very best
to make him a good wife, and strive my uttermost to love
him as he deserves; just as if this madness of mine had
never been. Fever-fits do good sometimes, they say; and
perhaps this one may turn me, a little sooner, into a sober,
sensible matron. You will trust me so far, I know; and
keep my secret, always?'

Dering's face brightened wonderfully. That good Maurice! In a case like this, he was as easily hoodwinked as
a child.

'I do trust you, heartily,' he said, 'and I am too glad to
do so; for if it were otherwise, my lips would be sealed.
It is the simplest question of honour.'

The bright fathomless eyes looked up into his face again,
with a wistful earnestness.

'Thanks—so many thanks,' she whispered; 'and I will
keep *your* secret too.'

The dark-red flush, that always showed when he was
much provoked or moved, mounted to Dering's brow: he
struck the butt of his gun sharply on the ground, as he
turned half aside with a short bitter laugh.

'So you have found me out too? I gave Paul's sagacity
more credit than it deserved. I'm worse than a schoolboy
in his first passion. I suppose my face has been telling
tales?'

'Only once,' she said. 'On Monday last, in Harlestone

Chase. I guessed something before; but I was never sure till then. And Georgie—does *she* know?'

In spite of all Ida's self-command, a tremulous eagerness in her voice betrayed her interest in that question.

'I hope and trust not,' Maurice answered. 'Some wild words broke from me—I can't recall one accurately—just before I got alongside of her, when I saw she was going to throw herself out of the saddle. But I don't think she could have heard; or, if she did, that she has remembered. Wittingly, I have never made the confession to her, or to any other; and, by God's help, I never will.'

A sudden gleam of crimson light, shooting through the cloud-pile in the West, fell full on his earnest face as he spoke these last words. With the firm resolve, there was mingled a certain reverence and devotion, such as you may see in a picture of old-time chivalry; showing how the good knight took upon himself the Vow, that could only be achieved through travail, and privation, and peril of death. Ida thought she had never loved him thoroughly till that moment. But no sign of emotion escaped her, save one long, low, painful sigh; so for a few seconds there was silence again, broken by Maurice.

'We need never speak of these things again,' he said, gravely, but very gently. 'There is no danger of mis-understanding between us henceforth. I do hope, we may still be good friends; at least, forgive me if I have said a harsh or rude word to-day. I've been rather sharply tried of late, you know.'

He held out his hand with the kindly courtesy that made his manner so winning; and Ida held it just long enough to return, decorously, its honest pressure. Their eyes met for a moment or so—steadily enough—but the girl's sank first.

'Let us go now,' she murmured, 'it is more than time; and never a word again of what has passed to-day. But, Maurice, remember!—friends—friends always.'

It may be that at the moment she spoke in sincerity. But when natures opposite as those two shall be joined in honest, harmless amity, the day will have fully come, when the wolf shall lie down by the lamb; and the asp's tongue, innocent of venom, shall lick the lips of the sleeping child.

So that strange pair walked slowly homewards. To the credit of both be it recorded, that they were able to talk on more than one indifferent subject before they reached the terrace, where the other two leant over the balustrade, also admiring the sunset. That same sunset easily excused their own delay ; both Ida and Maurice looked perfectly calm and unconscious, when they met the scrutiny of Paul Chetwynde's eye.

Now, it will appear to many grossly improbable, that an English damsel of good birth and breeding, should have so far forgotten maidenly dignity and reserve, as to cast her love, unconditionally, at the feet of a man who had never offered her more than the common courtesy and kindliness justified by long familiar intercourse. Some of these sceptics may possibly be not a whit behind their fellows, in the ordinary *curriculum* wherein worldly wisdom is learned.

I know that such instances of moral depravation and social aberration are extremely rare. But I know, too, that in the memory—if not in the conscience—of more than one reader of this page, there will rise up a silent witness to the evil truth, that—such things *have been*.

CHAPTER X.

DESDICHADO.

EARLY in the afternoon, some ten weeks later than the time we have been speaking of, a party of four, including the host, sate, after a late breakfast, smoking the digestive cigar in Paul Chetwynde's chambers.

They were very pleasant chambers; the look-out over the Green Park was endurable even on that chill November day; the furniture was rich and well-chosen, though not too costly for comfort; there were none of the precious trifles lying about that adorned the *tabagie* at Marston Lisle, but scarcely any appliance of luxury or laziness had been forgotten. Through the folding-doors, half covered by a heavy *portière*, you may catch a glimpse of a dining-room, panelled in dark oak, relieved by gilt mouldings and four admirable cabinet-pictures; it is the very size for a select party, and you begin to fancy there may be some truth in what people say—' If Chetwynde prides himself on anything, it is on his little dinners.'

Of the three guests we will take Gerald Annesleigh first; purely on physical grounds; for on any other, he certainly would not deserve priority. It is almost impossible to portray, with the pen, an exceptionally handsome person of either sex : I will not attempt it now.

Fancy a face, in which every feature was not only perfectly moulded, but harmonized perfectly with the rest; large lustrous eyes, in which the sleeping light was very easily awakened; dark glossy hair, carefully trained down to the uttermost curl of the wonderful mustache; a slight figure of admirable symmetry, inimitably graceful even in repose,—and you will have some faint idea of that wicked Prince Charming.

Truth to speak, Gerald Annesleigh has, from youth upwards, consistently abused his advantages of mind and body, on a scale that few men have a chance of imitating. Indeed, he has been going down-hill with a steady rapidity, ever since he began life as a Cornet of Dragoons, with good introductions, a fair allowance, and excellent expectations. All these he had exhausted long ago, except indeed the last, which he could not get rid of, though they were worked nearly threadbare now ; for he was heir to the title and estates of his uncle, the childless Earl of Dumfermline, who abhorred him above all living things, and had worried a whole firm of lawyers out of their patience, by driving them to look for a loophole through which the law of entail might be evaded.

The Earl had ceased for years to make his reprobate nephew any regular allowance ; but Gerald used from time to time, to wring out of him sums, more or less considerable, by putting on the screw of some disgraceful exposure, that would blacken yet more an already tarnished escutcheon. Annesleigh himself was famous for his cursing ; but upon these occasions, it may be doubted if the reverend senior did not match him in eloquence of malediction.

' Unfortunately,' as Gerald remarked one day, ' the Emperor is of a spare habit and lives low ; or I'd taken short odds about apoplexy before this.'

He had never yet appeared before the criminal bar of an offended country ; but from all other courts he was seldom long absent. Of course few fathers of reputable families

would allow Gerald to darken their doors; yet he had
never been detected in any of those misdemeanours that
exclude the sinner from the pale of society, at once and
for ever. For instance, there were ugly gambling stories
about him in half the countries in Europe; but no foul
play had ever been brought home to him; on the only two
occasions when he had been involved in a quarrel at cards,
he had contrived to throw the blame upon his adversary,
besides shooting him with infinite promptitude and dexterity. So he had gone on—and was likely to go on—for
many seasons; treading lightly and gracefully along the
slippery verge of the chasm, at the bottom of which lay
deadly dishonour, if not death.

Almost the prettiest picture I can remember, is one,
representing a fair child, about five years old, nestling
close to the knee of a very beautiful woman, looking up at
her from under wavy brown curls, with a glance, half play-
ful, half loving. That child was Gerald Annesleigh; that
woman, his mother—dead—through God's mercy, years
ago; ay, before her darling's locks were shorn, before his
glorious eyes had learnt to lie.

In characters utterly base, or wicked, or cruel, these
paradoxes are often found. The Eleventh Louis, you know,
never stirred without his leaden Madonna; Cenci, I doubt
not, was confessed and shriven occasionally; and Couthon's
spaniel was as well known in the Terrible Days as her
master. So, perhaps, it was not strange, that Annesleigh
could never be persuaded to sell that picture, though he
would raise money on it unscrupulously.

This peculiarity was once remarked upon by one of
those benevolent gentlemen who succour the distressed
aristocrat with a temporary loan, on the deposit of some

article of value, when personal security is not quite negotiable; this, in spite of his reversionary prospects, was often the case with Gerald, when he required money at a minute's notice.

'The first time as that picter came to me,' Mr Simmonds said, 'I offered a tidy sum for it,—right down. It aint often you get hold of such a bit of colouring now-a-days. The Captain had been dreadful hard hit on the October Meeting, and wanted cash for The Corner—bad. But he d—d me as handsomely as ever I heard him—the Captain's language is *very* moderate, you know, sir, when anything puts him out, and told me—' to keep my huckstering to myself, if I wanted to keep his custom; that I didn't know my own business neither, for it was the best pledge I ever took.' He was right, too. I've had that one a many times, but I never keep it long. I remember, that time he took it away the day after the Houghton settling.'

When the poor painting was *at home*, it lived always in a deep recess, over which a thick curtain could be drawn at pleasure; so that the image of the dead lady was not compelled to look on the orgies of drink or play, or darker debauches yet, which had gotten for those rooms such a terrible name. The most reckless of the female dare-devils, who make a mock at all holy things, human or divine, never ventured, a second time, to peer behind the veil.

That small, spare, silent man, with wrinkled, bloodless cheeks, thin, pale hair, and a meek, chronic smile, is Gerald's *umbra*—Penrhyn Bligh.

He inherited from his father an honourable name, a fair competency, and a weakly constitution. The two first he got rid of some time ago; and is trying sedulously to dissipate the relics of the last, by late hours, and constant devotion to the shrine of Absynthia Mater. Annesleigh was the prime—if not the sole—cause of the poor little creature's ruin. But, so far from bearing any malice thereanent, Penrhyn attached himself at once to Gerald's fortunes, and serves him still with a ready fidelity, believing that there is nothing alive equal to that superb Bohemian. We all know how Bertrand fares, when he is squire to Macaire. Nevertheless, Penrhyn is always helplessly miserable when not supported by his patron's countenance: he is quite content to accept more than his share of their common discredit, so that he may bask in the reflected light of the other's evil triumphs.

It would be hard to say, how Annesleigh himself feels towards his unhappy dependent; he treats him with a sort of contemptuous good-nature, and will not allow any one else to bully him; but never thinks it necessary to express any gratitude for the services he accepts, or any regret for the ruin he has made. It has been said, that there is no dislike more bitter, than that which the injurer nourishes against the irredeemably injured; but, when conscience is utterly seared, perhaps this sentiment is crushed into inactivity with the rest.

Next to Penrhyn Bligh—almost eclipsing the meek little *umbra* with his portly presence—sits the Great O'Neil, once a major of Carbineers, now a peaceful J. P. and D. L. in his native Corkagian county.

A tall, burly man, who carries his sixty years right gallantly; with a moist, merry eye, and a bold soldierly look still about his face, though his mustache was shaved when his papers went in, and his thick gray whiskers are carefully trimmed in orthodox 'cutlet'-fashion. There is a rich, racy roll in his voice, scarcely amounting to a brogue, just sufficient to round off more mellifluously the magnificent periods in which the Major delights to indulge. He has a very vivid imagination, and a keen sense of humour; but is so intensely good-natured that he seldom 'chaffs' much ; and would rather invent an absurd story against himself than against his neighbours any day.

So much for the company. Now for a specimen of their converse, though it is not particularly important or interesting. But it was necessary to bring these fresh personages before you, inasmuch as one of them, at least, had much to do with the fortunes of those whom you know already.

They were talking about the double marriages of Gascoigne and Luttrell, which were to come off in the ensuing week. The *venue* was fixed some miles from town; for, though Lady Versehoyle had consented to creep out of her warm winter-nest to see her daughter given away, she would by no means encounter the perils of a London November.

'Well, I do call it hard lines,' Gerald was saying—'I don't often care about going to church, or into *very* reputable society : here I've a chance of doing both at the same time. Why, I should live for a month afterwards in the odour of respectability, if not of sanctity. And Paul won't help me. Look now : I'll make a compromise, just for once : I'll leave my poor Pen. behind. What do you say ?'

'That would make a great difference, certainly,' Chetwynde answered, with a half sneer. 'But, even so, I don't think there would be room for you. A double marriage is

a serious thing; at least a hundred people will have to be
left 'out in the cold,' who have a better claim than you,
my virtuous Gerald. Why, you hardly know Philip at all,
and his bride but very slightly.'

'*Very* slightly,'—the other said, just a shadow of a sneer
gathering about his voice, and a wicked light glimmering
in his eyes—' of late years, at all events. But I met the
little Verschoyle down at Torquay, before she came out (I
was hunting that fat Cumberland heiress, who married the
crooked Indian man—cruel case, it nearly broke Pen.'s
heart)—they didn't look so sharp after her then. She was
quite the nicest thing I ever knew. After she was presented, we went each our own way. That Carew woman
fights very shy of me, and she's got eyes in the back of
her head, I believe; besides, I had a good deal of business
on hand just then. But I travelled a hundred miles to see
her at her first ball; and I've a fancy to see her at her
wedding.'

'You'll have to baulk it this time,' Paul retorted rather
sharply. 'I was not aware that your acquaintance with
Miss Verschoyle dated back so far. It's another reason
for your being left out next week. I'm inclined to believe
in the luck of auspices. It would hardly be giving a bride
a fair chance, if she took the vows under that evil eye of
yours.'

The good-natured O'Neil interrupted them here. The
signs of impending storm were plain to read; for Chetwynde's face and lips were set ominously; and Annesleigh's smooth white brow had begun to lour.

'Well, it beats me entirely, that whim of witnessing
weddings'—the Major was great at alliteration—' It's a
sort of morbid monomania, I verily believe, like visiting

vivisection-rooms. Gerald, ye born imp, what business have you dabbling in holy water? I'd sooner go to a friend's funeral than to his marriage, any day. His troubles are ended in one case : in the other they're just beginning.'

His audience smiled expectantly. Upon no subject did the Major wax eloquent so readily as on his own matrimonial troubles : he would descant upon these for hours together, with a bitterness not altogether comic or feigned. The partner of his bed and board was indeed a very awful lady—a sort of refined and dignified Xantippe—who tried her utmost, at all times and seasons, to keep the mercurial veteran below ' boiling point,' with very variable success.

The O'Neil nodded his head thrice, solemnly ; settling himself in his huge arm-chair, into a *pose* between the didactic and the oratorical.

' It is, now, almost a quarter of a century,' he said, 'since I proffered to a high-born female the priceless treasures of my heart and hand. For all these years, without fear or favour, have I been fighting the battle of the Henpecked Husband against odds that no bachelor can realize. You see the lines on my manly cheek, and think they're the wrinkles of increasing age. No such thing. You look on a brow like the brow of Prometheus ;—scarred by Mistress O'Neil's thunder. Now, I'm not a reprobate, like one of yourselves. I have troubled the peace of no man's household ; I never gamble beyond "golden crowns ; " and I carry my drink genteelly. But I object, on principle, to going to bed till I feel sleepily inclined. On the question of free-agency here, there broke out, five-and-twenty summers ago, a war that will only terminate with the existence of the belligerents. I've known that villain Gerald, forgetting the respect due to gray hairs, banter me on going home so early, when it wanted but an hour to dawn. Irreverent scoffer! Did ye guess at the retribution of the morrow? I read 'Zanoni' when it first came out; but I never realized its power till one night when I forgot my latch-key. When the door opened, there—tall and white against the black back-ground—stood the apparition of Mistress O'Neil. If Clarence had not shrunk before The Watcher on the Threshold, he would have owned a bolder heart than mine.'

The Major stopped to take breath here, and drew his handkerchief across his forehead, as if the bare recollection had brought back the sweat of fear.

'You temporize sometimes, I fancy,' Paul remarked, with a palpable 'drawing' intention. 'I've heard of excuses——'

The O'Neil drooped one lid, for a second, over a merry twinkling eye: it was a master-piece of winking.

'Excuses?' he said. 'Don't you know what happened a month ago, in the smoking-room at The Rag? Musgrave had just come back from India, and gave a dozen of us a right good dinner. About four, I made a move to go. Anstruther was next to me—you know the pretty, smooth girl's face: there's the making of a man in him, for all that.

' "Why, you are not going yet, Major?" he lisped out. "You've a capital excuthe to-night; friends don't come back from foreign, every day."

'I turned upon that unlucky youth with an inexpressible dignity of rebuke.

' "Sir," said I, "five years before your excellent mother was married, I began trying experiments on feminine credulity in the person of Mistress O'Neil—*née* Macdonald. And you presume to suggest an evasion to *me!* Tarry at Jericho till your beard be grown."

'I don't think the child slept sound in his cradle that morning.'

Even Penrhyn Bligh joined heartily, for once, in the laughter which rewarded the Major's tirade. Annesleigh had quite recovered his good humour. Indeed, he was too wise to quarrel with a useful acquaintance, such as Chetwynde had shown himself ere this, about what was really only a whim.

'Well, I give it up,' he said. 'The fair Georgette must receive my blessing at second-hand. By-the-by, who's going to be Gascoigne's best man?'

'Dering, of course,' Paul answered. 'I'm to squire the reverend Luttrell.'

'Dering of the —th; the riding man, you mean,' Gerald went on. 'I hope to G—d he won't go flirting or feasting too much, or do anything to shake his nerve in the week after. I shall back his mount in the Grand Military for pounds, shillings, and pence.'

So, they fell to racing talk, through which we have no need to follow.

CHAPTER XI.

THE LAST TEMPTATION.

ON the fourth day before the marriage, Dering rode down to Carhampton, where Lady Verschoyle and her daughter were staying. Gascoigne, who had been called suddenly away to Marston, had intrusted him with certain final arrangements; Maurice had also an errand of his own; he brought a wedding-gift for Georgie.

It was rather a gorgeous souvenir to come from a modest captain of horse—a broad, heavy band of flexible gold, with a medallion in purple enamel, bearing the initials of bridegroom and bride, interlaced in an intricate monogram of brilliants.

Lady Verschoyle was confined to her room with one of her nervous headaches, so the demoiselle received her visitor, alone. It was the first time they had so met, since the day of the race on Harleston Chase. During all this time there had subsisted between them, as I said before, a certain reserve and reticence, though this had been gradually becoming more and more one-sided.

Indeed, such a state of things did not suit the fair Georgie at all. When she had once been on a confidential footing with any one, she by no means approved of the relations being changed into distance or formality. Her friends and adherents said this was 'because she was a dear affectionate little thing;' her rivals and detractors imputed it to coquetry, pure and simple. Perhaps both were partly right.

In the present case, she thought that she had done quite penance enough for that moment of yielding to an imprudent impulse, and that it was full time Maurice should take his place again in the inner circle of her favourites. With all this, she felt not a shadow of disloyalty towards her affianced; indeed, she liked Philip better and better as the hours grew nearer when he would claim her as his very own; for scarcely a day passed without her having to note some mark of delicacy, or generosity, or kindness, on the part of her lover.

These anomalies are marvellous, I own; but they are not uncommon. Indeed it is one of the most curious of physiological studies, to remark how very close to the wind a thorough-paced coquette will sail, without any defined purpose of evil; nay, without any rash intention of risking shipwreck.

I say all this, to explain my poor little heroine's conduct on this especial afternoon—not to excuse it; for in truth she did behave with extreme naughtiness.

When Georgie had finished her raptures and thanksgivings—they were rather more gushing than the real beauty of the gift could justify—there was an awkward silence for a minute or so : she kept her eyes fixed on the bracelet as she turned it backwards and forwards on her slender wrist; all the while the delicate rose-tint rose brighter and brighter on her cheek ; at last she spoke, low, and, as it seemed, nervously, still looking downwards.

' I shall value this more than any one of my presents. Do you know why ? I take it as a peace-offering ; though that ought not to have come from *you*. Don't deny that, for weeks past, you have thought me stupidly cold and ungrateful. I don't wonder at your being vexed and disappointed, till you became formal too.'

Now here I appeal to the memory of my masculine readers to answer, whether some of the most complicated scrapes and painful interviews in which they ever were involved have not begun with some such self-accusation on the part of the Fair Penitent, accompanied by an imputation of animosity to her victim ? Disclaimers and denials of ever having taken offence, are worse than vain ; they

I

simply recoil upon yourself from the plaintive obstinacy they encounter.

Dering was cool and self-possessed enough on most occasions, and of late had been looking his position very fairly in the face; but this was rather more than he had schooled himself to meet. For a moment or two he was cruelly embarrassed; it did him some credit, that he should have recovered himself so soon. But he was not inventive or sagacious enough to steer clear of the aforesaid useless denials.

'I assure you, you are utterly wrong,' he began. 'I have nothing on earth to complain of. What can have put such a fancy into your head? My dear Miss Verschoyle——'

She interrupted him here; her full scarlet lip was pouting slightly, and the quick, petulant movement of her delicate foot kept time with her tongue.

'There, you *will* always use that formal address, though I do hate it so. Everybody that I like, and that likes me, calls me ' Georgie.' You are the most ceremonious of all the real friends I have. And yet, you are like an elder brother to Philip; and I—owe you my life.'

He answered her instantly, with a laugh rather cold and constrained.

'I didn't know you had such an antipathy to your surname. Now I think it such a very well-sounding one. You change it, and I start Eastward ho! so soon, that it seems hardly worth while to familiarize. I'll ask Philip what he thinks about it, if I come home again safe and sound.'

'But you did call me " Georgie " *once*, you know.'

The beautiful eyes were lifted now, though somewhat

coyly; and there shot through the silky lashes just one gleam of purple fire.

It was a home-thrust, certainly, and for the moment Dering's self-command was staggered; the effort it cost aim to regain it made his face seem hard and stern.

'I won't affect to misunderstand you,' he said, darkly. I hoped you would not have remembered a syllable spoken then. I believe that words uttered at such a moment ought never to be brought against one, in this world or the next. But they deserve some penance. *Now*, perhaps, you may guess why I have borne myself towards you somewhat distantly and formally. Trust me, it is better that we should bury every memory attached to that terrible day— bury them for ever and ever. You may write "All's well that ends well," on the tombstone.'

The grave earnestness of his voice and manner—without a tinge of bitterness, unless it were levelled against himself—utterly quelled the *diablotin* of coquetry in Georgie's breast. (I here repress a strong temptation, to illustrate by Ithuriel.) It was a line of defence she was quite unused to encounter, and it baffled her completely. Like most women of her stamp, she was very slow, on such occasions, to realize the harm she did or the pain she inflicted. Nevertheless, a vague misgiving did overcome her now, that she was wringing and torturing a brave honest heart that had always wished her well and been ready to serve her, merely to gratify the girlish vanity of successful fascination. She began to feel frightened and remorseful.

Before she could falter out a word, Maurice spoke again —still very gravely, but in a tone perceptibly softened.

'I think it better to end this, once for all, since so much

has been said already. Pray believe that I speak now, exactly as I would if Philip's hand were resting—where it has
rested so often—on my shoulder. You know how he trusts
me; but perhaps you *don't* quite know how thoroughly he
can afford to do so. The proof of it is, that I can venture
to be quite frank with you to-day. I have admired you
from the first moment we met, more than any woman I
have yet seen. But I never had a hope of winning you;
and, if Philip had never sought you, I should never have
asked you to share my uncertain fortunes. When your
engagement was announced, there was a change in me, I
own; and perhaps I felt one painful throb, when I heard of
it. But, I swear, there never was in my heart one spark
of bitterness or jealousy of Philip—much less a desire to
steal away one particle of your love from him. From the
very first I wished you both well, just as honestly as I shall
do next Tuesday at the altar. I have not quite shaken off
the old fascination yet, though I've tried hard enough,
God knows; but, for months past, I would no more have
connected you with a guilty or covetous thought, than I
would have trampled on my dead sister's grave. Those
rash words of mine were spoken, when we were both too
near the next world to stand on form or ceremony; and I
did forget duty in my great fear for you. There is only
one reason why I hope Philip will never guess what I have
been telling you now. He is so good and kind, that he
would be always reproaching himself with having stood
between me and the light. It is not so. I believe a year
or so of foreign service will work a thorough cure. There
is happiness in the after-time for me, as well as for you.
This is the longest speech I ever made. I know you

cannot be offended; but—so many thanks for listening patiently.'

Georgie's face was shaded by her hand, while Maurice was speaking; when she raised it, it was wet with tears— tears, springing not from bitterness or shame, but from pity, and sympathy, and gratitude—tears, such as a husband might see on his fair wife's cheek, and never doubt her loyalty. Though she honoured Dering, at that moment, more than any other living, not a spark of guilty passion lurked beneath : her feeling somewhat resembled the simple hero-worship, that many women have nourished for famous men whom they have never seen.

'Neither Philip nor I can ever pay half our debts to you,' she said at last, almost in a whisper; and held out a little tremulous hand.

Maurice held it for a second lightly, as he raised it to his lips, with the same gesture of rather old-fashioned courtesy that you may remember on a certain afternoon in the past. Then he spoke quite cheerfully, with the old merry light in his eyes.

'I've given up all hopes of making either of you reasonable on that point. Well, if you persist in giving me great credit for doing—as any other man alive would have done —my best, you shall pay me off by instalments. When Philip writes, as he will do every month, you can look over his shoulder, and put in a tiny postscript with any scrap of news you think I should care to hear. And will you pet The Moor now and then ; a good deal for me, and a little for yourself ? He stands at Marston while I'm away : I'll never part with him ; but he wouldn't do for India.'

'You know how glad I shall be to do all this—and more.'

While the words were on Georgie's lips, the door opened, and Lady Verschoyle entered. She had actually roused herself sufficiently to descend, and confer for a few minutes with Dering, as Gascoigne's plenipotentiary, anent certain arrangements for the Tuesday following.

So the subject that these two had been discoursing on, was sealed up between them, thenceforward for ever.

It was months since Maurice had felt so thoroughly light of heart, as when he rode homeward that afternoon. Indeed, though he had hardly realized it at the time, he had achieved a rare and exceptional triumph. He had actually made a woman his friend for life, by—telling her the simple truth.

There is no reason why we should linger over the details of the double wedding. The Dean of Torrcaster—duly 'assisted' of course—performed the ceremony with a stern austerity of demeanour that made it sound very like a funeral service; indeed, one of the subalterns, a slim spectacled curate, was so awed and impressed thereby, that he made two verbal errors in the small part he had to perform, thereby drawing upon himself a sharp reprimand in the disrobing chamber afterwards.

Dering played the bridesman gallantly. For one moment, just at the plighting of the troth, a vague misty feeling overcame him; so that his own father's words, spoken within a foot of his ear, sounded as though some stranger were uttering them from a long distance off; but his wandering glance met Paul Chetwynde's eyes, fixed on him keenly and anxiously. They had precisely the same effect on Maurice as the sight of cold water often produces on a lady preparing to faint; he recovered instantly, and had no relapses. Indeed he was rather brilliant than other-

wise at the breakfast, and conducted himself to the entire
satisfaction of the bridesmaid he had specially in charge.
If the truth must bo told, a phantasm, with chestnut hair
and brown eyes, and an erect martial bearing, for weeks
after mingled not unfrequently with that damsel's virginal
dreams.

Miss Verschoyle looked distractingly pretty, and changed
her name with not a whit more nervousness than was
decorous and becoming. Even the Dean of Torrcaster
softened into a cast-steel smile of approbation when he
congratulated her in the vestry : if he had been *very* much
pressed, it is possible the holy man would have bestowed
on that fair brow a single paternal salute.

And Ida Carew ?

Surely the most callous spectator there would have
shrunk and shuddered, if he could have guessed at the
tumult of conflicting passions, rioting and raging in that
wicked, wayward heart. Of the inward strife, the placid,
handsome face betrayed not the shadow of a sign. She
was always so pale that no change was perceptible here ;
yet, throughout the early morning, a weary sleepless look
haunted her face ; and, if her maid had told tales, perchance something might have been heard of ' red lavender,'
or some other among those mysterious feminine stimulants,
of which the vulgar male world is but little aware. She
brightened up as the day went on, and had never looked
more perfectly lovely than when she stood by the altar.

But, mark. At the very moment when she uttered the
vow—' to honour and obey,'—those wonderful, deep eyes
were lifted under the bridal veil, and shot one straight,
swift glance to the spot where, in the background of the
group, stood—Maurice Dering.

*   *   *   *   *

One scene more before we part with one of our characters for awhile.

Stand here with me, on the crest of the hill, and watch the finish for the Grand Military of 185—. A brace of minutes now will settle, who shall win and wear the Soldiers' Blue Riband.

The three leading horses—nothing else has the ghost of a chance—have just swept round the last turning flag into the straight run-in : only three fences and a flight of bushed hurdles are between them and the judge's chair. Only three fences : but they are laid tough and strong with the famous Gorsehamptonshire thorn that holds hind legs like wire.

Ajax is in front—a great raking chestnut, with a coarse head and ragged hips, but a rare jumper and galloper when the ground is not too deep. He pulled like a steam-engine for the first two miles, but it is as much as he can do now to get over the ridge-and-furrow without rolling in his stride. Ajax's rider is Captain Burstall of the Royals, one of the hardest—if not one of the best—men to hounds in broad England. His friends and admirers assert that his nerve is so extraordinary, that he has sometimes to steady, or, as it were, handicap himself, with a portentous cigar before starting for cover : otherwise, ' he would be a little above himself, and jumping everything.' He walks under eleven stone, but is built like a bull and very nearly as strong ; those brawny bow-legs grip the saddle like a vice.

About three lengths behind, is Mildmay of the Coldstreams, riding his own mare, Lady Agatha, and riding her right well. There is great craft and coolness behind the pale beardless face; indeed, that boy is very few pounds worse than the average of professionals even now, though not more than four years have fled since he ceased to be ' a pretty page.' The mare well deserves to carry the hopes and money of the Household Brigade; you might guide her with a silken thread, and she was never known to fall; see, how the ridge-and-furrow seems to melt away under her swift smooth stride.

Last of the three—he has been waiting in front from the start—comes our old friend The Moor, steered, also, by his owner.

The scattered murmurs and shouts at the Stand are deepening into a concentrated roar; not only comrades and partisans are shouting, but the Ring too waxes stentorian: it is strongly represented to-day, for it so chances that no other meeting clashes with the Soldiers' Race. The ' talent ' don't much fancy Ajax; of the other two the mare has a trifle the call in the betting; but the prevailing cry is—' No one names the winner.'

Some one *does* name the winner, though; and names him pretty often. The undaunted backer is no other than Gerald Annesleigh. He stands a cracker on The Moor, and has laid against everything else. Yet he still keeps piling on the money, in spite of the imploring looks and whispers of Penrhyn Bligh, who stands close by his patron's side, looking more white and nervous than ever, with the twitch about his mouth quickened painfully.

Ah!—it lies between the pair of them, now. Ajax's rider rather lost his head when he saw the winning flag straight before him, and was a little hard on his horse over the thirty-acre ridge-and-furrow. The second fence from home is a 'laid' one—black and firm as masonry. Ajax drags his hind legs, ever so little; the next instant there is a crash, that we can almost *hear*, and a confused heap struggles in the ditch yawning on the landing side.

The man is up first. Not hurt? What a question! Why, you might blow Dick Burstall from a gun, and he would rise up on his feet, with only a few immaterial contusions. Nevertheless, the chief of the ' Cut-em-down Captains' must wait for his Blue Riband till the next year.

It is the nearest thing between the other two. Twice Dering goes up to Lady Agatha's girths, and twice she slips away in front again, with, apparently, fatal facility. Louder and wilder go up the cheers of the Household Brigade, who are shouting as if the race was over; and still through the uproar cleave the clear ringing tones of Gerald Annesleigh.

' The Moor! The Moor! for any even money.'

Over the hurdles without a mistake. Half-way up the distance Maurice makes his last effort: this time he gets to the mare's head, and *keeps there*. For a second or so, the two run locked and level, as if they were yoked in harness; then the lean brown head begins to steal in front, just as it did in Harlestone Chase. Lady Agatha runs game as a pebble to the last; but The Moor runs the longest.

All over now. The Gilt Vase is fairly won; and the Guards shall only score a *proximè accessit* of the honours of this year.

Annesleigh's hand, that has been suspended over Penrhyn Bligh's shoulder for the last few seconds, descends with a force that brings the meek little man to his knee; but he looks up in Gerald's flushed face with intenso admiration, as the latter mutters in a voice rather hoarser than usual, with one of his own double-shotted oaths,—

'Landed, by ——.'

The victor's ovation among his comrades was only half over, when a man in his own regiment came up with Annesleigh, who wished for an introduction. Gerald's manner, when he was on his good behaviour, was singularly graceful and winning. Maurice was not insensible of its attraction, though common fame had prejudiced him strongly against the speaker; besides, he was in a humour to be pleased with anything just then. So he accepted the other's congratulations, and disclaimed his compliments with frank courtesy

'I'm very glad you trusted the old horse with your money,' he said. 'I knew we should be close up at the finish, if we were not quite out-paced. Indeed, I ought only to have been afraid of one in the race. Lady Agatha has a great turn of speed, and Mildmay rides like a professional. I don't really deserve much credit; one had only to sit steady, as it turned out. He is a very easy horse to ride. Would you like to look him over?'

'Very much,' Gerald assented. 'I hardly had time to glance at him when he was saddled, I was so busy up here. It was a real good thing all through; and a rare turn of luck for me. Say what you like, I have seldom seen a race better ridden, and I watch a certain number in the course of the year. Remember, if I ever have a chance of doing you a good turn, I owe you one.'

If you have patience to read to the end, you will see how that debt was paid.

When—after a night of heavy play, during which the

luck has been running dead against him, with never a turn in the tide—the crippled gamester walks slowly home through the brightening twilight, and, reckoning up his available resources, finds that he may not hope to renew the fight against Fortune for many a day to come, there mingles often, they say, with the bitterness of discomfiture, a strange sense of relief and refreshment—arising from the certainty that, now, nothing more can be hoped, or feared, or struggled for; that weary brain and strained nerves must perforce find rest for awhile.

Some such feeling as this shot through Maurice Dering's breast, as, a month later, he watched a cold January sun go down behind the Dorset highlands : he stood, then, on the deck of the good ship Indus, outward-bound.

CHAPTER XII.

BENEDICTINE DAYS.

Two years went by, bringing little of change to those who abode still in England ; yet they brought an heir to the broad lands of Marston Lisle. It was a very small baby, with Georgie's bright, soft hair, and Philip's dark, dreamy eyes, rather fragile and delicate to look upon ; but it must have had a remarkably good constitution, or it could not have supported the incredible amount of petting lavished upon it by all the female members of the family, with Aunt Nellie, of course, at their head. That infant's apparel was a perfect miracle of florid decoration ; yet its admirers ceased not to tax their ingenuity in the pro-

duction of new intricacies of needlework, to be offered to
their tiny sovereign.

Maternity did not make Georgie look a whit more
matronly, nor sober her in any way, materially. She was
very fond and proud of her baby, and it was the prettiest
sight imaginable to see them together; but she was not
disposed to sacrifice her time and her fancies to nursery
despotism. The spirit of coquetry was still alive and
strong within her; she would flirt, at times, quite as
scientifically, if not quite so openly, as in the old days; but
scandal had never yet been busy with her name, and the
world only did her justice here; for, of anything beyond
the indulgence of vanity, she was absolutely innocent.

Philip was thoroughly and completely happy. So far
from feeling jealous or sulky about these little *escapades* of
his fair wife, they rather amused and gratified him: he
looked upon each conquest of hers as a fresh social triumph
—simply a homage due to her wonderful fascinations. Indeed, before she slept, Georgie used to repeat to him some
of the prettiest speeches that had been murmured in her
ear during the evening; and certain Lotharios, in intention, would have been sorely discomfited if they could
have heard the trills of silvery laughter that often interrupted the narration.

Mrs Gascoigne achieved an immense success in the
country. Marston had always been a pleasant house; but
its attractions seemed increased, now, sevenfold. Even
Paul Chetwynde, in despite of the prejudices of which you
have heard, could not deny that this was entirely due to
the delicate Butterfly-Queen. She was an especial favourite with the womankind, from the curate's wife in her own
parish up to the Duchess of Devorgoil. That ample and

august lady—of whom Georgie pretended to be so terribly afraid—though she would shake her head at times,
and talk about 'thoughtlessness and want of dignity,'
would scarcely have had the heart to clip the wings of the
pretty 'light-minded bird,' or to tame her into frigid pro-
priety.

The aspect of things in the West was not quite so brilliant. The curse of childlessness, which for many generations had haunted the direct line of the Luttrells, seemed
still to prevail at Minstercombe. Neither was Ida's popular-
ity in the neighbourhood at all comparable to her fascin-
ating cousin's. To those honest Devonians she appeared
intensely proud and reserved: she was, in reality, only
listless and indifferent, and careless about dissembling,
when she chanced to be unusually bored. Only once, the
natural haughtiness of her nature spoke out.

There lived, not far from Minstercombe, an elderly
dowager of great influence and repute; the widow of a
deceased county magnate. She was a kind, good woman
at heart; profuse in her charity, and much given to hospitality of a formal, constrained sort: but she loved to patronize both high and low, and chose to be Lady Paramount
as well as Lady Bountiful. She was very ready on all
occasions with her dictatorial advice; but especially bestowed it on all young married females who came to live
within the limits of her rule. To such, on the earliest
feasible opportunity, she would deliver a set form of lec-
ture on Conjugal Duty—verbose, grandiloquent, Chaponic;
and hitherto all her victims had submitted unresistingly,
if not respectfully.

When Mrs Standishe paid her first state visit to Min-

stercombe, she prepared to play the Monitress, as usual:
she never repeated the experiment. Ida said very little,
and that little very quietly; but she contrived to quell the
ancient lady after a fashion that the latter never forgot or
forgave. She was firm in her friendships, and never unjust even when most deeply offended; so she did not
altogether withdraw her countenance from the house,
whose master she had known from boyhood. But, ever
afterwards, she used to sigh, with ominous significance, as
she mentioned ' *poor* Mr Luttrell's' name, and would
throw out dark hints of danger impending over that ill-
governed household.

Yet Geoffrey did not deserve much pity, as yet. It is
true that his careless joviality was somewhat abated, and
sometimes he would look quite grave and thoughtful; but
he was not unhappy, or even discontented; and if there
were a real change, he himself could not have analyzed or
explained it.

Ida's manner towards him was the same as it had always
been; perfectly pleasant and good-natured, but nothing
more. She was irreproachable in all points of wifely duty,
and was never irritable, or imperious, or exacting. Yet if
Geoffrey had questioned his own heart, he would have felt
a longing there to meet with some flaw in the calm perfection; some whim, that he might gratify—were it ever
so unreasonable; some outbreak of temper that he might
pacify—were it ever so groundless.

There was no room for distrust in his honest nature;
but the vague disappointment, that he used to shake off
so readily, began to grow more defined in its gloomy out-
lines. He never dreamt of murmuring or repining; yet he

could not always help feeling that he was casting away all
the treasures of his faith and love, to be repaid by a scanty
mite of cool, amicable regard.

His childlessness, too, weighed heavily, at times, on
Geoffrey's mind. It was not only that he longed for an
heir to his possessions and ancient name: he had a faint
idea—scarcely mounting to a hope—that if that one link
existed between them, it must needs draw his wife closer
to the heart that was so eager to take her in. Was he
right, there? I know not. In drama, or romance, the
crucial test of maternity never fails. But in real life——
Ah, me! it is better to let the question pass by

Certainly, their happiest days were those spent away
from Minstercombe. It is a sign ominous to a household's
peace, when the spirits of one or both of its rulers rise in
exact proportion to the distance lying between them and
home. This was certainly so with Ida: and, perhaps, with
Geoffrey—in a less degree Things went best with them
during their long visits to Marston Lisle.

Now, you know something of Ida's feelings towards her
charming cousin. It is scarcely probable that there was
much change here: her loves and hatreds were singularly
consistent and abiding. But dissimulation to such an
accomplished actress was the easiest of all tasks, now that
there was no tangible provocation to be encountered
daily.

Since that gray January day, when the Indus left her
moorings in Southampton Water, Georgie might make as
many conquests as she pleased:—Ida would grudge her
never one.

So she bore her part right pleasantly in the gaieties of
Marston, and was a very efficient aide to the fair mistress

of the revels. It was there, too, she oftenest met Paul
Chetwynde; for the latter was too lazy to travel into the
far West when he had a chance of lighting on his friends
nearer home. The Luttrells were never long in London;
for Geoffrey detested pavement intensely, and Ida was
never unnecessarily cruel.

Dering was creditably regular in his correspondence;
but it was rather unequally divided; the larger share fell
to Gascoigne and far the smallest to Luttrell. This did
not disquiet or chafe the honest parson in the least.

' I'm not good at scribbling, like you two,' he was wont
to say. with his great hearty laugh. ' I don't know why
the old boy should write to me at all, as I see all his
letters, if it were not that he guesses I like to hear, at first
hand, of his doings among the big game. How I *do* envy
him. And think of you fellows trying to stop him from
going out,' &c., &c.

Before Dering had been a full year in India he had
achieved no small renown as a *shikari*, and had despatched
to Marston the skin of a full-grown tiger, slain by him on
foot, fairly face to face.

Gascoigne used to contemplate that trophy, as it lay
before the hearth in his own room, with inexpressible
pride and triumph. He was never weary of telling the
story of the slaughter, mingling therein certain professional
phrases of Eastern veneric which he had contrived to
master. Each new guest at Marston—there were many
who had never seen a loaded rifle, and cared nothing for
sport of any description—was doomed to listen to that
tale: for the first time in his life Philip seemed not to
calculate on the possibility of his hearer being bored. Indeed, as Chetwynde once remarked, ' He couldn't have

K

been more insufferably vainglorious than if he had shot the brute himself.'

When only the family circle (in which Paul, of course, reckoned himself) was staying at Marston, they often used to gather round that hearth, as the autumn evenings were closing in, and talk of the strong hunter far away.

From childhood upwards, Ida Luttrell's notions of comfort had been rather *feline ;* she had a peculiar facility of curling herself up into corners, and never sate formally erect if she could possibly help it. On these occasions she used to nestle down on the tiger-skin, close to the savage head and white grinning fangs, with her head pillowed on Georgie's knee; her hand rested naturally on the ragged spot, where the heavy bullet had rent its way in to the life.

So she would lie, still and silent, her breathing low and regular as in sleep, while the others talked on. But, ever and anon, if you could have peered under the veil of lashes into those downcast eyes, you would have seen a flickering light there, that never came from the reflection of the fire.

CHAPTER XIII.

A SAFE INVESTMENT.

On a certain May morning, soon after breakfast, Chetwynde was sitting alone in his chambers, when his servant brought in a card, whereon was written, in a stiff, clerkly hand, ' Mr Thos. Brine.'

Paul had an exceptionally retentive memory for faces

and names; but now he was rather puzzled, and had to ruminate some seconds before he could identify his visitor. 'Brine—Brine?' he said. 'Why, surely that's the name of Serocold's managing clerk. What on earth can he want with me so early; and why don't he write instead of sending? Let him come up, Evans. I confess to feeling rather curious: it will turn out to be nothing, of course.'

For once Paul Chetwynde was *not* doomed to be disappointed.

There entered a short stout man, somewhat beyond middle-age, very decorously attired in black broadcloth; the self-satisfied expression of his smug, smooth face, rather neutralized the effect of a studiously obsequious manner.

'Won't you take a chair, Mr Brine?' Paul said. 'You come on business, I presume, from Mr Serocold.'

'Thank you, sir,' the other answered, as he seated himself. 'I *do* come on business—on your business too. But not from Mr Serocold. I left his office quite a month ago; at my own wish, I beg to assure you. Since that time I have been with Messrs ——' He named a firm rather eminent among the sharp practitioners of the day.

'I'm very glad to hear of that,' Paul replied, arching his eyebrows slightly. 'But would you be good enough to come, at once, to what interests me personally? I've one or two engagements this morning.'

He spoke more coldly and distantly than was his wont; but, in truth, he was by no means favourably impressed by the demeanour of his visitor.

Mr Brine did not seem to notice this; but went on in the same smooth, unctuous tone.

'Let me state, sir, in the first place, that I have no mercenary motives in coming here to-day. I don't expect to

K 2

be rewarded, except by my own conscience. But duty compels one to do disagreeable things at times. I'll come to the point immediately. But will you allow me to ask you one question, in confidence,—What is your opinion of Mr Serocold?'

'I decline answering that question,' Paul answered, more haughtily than before. 'I'm not in the habit of exchanging confidences with utter strangers, nor of favouring them with my opinion about third parties—professional or otherwise.'

The smug face opposite waxed somewhat sulky and lowering; but there was no change in the trained humility of the other's voice and manner.

'I beg a thousand pardons, sir. I had no intention of offending you. Would you mind answering *this*, then? Did you intrust £5000 to Mr Serocold some three years ago; and do you know how that money is invested now? I assure you I have reasons for asking; I can have no object in being impertinently inquisitive.'

'There's something in that,' Paul muttered; and then went on aloud: 'I certainly did intrust that sum to Mr Serocold about the time you allude to. I believe it's invested in Canada Bonds. I could tell, of course, by referring to my papers. But Mr Serocold holds a general power of attorney from me. All I know is, that I have received the interest quite regularly, and that satisfies me.'

'You are not hard to satisfy, sir,' Brine replied, with just the dawn of a sneer hovering round his mouth. 'But I dare say the interest would be paid regularly for some time to come. As to the principal——'

That marble head of Paul Chetwynde's was as cool about his own financial affairs as about all other earthly things;

but it must be owned that he felt rather more than curious just at this moment.

'What the d—l's the use of beating about the bush?' he said, with unusual hastiness. ' Can't you say in a dozen words what is wrong, if you know of anything ?'

He had not long to wait for the answer; and it was concise and explicit enough to satisfy any one.

' Every shilling was sold out a year ago.'

There came a sparkle of malicious triumph into the speaker's dull gray eyes, as he saw Chetwynde change colour, and drive the nails of his right hand into the leather of the arm-chair in which he was lounging.

But it was only for a second or two that his wonderful self-command failed. He did not speak till he had had time to reflect that, though the loss was a heavy one, it was by no means ruinous; he had still an income left amply sufficient for his wants, and for indulgence in most luxuries. After the first shock of vexation and surprise had passed, Paul began to realize the satisfaction that would accrue to one of his peculiar temperament, from having the austere sectarian so thoroughly on the hip. So he answered with perfect composure, though his brows were still bent heavily.

' If I understand you aright, you accuse Mr Scrocold of felony. Dangerous words, if they can't be substantiated. And you have known of this, since it was done. Isn't there some such thing as "misprision?"'

The other looked up into his face cunningly, but without flinching.

' I don't accuse Mr Scrocold of anything of the sort. Perhaps he has taken care to keep clear of felony. As for myself—we don't criminate ourselves in the school where I was bred. There are no witnesses to what is said here, remember, even if it is not to be considered confidential. But, Mr Chetwynde, if you'll be good enough to consider, I'm sure you will see you are taking this matter in a wrong light. I can have no possible motive except to serve you.'

Paul's keen, cold eyes shot at the informer one single glance, straight and swift as a sword thrust.

' Or to injure Serocold?' he said. ' How about that? I should like to know on what terms you parted.'

You will hardly find any scoundrel so case-hardened, as not to feel annoyance at being forced abruptly to descend from the position he has assumed, be that position ever so low already

Mr Brine was hugely disconcerted; and perforce took refuge in sullenness.

' I don't see what that has to do with this business, or how it concerns anybody except myself. I've said before, I left at my own desire. I've got my bread to make, and a character to lose, too, or I shouldn't be where I am. Suppose I didn't choose to risk both by staying in an office where such things were going on—where there might be a crash any day? Then, every one would have said— " Like master, like man." Now, I'm clear, and I mean to keep so. I warn you, Mr Chetwynde, if it comes into Court, it's no use calling me as a witness. I shall know nothing. You can easily prove if I've spoken the truth, by asking Serocold for your bonds. But if you'll take my advice, you'll make no criminal matter of it. You might get back most of the money, perhaps, if you managed well.'

' I shall take other advice before I decide on that,' Paul said. ' I don't like compromises in such matters. Besides, the chances of recovery must be small. Serocold was getting desperate when he ran such a venture as this.'

The ether shook his head mysteriously

'You're right enough there, sir,' he said. 'Serocold was insolvent twice over months ago. But he has powerful friends of his own persuasion, who would pay something to save scandal. Besides, I think he holds a secret or two, worth money'

Chetwynde pondered awhile in silence Suddenly a new thought seemed to strike him; and his face became more dark and troubled than it had been since the interview begun.

'What an idiot, not to have thought of that before! Why, half Philip's title-deeds may have been lying in that accursed office. And it was I who recommended Serocold!'

There was a shade of professional contempt in Mr Brine's smile; but it was comfortably reassuring.

'Don't alarm yourself, sir,' he said, promptly 'I can answer for all such being safe. Real property is not so easily convertible as bonds, and stock, and personal securities. You and a few more will be the only sufferers; and I fancy you will be the heaviest.'

The man spoke after his light; and, probably, meant what he said at the time: it was a simple question of pounds, shillings, and pence with him.

When, months afterwards, Paul Chetwynde became aware of all the cruel truth, he felt ashamed at having wasted so much pity on himself.

What was his loss compared to that of the scarred grayhaired man who had trusted the proceeds of his commission to Serocold for investment? He had won his way upwards from the ranks by hard, good service—(and hard pinching too, for he purchased one step)—till he got his

company,—only to find himself, at fifty-eight, nearly as
penniless as when he enlisted, with the addition of a stiff
shoulder, an ailing wife, and two helpless children.

How did the news fall on the weak, nervous devotee,
who had given all her dead husband's savings, and the fortune of her own child, into the hands of the austere pietist,
with no more doubt or suspicion than if she had laid the
money on God's altar? To *her* there was much mercy
dealt; for the blow killed her very soon.

But it fared not so well with the orphan. She had a
cruelly hard time of it in her first situation. The head of
the family was a chief of the Cottonocracy, who paid thrice
as much for the tending of his hot-house plants as for the
training of his olive-branches; he stood in extreme terror
of his butler, whom he had bribed away from a dukery,
and when he had endured more than wonted contumely at
the hands of that awful dignitary, was wont to descend on
the school-room, and relieve his feelings by bullying the
governess. Perhaps, a loathing of that intolerable servi-
tude, and a desire to win liberty at any price, spoke as
strongly as the voice of the tempter who lured the girl to
sin, and left her to shame. Years afterwards, you might
have heard a miserable unsexed woman—possessed, as it
seemed, by seven devils at the least—when the fury of
drink-frenzy was abating, and the maudlin stage was coming on, wailing out broken memories of how ' she had
been a lady once, and might have kept so still, if her poor
mother had not trusted all their money to a ——'

If Robert Serocold could have heard the awful maledic-
tions that closed the sentence, I think he would have
shivered on his prison-pallet, though the model cell was
warmed to a turn.

To return to our sheep, one of whom so lately found himself shorn.

Paul Chetwynde was so intensely relieved by what he now heard, that his humour became almost genial. He began to think that he had dealt to his visitor rather scantier measure of courtesy than may justly be allotted to the bearer of evil tidings.

'I'm sincerely glad you can say so much,' he said. 'For a moment—you see I know less than nothing about those things—I feared I had got Mr Gascoigne into a worse scrape than my own. I've taken your information rather ungraciously : it was well meant, I dare say; at any rate, I've no business to go into your motives. Pray remember, if you should repent hereafter of having told me all this gratuitously, I shall be ready to reward you according to my power—whether I save anything out of the wreck or not.'

The other shook his head negatively; but he appeared rather gratified by the half apology. So they parted, with few more words.

It may be well to say here, that Mr Brine never did return to claim any recompense. During the years that he had served Robert Sercold, dislike and fear had ripened into a steady enmity; though the worm turned late, it turned viciously at last. The man would risk nothing; and waited till he could expose his oppressor without compromising himself, or damaging his own professional prospects; but when he became comparatively independent, he did not dally long with the luxury of uncommercial revenge.

As soon as his visitor had withdrawn, and he had collected certain necessary memoranda, Chetwynde betook himself to the Temple, where dwelt a friend more learned than himself in the law. After a brief consultation, they sent for an eminent detective, whose office was hard by, and took counsel of the oracle. Eventually it was settled that Paul was to see Serocold, in the first instance, alone. But in the square outside was posted one of the most trustworthy of the subalterns; a staunch sleuth-hound, who, ere this, had kept the trail from one end of Europe to the other, till the quarry turned to bay at last, in very weariness and despair.

A sour-looking clerk took in Paul's name to his principal, and returned with a message to the effect that ' if Mr Chetwynde's business was not very important, perhaps he could make it convenient to call later in the day.'

' Mr Chetwynde's business *was* important; and he could *not* make it convenient to call at any other hour.' So he was admitted into the Serocoldian sanctum without further delay.

There sate the good man, with lips more compressed and a gloomier brow than usual; as if he had grave cause to complain of having been disturbed in more important business. Indeed, there was a judicial austerity in his whole demeanour, inexpressibly exasperating to one who knew as much as did his present visitor and late client.

' Will you be seated, Mr Chetwynde?' he said. 'I trust you will be as brief as possible. I am deeply engaged this morning.'

Paul sank into the chair thus indicated, simply from his inveterate habit of taking everything at ease, if not easily; if he had been condemned to be shot to death, he would certainly have preferred to face the platoon—sitting. But there was a set expression about his mouth, and an odd look in his eyes—half cruel, half scornful—that the other could not long have failed to observe.

' You will have to defer your business, whatever it is; and it depends on yourself whether this interview is to be brief or not. Possibly, the matter may be very easily settled. I want to sell out that £5000 of Canada Bonds; —at once, mind. I have a better investment for the money '

If you had seen Robert Scrocold's everyday complexion, you would have thought it scarcely possibly that its pallor could deepen: yet there was a perceptible change now: near the cheekbones and the angle of the jaw the dull white seemed marbled with a faint livid green. A very close observer might have noticed a slight shaking of the thin, callous hands, that shuffled some papers together, rather hurriedly; but there was no tremor in the hard grating voice.

'If you were more of a business-man, Mr Chetwynde, you would know that it is impossible to change your securities at a moment's notice. You say, you have found a better investment. I would advise you not to be rash. You will scarcely find any such that can be called safe, and will return you higher interest.'

' I'm very happy to say I'm *not* a business-man, as you interpret the word,' Paul retorted, without attempting to disguise a sneer. ' But, with all my ignorance, I happen to know that Canada Bonds are nearly as negotiable as bank-notes. As to the safety of investments—that's a matter of opinion. If you will hand me the bonds, you need trouble yourself no further in the matter. I will take the consequences on myself, and my broker can manage the rest of the business.'

His keen glance rested full on the other while he spoke; but Serocold met it with wonderful steadiness.

'You are the best judge of your own interests, of course. If you will call here at noon to-morrow, I will hand you over your bonds.'

'I prefer to-day,' Chetwynde answered. 'There is ample time. Will you be good enough to inform me where they are deposited?'

Then—in spite of all his audacity and craft—the lawyer felt that the evil moment was upon him. There came into his eyes a glassy, haggard look, fearful to see; it was more from habit than deliberate intent that he fenced yet a few seconds longer.

'Where are they deposited?' he said, hoarsely. 'At—my banker's, of course.'

Paul leant forward, with his arm resting on the table between them, till his face was only a foot or so from the other's. He spoke just as coolly and slowly as if he had been making the most ordinary remark.

'At your banker's? The proceeds of the sale, I suppose you mean. Haven't you got rid of all yet? For the bonds were sold a year ago.'

Paul had promised himself a little intellectual amusement in that interview. He had reckoned on some sport with the stratagems and evasions of Tartuffe so near his unmasking. But his patience—great as it was—yielded to the strain. He delivered that home-thrust at least five minutes too soon.

For some seconds after, the two faces remained opposite to each other, without recoiling an inch or moving a muscle —the one set in a pitiless scorn, too deep for anger—the other possessed by a blank, ghastly horror. Then the

lawyer locked his fingers tightly over his stony eyes; and
his head fell forward on the table, with a dull crash, such
as you hear when you strike horn upon wood.

Chetwynde sauntered slowly to the window, and looked
out into the square. There leant, against a lamp-post a
few yards off, the invaluable detective, poisoning the
fresh May air with the blackest of graveolent cigars, and
conversing with an infirm and palpably imbecile ticket-
porter, with a broad, benevolent smile on his florid countenance. A hoarse, guttural sound behind him made Paul
turn round. The lawyer had lifted his head, and was
trying to speak. At last the words came out of his dry
throat huskily.

'You know all, it seems. I guess where you learnt it.
I deny nothing. What do you mean to do ? '

He never wasted time in asking for mercy or forbearance: there was scant trace of either in the calm, implacable face that confronted him now.

' I mean to get my money back, if I can,' Paul said,
sternly. ' If not—perhaps, even, if I do—I make no terms
—I'll have money's worth to the utmost farthing, if I can
get it out of criminal law. If I didn't prosecute, it would
only be on the conditions that you wound up affairs, and
left the country immediately And all we, whom you have
robbed, must share and share alike. You don't suppose
I'm going to save myself at the expense of the rest, who-
soever they may be. I should simply be an accomplice in
the swindle. Without more paltering—what do you propose ? '

Once more the lawyer shaded his face with his hand;
when he uncovered it, it wore a cunning expression, as if
he saw a gleam of safety in the black horizon.

'I will not palter with you, Mr Chetwynde,' he said; 'I prefer telling you at once, frankly (you should have seen Paul's look when that word came out) that, from my own resources, I can make no restitution to you or to any one. But, if time is given, I have friends—substantial friends —who might make some sacrifices sooner than see scandal cast on the good cause, through the shame of an unworthy professor.'

'Friends!' the other retorted, with intense disdain; 'a proper recommendation—that they should be friends of yours! They must bring a better testimonial than that, and better security than a sanctimonious outside, and better argument than texts quoted glibly, if they wish me to treat with them. As to time—I'll give you till noon to-morrow; not an hour longer. As I said before, I will listen, but I promise nothing.'

The crafty look on Serocold's face darkened into malevolence again.

'You do not know of whom you are speaking,' he said, darkly. 'Cannot holy men hold the same faith with sinners? Is Scripture untrue because the Devil quotes it sometimes? There is one text you might remember— 'Judge not, that ye be not judged.' Mr Chetwynde, the time you fix is too short. For your own sake, you had better have more patience.'

'I don't intend to bandy words with you, much less discuss points of doctrine,' the other broke in. 'I will not extend the delay by ten minutes. I would never have granted it, but for the chance that others, besides myself, may possibly save something by a composition. We don't risk much in leaving you free till to-morrow; you will set your foot nowhere unwatched till then, and the faintest attempt at escape will be stopped by decisive arrest. Then, the matter will be out of my hands.'

The criminal winced visibly. He knew right well what these last words meant, for he had himself employed the same staff of detectives ere now. If he had nourished any vague hopes of escape, they died, there and then.

'Take your own way,' he muttered still more sullenly. 'I understand that you will not refuse to see any person that I may send to you? That is enough. I have no more to say, and no more to confess, if you stay here till to-morrow. I shall go to my house to-night; you can have me followed and guarded as you please.'

For the last few seconds Chetwynde had been regarding the speaker with something akin to curiosity.

Indeed it was worth observing; how, when the first shock had passed, the dogged devil in the man's nature re-asserted itself. There he sat—with the garment of righteousness that had masqued him these many years torn in shreds from his shoulders—dishonoured exile in his future, even if he escaped a prison; knowing well that in all the world there was no door that would henceforth be open to him without a golden key; knowing, too, the full extent of the ruin he had brought, not only on Chetwynde, whom he hated for his scoffs and gibes, but on others who had listened in timid reverence to his lectures and cowered before his admonitions, trusting him all the while as if he had been some stern angel: he sat, I say, contemplating this Past and this Future, and yet maintained the old, hard, austere demeanour. It seemed as though he must have swallowed some antidote to the poisons of remorse and shame.

' I don't suppose you *will* confess more,' Paul said, after

a pause ; 'and I don't know what good it would do, at
present, if you did. But, I own, I should like to know
what on earth became of all the money. I should not have
been quite deceived, I think, if I had not given you credit
for being rather miserly in your tastes.'

There was something in these words that goaded Serocold out of his sullen torpor ; a savage light rushed into
his eyes ; he shook his clenched hand aloft, as if threatening or defying Heaven, after mocking it so long ; and his
hoarse strained voice rose almost to a shriek.

'Gone——. Can I say, where ? Sunk in every pit-fall
that could swallow up money. And—why ? Have I not
been toiling and scheming while others were sleeping, and
pinching myself while others squandered ; ay, and praying
while others were mocking ? Have I ever yielded to the
vices or pleasures in which others delight ? What have I
ever spent on drink, or woman, or play ? Why, the very
income that you lose now would only have bought you
mere luxuries. I was always cautious, and took wise
counsel too. Yet nothing would go right : losing—losing,
always, till I came to—this. If I had won, I would have
made my name famous for good deeds. And we talk of
the justice of God ! '

Rhapsody was very foreign to the cold formalist's nature ;
yet, he certainly seemed to speak bitterly in earnest. It
is just possible—there are such strange anomalies amongst
us—that his fanaticism was only half a lie. If so, he was
not the first of his class that has tried to make austere
bigotry atone for deliberate dishonesty.

But an expression of supreme disgust swept across Paul
Chetwynde's face as he recoiled a full pace from the
speaker.

'You are going to try blasphemy now, I suppose,' he said, 'since cant has failed. You had better keep that tirade for the dock, where you are sure to stand sooner or later, whether *I* send you there or no. The devil take your insolence! You rob me, and I don't know how many more, and then boast that you " are not as we are ;" finishing up by denying Heaven's justice because your speculations have failed. By oath, you're a natural curiosity. But I'll not trust myself much longer in your society, for all that. By noon to-morrow, or—you know the consequences.'

So Chetwynde left the lawyer to his meditations, or devotions, without another word.

The amiable detective, who had just lighted another cigar, and engaged the ancient ticket-porter in another interminable story, took no notice of his principal as he passed: the slightest nod from Paul told him that he was to remain on guard. He was soon after joined by a comrade, if possible more florid and affable than himself. Robert Serocold was virtually just as much a prisoner now as if the manacles were on his wrists.

He knew that : he knew that if he were to dodge all over London all that night, a stealthy step would always be close behind his own, and one pair of sharp eyes, at the least, close to his shoulder. Far better to go straight home, and let them follow him, and watch every outlet from his house through which a dog could have crept.

Directly he was left alone, Mr Serocold began to write a letter, with slow, painful deliberation : he despatched this by a messenger as soon as it was finished. After this he never dipped pen in ink again ; making no attempt to arrange his affairs, nor even collecting the papers that lay scattered about the table and the room. There he sate quite motionless, with fixed, staring eyes, and a vacant expression on his face, till long after office-hours. He was often in the habit of overstaying the clerks; so they departed, now, unsuspiciously as usual.

At last he went out: there was no particular sign of perturbation about him; only his hat, instead of being set primly and squarely on his head, was crushed down low over his brows. As he passed the lamp-post, where the two detectives were still lounging, one of them, who knew him, saluted him civilly—'hoping he was well.'

The lawyer made no answer in words; but there shot from under his shaggy eye-lashes one look of deadly malevolence, and he muttered under his breath one curse, as bitterly blasphemous as ever was mouthed in Alsatia.

The glance and the growl only provoked a smile—of amusement, if not of positive satisfaction—from the persons at whom they were levelled.

It is needless to say that the earth-stoppers never lost sight of their fox till he went fairly to ground. Then they made themselves as comfortable as they could, consistently with unremitting vigilance; and waited patiently for a fresh signal, before beginning business in earnest.

CHAPTER XIV

HONOUR THY FATHER.

CHETWYNDE, as you know already, took things much more coolly than the average of his fellows. Nevertheless, it must be owned that the annoyances of the day seriously interfered with his appetite. As he was dressing, between seven and eight that evening, after the listless fashion of a man quite indifferent to the dinner in prospect, he was surprised by the announcement that the Dean of Torrcaster was in the drawing-room waiting to see him.

During the few minutes that elapse before Paul can appear before his sire, it may be worth while to sketch the exterior of the eminent divine.

A tall stout man; somewhat over the half-century, but with scarcely a tinge of gray in his strong wiry black hair and bushy eyebrows; more than upright in his bearing, for, sitting or standing, he carries his head always thrown backward; his complexion decidedly sanguine, yet not healthily ruddy; it looks as though the blood was forced at times too violently through the swollen veins; the features are not badly cast in a large mould,—but altogether it is a very unpleasant face to look upon. The coarse cruel mouth tells tales at once : that face might be sanctimonious, but never sleek or smooth. After one glance at the man, you felt instinctively that the slightest scratch in the thin outward varnish would betray a bitter savage temper beneath, not always restrained within the bounds of overbearing harshness.

One fact speaks significantly enough of the relations subsisting between the two : this was the first time the Dean had set foot in his son's chambers. When Chetwynde entered, he found his father scanning the objects around him with evident contempt and disapproval: of a truth the furniture and other appliances of Paul's chambers differed greatly from those to be found in the solemn rooms at the

Deanery, where everything was of the severe ecclesiastical order.

Paul did not take up the implied challenge ; but, after a salutation strangely cold on both sides, asked to know the reason of the unexpected visit.

The Dean cleared his throat twice or thrice before he replied.

'I have come upon very unpleasant business,' he said at last. 'I have received a note from Mr Serocold, stating the particulars of your interview this afternoon, and begging me to speak to you on the subject. I need not say how the intelligence has shocked and astounded me ; yet I have not thought it right to refuse his request.'

Paul's smile, it must be confessed, was anything but pleasant or conciliatory.

'You are the best judge, sir, of course,' he said, 'of what you owe to yourself and your position. But I should think it was about the first time that a common swindler has chosen a dignitary of the Church as his ambassador. Will you be good enough to tell me what you are empowered to propose.'

The Dean's brow lowered more and more while his son was speaking, till it settled into the black frown that had so often appalled a humble dependent, or faithful follower : with neither of these had he now to deal. He knew it, too ; but, from habit perhaps, even at that early stage of the discourse, he could not refrain from launching out in reproof.

'You speak with most unchristian bitterness, to say nothing of implied disrespect to me. Robert Serocold is *not* a common swindler. Up to the unhappy moment when, under great pressure of circumstances, he yielded to tempt-

ation, he has borne a character perfectly blameless. I am
not about to defend his conduct, or even palliate it. But
he assures me that he took the money simply as a loan,
meaning fully to repay it, after making calculations on
which he had a right to rely. If time is granted him I
believe he will make all the amends in his power; and I
believe grace will be given him to repent heartily; repent
in a way that *you* perhaps can hardly understand.'

Paul's smile was very nearly a sneer now.

' If you think proper, sir, to draw comparisons between
Serocold and myself—to my disadvantage—you can do so,
of course; but I distinctly decline to listen to them. I am
happy to say that I can *not* sympathize with his feelings in
any way—repentant or otherwise. About his intentions,
I shall keep my own opinion; nor do I see how they much
affect the question. Complete restitution—to others as
well as myself, for I can't suppose I am the only victim—
is the only amends he can make : he must leave England,
too, as soon as his affairs have been thoroughly sifted.
He shall have no further chance of plunder, this side the
Channel. As to time, the whole thing must be settled
reliably—so far as it is possible—before noon to-morrow '

The Dean's face flushed to crimson, and the lines round
his cruel mouth grew deep and set, as though drawn by a
graver's steel. He controlled himself with a mighty effort;
but if a child had been standing then between these two,
it would have guessed that the interview could not end in
peace.

' You are trifling,' he said, hoarsely. ' You know full
well that you ask for impossibilities. Serocold has no resources of his own, and those of such as would help to
avert a public scandal are limited, and cannot be realized

at a day's notice. He led me to believe that you would
listen to any reasonable composition.'

'You will find I am not trifling at all,' Paul retorted with
exasperating coolness. 'And if Serocold told you anything
of that sort, he lied, as he has been lying all his life long.
I said I would listen, but would promise nothing. I *have*
listened; and I am more than ever inclined to accept no
terms, but let the law take its course.'

The Dean rose from his seat with slow solemnity; the
room was only lighted by a single reading-lamp, and his
figure loomed impressively large, as he stood somewhat in
the shadow. He stretched out his right hand, with his
favourite gesture of menace and denunciation—he had
copied it, years ago, from a picture of Jeremiah cursing
Jerusalem—which, from the Torrcaster pulpit, had stricken
terror into the hearts of true believers as well as evil-doers:
poor Mrs Carew still saw it in her dreams, and would wake
a-trembling. The ponderous syllables came one by one,
like measured blows of a sledge hammer. The sonorous-
ness of the delivery was somewhat marred by a certain
thickness of utterance; but the whole effect was rather
imposing, albeit decidedly theatrical.

'I will bandy no further words with you. I command
you, on your duty as my son, and at peril of my lasting
displeasure if you refuse, to press this matter no further,
and to abandon all idea of prosecution, trusting to me to
make the best arrangements for your interests. You may
take five minutes for consideration; and then say, if you
will obey or no.' Then the orator resumed his seat.

Paul had not stirred in his chair, nor moved a muscle of
his face during that brief declamation: almost before it
was concluded, without turning his head or relaxing the

steady gaze that looked straight into his father's eyes, he laid his hand on a bell close to his elbow, and rang it sharply.

' You know Mr Serocold's house at Clapham, don't you?' he said to his own servant, who answered the bell.

The man assented.

'Take a hansom,' his master went on, 'and go down there as quickly as you can. You will find two men on the watch, outside. Say to either of them just these words —' Make the arrest at once.' Stay—I'll write them down and sign them. Start at once, and let me know when you come back. I shall be at the club, if not here.'

Chetwynde's confidential servant was one of those in-valuable menials—rarer than rubies—who set about their appointed tasks, be they ever so novel or strange, quietly and quickly, without remark or remonstrance; who, when business is in hand, never indulge themselves in thinking independently, unless specially ordered so to do. Had Evans not been endowed with this silent discretion he would not have held the place for ten days that he had occupied for as many years.

He had always heard Mr Serocold spoken of as a person of the highest repute; not a rumour, of course, had reached him of what to-day had brought forth; yet he went on his way to give orders for the arrest (for he understood the whole thing at once) of that respectable gentleman, just as unconcernedly as if he had spent all the leisure hours of his life in practising as an amateur detective. He did not even bestow a side-glance, before leaving the room, on the Dean's face, as he sate in a huge arm-chair rather without the circle of lamp-light.

Yet that face was worth looking at, to any physiognomist, not easily repelled by expression, but ready to take the rough with the smooth in his studies of human nature.

'That is my answer, sir,' Paul said, just as coolly as ever, directly they were alone again.

It is doubtful if the Dean heard the words: he was literally blind and deaf with passion, and too astounded to interfere or prevent the servant's departure.

For many years he had met with more deference from almost every one in anywise subject to his authority, than from his own son. But it had never entered into his brain to conceive that Paul would openly thwart or defy him. Society is wonderfully submissive to men of his stamp; those great bulls of Bashan stamp and stalk about, each in his own prairie, with little let or molestation, unless some rival, equally blatant and blusterous, chances to invade the domain. Perhaps Dean Chetwynde had never been actually bearded since he left college. Tyranny, within doors and without, religious and secular, had become as natural to that man as if he had been born with a hereditary right to despotism. All this made the blow fall heavier now: no wonder that it fairly staggered him, and for the moment shook his moral dignity from her throne.

It would be difficult, even if it were advisable, to transcribe the torrent of foamy invective that burst from his writhing lips when he found voice to speak. But I have too much respect for the most venerable of all institutions, to give more than the outline of a high clerical dignitary in a state of—let us say—self-oblivion. If the most zealous of the Torrcaster faithful could have looked upon their leader then, their fanaticism would have been cured on the spot: bigotry could not have survived the shame of recog-

nizing what a poor weak creature it was that they had so
long delighted to honour.

What made the outburst more horribly grotesque, was
the Scriptural tone that pervaded it. Scraps of texts were
mingled with broken menaces and incoherent abuse; indeed
the incongruities somewhat resembled those of Holy Willie's
Prayer, only that in this instance there was no hypocrisy
of aforethought.

At last the Dean stopped from sheer want of breath.
Putting flowers of speech aside, the gist of his invective
seemed to resolve itself into the often-repeated question,
' How the son dared to forget what he owed to his father?'

No living person had witnessed such an outbreak from
Dean Chetwynde; for he kept his temper, as a rule, within
decent and dignified bounds; always saturnine and severe,
and pitilessly fluent in reproof, he was never actually
savage. Yet Paul sate through the gust of passion perfectly unmoved; betraying no more emotion or surprise
than if he had been listening to the rant of a stage-player.

Yet the first-born was set there, face to face with the
sire that begat him—with the priest who sprinkled the
water of baptism on his forehead, who taught his baby-lips
to lisp their earliest prayer. And these things happened
not in the days of Carlos, or Curthose, but in the middle
of this severely civilized century; in this land of ours,
which delights to keep holy the Sabbath-day; whence,
year by year, they go forth by those armies whoso mission
it is to convert and soften the heart of heathendom.

' Forget what I owe to you?' Paul said in a low bitter
voice. ' I'm not likely to do that. It's a long score: too
long to be paid off on this side of the grave. If my spirit
was not crushed in childhood, it was not from the sparing

of the rod. You were liberal enough of chastisement, and always had a text to back it with : I never heard you quote that one about 'provoking the children.' How many kind words or caresses have I to thank you for? I swear—not one. I owe you more than this—a manhood without faith, or hope beyond the world's bounds. It was too late to look for another religion, when you had made me hate and scorn the one that you profess. Is it nothing, that the very words you have been saying would have a holy meaning for others, and sound to me like breaking bubbles of air? Do you wonder at this? Have I not seen you come back from preaching a charity-sermon, and bully your servant for giving a crust to a starving beggar-woman? And you talk about a filial reverence. Bah! There's no one to overhear us : it isn't worth while playing out the farce any longer. I am—what you have made me. An unnatural son—eh? Well, I've learnt to disbelieve in natural affection along with the rest of your creed!'

There was something awful in the suppressed passion of Paul's manner and tone : it told, at once, how many years the sullen embers of enmity had been smouldering before the fire kindled, and at the last he spake with his tongue. The Dean was fairly cowed : he could only mutter something, between a protest and a refusal to listen any longer. The other went on without noticing this.

'I have more to say : it will be as well to hear me to the end. I am speaking on these things for the first and last time. I could forgive more easily what you have done to me, if I did not know what you have done to others. Have I not seen you grinding the life out of that poor crippled sister of mine; magnifying her small failings into mortal sins, till she is half mad sometimes with terror and remorse, and dare not call her soul her own? Besides this—I loved my mother dearly.'

At these last words the elder man raised his head, that had sunk nearly to his breast; a vague fear was mingled with the fury in his bloodshot eyes; and his voice shook a little, though it was hoarse and deep as a tiger's growl.

'What do you mean? Do you dare——?'

He had better have kept back the challenge, or crushed it between his grinding teeth. When Paul spoke again, his face was fearfully changed: it was, now, far the darker and more threatening of the two.

'What do I mean? I'll soon tell you. I mean just this. I knew all along of the tyranny that drained my poor mother's life away. Have I not lain awake for hours together, because I could not sleep for her sobbing and moaning that came to me through the wall? She never murmured in this world; but I am sure her complaint has been heard somewhere ere this: for I do believe in Eternal Justice, though not as you would teach it. I knew all this: and four years ago, I learnt something more.'

Paul's voice sank almost to a whisper, here; but every word was so terribly distinct, that it might have been heard a hundred feet away.

'I know, now, how my mother died, and why Janet was born a cripple.'

The colour died away in Dean Chetwynde's face—not gradually, but instantaneously, as it might do in a head that has just fallen under the guillotine: his cheek remained ashen-white, veined and flecked here and there with dull purple. His mouth opened twice or thrice convulsively, but the dry swollen tongue could form no intelligible syllable: and all the while his great limbs and frame were shaking as in an ague-fit.

After a minute's pause, Paul went on with the same cruel calmness—far harder to bear than virulence of reproach.

'You remember Julie? Of course you do. I don't wonder you got rid of her the day after my mother's funeral. You had better have sent her the alms she asked for to keep her through her last illness. She sent for me to the hospital, and—she spoke out before she died. She told me how she found my mother in a fainting-fit, that evening in the library—ah! I see you've not forgotten it. That long inscription on her tomb in the cathedral says nothing of the push or blow—which was it?—that killed her. Did the doctors guess nothing when they found her in premature labour; nor the dead-nurse when she laid out a corpse, with a black bruise on its breast? I dare say that gentle saint forgave you, if she had strength to speak; and Janet would forgive too. But *I* never will—by the Eternal God. And you come now to command me to let your precious disciple go free—trusting to *you*, to guard my interests? No—my leading-strings were snapped rather early. You can give him spiritual consolation in prison, if you like; or comfort him with your countenance when he stands in the dock; but you cannot help him, here. Now I have said my say.'

If the most vindictive of the many weaklings whom the clerical despot had overborne in his pride of place could have stood in the room just then, the measure of retaliation would surely have been filled to the brim.

It would be difficult to find anything, in earth or heaven, less impressionable than the conscience of a hard, heart-

less man, who has worn for many years the outer garment
of the ascetic. Yet callosity, simple and absolute, is, perhaps, comparatively rare. In the toughest moral hide
there may be one gall which will rankle incurably.

The Dean of Torreaster could look back on the long
weary days of his meek wife's martyrdom without a throb
of self-reproach; but he always thought of that single fatal
night, if not with remorse, at least with intolerable shame.
As he walked up the cathedral nave, his eyes never rested
for a second on the little side-chapel, wherein lay a fair
white effigy, supine with folded palms. When he chanced
to hear of the French waiting-woman's death, he felt a
great relief in the certainty that the black secret would
be buried with her. Now—he knew that it had been revealed to the one man alive that he would least have
chosen for the confidence. He had found it, of late, very
hard to meet, with undisturbed self-complacency, his son's
keen, cold eyes: how much harder would it be, now
that he could wonder no longer at their animosity and
scorn!

On a table, close to the Dean's elbow, there stood a tall
glass pitcher of iced water and some goblets. He filled
one of these till it overflowed, and drained it eagerly, at a
gulp. Slowly and sullenly the torpid blood flowed back
into its channels and mounted in his face; but his breathing was still thick and laboured. At last he rose and
walked towards the door, staggering a little and groping
his way, like one drunk or purblind.

He paused on the threshold, and facing round, with his
hand on the lock, spoke for the first time in a dull, heavy
voice. It seemed as if he hardly realized the meaning of
his words, but was rather actuated by one of those nervous

impulses, which, at certain crises, make a man feel that he must say something, whether it be relevant or no.

'Your blood be on your own head.'

'Amen,'—quoth Paul Chetwynde.

It was afterwards somehow tacitly understood between those two, that appearances were to be kept up before the world. Paul still paid brief ceremonious visits to the Deanery. But, in life, they were never again alone together.

On what grounds the criminal had ventured to claim the Dean's intercession, was never fully known. When, three years later, the reverend man, stricken suddenly by apoplexy, departed this life in great haste, and intestate, Paul found among the mass of papers abundant evidence that his father had been deeply involved in the speculations wherein Serocold had sunk other fortunes besides his own. Perhaps there existed between the lawyer and his client a stronger bond than a community of financial interests; and perhaps the latter had been intrusted with something beyond mere professional confidences. But the clue to the possible mystery was never found. Serocold was probably satisfied that the Dean had done his utmost to save him; at any rate, he was not the man to make unprofitable revelations about himself or others. They got little out of him, either before or after his trial; and, when he caught the jail-fever in the second year of his imprisonment, he confessed nothing even in delirium, and died at last as mute and sullen as a bull-dog.

In the dock the lawyer pleaded 'Guilty' at once; but asked to be allowed to say a few words, before sentence was passed. He then expressed himself much in the same terms as in his own chambers, when he so provoked

Chetwynde. But he seemed more anxious to claim exemption from the vulgar herd of criminals, than to mitigate or explain away his actual offence. He wanted to make his case paradoxical and exceptional.

Melancholy to relate, the plain, practical jurymen would persist in regarding Robert Serocold as a very ordinary swindler: and the judge, though his solemn face betrayed no irritation or disgust, confessed afterwards that he was moved by the pietist's self-laudation to double severity of punishment.

CHAPTER XV

UP IN THE HILLS.

LET us travel, now, a thousand leagues Eastward Ho !

A deep irregular gorge ; shut in on either side by a steep spur of the great mountain range that looms all around, dark against the sky-line; almost choked up, in parts, by low trees buried in creepers, and stubborn brushwood, and tangled grasses ; with masses of a yellowish-brown stone cropping out here and there. Just such a scene, in fine, as you may see repeated, day by day, as you wander through the hill-country of India.

At certain points, when the rock comes too near the surface to allow rank vegetation to take hold, are small clearings, like a natural glade in our English woodland. Opposite to one of these, half-masked by a huge boulder, a hunter is sitting, with one rifle across his knees, another by his side.

We recognize an old acquaintance, though his cheeks

look wonderfully tanned and brown under the white
linen swathed round the close felt casque, and there is a
burnt reddish tinge in his chestnut beard, as if it had
passed through the furnace-heat of many fierce sun-rays.
But the clear, honest eyes are not a whit changed, nor has
one line of the face grown harder.

It is the same Maurice Dering, all over, whom you saw,
two years ago, waiting on the 'rocketers' at Marston
Lisle.

He is quite alone on his post; but two of his comrades
are already ensconced in their several stations within a few
hundred yards; for at this point it is almost certain that
their game will break. It is a noted cover for bear; and
they are to shoot at nothing else to-day.

Maurice's favourite *shikari* had been disabled early in
that week by an accident. The man who ought now to
have been at his elbow was a comparative novice in wood-
craft. Old Kurreem would never have brought out bullets
three sizes too large for the second rifle that now lay un-
loaded and useless by the hunter's side. Dering was
noted for his success in managing his followers, whether
actually in his service or not. The great secret of this
was, that though always firm and decided in his manner,
he never by any chance lost his temper with a native, nor
condescended to use threats or abuse. On the present
occasion he did not rebuke the lad's mistake very sharply;
but simply told him to be more careful for the future, and
despatched him to the tents, which were not far distant,
to change the bullets; for neither of Maurice's comrades
had any to fit that particular rifle.

The young *shikari* was silent and reserved, as are most
of his kind; but his large bright eyes told plainly enough

how he appreciated the Sahib's forbearance. He became famous in after-days; a bolder or more faithful henchman never trod on Indian soil. Was he thinking, I wonder, of that especial morning, as, years later, he lay, when all crushed and mangled they had dragged him from the tiger's fangs; when he took Maurice's hand in both his own, damp already with the sweat of the death-agony, and kissed it so thankfully and humbly; and then—glancing aside at the bloody writhen mass of brindled fur, that, awhile ago, was the dreadful Man Eater—went heaven-wards with a smile on his thin lips, and a gleam of triumph in his black falcon eyes?

But if there was no displeasure or discontent on Dering's face as he sate there musing, it surely was much more pensive and grave than could be accounted for by the occasion. Indeed, it was evident that his thoughts were not, just then, with the game. He held in his hand an open letter, which had come to him that morning; as he turned the pages backwards and forwards, his brow darkened with anxiety.

That letter was from Philip Gascoigne; it was much briefer than usual; besides this, though it was as affection-ate as possible, it was marked by a certain reserve and constraint that puzzled Maurice sorely.

'What on earth does he mean by that?' he muttered half aloud, as his eye lighted for the third time on one of the last sentences. 'Surely he's not been ill; his wife would have mentioned it, even if Philip had kept it back. And what can have happened to worry him?'

The words ran thus:—

'This is the stupidest scrawl you have ever had from me. And I'm afraid the next won't be much better. I

M

feel as if I should not be in real scribbling form for some time to come. Georgie must make her postscripts longer; that's all.'

In truth, the postscript to-day was a good half of the letter: yet it did not convey any very important news; relating chiefly to the fair lady's triumphs at a certain fancy-ball, where she had appeared as Diane de Poitiers. She gave an elaborate sketch of her own costume, and mentioned, casually, that Captain Annesleigh's had also been much admired: he had been her partner in the *Moyen-age* Quadrille, in the character of the Second Henry.

Maurice bent his brows slightly as he read that last name; as men will do who are chasing some vague unpleasant recollection.

'Annesleigh?' he said, meditatively. 'Of course; I remember. That's the man who backed me for such a cracker in the Grand Military. Pleasant enough to talk to; but not to be trusted, I dare swear. There are some ugly stories about him. I wonder if he visits much at Marston? If so, they are derogating fast. I've a good mind to give Philip a hint of what I've heard when I answer this. But Paul knows more about him than I do: he'll take care to keep everything straight. *That* Diana, too, of all Dianas——a nice character truly: I wonder they allowed her to take it.' But his own frank smile came back to Maurice's lip, and his eye brightened with pleasure, as it rested on the last paragraph of all.

'The Moor is *so* well. I see him every day, after breakfast, wet or dry. He likes me now better than he ever liked you. But he sends you his love nevertheless. And he wants you home again, as much as—we all do.'

A very fair vision rose up before Dering as he read: a

vision of golden tresses mingling with a black flowing
mane; of a strong brown neck and swelling crest, bowed
curvingly to meet the caress of a little white hand: just
such a group as we fancy, under the torches, in the court-
yard of Linteged, when the dawn of Duchess May's wed-
ding-night was near the breaking; when the red-roan
charger had so lately been lightened of his double burden;
and the furious hoof-thunder had scarcely ceased to roll
through the pauses of the rain,—

On the steed she laid her cheek, kiss'd his mane and kiss'd his neck.
'I had rather died with thee, than lived on, the wife of Leigh,'
    Were the first words she did speak.

Ever since he sailed from England, Dering had put his
thoughts, on one particular subject, under very rigid discipline. They were, indeed, perfectly drilled now. These
postscripts no longer evoked that fluttering at the heart
and quickening of the pulses that, at first, could not be
denied or dissembled. If, in Maurice's recollections of
Philip Gascoigne's wife, there still mingled a sentiment
more tender than friendship pure and simple, they were
surely guiltless of any taint of covetousness or repining.

Even so, O Benedict, my friend, may you sometimes
think of the delicate white flower that you would fain have
plucked in the days of your gipsyhood, had it not withered
too soon, without treason to the Queen Rose to whom you
have since sworn fealty—that brilliant Beatrice, whose
empire had been waxing stronger from the very day that
she condescended to become your blessing and crown.

Yet perhaps it was scarcely prudent in Maurice to allow
his fancies to stray as they did just then: the reins of the
discipline whereof I have spoken were certainly relaxed

for the moment; and the dreamer fell into a reverie, dangerously sweet in its very sadness. He could not refrain from one long, low sigh.

How that musing was broken, and how that sigh was answered, you are going to hear.

Whatever grounds he might have had for meditation on that especial morning, Dering was too thorough a sportsman to have yielded to a fit of abstraction, if there had been any immediate prospect of his rifle coming into play. The bears in these parts are generally very hard to move and loth to break cover; the beaters had not long got fairly to work, and their shouts still came faint and distant from the upper end of the gorge.

But Maurice's senses, naturally keen, had been so wonderfully sharpened by forest-practice, that a leopard would scarcely have stolen past him unnoticed, within fair earshot. A smothered, crackling rustle in the brushwood hard by was more than sufficient to recall those wandering thoughts, and bring him alertly to his guard. He was on his knee, quite ready for action—still half-masked by the boulder behind which he had been sitting—a full minute before the game broke cover in the clear ground before him.

He compressed his lips in silent disappointment, as two bear-cubs, about three parts grown, thrust their way through the tangled grass and branches, waving their brown-black heads restlessly from side to side as they blundered on, with the half-scared, half-savage expression in their little bright eyes peculiar to their race when molested.

Maurice had hoped for a worthier antagonist. But he never dreamt of letting this chance pass. Besides, bears are very like men, and if allowed to run away, are pretty sure to fight another day, when it is not so convenient to other parties concerned. Hunting parties were not so frequent then as they are now, and the brutes were rather in the ascendant in these parts. So—muttering between his teeth, ' It's rather chicken-slaughter,'—Dering raised his rifle and fired twice in rapid succession. The leading cub rolled over, stone-dead and scarcely quivering; for the heavy conical ball had crashed right through its innocent young heart. The other dropped too, but lay tossing and struggling in a longer agony; the smoke of the first barrel hung slightly, and the bullet struck about an inch too far back.

Almost simultaneously with the last shot, Dering rose on his feet, and began re-loading with mechanical quickness and precision. But before lead touched powder, there was heard another sound, that struck rather startlingly even upon his nerves, inured as they were to all sorts of peril.

It was a savage, guttural growl, almost deep enough to be called a roar, half menacing, half piteous; in it spoke not only the fury of a wild beast hungry for battle, but the agony of a mother scenting the blood of her offspring. Neither was it the natural voice of the brute; for the Indian *ursa* is not prone to loud expression of emotion; and in the extreme of anger or pain rarely gives vent to more than a hoarse, grunting murmur. Then the tangled jungle broke away, as dry withy-bands yield to fire, and a huge she-bear crashed into the glade, rearing nearly erect, as she confronted her enemy.

Just such a figure, the children, shrinking and shrieking, saw issue from the wood of Beth-el, when their bantering of the bald-headed Prophet was about to be so incomprehensibly avenged.

It is very true that, compared to the terrible Grizzly of the Far West, the Eastern bruin is a tame, harmless animal: nevertheless, there are men alive who can tell you, that it is no child's-play when he closes in earnest: his claws are sharp and strong enough to tear a scalp away, as easily as you would strip a Tangerine orange of its rind. Remember, too, that the brute was maddened now by the philoprogenitive frenzy that makes the most pacific of living creatures bitterly dangerous.

But Dering's self-possession never deserted him for a second. He drove the ball home, strongly and steadily, and threw a cap on with inconceivable quickness: then he blew a long, shrill blast on a whistle that hung to his button; there was a peculiar note that gave at once to those who heard it the preconcerted signal of imminent danger. Maurice knew his comrades well, and could rely on help coming as soon as feet, swift and nimble, could bring it; besides this, he had one barrel loaded, and had great confidence in his shooting: so he awaited the onset in perfect calmness if not in comfort.

But, for a little space, the onset was delayed. After that first glare into his eyes the creature never seemed to notice her enemy: her whole attention was riveted on the cub that still lay writhing in the death-agony It was pitiful to see her stooping over it, and fondling it with her head and fore-paws, moaning, all the while, as if her heart was breaking.

Unnatural and romantic as it may seem—to save his life thrice over, Dering could not have shot her just then. But he had not long to hesitate. All at once the cub ceased struggling, and, stretching itself out with a slight shiver, lay stone-dead. Before the last breath was fairly drawn, the old bear reared herself up once more, and, with a growl more terribly significant than that which had heralded her appearance, dashed in, straight and swift, to her vengeance.

During those few seconds Maurice had stepped back a pace or two, and stood now fully prepared. When the brute made her rush he brought the rifle steadily to his shoulder, and fired at once, sighting her right between the eyes. The bullet did not swerve from its mark one hair's-breadth, but the abrupt movements of the animal made the slope of the forehead uncertain; the ball glanced upward, inflicting only a deep flesh-wound that did not even stun.

Dering had just time to draw a short hunting-knife, and to throw his left arm up instinctively to guard his face and eyes : then man and beast went down together, locked in a death-grapple—the first-named undermost.

Some persons resuscitated from drowning have said, that a perfect diorama of past events and familiar faces passed before their minds' eye, during the last struggle for life. It was not so with Maurice : his recollections of what ensued were always remarkably vague. Yet, one thing he did remember. Over the growls of the savage brute above him—over the shouts of the men that were leaping down madly to his rescue—he heard, quite plainly, as if some mocking devil were whispering them, those last words that he read before he fell a-dreaming.

'And he wants you home again, as much as—we all do.'

It seemed as though the weakness of allowing thoughts

to stray on long-forbidden pastures, was being punished right sharply, and with brief delay.

But all coherent feeling was soon merged in a strange excitement, which Maurice never chose to speak of in after days, and never could recall without shame. The simple truth was, that he was become drunk with the scent of blood in his nostrils—blood not all his own. The pain from the savage fangs and claws that ceased not to gnaw and rend his flesh—the horror of the hot noisome breath that mingled with his own—the happy Past, the dreadful Present, and the dim Future—each and all were forgotten in a brief delirium, not exempt from a fierce wild joy, as his right hand kept plunging into the side of his enemy, searching for the life that lay so deep. He did not even feel faint or wearied, up to the moment when sudden darkness swept across his eyes, while the weight above him seemed to grow more deadly heavy : after that, it was all blank and void.

The man who held the post next to Maurice Dering's was a major in the same regiment : he was not only a thorough sportsman, but a tried and famous soldier. One exploit of his in the Sikh war will not easily be forgotten.

He had been ordered to charge with his corps of Native Cavalry. Whether it was treachery or a sudden panic that affected the Sowars (who would fight well enough as a rule) was never clearly ascertained; but they began to rein up and fall back one by one, till, within two hundred yards of the enemy's front, the three European officers found themselves virtually alone. It was a critical time; for there had been some awkward mistakes made, of late, in cavalry movements. Those three men knew that death was before them, and dishonour behind : they never hesitated for a second, but rode straight on, with a cheer; breaking through the irregular line before them as they would have 'swished' through a bullfinch in the Shires. Reginald Errington came back with five wounds in him; and came back—alone.

But he said afterwards—he had no more vainglory in him than a child—that, while he was galloping on into the jaws of a bloody grave, he felt nothing like the faint heart-sickness that oppressed him, as he struggled over the few rods of rocky jungle that separated him from the scene of the death-struggle. When he reached it, he saw at the first glance that he had come too late to give any material aid. That confused heap, in which man and brute were mingled after a horribly grotesque fashion, weltered in a crimson pool—quite still and mute.

The heart of the strong swordsman, who had slain a human hecatomb on fairly stricken fields, melted within him, as he stood there, breathless and panting—more from excitement than exhaustion. He could find no voice to speak; and only signed to his own *shikari*, who had reached the spot nearly as soon, to help him to drag the corpse of the bear away   For a corpse it was; nearly drained of blood that had poured through three-and-twenty wounds. But for the other?——

In that inert, flaccid mass, livid white, save where it is furrowed with fearful gashes, who would recognize the strong hunter that went forth with the dawn, conquering and to conquer?

Reginald Errington turned away his face, and groaned aloud. Maurice had been wonderfully popular in his new regiment ever since he joined; but similarity of tastes in other things besides shooting had made him the peculiar

ally of the man who knelt beside him there, with a dimness
in his honest eyes, and a choking in his great bearded
throat. The two had had some extraordinary days already,
at the big game; and only the night before had been
planning an expedition far into Cashmeer. And this was
to be the end of it!

No,—not quite the end; for as the other hunter and
some more of the attendants came up, Maurice stirred
slightly.

Of all thanksgivings that have gone up to the Throne of
Mercy, there never was one more sincere than the two
syllables that broke from under the Major's huge grizzled
moustache, as he sprang to his feet and called for 'water!'
Fortunately this was ready at hand : they dashed it over
Maurice's face repeatedly ; at last he opened his eyes, but
closed them again instantly, and relapsed into a dead faint.
Then they began to chafe his forehead and hands with
brandy : so, after a while he revived slowly, and this time
in earnest.

But the process of recovery was long ; while it was proceeding, Ahmoud returned from the tents with the proper
bullets. The lad's silent, stoical nature was quite transformed, for the moment, in the bitterness of his remorse :
he would have it, that he alone was the cause of the
disaster. Indeed, the first intelligible sounds that forced
themselves into Dering's dizzy ears, were the wailings of
the delinquent, as he imprecated curses on the graves of
his deceased parents for having begotten so ill-omened a
son; and the first decided expression on Maurice's face
was compassion, as he turned his head, with a painful
effort, to smile on the self-accuser.

He spoke, too, before any of the others, beginning in a faint whisper, though his voice strengthened rapidly.

' A sharp tussle ; but I believe I'm all right, barring some deep scratches. *The bear's all right, too—isn't she ?'*

Reginald Errington quotes those first conscious words of Dering's to this day, as an illustration of the strength of his own ruling passion ; and I believe he would sooner part with the last of his ancestral acres, than with the rusty ragged-looking skin which he treasures as the trophy of that day

---

CHAPTER XVI.

THE LAST LOVE.

THE hurts, of which Maurice Dering spoke so lightly, though not church-door wide nor draw-well deep, were serious enough to confine him to his couch for many days. Yet he was recovering fast, when he, unluckily, caught the low fever prevalent in those parts, which threw him back again to death's door. When his iron constitution and case-hardened frame carried him through this last peril, he was fearfully weakened and altered.

It would have been difficult to find better quarters for a sick man than the bungalow to which Maurice had been carried as soon as he could be moved. It belonged to the chief magistrate of the district, who had arranged for Dering and Errington the *battue* that so nearly terminated

disastrously : he was, indeed, the third hunter above alluded to, who has, so far, been left nameless.

Mr Drummond was a civilian of the *ancien régime*, and
represented that nearly extinct class very creditably. He
came out as a griffin in those days when there was a real
aristocracy in our Indian Empire—when its highest honours
were almost hereditary in certain powerful families—when
a Directorship was worth more than a close borough—when
the Biennial Stakes for Competition-wallahs had not yet
been founded. In spite of certain prejudices, and a punc-
tilious regard for forms and ceremonies, peculiar to the
school in which he had been brought up, few men in his
Province were more respected and loved. Temperate as
an anchorite in his own person, he was famed far and near
for a royal hospitality; he discharged duties, varied and
important, with untiring patience and rigorous impartiality,
yet he always found time to carry out his favourite pursuit
on a scale that few could rival ; that unerring rifle of his
had saved more than one life, and many a light-weight had
reined up a beaten horse, while old Patrick Drummond, a
hundred yards ahead, was drawing out the 'first spear.'

May the turf lie light upon his grave ! For he was one
of the very few, who, being themselves strictly virtuous,
are solicitous that the rest of the world should not be
stinted in their cakes and ale.

In this pleasant sojourn Maurice passed the long hours
of a gradual convalescence. He rose up at last, almost
himself again—physically. But some old feelings had
utterly died within him, and new ones had sprung up beside. As he lay half-dreaming in the soft, cool twilight of
his shaded room, his senses floating in the calm languor
that ever follows a spent fever-storm, a wonderful peace

seemed to possess him : he had not forgotten the past, or any of its ties; but all its pains and sorrows were as though they had never been.

In one word—the spring of the emotion that would, till very lately, stir within him at the sight of Georgie Gascoigne's hand-writing or the mention of her name, was broken for ever and ever. Passion he had vanquished long ago; but never till now could he offer her friendship, pure, simple, and fraternal.

This negative state soon began to pass into the positive. If the sweet little sorceress had stood before Maurice again, wishing to re-knit the broken spells, she would have found herself powerless as repentant Maimouna. More than this —she would ere long have been aware of the presence of another fair White Witch, exercising gramary more potent than her own; though it was innocent and holy—such as never was learnt at the feet of Magian.

Let us drop metaphor, and say at once that Maurice Dering—having had some trouble with his heart when left to its own devices—began to think seriously of handing it over, for safe keeping, to one that was right worthy of the trust.

Every one wondered why Patrick Drummond had never married; but no one was disposed to quarrel with his choice of celibacy. No legalized mistress could have presided over the hospitalities of that pleasant house more genially and gracefully than did the widowed sister of its master. She had held the keys of office for many years; and Alice Leslie, her fair daughter, had just come back to her from England, after a three years' leave of absence on urgent 'finishing' affairs.

I suppose, after severe illness this weak clay of ours is

especially plastic and ductile, so that it will receive almost any impression, and retain it, sometimes, as it hardens once more. On no other hypothesis can we rationally account for the contracts entered into by certain of our brethren, weak though they may be. It is the same story over and over again. If you chance to marvel at one of these Mezentian matches, some friend of the family is sure to say—half apologetically—

'Oh, you know, her people were very kind to him when he was laid up at——(naming some place "on the further side of God-speed") with that terrible fall over timber."

Kind? From such disinterested Samaritans may Heaven keep me and mine!

Or—'He never would have got over that *malaria*, caught at Ancona, if it had not been for dear Lady Matchbury, who found him at the Albergo d'Espagna, quite by accident, as she was changing horses, and nursed him like her own son.'

Her own son? Her son-in-law you mean. And—quite by accident, was it? As if we had not heard how the rotund mother and rubicund daughter stuck to poor Charlie Glenlyon's trail, through Germany, and Switzerland, and Sardinia, till they ran him fairly to ground in the Holy City at last! Did he not flee for his life, or—what he valued more—his bachelorhood, to Ancona, with a wild idea of taking ship from that unfrequented port to an unknown land; knowing that his only chance of baffling that staunch pair of braches was to 'take to soil'? By accident! —as she was changing horses at the Albergo? *Altro!* If that knowing and avaricious old aristocrat ever gave a double *buona-mano* in her life, it was to the postilion who drove the last stage that lay between her and her victim.

Do you suppose that if Charlie had been clothed and in his right mind he would have yoked his fortunes to those of that stout and stridulous young person, who rolls when she walks, and screams when she talks, and squalls when she sings—he, who always raved about willowy waists, and upheld a low, sweet voice as the most excellent thing in woman? Orazio mio! There are more philtres on earth than are dreamt of in your philosophy.

I confess that recollections of others' wrongs have led me far astray from my subject. These observations are singularly irrelevant : for no sort of unfair influence was exercised now on Maurice Dering. Indeed, any man, however wise, or steadfast, or strong of heart, might have been proud of winning sweet Alice Leslie.

The enchantment came over Maurice, not suddenly, but very slowly and surely. He began by feeling intensely grateful for all the small kind offices of womanly thoughtfulness that came specially from *her :* then he became sensible of a subtle attraction in her voice when she talked or sang. When the girl was playing chess with her uncle, her great brown eyes used often to turn from the game towards the invalid's sofa, to see if he wanted anything. After awhile each of these glances sent a strange thrill of happiness through Dering's veins ; and he used to watch eagerly till another was vouchsafed him, and consider himself ill-used if it were long in coming. One day, a comrade, who had turned out of his way to see how Maurice fared, grew honestly enthusiastic on the subject of Alice's grace and beauty. After his visitor was gone, the invalid had a fit of bad spirits—not to say, bad humour —that lasted for some hours. It was not that he felt chafed, because that particular man chose to express admiration so freely. But he began to realize what a dreary thing it would be, if some one were to come and win the fair girl before his eyes, and bear her far away, so that they might never meet again till both were old.

On one especial evening he had begged Alice to sing to him; her voice was wonderfully adapted to the ballads in which Maurice especially delighted. At last, she opened 'The Silent Land.' The sweet, plaintive tones went straight to Dering's heart, seeming to beseech him not to palter longer with its secret. They were alone in the room, when Alice closed the piano, and came to his sofa to arrange the pillows;—Maurice took the little hand, as it wandered very near his cheek, and laid his lips thereon with passionate earnestness.

The virginity of a strong honest heart passed into that caress; for such an one Maurice had never bestowed on any woman, alive or dead. If his love for Georgie Verschoyle was mad and hopeless, it had at least the merit of keeping him pure and true.

That *this* love was not hopeless—if he had not guessed it before—he knew, before he unlocked his clasp of those slender trembling fingers.

Alice had heard her uncle so warm in Dering's praise, that she had been prepared to admire him before they met. The sharpest pang that had ever lighted on her innocent life shot through her breast, as she saw his face so drawn, and thin, and pale, when they carried him into the house from his litter. While she watched his recovery, her simple hero-worship had waxed into a deep, uncalculating, *womanly* devotion. If he had left her, without one word warmer than kindness and gratitude, she would never have reproached him, even in thought; but it would have gone near to break her heart. No wonder that she felt faint with joy, when she knew that, henceforth, she might love without shame, and hope without fear.

Though the happiness of this pair was never perfect till now, we will not tarry with them here, but march straight onward to our goal. Such 'passages' it is impossible to transcribe faithfully, unless they be of the staid and sober sort, which can interest only the parties concerned. Furthermore, I think that you will be glad that we did not linger over this scene, before all the story is told.

When Dering confessed to himself that it would be mad presumption if he nourished an idea of winning Georgie Verschoyle, he only looked his own position—and hers—fairly in the face. But circumstances were changed now A troop in India is a very different thing from a troop in England, and will ' carry a wife ' well enough ; especially if —as in Maurice's case—there are moderate private means in the background. Neither could sweet Alice Leslie's matrimonial prospects be compared to those of a beauty-regnant at home.

Nevertheless, Dering did anticipate certain prudent scruples on the part of the elder powers. And so it turned out : he met, not with denial, but with demurrer.

Patrick Drummond was open-hearted and open-handed to a fault ; but he had been born and bred north of the Border, and, at a pinch, could show himself both wary and worldly-wise. He was really attached to Maurice, and thought him fitter than any man of his acquaintance to be trusted with Alice's happiness. But he knew that his niece's own fortune would hardly have provided some women with their *trousseau :* he himself could help but little, for, having no occasion to lay money by, he had

N

always lived up to the verge of his ample income. Besides, Alice was so very young.

Dering owned a godfather in England—an eccentric old bachelor with great possessions—who had already been very kind to him, in a capricious way : for instance, he made him a present of his troop. This reverend senior had a weakness for being consulted, whenever his *protégé* meditated any important step ; it was more than probable that he would take serious umbrage if Maurice were to contract himself irrevocably, without previously advising him of such intention. The sagacious Scotchman could in nowise countenance the imperilling of such fair expectations.

For many months to come, regimental duty for Maurice was out of the question. Indeed, all the surgeons were inflexible on the point of his spending the next hot season at least in a more bracing climate than could be found anywhere nearer than the Upper Himalayas. In any case, it must come to a separation of the lovers for a period of several months.

In fine, Mr Drummond decided (Mrs Leslie, of course, played up to her brother's suit, as she had done all her life long) that Dering should go home, on eighteen months' sick leave, to be shortened to a year if circumstances should allow. Meanwhile, no engagement was to be announced to the world in general, though the parties principally interested might make what unauthorized contracts they pleased.

All this was so perfectly reasonable, and so very kindly expressed, that Maurice had not a word to urge in objection. A modified consent was all he had a right to expect ; and this he had obtained, at once : so all the terms

of the treaty were settled without useless discussion. If
Alice Leslie's heart sank within her at the prospect of long
loneliness, be sure she never murmured, even to herself;
repining, now, would have weighed on her innocent conscience like wicked ingratitude. So she bore up bravely
enough till the very day of her lover's departure; when
she broke down utterly, and almost unaccountably.

When Maurice first saw her face that morning, he was
painfully struck by its expression: not only sadness was
there, but a vague terror as well; and the beautiful brown
eyes looked wild and scared. That peculiar expression
passed away very soon; but all the day long the girl was
deathly pale, and she would start and shiver at times without any apparent cause.

The lovers were never alone together till just before
Maurice's departure, when the ruling powers granted one
half-hour's space of undisturbed solitude. It is only with
a few minutes of that solemn interview that we have anything to do.

They were standing on the brink of a deep clear pool,
fringed with broad-leaved water-plants, and flecked here
and there by ripples from rising fish; behind them rose a
thicket of flowering shrubs, linked together by many
chains of creepers, overshadowed by tall feathering palms;
all round them was the whisper of the cool evening breeze,
just then beginning to wake.

It was after a pause of some seconds that Alice spoke:
there was a change in her voice; the tones that had been
low and sad throughout were tremulous and awe-stricken
now.

'I want to tell you something, dear, before you go,' she
whispered. 'I know I am very weak and foolish, but you

won't laugh at me—now or hereafter. Last night I had
such a dream—ah, such a dreadful dream! '

The strong arm, that was wound so fondly round the
girl's slender waist, could not avert nor arrest the shiver-
ing-fit that overcame her again.

Maurice bowed his head, till his cheek was laid on the
smooth brown hair, and drew his betrothed closer to his
heart; as if he would teach her where to look for rest.

' Tell me all, my darling,' he said, cheerily; ' even if it
pains you—tell me all. You are not strong enough to
carry a secret, though it be no heavier than an evil dream.'

Alice stopped shivering then; she looked up in her
lover's face, and drank a long draught of courage from
those clear honest eyes.

' Yes, I can tell you, now,' she went on in a firmer voice.
' I dreamt we were standing together, just about this hour
of the evening; only it was in England, I think, and we
had no thought of parting. I cannot remember what
words passed, but I know you were as kind and good
as——you always are; and I loved you just as dearly. I
think I was telling you so, when I saw a hand laid on your
right hand—I was holding your left fast—that tried to
draw you away. I knew it was a woman's hand—the
fingers were so white and slender—before the figure showed
itself from behind your shoulder. It was only a figure, for
I never saw the face; something misty and black, like a
hood, kept waving round the features, and kept them
always in shadow. Yet, somehow, I knew that the woman
was beautiful and dark and pale. And still she tried to
draw you away, and still I held you fast, and I cried out—
" Ah, Maurice, don't listen; tell her to leave you; tell her
you are all mine." And your lips moved, but no words

came: and I felt that you were true to me, darling,—true all throughout,—but that you were under a wicked spell. Then I grew very strong and brave.

' " He *is* mine," I said : " by God's help I will keep him, in life or in death ! "

' The figure dropped your right hand, and passed swiftly behind you, till she stood close behind me. Just then I became aware that we were standing on the brink of a chasm, so very deep that the bottom was a mass of gray vapour, and out of it there came smothered growls, as if wild beasts were chained there. Then the woman said in my ear (her voice was very sweet and musical, though she was so wicked and cruel) :

' "If not mine, never—never yours !"

' And she pushed me over the brink before you could save me.

' And as I fell—ah, Maurice, hold me fast !—the growls from below rose into an awful roar, and the vapours swept away ; and I saw a crowd of horrible creatures, something like men, with black faces and white grinning teeth, waiting to seize me. Can you wonder that I woke shrieking, or that I have been frightened ever since ?'

Poor Alice's courage only just carried her through. As she spoke the last words she buried her head on her lover's breast, trembling like a netted bird, and broke into passionate weeping.

Maurice Dering was not in the least superstitious; and, as you know, his nerve was exceptional; but a painful thrill shot through him as he listened.

He had not forgotten a certain hour, just before sundown, when a woman—beautiful, dark, and pale—held his hand and sought to draw him aside from the path of honour, by proffer of her love. It is true, that he had no cause to look back at that interview with shame or remorse : nevertheless, the reminder of it, at that especial moment, savoured strongly of ill omen. There were unpleasant coincidences in Alice's dream. It was only by a strong effort that he could summon up cheerfulness sufficient for the emergency. He did not try to laugh the girl out of her terrors, but soothed and reassured her gradually by the gentlest endearments and caresses—as for promises, she needed none. At length, he succeeded perfectly.

When Maurice took his last look of that lovely face, lighted up by the last level rays of a westering sun, there were no tears there, save those of a natural sorrow : the sweet sad smile of loving adieu still lingered on her lips.

When he sees that face again, it will be radiant with another light; the tender lips will still wear a smile, but a smile of welcome ; and there will be no traces of tears, that long ago have been wiped away, for ever and for ever.

CHAPTER XVII.

CONFESSIONS.

LET us see, now, how those who tarry at home are faring: to do this, we must look some months backward. The third October from that in which this tale began, found Chetwynde and Luttrell once more at Marston Lisle. The two were crossing the park, on their way home from shooting, late one afternoon—Gascoigne had left them some

hours ago, on pretext of business—when Geoffrey thus delivered himself of the results of long rumination:—

'There's something amiss with Philip, I'm quite certain.
His shooting was never first-rate; but did you ever see
anything like it, this morning? It wasn't only that he
missed almost everything; but he shot so wildly. You
must have noticed it, Paul?'

'I did notice it,' the other said, gravely. 'And Philip
was aware of it too. I never saw him vexed before, about
his own misses. Don't you remember, that I never chaffed
him once, all through the morning? That was the reason
of my forbearing. Yes, there *is* something on his mind;
and it's very unlike Philip—keeping his griefs to himself.
I wish we could guess without asking him a point-blank
question. Do you think he can be getting uncomfortable
about Annesleigh? I don't believe the little woman means
any harm; but I wish he wasn't coming here next week.
There's a taint of sin in the atmosphere wherever that
smooth-spoken desperado happens to be. It will be a
good day for honest, or comparatively honest, people, when
the Devil claims his own. Gerald must have been waited
for, *down there*, this many a year.'

The parson shook his head remonstratively.

'Hush, Paul,' he said; 'harsh words won't help us,
much less blasphemous ones. What do you or I know
about the time when a man's soul is due? Annesleigh is
as bad as bad can be, I dare say, if half the tales about him
are true. But perhaps Marston itself is the real temptation to him. So few reputable houses are open to him
now. At least, I never saw anything——'

'Of course you never saw anything,' Paul broke in,

rather crossly. 'You never do. Why don't you ask Ida about it?'

Geoffrey turned short round on the speaker, with a comic perplexity in his broad blue eyes.

'There's no pleasing you people,' he said. 'My dear Paul, I *did* ask Ida about it—once. If it's all the same to you, I won't repeat the experiment. She never was so near being really angry with me. She has a knack, you know, of putting people into false positions, when they vex her. In about five minutes I felt a thorough scandal-monger, though I started with the best intentions.'

Chetwynde shrugged his shoulders, as was his wont when he did not think it worth while prolonging a discussion, and walked on in silence. But, when they reached the house, he left Geoffrey to settle the morrow's programme with the head keeper, and went straight to Gascoigne's *sanctum*. Philip was sitting in a low arm-chair, drawn up close to one of the windows—his head leant on his hand, and turned towards the darkening landscape—evidently rather drowsy, or in a deep reverie; for he never moved at the sound of the opening door, or the entering footstep.

Now, that same hour of equinoctial twilight—if you happen to be in weak health and poor spirits—is a very trying one to encounter, alone. The phantasms that arise, then, are seldom ghastly, or terrible, but they are inexpressibly dismal and discouraging.

The peculiar light and the peculiar attitude may have had something to do with it, but the instant that Paul crossed the threshold he knew that his suspicions, relative to some unknown trouble of Gascoigne's, were only too well founded.

Philip never rose till his friend's hand touched his shoulder : then he raised himself with a start, and began to ask hurried questions, as to the sport since he left the others, &c., &c.

Chetwynde answered all these with perfect composure ; then he led up, quite naturally, to the arrangements for the following week.

'We can't beat that ground of Durden's till Thursday,' Philip observed. 'It's about the best we have, for mixed shooting ; and Annesleigh only comes in time for dinner on Wednesday.'

Paul drew up a broad footstool close to Gascoigne's elbow, and sat down before he replied—deliberately—

'Annesleigh comes on Wednesday ?—to be sure he does. Now—Philip, old man—well as I know you, I don't want to interfere, impertinently, with your family arrangements. But just let me ask you one question. Do you think that's a nice sort of man to be running tame about a house ? I happen to know, that he domesticates himself with extraordinary rapidity.'

Gascoigne turned half round, and looked at the speaker with a languid wonder.

'Why, I thought he was one of your favourites, Paul,' he said. 'The only time I ever saw him, before I married, was in your chambers. And he's always quoting you ; as if you met perpetually in other places than here.'

Chetwynde ground his teeth impatiently.

'He is not an especial favourite of mine, though I meet him often enough : and if he quotes me, it's as Somebody quotes Scripture—for his own ends. But that's not the question. What does it signify whom *I* herd with ? I was speaking of "houses," not of "chambers," and of people who have ties and duties to attend to such as I shall never own. Once more, Philip—I don't want to be impertinent —-but do you think you are wise in letting such a marked black sheep run at large about the Marston pastures? He's been here pretty often of late.'

When he turned round once more, vexation mingled with surprise was on Gascoigne's face. It was not that he objected in the least to Paul's interference; but he was evidently sorry that his friend should disquiet himself in vain. He knew right well that Chetwynde never spoke thus earnestly, without bitter earnestness at heart.

' Don't be absurd, Paul,' he said quietly. ' You never *can* meddle "impertinently" here. Were you not sworn in of the privy council long ago? I believe the honour of Marston is just as dear to you as it is to me. But you do look at things, and people, too much *au noir* at times. I don't admire Annesleigh particularly, and never should trust him too far; though I think he has been trying to become more respectable for some time past. He told me, the other day, that he was " going into steady training for the Upper House." There may be some truth in it, for his uncle's health fails more and more. I've never heard of his getting into any scrape for the last two years; that's negative praise, anyhow. He's always an ornamental piece of furniture, you must admit; and he will be especially useful just now for these *tableaux* which are to eclipse the Molton ones. After all—who is in danger? Annesleigh has never tried to borrow money of me: he amuses Georgie; but I don't think she even flirts with him. If she did, I am sure I should have heard of it.'

These last words were spoken in such perfect simplicity and good faith, that Paul would hardly have had the heart to hint a suspicion, had he entertained such, which really was not the case.

'Perhaps I *am* unjust,' he said, slowly. 'But you've heard the proverb about pitch as well as I have. It would be a pity if the scandal-mongers should see a speck on your wife's white hands, though you and I know them to be as stainless as snow.'

Gascoigne threw back his head, rather disdainfully.

'The scandal-mongers! If *we* cannot afford to defy them, we have lived all our lives in vain. But, Paul, you are wrong again, here. It was not Georgie this time who suggested that Annesleigh should be invited, but Ida. I thought she was curiously eager about it, when she spoke to me.'

Chetwynde whistled, long and low.

'Ida, was it?' he said at last. 'That alters the case materially. If it comes to a match between her and Gerald, I should like to back her, at odds. I think she has that race, with several pounds in hand. There's not another woman in England that can take care of herself so thoroughly.'

This was the deliberate opinion, remember, of a man endued with no ordinary perspicacity; founded, too, on the familiar experiences of many years. In good truth, the miscalculations of science are often more wonderful than the blunders of ignorance, and lead the judgment much farther astray.

So, for a few seconds, Paul sat silent and pondering. One thing was evident, Gerald Annesleigh was not the *bête noir* that haunted Gascoigne; yet that something weighed heavily on his mind was equally clear. Even during that brief interval Philip had sunk back into his old posture of

listless melancholy ; and though objects were barely dis-
tinguishable, his eyes had reverted to their dreamy outward gaze. At last Chetwynde leant forward, laying his
hand lightly on the other's shoulder—the room was nearly
dark now,—and spoke, almost in a whisper.—

'Won't you tell me what it is ? You know *anything* is
safe with me.'

Philip shivered slightly, but did not attempt to shake off
the kindly pressure.

'It must come, sooner or later,' he said, in his own low,
musical voice. 'As well now as at any time. My dear
old Paul, you don't deceive me with your cynicism; what
I've got to tell, will hit you as hard as any of them. Have
you never guessed that, for months past, I've been getting
weaker and weaker, and more and more blind ? I could
not tell rabbits from hares, to-day. I've tried to delude
myself into thinking that it was only the old *malaria*
bothering me again. But delusions are over, since I saw
Ferrand last week in town. He cannot quite define the
nature of the disease, but he told me fairly—he don't
mince matters, you know, and I like him the better for it
—that there is something radically wrong with the spine.'

The hand that rested on Gascoigne's shoulder shook like
a dry leaf in a strong breeze, and through the gathering
darkness there broke a sound strangely like a sob ; it came,
not from the breast of the last speaker, for—his confidence
once made—he sat mute and statuesquely still.

'My God !—is there no hope ?'

The force that Chetwynde put upon his voice, to prevent
it from failing utterly, made it unnaturally hard and cold.

'Of ultimate recovery—little or none,' Philip answered,
quite steadily. 'But the decay may be very gradual, and

I may linger long between the different stages; this, the first one, is generally more rapid than any, except the last. I never had much nerve, you know; but I think I should have borne up better, if it had not been for thinking, what a trouble and burden I shall most likely be to every one that I wanted to make happy. That's very, very hard. God help me! I cannot see my way through the darkness.'

'And your wife knows nothing of this?' Paul asked, still in the same hard, constrained voice.

'Not a word,' Gascoigne answered eagerly; 'and I trust to you to help me here. The secret shall be kept from her as long as I have strength to stand upright. My own sweet Georgie! Imagine her being condemned to humour a sick man's fancies, and watch the changes of his pulse. Six months of nursing would take all the bloom from her beauty. And is she not lovely now—and happy, too? The world never saw such a charming *châtelaine*. She shall enjoy the last month of our plenty, as royally as the rest, though the famine-years must needs come.'

The twilight deepened more duskily, yet the pale, delicate face seemed to brighten. In truth, there was a light upon it, that has hovered, ere this, round the brow of others, whose spirit was as strong as their flesh was frail to endure —a light that shone, perchance, in dark, damp, amphitheatre cells, when, without, the sun glared down on crimson sand, and the voice-thunder out-roared the lions.

You may call this comparison over-strained, or irreverent, if it so please you. I write as I believe. I believe that, though the age of miracles is past, the age of martyrdom will last till the death of Time. I believe that some now living—though their suffering was not for conscience-sake

—who have borne their heavy cross unrepiningly and un-
selfishly, will, one day, not stand far from the foremost rank
of the Noble Army.

The change on Gascoigne's face did not escape Paul Chetwynde; he understood and appreciated it, thoroughly.
The last barriers of his calm philosophy—they were but
flimsy out-works after all—gave way, and his strong,
earnest nature broke out. He dropped his head on his
hand, and groaned aloud.

'And—with all this on your mind—you can be anxious
about the *tableaux* they are to act next week, and can
settle what ground we are to shoot to-morrow? Ah,
Philip, Philip! you put the stoutest-hearted of us all to
shame. And if the worst come to the worst—though I *will*
hope for the best—do you talk about being a burden to
any one? You never were really ungenerous, in all your
life before. I'm not going to speak of Geoffrey; nor of
poor old Maurice, if he ever comes back; nor of Aunt
Nellie; nor even of your own wife, to whom you do scant
justice, dearly as you love her. I'm going to speak of myself, if you've patience to hear it.'

Gascoigne did not answer, it was too dark now for the
other to see his eyes, but he drew Paul rather closer to him,
by the hand that still rested on his own shoulder.

'Listen, then,' Chetwynde went on, quite calmly now.
'You know as much as any one of my past and present,
but you don't know all. It would do you no good to
know it, or I would tell you every word. It's enough to
say, that it stands thus with me: I sit here, with four-and-
thirty years told, and neither duty nor honour binds me to
any living man or woman—not duty, because there is a
wall built up for ever between the Dean of Torrcaster and

me ; not honour, because I never have asked, and never will ask, any woman, gentle or simple, to share such an existence as mine. Philip, I don't hope much, or fear much, for reasons that you may easily understand; but— I *believe* less, for reasons, or no-reasons, that you have been spared the knowledge of. I'm not going to make my moan now; or attempt to lighten your burden by weighing it against my own : one is physical, the other moral ; the comparison wouldn't stand for an instant. But if you only could guess the dreariness of having nothing *absolute* to rest upon—no unalterable and incontrovertible creed. If you have not this, the subtlest disputant gives you your *Fiat Lux.* It is not enough to believe in a Supreme Being —I do that—you must worship Him after set forms and ceremonies: you must believe His written, no less than His unwritten words. I struggled hard—I swear I did— struggled like a drowning man, when those doubts and disgusts first came upon me ; for I guessed what it would come to ; but they beat me, at last. I've thrown up my hands, now, and float where the stream chooses to carry me. Did you ever hear me cavil at another's religion, or try to draw any one into controversy, or even scoff at fanaticism ? I'll tell you why I never did so. I'd sooner see a man a confirmed drunkard, or gambler, or profligate, than a sceptic. There's a chance of recovery, if ever so faint, for all the others ; for the last—none. Do you want to know whose fault it is, that I am what I am ? My own, I suppose. At least I accuse no one, nor will I ever. There : I told you I should try your patience. You are my only confidant, and I don't think I should have spoken out—even to you—but for this. I want you to realize how utterly alone I stand in the world. Isolation is independence, at all events. Once more, I would not interfere with those who have a better right to take care of you. But, understand, from this time forward, so long as you and I shall live, you have only to say ' Come,' and I will be with you as quickly as steam can bring me, and stay by you till you tell me to go. Promise me this, at least : you will not scruple to use my hands and eyes, if your own should fail ? '

Gascoigne sighed heavily ; there was a deeper melancholy in his voice as he answered, than when he had been speaking of his own sorrows.

' Poor Paul ! I never guessed at this. It is very dreadful. You are ten times more to be pitied than I. But though what you have told me has pained me more than I can say, it has not made me distrust you a whit. Here is the proof. There's the draught of a fresh will in the house now, where you are named as Cecil's first guardian, should he be left fatherless. I sign and seal that will to-morrow. And, otherwise—as you say, so it shall be. While we both live, I'll never scruple to ask you to help me at my need. As to what has passed to-night, do you keep my secret—as I will keep yours—till the time comes when it *must* be told. ' Unto the day the day : ' perhaps for both of us there are better things in store than we dream of now.'

So with no more words, and only one brief hand-clasp, those two plighted their faith. A hundred seconds later, when lights came in, not a ruffle of emotion on either face betrayed that between them there had passed almost the saddest confidences that man can intrust to man.

All that autumn through, the gaieties went on bravely at Marston Lisle.

The *tableaux*, before alluded to, wore eminently successful, utterly eclipsing the glories of Molton; the most
picturesque of them all was ' Sir Galahad's Dream,' wherein Gerald Annesleigh (save tho mark!) playod the Maiden
Knight; while Georgie, and Ida, and two other damsels
almost as fair, watched his sinless slumber.

So autumn glided pleasantly into wintor, and still Philip
Gascoigne's secret was kept. Nearly a year must pass
before you meet any of these our characters again; but
when they next appear it will be *en masse*, and—for your
comfort—they will be ' forming up ' for tho strong business
of the last act.

CHAPTER XVIII.

UNDER THE ELMS.

A soft still evening follows a broiling August day. Tho
air is fresh and cool; but, even now, there is no rustle in
tho leaves of the solemn elms. To meet or find a breeze,
you must mount some hundred feet, and couch among the
heather, on the crest of one of the hill-ramparts that fence
in to the north the long rambling street of Spa.

The season is at its flood, just now; almost every civilized nation has sent hither traders or travellers, to buy or
sell, or look at the raree-shows of the tiny Vanity Fair.

Here is Princess Czernikoff, the white sorceress of the
Ukraine, who for thirty years or more has kept alive her
terrible renown. There were wicked whispers about her
before she stood at the altar—a bride, in her eighteenth

summer. What was the story about her father's handsome secretary, who was such an accomplished musician? He was a serf to be sure; and serfs have no business to play false notes at state-concerts; yet it surely was hard measure, to make him shriek his life out under the knout that night of the wedding. Since then, for that pale, green-eyed woman, in half the countries of Europe men have drawn swords and died; and she will do more mischief yet, though she verges on the grand climacteric. Wherein lies the secret of her fatal fascination? The world in general, and her rivals in particular, are never tired of asking that question. Simple as it seems, it has never been answered yet. The Czernikoff's victims tell no tales.

Here, too, is Sofie Lichnöffsky, the lovely Polonaise, almost as celebrated and dangerous in her way; who has become *quite* irresistible since she grafted the patriot upon the coquette. When the languishing look in those glorious dark eyes is more *prononcé* than usual, her friends say it is the natural melancholy of an exile and martyr; when she falls into a fit of abstraction (as she will do when the converse interests her not) she is supposed to be meditating on the wrongs of her country. Of course, both on political and private grounds, she and the Czernikoff are mortal enemies. Neither will accept of divided male allegiance; it is clearly understood that the briefest interchange of courtesies with the enemy, will be treated as desertion under arms, for which there is no forgiveness. The star of Poland is rather in the ascendant just now; for Sofie has succeeded in seducing from the opposite camp one of its chiefest paladins—an extraordinarily handsome Magyar, whose iron constitution and enormous revenue may possibly last about five years longer, at his present rate of expenditure.

Here, too, is the fair Fitz-Eustace, who has only lately abdicated the sovereignty of Southern beauty in favour of her fairer daughter. It is so long since they crossed the Atlantic, that they must have forgotten the sound of the rollers. There is a husband and father 'out there'—quite orthodox and authenticated—who ministers lavishly to their numerous requirements; but the worthy planter dwells peacefully among his own black people—deferring, from year to year, the pleasure of seeing his Carolina Roses in bloom.

Nor is Hélène de Lauragais—*née* Du Château-Mesnil—absent; the eloquent *Marquise*, who can talk as fast with her eyes and her lithe fingers as with her pomegranate-flowers of lips. It is whispered that a certain Great Personage has looked upon her of late with favouring eyes; since that report—true or false—prevailed, the fair dame's social importance has become almost oppressive to her; for her frank, gay spirit is prone to recreate itself in the amusement of the hour, and is not often troubled with *arrière-pensées.* Now, whithersoever she may bend her steps in these her summer pilgrimages, certain grave and reverend seigniors, representing each some European cabinet, are sure to cross her path accidentally. It is not bad sport to watch her, responding to the stiff courtesies of some gray-headed statesman, whom even the reckless *Marquise* cannot afford to dismiss off-hand—her eyes flashing impatience all the while—her tiny foot keeping time to a favourite *valse,* now drawing very near its end.

o 2

So much for the womankind. The men are not worth wasting many words upon. The usual lot is fairly represented.

Mendez, the colossal Spanish gambler (who, if he plays square at any game—*Trente et quarante* included—is the most maligned innocent in Europe), has come across for a week's change of luck from Homburg, where two unlucky (?) croupiers running have made a large gap in half-a-million of winnings. He punts in just the same form as ever; placid and imperturbable while fortune favours; clamorous and quarrelsome when the tide fairly turns: a *roturier* from head to heel.

Look across the board of green cloth and you will see a refreshing contrast. That sallow man, with sharp, projecting features and weary eyes, who looks forty though he was a legal infant twenty months ago, is the great Belgian magnate, Prince Amadeus LXVI. You see he plays quite as high as the Spaniard, but does not deign to cast down his own *rouleaux*, or amass his own note-piles: all that is done by the grave secretary, behind whose chair the Prince stands, apparently a disinterested spectator, though he will murmur now and then, without bowing his head, certain mandates as to the game. That youth, at least, *se ruine en grand*.

Then there is, as a matter of course, the stout English *millionnaire*, who could buy up the whole Redoute—including the Bank—if it so pleased him; playing for five franc-pieces, or louis at the most; bursting into a sweat of agony if he loses thrice consecutively, and getting purple with triumph if he follows a *série de cinq* on his kindred colour.

You don't care to hear about the Italian with the fierce

brigand-face and silky manner, who has always lost his last
available *scudo* just before you met, when on the point of
realizing a fortune by the marvellous martingale that only
wants capital to be infallible ?   Nor of the venerable man,
with the long white beard, and devotional aspect, who
always crosses himself when he sits down to play, and then
places by his card a small slip of dry wood, which might
be a holy relic, if it were not a slip from the tree at Homburg, where, last summer, they found the Russian suicide
hanging ?   Nor of the ancient female—rather the reverse
of venerable—who will punt away for hours at a time,
without once intermitting a dreadful mumbling murmur,
that issues from under a cavernous black bonnet, like an
oracle of Trophonius ? You never guessed of what nation
or language she could be, till last Sunday that portentous head-gear nodded close to your elbow, and you
heard that malignant grumble still going on, as if a witch
had strayed into the tabernacle unawares, and felt it in-
cumbent upon her ceaselessly to curse the clergyman.

No—these personages might make rather curious studies
in their way, but with them we have little or no concern.
We are more interested at present in that group sitting
under the elms at the lower end of the *allée* on this same
August evening.   Almost all the principal actors in this
drama of ours are there; though Geoffrey Luttrell is
absent, as he was through its opening scenes.

The most prominent figure—simply because it is so
sadly changed—is that of poor Philip Gascoigne.

He had borne up, as he said he would, to the outermost
verge of physical endurance ; but, months ago, it became
impossible to keep up appearances longer ; the daily effort
perhaps only hastened the break-down : he is a confirmed

invalid now, and can only totter a few paces without the
help of a strong arm.   He had no pain to suffer, beyond
the misery of utter lassitude and prostration ; and he kept
up his spirits wonderfully : indeed, he had seemed better
in every way since he had been at Spa, after the fatigue
of the journey was once got over.

Close to Gascoigne's shoulder sat Maurice Dering; a
trifle thinner than of yore, with a white scar here and
there showing through the deep bronze of his cheeks and
lower brow : for the she-bear's claws scored sharply where
they *did* come home.   He had been terribly shocked on
his return, to find Philip in such a condition, for he had
not received the slightest intimation of it ; but—thinking
for his friend very much as he would have thought for himself—he decided that to brood over things was the worst
possible course for all.   The natural elasticity of his temperament taught Maurice never to despair on his own or
on other's account; and he had actually, by this time,
brought Philip, and—what was harder still — Philip's
familiars, round to a view of the case far from gloomy.

Giving Maurice all the credit for pluck and good intention that he deserves, it must be owned that he had
peculiar reasons for feeling cheerful and benevolent at that
particular time.   The eccentric godfather above-mentioned
had shown himself wonderfully tractable and amenable to
reason.   He had listened graciously to the recital of
Dering's matrimonial schemes ; and, without actually com-
mitting himself, had held out certain vague half-promises
of a most satisfactory character.   But he stipulated that
the engagement should still be kept a profound secret
(why—he himself, perhaps, could not have told), and
begged that Maurice would not attempt to curtail his

leave. This last request was founded on the state of his own health, which was really precarious. The god-son did not think it well to discuss matters over-much; nevertheless he had no notion of obsequious submission. With regard to the engagement, he consented readily that it should not be mentioned to any one except Gascoigne, Chetwynde, and Luttrell.

'There never was but one secret between us,' he said to himself, 'and *I* won't make another, if I know it.'

He was so firm on this point, that the senior was fain to yield; but he insisted that the wives should not be admitted into the confidence. When Maurice assented to this, it seemed to him a perfectly reasonable condition; beyond this he scarcely thought on the matter.

It might have interested him more, if he could have seen just a little further, backwards and forwards.

The others, with one exception, are much the same as you left them. The lines have grown harder, perhaps, round Chetwynde's braced lips, and his brow is more ready to contract, more slow to unbend, than of old. But dear Aunt Nellie does not look aged by an hour: her face was always rather a sad one; a little of more sorrow or anxiety leaves no traces there. Ida Luttrell meets you—as she met Maurice Dering two days after he landed from India —placid, indifferent, and inscrutable still.

> Shall the last ever loveliest be?

says a parlour-poet of no small renown.

Yes, for—in spite of a change that you only begin to appreciate when you have scanned her narrowly—loveliest always is sweet Georgie Gascoigne.

What a change it is, after you do thoroughly realize it! Yet it is rather moral than physical.

It would be hard to single out each detail, or to prove your conclusion by individual instances ; but, somehow, you are sensible that Georgie's whole character has seriously deteriorated.   Indolence has sunk into lassitude ; instead of the timid, coaxing ways that were so charming, you notice a frightened nervousness more painful than pleasant to deal with ; the pretty waywardness of a year ago has waxed now into self-will, always obstinate, some-times passionate.

When Mrs Gascoigne was first made aware of her hus-band's state, she betrayed a sorrow and sympathy that, doubtless, were perfectly sincere.   She began by being everything that is affectionate and attentive—indeed, up to the present time, she could not be said to have been neg-lectful of any of her duties—but gradually her temper grew more fitful ; she would be impatient and peevish, at times, with others ; though with Philip — never.   This was especially the case after the inauguration of the London season, when they still abode at Marston.

Gascoigne was not insensible to the change ; but it did not surprise him much, or vex him seriously.   He thought his pet was naturally dull in the great country house, long void of visitors, and that she missed the social excitement that she had been accustomed to from childhood, and that all her intimates were now enjoying.   So he pretended that it would be better for him to be always near his con-sulting physician, and moved his whole establishment up to their pleasant town house in Park Lane, where Ida Luttrell soon joined them—alone.

Then Philip became very urgent in his endeavours to prevail upon his wife and her cousin to go into society, much as usual.   His arguments to this effect were exceed-

ingly ingenious, and palpably sincere. It is not worth
while to go through them now : it is enough to say that
Georgie yielded, at first with seeming reluctance, afterwards with indifference.

But things did not improve, as the poor invalid had
hoped. The more Georgie went out, the more fitful was
her humour at home. At last she became subject to
violent weeping fits, without any apparent incitement ;
but of these Philip was, mercifully, kept in ignorance.
Her brightest time was immediately after Dering's return.
She was unaffectedly glad to see him again : they met, too,
without the faintest embarrassment on either side, though
they met alone.

All this while, Ida's influence over her cousin grew
stronger day by day, till the latter became absolutely helpless in her hands. The self-possession and self-assertion
which had stood well by Georgie in many a coquettish *im-
broglio*, had utterly deserted her now : she never seemed
at ease, unless under the wing of her ally. Sometimes,
when the most ordinary conversation was proceeding, she
would glance over at Ida in an eager questioning way, as
if doubtful whether she had not gone astray in her talk.
At such seasons, a very close observer might have noticed
Mrs Luttrell return the telegraph with a strange look,
almost impossible to define. It was not reproachful—far
less was it menacing. I think I have seen something
similar in the grave benevolent eyes of a certain eminent
physician, presiding over an aristocratic asylum where
everybody is cured by kindness, when one of his patients
began to talk—not wildly—but rather too rapidly for decorum.

Still, as was aforesaid—whatever she might be with

others—his wife was always tender and gentle with Philip : she never seemed in a hurry to escape from his room, and would break any engagement to sit with him, if he happened to be at all worse than usual, or especially in need of comforting. As for flirtations, she had, apparently, forgotten the meaning of the word. Society, with whom she had always been a favourite, said that 'Mrs Gascoigne behaved beautifully.' Did you ever know Society wrong?

So, under the elms, on that August evening, sat very much the same group as might have been assembled under the beeches at Marston Lisle. Others joined them from time to time, and, after lingering awhile, lounged on again : but these it is necessary to weave into the thread of the story in the discourse; on the same principle that has induced me to omit all mention of brothers and sisters and other kinsfolk attached to the actors, who have nothing to do with the *peripeteia* of our piece.

The habits of Spa, as every one knows, are early, if not simple : to these, in a measure, the Gascoigne party accommodated themselves; dinner was over with them some time ago, though the sun had scarcely set; and round the heads of Dering and Chetwynde thin blue smoke-wreaths were already curling. Hitherto the conversation had been very desultory, and, to us at least, uninteresting.

'By-the-by,' Philip remarked, after rather a long pause, 'I wonder what has become of Annesleigh. Has any one seen him since last night? Those Delaval girls were to have a riding-party, over the hills and far away : I suppose *la belle Diane* has tied him to her bridle-rein.'

'I saw him twice to-day,' Paul answered, indifferently. 'He was at his devotions each time; but he was wooing a female more fickle even than the Delaval "dasher." Per-

haps he would have succeeded better with the damsel than
with the dame; for the dame was—Fortune.'

'How fond you are of dark speeches, Mr Chetwynde,'
Georgie interrupted, with somewhat of her old petulance.
'Wouldn't it have been just as easy to say, that you saw
Captain Annesleigh playing and losing heavily?'

Paul shot one of his keen covert glances straight at the
fair speaker.

'Just as easy, my dear Mrs Gascoigne; but if a humble
individual chooses, at rare intervals, to indulge in a small
parable, I know no law, human or divine, that forbids it.
I was not aware that any one here present was specially
interested in Gerald's luck. Besides, I'm not at all sure
that he *was* losing heavily: his own face is a bad weather-
glass; I only draw my conclusions from poor Penrhyn
Bligh's. "Talk of the ——" I beg all your pardons; but
what a wonderful proverb that is. I can't remember
having seen it better illustrated.'

In very truth, the subject of their talk was just then
within fifty yards of them, strolling down the broad walk
under the elms, with the indolent grace habitual to him;
only now and then you might have heard a small lump of
gravel crunched viciously to powder under a grinding heel.

There was a gay smile on the new-comer's handsome
lip, as he lifted his cap, saluting the whole group courteously, and subsided into a vacant chair that chanced to be
next to Ida Luttrell's.

'How are you, Annesleigh?' Gascoigne said good-
naturedly. 'We were just talking about you. I thought
you had been a votary of Diana to-day, till Paul said he
had seen you—not so profitably employed.'

'Paul was quite right—as he always is,' Gerald answered with perfect composure. 'Not so profitably, certainly; for if I had kept my engagement, I should only have wasted time instead of money. Don't somebody say, they are synonyms? *I* never could find it out. But I'm glad you were talking about me. Perhaps some one will be good enough to administer a slight restorative, in the compassionate line? I'm childish enough still to like it; and look for it, when I'm badly beat.'

Ever since Annesleigh's first appearance, the colour had been rising and falling fitfully in Mrs Gascoigne's cheek; at those last words of his she flushed almost painfully, and leant forward, with eager lips half parted. It so chanced that no one, save her cousin, noticed the impulsive movement. That strange side-glance of warning darted like an electric spark from Ida's phosphorescent eyes, as she too leant forward, so as nearly to screen Georgie's face; and spoke—her own brows contracting.

'Is losing at play the only thing in which monotony does not become wearisome? You will have to go elsewhere for your favourite opiate, soon, Captain Annesleigh, if you draw on our compassion so often and so heavily. It is positively true, that *I* have none to spare to-night. I think you are only punished as you deserve for breaking your engagement to lionize Amblève; to say nothing of your own vow of total abstinence from the tables during this week.'

She turned her head imperceptibly, as she threw herself back with a marked impatience; and five words, sliding through her lips, reached only the ear for which they were destined—'Again, mad—false—and cruel!'

Gerald answered what was spoken aloud, unhesitatingly; and still he smiled his careless, rather defiant smile.

'My dear Mrs Luttrell, you are incontrovertible, as usual. But let your justice be tempered with mercy. If I have erred, I have suffered; and I shall suffer more before I sleep: for I have yet to make my peace with the great goddess Diana. If she does not resort to *la main forte*, I shall esteem myself luckier than I deserve. Besides, I'm doing vicarious penance for my sins at this moment, in our lodgings; where my poor Pen is casting dust upon his head, and moaning till I don't believe there's a dry eye in the house: even our hard-featured old landlady had melted before I left; and there's a *femme de peine*, extraordinarily fat and foolish, who must be hysterical by this time.'

The cloud was not lifted on Ida's brow, and Mrs Gascoigne's cheek grew paler yet. But though neither Dering nor Chetwynde had any great liking for the speaker, the gay dare-devilry of the man wrung from both more admiration than they would have cared to express: a *really* good loser is so exceptionally rare; they would have wondered yet more, had they known the exact state of Gerald's finances. He left England, with every shilling paid up at The Corner; but Goodwood had drained every available resource to the uttermost drop; luck at play with him, now, was a question of social life or death.

Philip Gascoigne murmured something about 'being ready to help, if Annesleigh was really in a scrape.' But the other interrupted, before half the sentence was completed—

'Thanks—a thousand times,' he said, more earnestly than usual. 'It's only too kind of you to offer such things. But, I'm in no such need at present. Perhaps the tide will turn before it leaves my boat quite high and dry. I mean to pull it all back on the September races here : that is, if Dering will ride. We shall have an animal in that will be hard to beat over this country: and we might bring off another *coup*, nearly as good as The Moor's. By-the-by, Dering, I want to ask your advice about these same races. I won't keep you ten minutes; but I never could talk business in company.'

So the two strolled away together.

As Gerald rose, he murmured a few syllables in Ida Luttrell's ear; she bent her head ever so slightly in answer. But through the rest of the evening she was unnaturally grave, and almost absent; also, the cousins held a cabinet council, for a long hour before they slept.

CHAPTER XIX.

CONSPIRATORS.

EVERY sojourner at Spa will remember a certain Temple, perched on the narrow *plateau*, where the zig-zags of one hill-side culminate and converge. It is a very unassuming little fane, of the Early Cremornesque order of architecture; and affords not a pretence of shelter from either wind or sun. Nevertheless, it is rather a central point, and not to be mistaken; therefore, the more convenient for *rendez-vous*.

Some time before noon on the following day, Mrs Luttrell might have been seen, loitering slowly along in this direction: she carried a book in her hand, but had not yet opened its pages; indeed, there was an anxious, worried look on her face, told plainly enough that study was not her object in seeking solitude. Solitude—comparatively speaking—she was sure to find: those tempting woodland walks are almost deserted till late in the afternoon. The active ruralizers urge some of the multitudinous ponies far afield over the *bruyères*; the invalids have exhausted their energies in a matinal toil up to the Fountains; the inveterate *flâneurs* of Pall Mall or the Boulevards stroll complacently down the level *Allée*, without dreaming of breasting the hill.

As Ida neared the Temple, she saw a tall graceful figure leaning against one of the pilasters—a figure that she recognized at the first glance. She had never expected that Annesleigh would miss the appointment; nevertheless, she drew back for a moment, as if in doubt; and ground her white teeth angrily as she at length drew near.

He saluted her very courteously, and cast away the cigar he was smoking before he came to meet her. They turned aside, as if by mutual consent, into a path less frequented than the rest, which skirted the wood, and led on over the heath, ascending still into wilder forest-ground. For some seconds they walked on in silence: Ida spoke first.

'I did not like to refuse to meet you. But I scarcely know why I have come. I fear I cannot help you any more. How could you be so mad yesterday—and after all you promised?'

Gerald laughed—a low, musical laugh, yet not a pleasant one.

'You, who have read so much, must have read about "dicers' oaths." When I broke mine, yesterday, I thought perjury would have paid itself by a succession of *séries*. I won't trouble you with a detail of deals; but indeed I had won a good stake twice; once almost enough to have squared all accounts here. I'm glad you don't say, "Why didn't you stop?" *You* know, as well as I do, why I didn't do so; but many women would have asked the question, notwithstanding. You can't help me any more? I'm sorry for that; but try and think a little. I'm sure you would, if you could.'

A coward—had he been ever such a villain—would have shrunk from the dark glance of hatred that escaped from under Ida Luttrell's eyelashes. But Gerald Annesleigh never knew what fear meant; and, moreover, had confronted, in his time, every phase of woman's passion.

'I would help you if I could,' she said between her teeth. 'You think so—while you keep those fatal letters of mine. You are partly right; yet only partly. Fail in your part of our compact—and see how long your hold on me will last. But you have played your game fairly—so far,—it is *your* game, remember, and has always been, though I have backed you. I will try my uttermost to serve you now. I'll go to the bankers and see if they will let me have some thousands of francs without drawing at once on England. I don't think they will refuse, especially as Philip Gascoigne has so large a credit there. I like you better for not taking his money last night; perhaps you will win all back before Geoffrey comes to fetch me (she never shivered as she spoke that name); if not, I must tell him I have been playing, or have made you play for me; or—whatever lie comes uppermost. Let that pass; it is my concern, not yours. I think I can help you this once; but remember—lose or win—this is the very last time.'

Gerald looked steadily in her face, and saw that she meant every word; but his thanks were not the less warmly expressed. Thenceforward their talk became more low and earnest, but it shall not all be recorded here, though Georgie Gaseoigne's name recurred perpetually It shall not all be recorded, simply because a more revolting spectacle than a deliberate seducer, is a woman aiding and abetting her sister's dishonour.

'And you've wrung nothing decisive from her yet?' Ida said at length. 'There is little time to be lost. If Philip Gascoigne is helpless and unsuspicious, his friends may be neither one nor the other. I believe they would not hesitate at crime, sooner than see him wronged.'

Gerald Annesleigh laughed out loud. To speak the truth—base and depraved as he was—the calm cynicism of his female confederate had had rather a depressing effect upon him, during the last quarter of an hour. It was quite a relief, to hear of a prospect of physical danger.

'His friends?' he said, carelessly—'they're only men, and don't count. I wish one could defy the women as safely I'm more afraid of those green eyes of the Czernikoff, than of all the others in Spa put together. She owes me an old grudge; and those are the only debts she ever pays. Not hesitate at crime? Legalized murder, I suppose you mean: that's the last nickname for duelling. Well, I shouldn't mind exchanging shots with Paul Chetwynde. But I'd rather shirk Dering if I could; not because he's the most dangerous, but because—What's the matter, Mrs Luttrell?'

He might well ask the question.

In place of the cool conspiratress, who for the last half-hour had been plotting and planning at his side, there stood a passionate woman trembling in every limb; her face unnaturally white, like steel heated sevenfold; her black eyes blazing with implacable menace and wrath. As she spoke almost in a whisper she clutched his arm with her slender fingers till he fairly shrank from the pain.

'You—you meet Maurice Dering—and for *her* sake? You had better cut your right hand off than lift it against him. You know something of what I am capable when I hate: if you harmed Maurice, you should know *all!*'

Annesleigh was rather startled at first, by the intense passion that he had unintentionally provoked. But he recovered himself almost instantly feeling rather ashamed of the momentary weakness; he extricated his wrist from Ida's grasp, gently but very decidedly; and there was an inflection of sarcasm, scarcely suppressed, in his voice, as he answered,

'My dear Mrs Luttrell, it is never remunerative to be over-hasty If you had only allowed me to finish my sentence, you might have spared yourself all that excitement. You would have heard, that I d rather shirk Dering—not because he's the most dangerous, but because I like him: though, I might have added, I doubt if the feeling is reciprocated. Are you satisfied now?'

Ida's self-possession returned, but less quickly than her companion's. Before he had finished speaking, she was walking on by his side just as composedly as ever. If she guessed that she had betrayed another of her secrets to Gerald, it is certain that she was conscious of no fresh shame; she was strong in the calmness of desperation there. *He*, at least, could think no worse of her, than he was bound to think already.

'Yes, I am satisfied,' she said, with her wonted deliberation. 'I was too foolish to take alarm at all. With the commonest caution, there need be no danger from any quarter. We will separate here, if you please. You shall hear what I have done at dinner. That will be soon enough.''

Gerald's salute at parting was as courteous as it had been at meeting; but, as he wended his own way home through the forest paths, his musings broke out aloud, rather incoherently, through the smoke of a fresh cigar.

'Did anybody ever see such a born *diablesse?* I thought I was up to a thing or two; but sometimes she makes me feel like a school-boy. Ah, *signora,* you have let another mouse out of the trap this morning. I knew how you hated your fair cousin; but I never guessed how you loved Maurice Dering. That rather complicates the question; only, I really believe, there's no chance of a row. The odd thing is, that all this encouragement—and substantial help, too—is given me, when I wanted no encouraging. I've set my heart on winning that delicious little creature ever since I first set eyes on her. I shall be in clover when the old man dies, and I don't see why I shouldn't make her happy enough, if she can stand the *esclandre.* I can't well fail now, especially with such a backer as I've got. I've a sort of idea, that Ida must exactly resemble a certain Countess of Shrewsbury of unblessed memory. I feel certain that she'll beat the banker; and I ~ no scruple in borrowing from *her*, though I wouldn't touch Gascoigne's money.'

Now, though all this was coarsely expressed (as was Gerald's wont when he soliloquized), it was, perhaps, neither unfair nor untrue.

Yet these last words were spoken of one who had

wedded into a family, on whose honour no stain had rested for centuries,—of the wife of one of the most honest and simple-hearted men that ever breathed God's air,—of a woman who, if physical innocence was the sole test of purity, might have cast the first stone at an adulteress brought to judgment.

CHAPTER XX.

ON THE VERY VERGE.

THE second evening after these things were said and done, there were great doings at the Géronstère. The paternal Administration called the entertainment, a Grand Feast of the Children; but in point of fact, those innocents were very much in the minority (as they invariably are at Spa), and, after night set in, did not greatly intermeddle with the pastimes of their elders.

It was a picturesque scene altogether, in spite of a certain tawdry flimsiness of decoration. It was pretty to watch the many-coloured chains of lamp-jewels streaming away, in all directions, from the central blaze, through dim forest-paths, till their last faint sparkles merged in the outer darkness. Most of the celebrities of the place were there, gorgeously or tastefully apparelled, each leading her string of willing captives, and keenly alert for fresh live-booty.

Helène de Lauragais had thrown state-craft to the winds, for that one night, and meant amusing herself in earnest; to which end she had bestowed intense consideration on her engagement-card, till each valse and mazurka was parcelled out with a scientific regard to the capabilities of her cavaliers, and her own powers of endurance.

The Czernikoff had not put in an appearance yet. Few marvelled at her absence, for her caprices were proverbial. But—

' *Elle porte donc toujours ton deuil, cette pauvre Princesse?*' murmured the plaintive Polonaise, in the ear of her latest favourite.

The Gascoigne party—excepting Philip, of course—were all present. There, too, was Gerald Annesleigh, looking superbly handsome, and radiant with good spirits. Even the Lichnoffsky was compelled to admit to herself, with an injured sigh, that the palm of masculine beauty could not, that night, be fairly conceded to her own Magyar.

Almost up to the moment of starting, Georgie Gascoigne had professed uncertainty as to whether she would go or remain at home with Philip. It was only to his earnest entreaties that she appeared at last to yield, rather unwillingly. However, when she once got fairly launched into the bustle of the *fête*, her wayward humour changed, and she threw herself into the spirit of the scene with more verve and gaiety than she had often shown of late.

The evening was far spent when Paul Chetwynde (who never danced) stood alone, just without the circle of the platform lights, watching a brilliant mazurka in which only the cream of the cream ventured to mingle. Suddenly a tiny hand was laid on his arm, and a low *trainante* voice whispered in his ear—

A pretty spectacle, M. Chetwynde, is it not? But I

would see *all* the wonders of the Géronstère to-night.
Will you be my cavalier for a little while?

The Princess Czernikoff spoke perfectly good English,
with a slight foreign accent, and an occasional peculiarity
of idiom. Was any civilized language strange to that
wonderful woman? Nay; I think, if she had taken it
into her head to bewitch a Japanese ambassador, or a
Black-foot brave, she would have uttered the charm in
their own barbaric tongue.

She and Paul were old acquaintances—nothing more.
They met always with mutual satisfaction; and parted
without a semblance of regret. For the last dozen years
Chetwynde had amused himself with watching the Princess's
intrigues, from a disinterested distance; while his cool
causticity was very agreeable to the fair Russian's mental
palate, on which most conversational delicacies had begun
to pall.

So he was quite ready, now, to follow whithersoever she
should choose to lead; and they strolled slowly away;
turning down—by chance, as it seemed—into the first
vista of coloured lights that led forest-ward.

Before they had walked many yards, the Princess made
her companion understand—she had mysterious ways of
conveying her will, without putting it into words—that she
was not, just then, inclined to talk, or be talked to. Paul
never forced conversation at any time; so he was quite
content to humour her now

They had nearly reached the end of the walk, where
the lamps terminated abruptly, when a significant pressure
on Chetwynde's arm admonished him to turn into a side
alley winding to the right, which almost immediately di-

vided into two still narrower branches—neither of them
lighted.

Paul felt certain he had been brought hither for some
purpose : nevertheless, when he heard a murmur of voices
through the dense foliage in the paths that, for a short
distance, ran almost parallel to that which his companion
had chosen, a natural contempt of eaves-dropping overcame all curiosity ; he half-faced to the rear, evidently in-
tending to withdraw.

But those lithe slender fingers tightened their grasp,
earnestly, on his arm; he heard a faint whisper—less be-
seeching than warning—' Wait, I pray you, wait '—and
looking down, he saw the glimmer of the feline eyes, as
they shot evil glances through the darkness.

Three seconds later, Paul could no more have stirred
than if his feet had been nailed to the ground where he
stood : the blood rushed back to his heart, as it had never
done but once before—when he was told, suddenly, of his
mother's death. For he heard these words murmured, between sobs, by a voice he knew right well—

' Ah, Gerald—have mercy. How can you press me so
cruelly ''

It was Gascoigne's wife who spoke. And at that very
moment, Philip was sitting alone ; quite happy in recollect-
ing how his arguments in favour of the *fête* had prevailed,
and in fancying how his pet was enjoying her evening.

The answer came in Annesleigh's rich mellow tones ;
and Chetwynde felt his quiet companion shiver ever so
slightly

' Sweetest, I would not be unreasonable for worlds—
much less cruel. But I have hoped and feared and waited

too long : I *will* have something real to rest upon. This must end one way or the other—and soon. After all, it rests with you to say—' Go.' Then I will never trouble you again after to-night. Many women would think that promise worthless. But *you* know better. You know, that you may trust the broken-down *vaurien's* word.'

The bitter sincerity of those last words could scarcely have been assumed. Paul Chetwynde, thinking over these things in the after-time, in despite of his hatred of the speaker, could not bring himself to believe that he was acting just then. The love of a man like Annesleigh is always tinged with selfishness and tainted with intent of dishonour; but the passion is sometimes strong enough in itself to need no deliberate falsehood to back it. Though Gerald felt that poor Georgie Gascoigne was most unlikely to accept the alternative he had just proposed, it is possible that he believed himself honest, in giving her that last chance. Nevertheless, he had played his evil game too often and too long not to know, when the odds were so overwhelmingly in his favour, that he could well afford to be generous.

Something else, too, he knew.

Many women—not over cold or calculating—looking at his ruined fortunes and wicked notoriety, would have shrunk from compromising themselves, irretrievably, with the incurable Bohemian : for such a step involved, not only sin, but a shame with which Europe would ring. But the thought of this only drew Georgie Gascoigne closer to his side. The romance that had sprung up, years ago, in her girl's heart, had slumbered for a while but had never died; and of late it had waked again in perilous earnest. She had deluded herself into believing all the rest of the world hard and ungenerous, because it refused to pity or sympathise with Gerald in his misfortunes; and she grew reckless in her wish to make him all possible amends. In spite of her miserable folly and guilty imprudence, it was not really love that she felt for her tempter. With the compassion of which I have just spoken, there mingled a sort of fatal fascination, while she was under the glamour of his eyes, which, in soberer moments of solitude, she was still strong enough to remember with scorn. But the spell held her fast, just now; and when she spoke again, her voice betrayed more plainly the gathering tears. Yet, still she tried to escape from the cruel strain into which Gerald strove to force her.

'Why will you speak of yourself so? It kills me to hear you talk lightly of your troubles, when you will not let me help you—as I would, and could.'

'You are a child still, darling,' Annesleigh murmured low, in his softest tone—yet not one of his listeners lost a syllable. 'Don't you remember that afternoon at Torquay, when you first heard that I was a hunted man? You brought me a tiny purse, with all your quarter's allowance in it, and wanted me to borrow. I took the purse; and I have kept it; but I gave back the sovereigns. So it shall be, now. I will accept nothing from you, but—what I have asked hitherto in vain. And this night shall decide whether you will give all—or none.'

It was Paul Chetwynde who was trembling now—trembling till the leaves around him rustled, and the hand, still on his arm, tightened its grasp warningly. In spite of his natural coolness and acquired habits of self-restraint, he could scarcely refrain from breaking in on the interview. For two reasons he forbore: first, because he felt that any

esclandre in such a place would damage Georgie's reputa-
tion irretrievably; secondly, because it was necessary that
he should know how far her infatuation would carry her:
he still believed that it would stop short of guilt. So he
forced himself to listen, quietly, to the low broken words
that came next.

'Have you no mercy? Will you not spare? If it were
only my own sin and shame, perhaps—— But there is
Philip, so kind and trusting and helpless; and my poor
little Cecil——'

The piteous agony of her pleading might have moved
Belial himself to relenting, if not to remorse : nay, it made
even Gerald Annesleigh waver. But he was as ruthless in
self-gratification, when his passions were fairly roused, as
Machiavelli may have been in statecraft: besides, he had
listened, unheedingly, to like appeals before—if not quite
so earnest—and had made a mock at them afterwards in
the midst of his wicked triumph : he fancied, too, the cold
scorn of Ida Luttrell's eyes, when she should hear that he
had thrown his weapons down when the day was so nearly
won. The reaction from the momentary weakness—as *he*
would have called it—made him more stubborn than ever;
and he spoke sullenly, if not threateningly.

'You ought to have thought of all that before ; yes;
before you made me, or let me—it's much the same thing
—love you desperately. It's too late to ask me to be
generous, now. You can answer as you please; but you
shall answer, at once. I'm not afraid of your breaking
your word. Will you promise to be mine; or do we part
here—for ever ?'

As I said before, fear had much to do with the fascination that Gerald exercised over his intended victim. If

Georgie had had any set purpose or plan of resistance, she would never have remembered it then : in a vague helpless terror she felt that the toils were closing round her, and that there was no escape. Almost mechanically, the words broke from her quivering lips—

'Give me time—only a little time.'

Gerald saw that it would not do to push intimidation too far; his companion was getting so nervous that she might at any moment become hysterical; and of all earthly things he detested 'a scene' the most cordially.

'Darling—perhaps I have been too hasty,' he said in his gentlest tone. 'I have had so much to make me desperate of late, you know. See now: I will be patient for forty-eight whole hours. Then you shall answer me once for all; and, meanwhile, I will not say one word that all the world might not hear. Don't think me a worse savage than I am : I would not frighten you into anything.'

Georgie was so weak and helpless and weary, that she could only murmur some incoherent syllables of gratitude, without realizing their meaning. Then she began to beg and pray that Gerald would take her back to the others instantly—instantly; she was sure they had missed her already.

Common prudence told Annesleigh that risk enough had been run, for that night: so he made no demur; and only tried to soothe her into composure, with low soft words of endearment. Just before they emerged into the light of the broader alley, Gerald stooped suddenly, and would have kissed his companion's forehead. But she drew back, so quickly, that the lips never brushed her brow, murmuring :

'Not yet—ah! not yet.'

It was well for her that so much of prudence and self-respect remained; for if the caress had been completed, it is probable that the cup of Chetwynde's patience would fairly have overflowed. As it was, he remained perfectly mute and motionless, till that other pair had turned a corner of the path that hid them from sight: then he breathed hard and deep, as divers do after a lengthened plunge, and spoke—still in a suppressed voice, though they were quite alone.

'Your object in bringing me here?'

'You cannot guess?' said the Russian—calmly, but *so* bitterly. 'Yet I gave you credit for more penetration than the rest. Did you think I pitied that pretty puppet with the golden hair? I tell you, I would not have stirred a finger to save her. My interest is in that charming compatriot of yours—the man who trades on his fair face, and bright false eyes, and soft lying voice, as merchants trade on their capital. He plays on the folly of us women, like a *boursicotier* on *la hausse et la baisse*. *Il s'imagina de m'exploiter* in Paris, the winter that is past. Do you begin, now, to understand?'

In the midst of his trouble, sprang to Paul Chetwynde's lips the familiar sarcasm.

'Pardon, Princess. I was not so dull as to impute to you disinterested kindness. You would have scorned such a weakness, I know, in the year of your "first communion." I did, partly, guess the truth; but it would have been insolence to affect certainty. So you, too, have a debt against Gerald Annesleigh? Be comforted: I think all his scores will be paid, ere long; it is full time.'

'A debt?' she said. 'Yes—but you know not how

deep a one. Listen. I do not tell you how our *liaison*
began : this is how it ended. One night he had lost more
than he could pay—apparently he always loses now. He
came to me in his distress and I thanked him for so
coming ; I thanked him, on my knees. I had not enough
at my banker's ; but the next morning, I pledged my
diamond *suite*—you remember it—the gift of my Empress,
and brought him the money before noon. He blessed me,
and called me his " angel and saviour." Even then, he
was betraying me. My rival was a *coryphée* of the *Acadé-
mie*. At times he will indulge in an unprofitable intrigue.
The following week all my letters—the letters that he
swore were burned—came back to me. On the envelope
was scrawled, in a vulgar feminine hand, '*Avec les com-
plimens sympatiques de Mdlle Cerisette.*' I do not know
that he was privy to the insult ; nay, I think he feared the
consequences, for he quitted Paris soon and suddenly—
deserting his last fancy as he had deserted me. Am I
therefore to forgive it ? *He* does not so calculate. We
meet—as you have seen us ; and no word relating to our
past has been spoken. But, if Gerald Annesleigh knows
how to fear, it is when our glances cross. All these
months I have waited ; for I would not risk an incomplete
vengeance. I believe the hour has come. Is it so, or
have I misjudged you ?'

While she was speaking, they had moved gradually
back, out of the deep shadow, into the lighted *Allée*. It
seemed as though the haughty impenitent sinner cared
not that darkness should cover the avowal of her sin and
shame. Her wicked glittering eyes gazed up eagerly in
her companion's face ; they read an answer there before
he spoke.

Paul Chetwynde's countenance could be stern and pitiless enough at times, but no living man had seen it as it was now—set, like a steel mask, in pale implacable resolve.

'You have not misjudged me,' he said, speaking low, through his teeth; 'and you have chosen your time right well; your patience is likely to be rewarded. Nothing is certain—not even retribution; but I do believe that yonder scoundrel's reckoning-day has come, unless the devil takes unusual care of his own. And, Princess, I care nothing for your motives. I shall thank you while I live, and will always serve you when I can, for what you have done this night.'

'I need no thanks,' she murmured; 'and,—if I have been wise in waiting,—the end will show.'

Her manner and tone very much resembled those of a modest philanthropist, who has just performed a benevolent action, and wishes to escape from gratitude.

They mingled with the crowd round the *paraquet*, and separated immediately afterwards, without another word on what they had seen.

Annesleigh had disappeared; and Mrs Gascoigne was sitting by her cousin, looking strangely white and weary. Paul was not surprised at hearing her whisper, a few minutes later,

'Ida, darling, would you mind going home now? This is not very amusing: and my head is aching so.'

Mrs Luttrell assented readily; perhaps she was only too anxious to be alone with Georgie: her keen eyes had seen, long ago, that a decisive blow had been struck that night; and she had not misunderstood Gerald's covert smile.

Chetwynde and Dering placed the fair dames safely in

their carriage; but when the latter was going to take his seat therein, as a matter of course, Paul interfered——

'Ida, I think the road is safe enough for you to dispense with an escort home. I want Maurice, particularly, to walk home with me.'

So it was arranged, without any demur or difficulty.

CHAPTER XXI.

JUDGMENT.

As the carriage drove off, Maurice turned quickly round: he guessed at once that something evil was in the wind; and the gloom on Chetwynde's brow did not tend to re-assure him.

'What is it, old man?' he said. 'Let us have it out—and quickly.'

The other did not tax his patience long; before they had walked half-a-mile Dering knew all that it was neces-sary he should know. It would be difficult to exaggerate his astonishment and anger. Giving Georgie Gascoigne credit for much frivolity and a little recklessness, he had never imagined the possibility of her coming within the shadow of dishonour. Treachery to Philip—so utterly trustful and helpless — seemed to Maurice almost too shameful for belief. Yet belief was forced upon him; for he knew that Chetwynde's evidence was only too con-vincing and clear.

Cool and determined as he was in all emergencies, he could, at first, not quite collect his thoughts.

'What is to be done?' he said, rather vaguely and dreamily, as if he were speaking to himself.

The answer came, instantly, brief and stern:

'Gerald Annesleigh must die.'

Dering never shrank or started; he only listened earnestly while Paul went on.

'Yes, half-measures are worse than useless here. If one were to carry off that poor pretty fool to the end of the earth, she would never be safe from *him*. It would only be putting off the evil day a little longer. Don't I know that devil well; how he will override every law of God and man, if it stands between him and his desire? You could no more check him, now, than you could stop a hound running at view. There's no chance for her while he is above-ground. It can be no heavy crime to rid society of such an enemy: if it be, we must risk it. I wish I could take more than my share of the guilt.'

'You are right,' Maurice said. 'It's a case where one must act rather by the light of nature, than by any written laws. It's no use shutting our eyes to it, Paul; the divines would be all against us here. But I, too, say—we must risk it, and trust to Heaven's mercy for the rest. There will be no need to draw lots about who is to strike the blow. It must be me, of course.'

He spoke very gravely and steadily; and his brow was clouded rather with sadness than with anger.

'I fear so,' Chetwynde answered, with something like a smothered groan. 'I'm no use with the pistols; and your practice is perfect, unless your hand has lost its cunning in India.'

'Lost!' Maurice said, with a short, hard laugh. 'You would be surprised to see how much it has gained. When

I was getting better, I used to sit under Drummond's verandah, for hours, shooting at all sorts of marks. I got to real feats at last. We shall fight *à la barrière*, I suppose. If Annesleigh does not shoot first—and straight—I tell you his chance is no better, now, than if he were lying in Newgate under sentence of death.'

A moody satisfaction gleamed through the discontent of Paul Chetwynde's face.

' I like to hear you speak so confidently ; but it's no use your blinking the question—I wish *I* could. You run a fearful risk. Gerald Annesleigh has been out three times, and never missed his man ; and he'll be more murderous than usual this time. There's not a more ruthless savage alive, when he's thoroughly roused.'

' Well, I don't know about that,' Maurice answered, slowly and rather reflectively. ' There's a risk, of course, and I dare say he won't throw a chance away. But I fancy he's had a sort of liking for me since he won that big stake on The Moor. I shouldn't wonder if he were to try to disable instead of kill. He has never seen me shoot ; and won't guess that I can use my left hand as well as my right. This will make the provocation more difficult ; and I never yet picked a quarrel with any one. I hate that part of the work worse than all the rest. But it has to be done. They say, he's quick enough at taking a hint of that sort.'

So those two went on discussing a hazard on which two lives depended, with more calmness than many judges display when the Black Cap is donned. This will seem absurdly incredible, if you have not realized the peculiarities of their several characters, as I have tried to portray them. They talked on, long after they reached home, and far into the night ; but through this discourse it is not necessary that we should follow. Finally, they decided on something like a definite plan of action; and then went, each to his rest.

Of all those nearly concerned in what the morrow might bring forth—with the exception of Philip, who was still in the bliss of unconsciousness—Dering and Annesleigh slept much the most peacefully. Georgie Gascoigne (who had shared her cousin's room of late) lay trembling and sobbing, till weary exhaustion brought broken slumber: Ida was scarcely less wakeful, though she scarcely spoke or stirred; and Paul Chetwynde's busy brain found no respite, even in his brief troubled dreams.

But, if Dering rested well, his waking was not so enviable; for nothing is more disagreeable than opening one's eyes with the consciousness of uncongenial work before one. This was certainly the case with Maurice; and he spent the whole of the day in a state of complete discomfort. Anything like unprovoked quarrelling was so entirely out of his line, that he was fairly puzzled how to set about it. Indeed, chance, rather than design, accomplished late in the evening the desired end.

Annesleigh had spent all the afternoon squiring 'those Delaval girls,' with one of whom he had carried on a running fight of flirtation for some time past. He appeared in the Redoute soon after dark; and began playing almost immediately. At first he won; but finally a fatal zig-zag of colours came, setting all *tableaux* and calculations at nought, which brought most of the deep players to the very end of their resources. Curiously enough, just at the beginning of the intermittences, Gerald chanced to look up, and caught Maurice Dering's eye fixing him from the opposite side of the table. Like all thorough-paced

gamblers, Annesleigh was superstitious in a certain way :
he believed in Luck, just as implicitly as he disbelieved in
Revealed Religion. He could not get rid of an idea, that
that steady gaze was inimical to him ; or, at least, had
somewhat to do with his evil fortune. More than once, he
half rose from his seat, meaning to speak to Maurice ; but
a fear of ridicule held him back. Ere long, the decisive
coup came : Gerald had not a gold piece left to stake. He
never moved a muscle, nor did he betray annoyance, even
by a frown : yet he was nearer absolute ruin—and he
knew it—than he had been for many a day. Still he was
savagely bent on fighting on, so long as he could find one
shot to fire. Looking round—coolly and warily, as a
strategist might, in sore need of reinforcements—his eyes
lighted on a man, standing close to Dering ; this man had
also been playing and losing, though not heavily.

Lord Carisbrooke was very young, remarkably good-
tempered, good-natured, and good-looking ; indeed, barring
a slight hereditary propensity to drink, few sub-lieutenants
of horse are so ' well-conditioned.'

Annesleigh had the true instinct of the Bohemian bor-
rower : he could tell, at a glance, whether a person was
likely to ' part ' freely : he guessed this to be a safe ' draw.'
So, he walked quietly round to where Carisbrooke stood ;
and, drawing him a little aside, asked for the loan of ' a
hundred Napoleons, or so : ' very much as he would have
asked for a light to his cigar. Though the other's revenue
by no means kept pace with his profuse expenditure—
in truth, his budget at the year's end might have given
the great Chase a lesson in financial audacity—it is certain
that he would have consented, now, readily ; simply from
a constitutional incapacity of saying ' No,' without due

preparation. But, before he could speak, Dering, standing by his shoulder, spoke rarely and sternly.

'Don't do anything of the sort, Carisbrooke. You've lost enough for one night, without throwing more money away.'

The insult was so direct and sudden, that Annesleigh could not suppress a slight start; but he answered it in his coldest tone.

'Carisbrooke, I can't congratulate you on the manners of your Mentor. Captain Dering, you imply that I wish to borrow, without the means or intention of repaying?'

'Clearly, I do,' Maurice said. 'At least, I'm not certain about the means: I am, about the intention.'

A dim suspicion of the truth dawned upon Annesleigh, as Dick Lowell's warning came across his memory. His glance at Dering was so keen and significant, that the latter felt himself flush under it.

'We had better finish this pleasant discussion elsewhere —if we finish it at all. But I fancy you've said enough for your purpose already. Carisbrooke, thanks all the same: I knew you were going to part with that hundred. Perhaps it's as well as it is: that money might only have followed my own. Au revoir, Captain Dering:' and so, Gerald Lloyd lounged listlessly away.

Carisbrooke had not seen much of life yet: of its dark side comparatively nothing. But he guessed that evil deeds were about to be done: and was greatly disquieted that through him the offense should have come. Dering stopped his excuses and misgivings at once.

'My dear Carisbrooke, there's no earthly reason why you should blame yourself, or thank me. I interfered, simply because I didn't choose to stand by and see a robbery brought off. I only insist on ono thing—that you don't open your lips to any ono on the subject, till I give you leave. I think you owe me that much, for saving your hundred.'

The other gave the promise, but rather reluctantly. He played no more that night, nor for many a night after; and his solitary cigar, as he walked up and down the deserted *Allée*, musing gravely for the first time in his life, smoked strangely bitter and tasteless.

It is no light matter that will distract the attention of the *galerie* when heavy play is proceeding : in the conversation just recorded, not a tone had been raised in anger; so, what looked like a 'very pretty quarrel,' still remained a secret to all but the principals.

Dering found Chetwynde in another part of the Redoute. As soon as their eyes met, the latter rose and followed Maurice down-stairs : neither spoke till they were in the open air. Then Dering drew a long breath, very like a sigh.

'It's all settled, Paul; or will be, to-night. He deserves all he'll get, no doubt; but—I wish I didn't feel so very like a *spadassin*.'

'I know what you mean, right well,' the other answered, rather sadly 'It's an evil business, look at it how you will; but—once more—I'm more guilty than you, if guilt there be. How did it happen ? '

Maurice told him as briefly as possible.

'Do you know,' he went on, 'I'm certain Annesleigh guessed the truth, and saw through that pretext for a quarrel, at once. If so—to give the devil his due—he behaved perfectly. I believe we are not more anxious than he is, to keep Georgie's name out of the whole affair.'

'I dare say it is so,' Chetwynde said, with a touch of his old sarcasm. 'Gerald Annesleigh has the knack of doing a black deed more gracefully than any living man. If he committed a murder, the victim would testify to his courtesy with the last breath. If you had seen him harden himself against that poor child's prayer for mercy—as I did—you wouldn't give him credit for much human-kindness or forbearance. We had better go home now : some one will come on his part before long, depend upon it.'

Indeed, they had not long to wait.

Before Annesleigh left the Redoute he had found and commissioned his second. It was no other than the Baron von Rosendahl, of terrible renown ; who had been 'out' about as often as Bussy d'Amboise, and was an authority throughout Europe on the minutest points of duel-law. This eminent person soon presented himself at Dering's lodgings ; and then and there, with due decorum and solemnity, arranged with Chetwynde the preliminaries of a meeting, to take place early the next morning, just across the Prussian frontier.

When Annesleigh had given instructions to his second —they were very simple and concise—he walked quietly to his hotel, where Penrhyn Bligh sate solitarily over scarcely-watered cognac. Gerald had fancied, of late, that the white anxious face of his *umbra* brought him ill luck at play, and had forbidden his attendance on such occasions. So the poor little creature—for whom society, viewed otherwise than as a source of profit, had no charms —was fain to content himself with hearing of the chances and changes of the cards ; that is, if his senses were not wandering on his patron's return.

Bligh looked eagerly into Gerald's eyes, as the latter

entered; but they told no tales even to him. He sate
down; and, filling a goblet with his wonted deliberation,
drained a deep draught of cognac and water, very slowly,
evidently relishing it.

'I fear you've lost again,' Penrhyn said, at last, more
timidly than usual; for, watching closer, he marked a dark
set look on the other's face, that he had seldom, if ever,
seen there. 'How much is it?'

Annesleigh laughed a little low laugh, as he answered,

'Lost? Yes, of course I've lost. But, my Pen, I don't
quite know how much it will come to; nor shall I till to-
morrow's over I mean to go to bed early, all the same;
and so ought you, if you want to see me through it decently I've got to fight Maurice Dering soon after day-
break. Von Rosendahl acts for me; I wouldn't trust
those hands of yours with loading; it'll come to closeish
shooting I fancy, and a few extra grains of powder might
spoil all. But you'll go with me to the ground, of course?'

Weak, and wicked, and despicable as he was, few could
have looked, then, unmoved, in Penrhyn Bligh's face: it
was so piteously eloquent in its grief and terror, that
something between remorse and compassion stirred within
Gerald Annesleigh's marble heart.

'Cheer up, old man,' he said, more kindly than he had
spoken for years, 'you couldn't be worse if a hanging-
match, instead of a fair fight, were coming off. I told Von
Rosendahl that we meant *business*; so I know exactly how
he'll fix it He'll put us up back to back at forty paces;
we shall wheel at the word, and fire when we like within
fifteen paces of advance. The *barrière* always suits me best.
I've no idea how Dering shoots—well, probably, as he does
most things. Mark this: I don't mean killing, this time.

I shall hold my fire till I'm within thirty yards; for I'm
not dead-certain beyond that. If he don't shoot and disable me before that, I'll break his pistol-arm as sure as
you live. If he wounds me slightly first, I won't try to hit
him at all. But you haven't heard how it happened.'

Bligh appeared to listen eagerly to the brief recital that
followed, but perhaps he scarcely heard a syllable; his
eyes were still glazed and fixed in a haggard terror. At
last he moaned out, half intelligibly—

'What *will* become of *me* ?'

There was a terrible simplicity in the words that might
have made you forget their apparent selfishness. In truth,
was it not as sad as shameful to see a rational being, born
to free-agency, so helplessly dependent on another; and
that other—one like Annesleigh?

When Gerald answered, though he still strove to speak
lightly, it was clear the mocking spirit was dead within
him for the nonce.

'It would have been a thousand times better for you, if
you had never seen me, Pen. But, as it is, I don't see
who would look after you and your morals, if anything
happened to me. Don't you think of that. It would be
too hard lines for both of us, if my number were to be
wiped out just when the Emperor is breaking fast, and I
might do something for you as well as myself. I'm not
going to give you any instructions to-night ; for you would
remember nothing. Yes, you can remember this. In
case of the worst, you'll find a letter in my travelling-bag.
Do exactly as it tells you. You'll find jewels enough to
carry you home, with the few louis you have left. Now,
I'm going to send you to bed, after one more glass. I've

set my heart on your looking respectable on the ground to-morrow.'

Bligh brightened up a little, under the influence of the other's confident manner; but a more dejected and miserable man seldom laid head on pillow His physical courage was rather below par; but it is certain, that he would have readily taken all the danger on his own frail shoulders.

After Annesleigh had seen Von Rosendahl, and settled all necessary arrangements, and written half-a-dozen letters, he sate, musing, for awhile, more gravely than despondingly. It may be that during that brief interval between recklessness and oblivion, some solemn thoughts may have passed through that wild, wicked heart; regrets, too, not utterly wasted, and vague schemes of amendment never to be realized.

Who can tell? Though the probabilities are fearfully on the side of justice, we may not deny that the mercy which smiled on the Thief's death-pang may possibly be extended to those who need it yet more sorely.

CHAPTER XXII.

EXECUTION.

ONE of these quaint little valleys, between steep wooded hills, that one sees only in the Ardennes, where the meadow sward keeps its tender emerald-green long after the upland pastures are parched berry-brown, thanks to the streamlet whose rippling murmur summer heats are powerless to

quell—a light breeze rustling through the leaves of dwarf
oaks and birches—over all, the clear crystalline atmosphere
of an early August morning.

On the narrow strip of level ground between the water
and the wood, two men stand back to back, at a distance
of forty paces, measured with unerring accuracy by a practised stride : they are the principals, as you may guess, in
the barrier-duel that is just about to begin. Somewhat
aside, about midway between the two, is a group made up
of the seconds, an Austrian army-surgeon, and Penrhyn
Bligh.

The Teutonic faces are stolid and passionless, as if they
were carved in beech-wood; but Chetwynde's is deathly
pale ; though its set, steadfast expression contrasts strongly
with the nervous agony that convulses Penrhyn's features
in a grotesque horror. No word had passed, when Paul
led Dering to his station—only a long hand-gripe, during
which neither pulse fluttered or trembled.

Look at the two men, as they stand—motionless as
statues—waiting for the signal to be given. Their attitude
is nearly the same; both right arms are bent back, so that
the pistols point upward perpendicularly ; but Annesleigh's
left is braced athwart his chest, so that the hand supports
the other elbow, while Dering's hangs easily at his side.
Maurice's lips are more firmly compressed than usual, and
the grave composure of his face is perhaps not altogether
devoid of anxiety. On Gerald's brow there is not a cloud
of concern—much less of apprehension ; the musings of
last night have left no trace behind ; in spite of the incon-
gruity of time and place, surely some pleasant passing
thought must provoke that half-smile.

The Baron von Rosendahl had won the toss—his luck

on such occasions was supernatural—and was to give the signal. He gave it almost immediately; smiting his hands together, in one sharp abrupt clap, that sounded like wood striking on wood.

The men wheeled, and stepped out forward, exactly at the same instant. As Dering set his foot down on the third pace, he levelled and fired.

Annesleigh halted on the shot, just as a troop-horse halts on the trumpet-call; he stood for a second or more—steady as a rock, only moving his left arm slightly lower on his breast; then he raised his right slowly, still keeping the pistol pointed upwards, so that the barrel stood out in relief against the sky. Paul Chetwynde saw that in hand and weapon there was no more tremor than if they had belonged to a marble effigy: his pulse stopped beating then; for he felt that Maurice's life was at the mercy of one who, in hate, as in love, had never been known to spare.

Annesleigh's voice rang out, through the clear morning, distinct and loud—but there was not one strained note in its music——

'Dering—we're quits at last.'

As he spoke, he fired straight upward; and the next instant, without a shiver or a stagger, crashed heavily forward on his face.

The first sound that followed, none that heard it will ever forget—like the howl of some tortured animal than a shriek of human agony: it broke from the writhen lips of Penrhyn Bligh. Though he swayed and tottered as he ran, he was the first to reach the wounded man's side, and strove vainly to raise him, with powerless shaking hands.

When they turned Gerald over, a thin red stream was

trickling sullenly down his left side.   The Austrian surgeon shook his head ominously: he had had long practice in bullet-wounds, and detected, at once, fatal internal bleeding.

The handsome face was lividly pale already; but not one of the features was distorted: if it had not been for a slight quivering of the lids, you might have thought that the great dark eyes, half veiled by the trailing lashes, were only weary   The eyes unclosed, however, almost as soon as they raised him: they lighted first on Maurice, who stood by—looking very sad, if not remorseful.

'Stand back—all of you—for two minutes,' Gerald said faintly   'I *must* say a dozen words to Dering—you'll hold me up, won't you?   It's no use looking at the wound: I knew I was a dead man, directly I was hit.   Take Pen away; or don't let him moan so.'

They did as they were bidden, though Von Rosendahl frowned gloomy disapprobation of such a violation of duel-punctilio as interchange of confidences between principals. As Dering knelt down, supporting his enemy's head on his shoulder, the cold sensation of blood-guiltiness tightened its hold on his heart.

'You'll believe me,'—Annesleigh went on—'for you can't help it; it can do me no good to lie.   Of course we know what was at the bottom of this.   She's weak and rash sometimes; but, I swear, she's as innocent—so far— as my dead mother.'

He spoke with a painful effort, hesitating between each word, in a way that letter-press can hardly represent.

'I do believe you,' Maurice said, sadly, 'and I know she is both weak and rash.   To keep her innocent, I have taken your blood on my head.   God forgive me!   It looks cruelly like murder now.'

'You did well,' the other murmured.   'There need be

no malice between us. I always liked you, and I *did* spare you to-day. Ask Pen what I said last night. He'll give you some papers soon : do what you like with them. I believe my last deed is a good one, though it goes against the grain. If you ever feel sorry for this, or think you owe me a turn, give poor old Pen enough to keep him decently: he won't trouble you long. I'm going fast—look here— I'm not a bit afraid ; but—I think I'd die easier if you would give me your hand—just once.'

The man that would have rejected that petition would have owned a harder heart than Maurice Dering's. As the pressure was exchanged, the shadow of his old sweet smile played round Gerald's lips; and his eyes closed for a second or so. When he opened them again the death-film was gathering there fast : it was evident that his ear guided him, as he beckoned feebly to Bligh.

The miserable creature tottered up, and casting himself on his knees, broke out again into sobs and meaningless wailing.

'Hush, Pen,' Annesleigh whispered, in a voice barely audible. ' Can't you say " Good-bye " quietly ? It's hard, on both of us. I'd have made a man of you again, if I had ever come to my own. I wish I hadn't bullied you so much. I wish—too late—though—too late. Only, re-member——'

Here his voice failed utterly ; he closed his eyes once more, and the bystanders, except the surgeon, whose finger was on his wrist, thought that all was over. Suddenly the heavy lids stirred and were lifted ever so little ; and the lips began to move. Dering, who still supported Gerald's head, leant forward to catch those last faint syllables ; slowly they dropped out—one by one—

' How—the—Jews—are—sold ! '

As he spoke, his face seemed to light up, for an instant, in a flash of scornful triumph; then a change swept across it, as if a grayish veil had been drawn swiftly down: a slight choking in the throat, and a shiver that was scarcely a struggle, told of the flitting of that wicked wayward soul.

Though Gerald Annesleigh's latest word was a mock, a truer one was never spoken. Considering that nothing politically important was affected, few more costly shots have been fired than that one whose echoes had scarcely ceased to ring. All the insurance policies on the dead man's life were only waste paper, now; for all the colossal sums raised on his reversions, that little lump of lead had given quittance in full. There arose wailing among The Tribes, such as hath not often been heard since the days of the Captivity; and one or two plaintive capitalists still refuse to be comforted.

There was silence for a moment or more among those who watched the death-pang, only broken by Penrhyn Bligh's suppressed sobbing; for—obedient to the very end—he had crushed down clamorous grief. Chetwynde spoke first.

'We must not linger here. We ought to have been back over the frontier by now; and we can do no good by staying. Yet—I don't like——'

They all knew what he meant. Though Gerald Annesleigh was far beyond human help or harm, it seemed brutally unfeeling to leave him lying there alone. In truth, the strange fascination that had made the dead man so fatal to his kind, still seemed to abide in the sad, solemn face, that rested where Dering had laid it gently down— not a sign of anger or pain marring its unearthly beauty.

But the Baron Von Rosendahl was a very practical person, and case-hardened by murderous experience.

'*Vous avez raison, M. Chetwynde ; il ne faut pas se dé-
couer pour les morts. En sus, M. Bligh, peut soigner le
transport et l'enterrement de son pauvre ami. Il ne risque
rien ; puisqu'il n'a pas servi en témoin.*'

'He is not fit ——,' Paul said, laying his hand, mechanically, on the mourner's shoulder, as he knelt, bending over
the corpse, his face buried in his hands.

Neither the words nor the gesture were unkindly meant ;
but they seemed to wake in Penrhyn Bligh the wrathful
devil that had slumbered for many a year. No one would
have thought that those weak, pale eyes could glare so
savagely.

'How dare you touch me ? ' he said, in a hoarse whisper,
'or meddle in *our* concerns ? D—n you ! You're not
satisfied with murdering him ; you can't leave me to do as
I like with his corpse.' The bitter blasphemies that followed are not such as can be written down.

Chetwynde saw that it would be useless to linger : argu-
ing with Bligh in his present state would have been like
trying to convert a maniac. He took Dering's arm, and
drew him away, after the Austrians, who had already
moved off.

All Maurice's arrangements, providing for a fatal termination of the duel, had been made over-night. Honourable
homicide is a venial crime enough in these parts ; nevertheless, for many reasons, he chose not again to present
himself in Spa. He went straight to the station—avoiding
the main street of the town—where his servant was waiting for him, and travelled direct to England, without stop-
ping on the road. He and Chetwynde talked long and

earnestly on their way back; but their converse does not bear materially on the story; so I omit it, just as I forbore to allude to the husbands of the Lichnöffsky or the Laura-gais—excellent personages in their way, but, by the world, completely ignored.

When Paul Chetwynde told Princess Czernikoff of that morning's work, she heard him out with a hard smile on her lips, and nodded twice or thrice approvingly at certain points in the story. She was also careful to discover, where the body was likely to have been conveyed.

Twelve hours after Gerald Annesleigh died there stood by his corpse a stricken, haggard woman, with an awful agony on her livid face, driving her sharp nails into her quivering flesh, cursing herself, that had willed—the hand that had wrought — the God that had permitted the slaughter. Just so, over the wicked Earl, may have raved the miserable avenger, who

> Hated him with the hate of Hell,
> But loved his beauty passing well.

The tidings came upon the Gascoigne party like a thunder-stroke. Even Ida was, for the moment, bewilder-ed by the suddenness of the blow. This soon settled down into a sullen despondency, such as a captive might feel when the iron bar, that has nearly set him free, breaks in the wards of the last lock. Surely, too, her hard heart was not exempt from a dull, vague remorse, as she remembered how, twice or thrice, Gerald Annesleigh had seemed to hesitate in his evil path, as if foreboding whither it would lead; so that, perchance, he might have turned back, had *she* not been near to goad him on to his doom.

It was from her that Georgie learnt the black news; and

she witnessed, alone, the first hysterical outbreak of the poor child's grief and horror. Ida's stern self-possession, and strange influence over her cousin's weaker mind, triumphed at last. None other in the household saw Mrs Gascoigne till she was comparatively quite composed; her face, then, betrayed no more violent emotion than would be natural to any soft-hearted woman, brought suddenly in contact with a violent death. As was aforesaid, she had never loved Gerald Annesleigh; it was a feeling quite undefinable, originating in absurd romance, and deepening into helpless fascination, not devoid of fear. After the first spasm had past, a certain sensation of freedom and relief possessed her, though she would never have owned it. Surely some feeling of thanksgiving mingled with her prayers of contrition and intercession for the dead man's soul. One remorse she was spared.

With that innocent false-logic, wherein our sisters excel the sophists, she had forced herself to accept Paul Chetwynde's version of the quarrel; and never suspected that her own honour had been redeemed at the bitter price of blood. But, though conscience was silent here, Georgie Gascoigne knew that she had been saved—once for all. In life, no woman should need two such warnings. In good truth, the vow of prudence that she took upon her, that terrible day, never afterwards was near the breaking.

Philip was dreadfully shocked and pained. He was sorry, of course, for Annesleigh, for whom he had conceived rather a liking of late; but he was sorrier yet for Dering. Only yesterday he would have laughed at the idea of that kindly nature's incurring the burden of blood-guiltiness, on a pretext apparently so slight and shallow. He did not judge his friend hardly, nor like him a whit the

R

less; but he felt that they never would see again the cheery, genial Maurice of the old time: on that honest right hand there ever must abide the one stain, over which the waters of this world have no power. Neither could Philip absolve Chetwynde of criminality, and told him so.

The latter absolutely declined to discuss the question. When the other, thoroughly mystified, begged at least to know if there were nothing more below the surface of the quarrel, Paul replied,—'That there had been ill-blood for some time past between Dering and Annesleigh; that he wondered Philip had not noticed it; and that natural antipathies were just as good a reason for fighting as any other.'

Chetwynde was always especially cynical, when his case was weak. Gascoigne was not convinced; though of the truth, neither then nor later, did he entertain the faintest suspicion.

'I can't argue with you,' he said, sorrowfully; 'but I know you are bitterly wrong, and so Geoff would tell you. How do you suppose *he* would take this? No; I never noticed anything of that sort—I notice so few things now. I always fancied poor Annesleigh rather like Maurice. You say, yourself, he fired in the air. Let us get out of this accursed place before night; my dreams would be spectre-ridden here. I'm certain Georgie would wish to go. Poor darling, she's as much shocked and grieved as I am, which is no small word. Something ought to be done to help that unhappy Bligh.'

'I've provided for that,' Chetwynde answered curtly. 'Yes, on all grounds, it is better to move—homeward, of course.'

Ten days later the party that you saw sitting under the elms at the *Allée*, sate—sadly diminished and altered—under the beeches of Marston Lisle.

CHAPTER XXIII.

MISERRIMUS.

IN all his life, up to the fortnight immediately ensuing on these events, Maurice Dering had never known what 'low spirits' meant. The depression and self-reproach under which he laboured, was not lightened by a visit from Geoffrey Luttrell. The parson was not unduly harsh or severe; but he spoke very plainly and decisively, not attempting to disguise his abhorrence of the deed that had been done, or his grief on hearing that his friend had so fallen into temptation.

More than once Maurice was tempted to reveal the real cause of the fatal quarrel; but it was not his own secret, and he forbore. So they parted—not in unkindness—yet with the sense of a barrier between them that had never existed till now, and that might be long in vanishing away. Geoffrey was on his way to Marston, where his wife was awaiting him.

Maurice still remained in town, chiefly because a man in his set could find no more solitary sojourn in early September. He did not feel equal to affronting the curiosity of society, as yet; for, though few regrets were wasted on Gerald Annesleigh, his death created a very marked void, and no slight notoriety was certain to attach to his slayer.

One morning Dering was sitting alone, rather more pensive than usual : he had just finished a letter to Alice Leslie, and another to her uncle. He preferred their hearing the truth—or as much of it as he dared to tell—from himself, and without delay. From the first, he had never disguised from himself, that the stain of blood on his hand might make him unworthy again to clasp that other innocent palm, that he had pressed so often and so tenderly. His happiness, not less than his life, was at stake when he faced Annesleigh's pistol.

In both letters he did not dissemble his regret; yet he did not altogether abase himself: he only prayed them to judge him as mercifully as they could—though the *whole* truth he might not tell—and promised to abide by their decision, without murmuring.

The last letter was scarcely finished when there came a weak, wavering knock at the street door : a minute later, Penrhyn Bligh entered.

The sight of that ghastly face and tottering figure, smote Dering with a pang of compunction, sharper than he had yet felt. Instinct told him that his hand had, unwittingly, dealt the finishing stroke to an incomplete ruin. The ship was stranded long ago, but never quite broken up till that last gale.

The frame that had always been spare and thin, was now shrunken and bowed like a man's in extreme old age; the scared eyes kept blinking through their scarlet rims, as if they abhorred the light; the timid chronic smile hovered no longer about the feeble mouth ; it was replaced by a convulsive twitching painful to see; and the tremulous fingers would not rest for an instant.

Bligh tossed down a sealed packet on the table, and

spoke in a shrill piping voice—hurrying his words together, as children do who are afraid of forgetting their lesson.

'I ought to have been here before: but—but I couldn't get further than Liège. It knocked me down there. I came as soon as I could stand: indeed I did. I hope—I hope I'm in time.'

'Don't excite yourself,' Maurice said, gently. 'And do sit down. I see you have been very ill. What was it?'

Penrhyn laughed a sharp hollow laugh, like a dog's bark. He did not take the offered chair, but stood, swaying to and fro, griping the table with both hands alternately. It was evident that he answered mechanically, and was speaking rather to himself than to Dering.

'What should it be—but the old thing? Only the "horrors" were worse this time. I never shut my eyes in the dark, now. It's bad enough, by daylight—to be waked by that woman screaming in your ear, just as she screamed the night before we buried him—let alone what you see in your dreams. I wonder if they *are* dreams. I'm getting beat fast: I've got to *fight the snakes alone*, since you shot him.'

He stopped abruptly, and began glancing over his shoulder, into one corner of the room, with wild frighted eyes. Something like terror came over Maurice's stout heart: to save his life, he could hardly have spoken just then. He took up the packet, and was just breaking the seal, when Bligh passed swiftly round the table, and clutched his wrist.

'Can't—can't you read?' he whispered, hoarsely; pointing to these words under the address—

'Open this—alone.'

Maurice laid the packet down again, with a sigh.

'I can do nothing right, it seems. Now, do take what I am going to say—as I mean it—in kindness. I promised *him*, that I would help you whenever you needed it. You *must* need it now. It would make me much happier if you would let me serve you in any way.'

Penrhyn drew himself together, with a painful effort, and, for a moment, stood up straight and steady: his eyes met Dering's without flinching, and his voice hardly quavered at all.

'Look here,' he said. 'I'm not proud; and I'm as hard up as man can be. I'd go into a robbery to-morrow, and thank the devil for being put on. But I'll stand at The Corner and hold my hat for pence, sooner than take a shilling from you. D—n you: is that plain enough, or shall I make it plainer?'

Maurice shook his head, sadly: he could no more have been angry with the unhappy being before him, than he could have struck an infant in arms.

'Yes, it's plain enough,' he said—'plain enough, that I may repent; but can make no amends. I cannot guess what that packet holds; but I thank you for bringing it. Will you let me send you home, at least? You are not fit to go alone.'

The momentary ferocity had died out of Penrhyn's face, and the old expression—imbecile when it was not frightened—had returned. He shook his head feebly, as he turned and made his way to the door. Before he reached it, his wandering eyes lighted on a liqueur-case, that stood half-open on a side-table. For a moment or two, it seemed as if he would have resisted the fatal fascination; but it was too strong for him. He staggered up to the table, and poured out a large glass of raw spirit. When he had drained it at a gulp, he broke out into that horrible laugh again.

'I told you I'd take nothing from you,' he said. 'I was bound to lie; for—I didn't want to have a shaking-fit *here.*'

The door closed behind him, without another word passing; and so Dering was left alone, with the dead man's message before him.

For several seconds he sat, gazing fixedly at the superscription; addressed in the firm flowing hand, that every usurer of note in broad England knew to his cost.

But to Maurice, the handwriting of the letters within the envelope was yet more familiar. He started in displeased surprise as it caught his eye: no wonder—it was Ida Luttrell's. On a slip of paper, Gerald Annesleigh had written—

'Use these or not, as you please. But read them through: there is no treachery in your doing so; I take all that on myself. I hate myself at this moment; but I see no other way of helping that poor woman: she will never be safe while she is in her cousin's power. I have not left one word of leave-taking for *her*: she had best hate my memory. I may be all wrong: but I mean right —for once. Rather late in the day—isn't it? Farewell.

'G. A.'

As he read on, the frown darkened on Maurice Dering's brow, till it was black as midnight: he cast down the last letter, with a groan of horror and disgust. There were six, with dates extending nearly two years back; and the proofs were damning beyond possibility of doubt.

Ida had not only been cognizant of Annesleigh's designs on Georgie Gascoigne, but had aided them both by counsel and connivance; she more than once suggested plans for the meeting of those two, and had actually furnished Gerald with funds to bring him to Spa, besides helping him to pay his play-debts there.

There was a deliberate depravity, and pitiless malice, and shameless cynicism about the whole conspiracy—for such it really was—far beyond what it had ever entered into Maurice's honest heart to conceive. For the moment he felt thoroughly bewildered. It seemed the very wantonness of crime. What earthly object could Ida have in plotting or abetting her cousin's ruin? And how was he to act? He no more thought of keeping Ida's evil secret, than he would of standing by to see felony done. Yet it was impossible to touch her without striking Geoffrey Luttrell to the very heart's core.

With all this misery, doubt, and difficulty, mingled that nervous eagerness to face the worst at once—common to most men of his sanguine temperament. He relied on Chetwynde's judgment far more implicitly than on his own, or that of any other living person. He resolved to seek that counsellor at once.

So a train, early that afternoon, carried Maurice Dering down to Marston Lisle. He had previously telegraphed to Paul to meet him at the station, about three miles from the house; begging him also to keep his coming a secret from every one.

Chetwynde's disgust and surprise at Maurice's revelations fully equalled the other's; but these reached their climax when Dering made a clean breast of what had

passed between himself and Ida. The vital urgency of
the case compelled him to act, just as a criminal does with
his advocate—making no half-confessions. During these
few minutes Paul's self-reliance—not to say self-esteem—
sank so many degrees, that it never afterwards fairly recovered itself.

'What a blind idiot I've been all these years,' he said,
in a low bitter voice; and I held myself a fair physiognomist and judge of character. Her motives puzzle me
still. Wait——. By G—d, I have it. Fancy, not thinking of that sooner. It's as plain as daylight.'

Maurice looked inquiringly, and rather wonderingly, at
the speaker. After a second, Chetwynde went on.

'Don't you see it? Hate and love were both at work—
if you can call that she-devil's passion love. She hated
Georgie, because she fancied she had once stood between
herself and you; and thought it might be the same over
again. I suppose she gives no man credit for constancy
in resistance to temptation. She wanted Georgie ruined,
and out of your reach, before you came back. Even if she
had not feared that pretty fool, she forgives no more than
she forgets. But explanations are not excuses. It's the
most infernal case I ever heard of.'

'It must be,' Dering answered sternly; 'for, if you have
guessed right, it does not soften me a whit. She don't
deserve to be spared.'

'Spared!' the other retorted with intense contempt.
'She should have short shrift if she alone were to be dealt
with. But there's poor Geoff to be considered. I believe,
on my conscience, this will go near to killing him.'

They consulted long and earnestly, walking through the

green by-lanes that led to a side-gate of Marston park. By the time they reached it, they had settled their course of action.

Chetwynde was to go up to the house, and bring Ida to a certain sheltered walk through a remote shrubbery, where Dering was to await them. Paul was to be present at the interview.

It seemed as though some strange fatality hung over the most painful hours of Maurice's life; for once again his nerve and firmness were about to be sorely tried, and— the day was hard upon sun-down.

CHAPTER XXIV

UNDER THE BEECHES.

CHETWYNDE found Mrs Luttrell in the garden, alone, for Georgie had hurried back to her husband directly they came in from driving : she had been unusually attentive to Philip of late, and would never leave him for more than an hour or two at a time.

Paul had not patience to invent pretexts : he told Ida, abruptly, that some one was waiting to see her on urgent business, and that she must come with him immediately. The cold sternness of his voice and manner was not to be misunderstood. That vague feeling of insecurity that had haunted Ida ever since Gerald Annesleigh's death became terribly definite, now ; but her stubborn spirit rose to the emergency: she followed Chetwynde without demur or objection, and only asked one question,—this was when they were crossing a strip of open paddock between two belts of shrubbery,—

'Won't you tell me who it is?'

Paul shook his head impatiently : she pressed him no further; and their moody silence was not again broken till they reached the appointed place of meeting.

Dering was leaning against a tree—his head bowed low on his breast—his hat crushed down over his brows so that his face could hardly be discerned : the despondency of his whole attitude would have struck the merest stranger.

At sight of Maurice, Ida felt that her worst fears were more than realized : she had fancied that possibly Penrhyn Bligh might have become possessed of her secret and betrayed it; but she had never dreamed of *this*. Her heart stopped beating for a second or so, and then began throbbing madly; a wild desire possessed her, to fly anywhere rather than be confronted with him; she halted, and had actually half turned round, when Chetwynde, as if he guessed her intent, laid his hand gently, but very firmly, on her arm; she yielded to the impulse without a struggle; but all her marvellous self-command could not repress one low piteous moan.

Dering lifted his head as they drew near : the first glance at his face told Ida that she had scant mercy to hope for. Then she grew stronger, in that awful courage of despair, that has enabled so many weak arms and hearts to hold their own, for awhile, against the heaviest odds. She never shrank or shivered as Maurice came forward to meet them; and her great bright eyes looked into his with a steady earnestness that was neither suppliant nor defiant.

Dering held an open letter in his hand : he held it out to Ida, striking it sharply with his forefinger.

'Do you recognize your own handwriting, Mrs Luttrell?'

With all the humiliation hanging over her, she was still too proud for useless denials.

'Yes; I wrote it,' she said, simply. Having spoken, she drew back a pace or two, and stood, with downcast eyes, and hands locked firmly before her—on her face that pale resolve which is *not* resignation; just as a criminal, who has pleaded ' guilty,' with nothing to urge in extenuation, might wait to hear his sentence read.

'Is it possible'—Maurice said—his voice shaking with passion—' are you made of flesh and blood like ourselves —that you can acknowledge such a letter as this, just as coolly as if it were a note of invitation? Why—I am speaking selfishly now—don't you know that, to stop the plotting which you aided and abetted, I have taken the sin of murder on my soul? For murder it was—call it what name you will,—I see that, plainer and plainer every hour. Of the wrong meditated — ay, and wrought too, against others, I dare not speak or think.'

Then Chetwynde's cold measured tones came in : he stood somewhat backward; almost midway between the other two.

'I have the same right as Maurice to accuse you; for my share of blood-guiltiness is the same. I advised and planned the slaughter; and would have executed it, if I could have trusted my hand and eye, as I could trust his. But neither he nor I had—or ought to have had—any special claim on your forbearance. Did you ever think of Geoffrey—who never thwarted a whim or quarrelled with a word of yours—who trusts in you as he trusts in God's mercy—when you dragged his honour, and yours, through the mire of Annesleigh's intrigues? Ida—I have known, and liked you, since your childhood; and it has all come to this; that I must speak such words without pity, and you must hear them without resentment. Ten thousand times over, I would rather have seen you dead.'

She looked from one to the other with vague dreamy eyes: and the listless indifference, habitual to her when not much interested in conversation, began to settle down on her face.

'Dead?' she said, softly. 'Yes—that would be better. But—as it is—what would you have me do? I make no defence; and I am quite helpless, you see.'

In truth, if you could only put the thought of her guilt, for one moment, aside, there would have been a piteous disproportion in the odds; it was cruel, to see that little frail delicate creature matched against those two strong, stern men. When Right is Might, it sometimes hardly obtains undivided sympathy.

'I will tell you what Maurice and I have resolved on,' Chetwynde answered. 'About sparing you, there has been no thought; about sparing Geoffrey—much. It is clear that your intimacy with Philip Gascoigne's wife must be broken off, at *any* cost. This must be your last visit to Marston. Now, if this can be done, without letting any other person—not even Geoffrey—into this miserable secret—so let it be. There are difficulties and dangers innumerable about it: if any woman living can surmount them, you can. You may use any fair means, and make any fair excuses; but, I warn you, of plots and conspiracies we will have no more. Will you make the trial, on your own risk and resources, or shall the matter be settled abruptly, this night?'

She paused for a few seconds, pondering gravely.

'Yes, I will make the trial—it *is* for Geoffrey's sake, though you will not believe me; yet, it may be only putting off the evil day a very little longer. I can make no promises, even if you would listen to them: but I suppose I shall do my best.'

Dering's eyes were cast moodily down, while she was speaking; but Chetwynde's more watchful glance never left Ida's face. From the very first he had failed to detect there one sign of contrition or shame, and this had chafed him sorely; now, he thought he could perceive the glimmer of an unholy hope—the dawning of a wicked triumph. He may possibly have been deceived in the change of Ida's expression; but a change there certainly was. His own brow—dark enough already—lowered visibly: he set his teeth hard; and, when he spoke, there was undissembled menace in his tone.

'One thing more. You must have noticed that hitherto there has been no question as to your motives in plotting Georgie Gascoigne's ruin. Shall I tell you why I asked you nothing? It was because I know all your shame— yes—all. I know what grudge in the past lay at the root of your hatred; what temptation in the future led you to combine against her honour. I know——'

She broke in here, with a cry, so piteous and agonized, that it sent a shiver through both her hearers, steeled though they were against relenting.

'Not that,' she moaned, 'anything but that. Tell everything to Geoffrey—to Philip—to all the world. But, Maurice, you *won't* let him taunt me so, before your face. Ah, how *could* you tell him?'

For the moment the positions of accuser and accused were changed. Maurice felt himself the culprit: those plaintive tones smote upon his conscience as if he had been guilty of base betrayal of confidence. Instinctively his fingers closed upon what they held; the touch of those infamous letters brought back all Dering's firmness; he spoke quite steadily.

'You are right, in this at least. Paul shall not say one other word on that subject. I—but very few. I had hoped those wild fancies were dead long ago. Yet it might have been better you should have known sooner, that in India I pledged myself—hand, and heart, and soul —to one whom I love, not better, I think, than she loves me; who will, I hope, ere long be my darling wife.'

Late, very late, but fearfully complete. Ida's punishment had come at last.

False wife—false friend—double traitress; she was all that, and more; yet scarcely any human creature could have forborne from pitying her, as she drank the first bitter drops of retribution. With the death-cry of her wicked love and mad jealousy, mingled the voice of a mocking devil; murmuring that the shame and sin had all been incurred in vain. The piteous pleading vanished from her face, as it hardened like a white flint-stone.

' That woman's name?'

If you never heard Rachel whisper, I can give you no idea of the intonation with which those three words were spoken.

'Her name matters nothing,' Maurice said. 'And I would no more think of uttering it at such a time as this, than I would tell her one word that has passed here. By God's help, I will keep her clear, even from the knowledge of any sinful or shameful thing.'

Now, mark how it stood with Ida Luttrell. She knew

that she had fallen to the lowest depth in the estimation of
those who were privy to her guilt : she knew that, if she
escaped open dishonour in the sight of others who ought
to have been yet nearer and dearer to her, it could only be
at the price of weary dissimulation and endless invention
of pretexts : she knew that, if, after all the scheming, the
black secret oozed out, the last state would be worse than
the first, for even Geoffrey must, then, needs shrink from
her side, if he did not cast her utterly adrift : she knew,
too, that the Fiend's arch-juggle had been played over
again ; the sinner had sold herself for a shadowy bribe,
when the real treasure had been given long ago to another.
Yet—it was not remorse or shame that was tearing, now,
at her heart-strings.

She only thought of the broad deep gulf that had been
opened, that day, between herself and Maurice Dering—
never, while they lived, to be closed again : she would
have borne up stubbornly to the very end, if she had
not marked the reverent tenderness of his manner and
tone, when he spoke of the woman who had won his love.
There are limits—as the ancient tormentors could have
told—to mere human endurance, physical or moral : at
that last turn of the rack, Ida's gave way.

Her whole nature seemed suddenly transformed : her
eyes blazed out, with a wild fierce light ; her voice vibrated
like a chord struck when it is strained to breaking ; and
her slight frame trembled with passion, till the plumes of
her *aigrette* quivered again.

'You will not speak her name ? I will learn it, very
soon. Maurice Dering—do you know why ? You may
trample me under your feet, as you will—you may make
me a mark for all the world to scorn—and I will worship

you to my life's end. But the woman that you love—I *may* hate her, as I *do* hate—with all my heart, and soul, and strength. Whoever she may be—if you change and love another, it will be still the same. I will harm her if I can. And, now—before she can be yours—I pray that death and dishonour may overtake——'

Her utterance was so rapid, that Paul Chetwynde, who would have checked her, as soon as he recovered from his first astonishment, had not time to do so, before Ida stopped abruptly

And this is why she paused.

She saw a sudden horror sweep across Maurice Dering's face, as he stood fronting her, that she knew was not roused by her own wild, wicked words; his eyes were fixed too on some object behind her. Before she could turn, a voice—utterly strange to her—spoke, close to her shoulder.

'Ida—are you mad, or—am I?'

CHAPTER XXV

ANGINA.

Yes, the voice was utterly strange, not to Ida alone, but to Dering and Chetwynde. Yet all had heard it a thousand times, speaking kindly or cheerily ; and to one, it had been, very often, prodigal of tenderness. Nor was the change to be only momentary : the old round jovial ring of Geoffrey Luttrell's voice was dead for ever.

He was returning from shooting, when he saw his wife

and Chetwynde cross that open strip of paddock; very
naturally he followed them, and came up unperceived, just
in time to hear the last few words of Ida's terrible outbreak.

Hard and intrepid as she was, the unhappy woman fairly
quailed, when she turned and saw her husband's face. A
month of deadly sickness might have worked less ravages
there, than those few seconds of agony.

Geoffrey looked from one to the other of the group in a
stunned helpless way, when he found his first question un-
answered.

'Will no one tell me what this means? Is it my wife
that has just been speaking, to the oldest friend I have on
earth? Let me have the truth—and quickly. A very little
of this will drive me mad.'

Ida stood still and silent—looking white and scared, with
her left hand pressed tightly to her side. Dering's face
was buried in his hands; but Paul Chetwynde, with a vast
exertion of will, forced himself to answer.

'My poor Geoffrey! We meant to have spared you
this:—indeed—indeed, we did. But it is too late now.
You must know all. Your wife has been very guilty.'

Luttrell drew himself up—neither haughtily nor wrath-
fully; but with a firmness not devoid of dignity, such as
might become a priest in execution of his duty.

'Then I will hear it from herself,' he said. 'Whatever
her sin may have been, you are not her judges. She shall
ask God's pardon first—then mine. I trust that both may
be granted; but—however that may be—I know this: no
created being shall stand between me and mine.'

As he spoke, his arm went round the pale shrinking

woman at his side; and he drew her closer to his heart; fronting those other two with something like defiance.

A revulsion of feeling, strong as sudden, came over Ida Luttrell then. She did, at last, value aright the true, tender, honest heart on which she leant; the old unholy passion gave place, for a moment, to the fresh pure love, as a fiend may fly before an advancing angel; though he never knew it, poor Geoffrey did really attain what he had struggled for so long and patiently; his wife, as she lay then in his embrace, was his very—very own.

'My dear kind darling,' she murmured. 'I don't deserve——'

A choking catching of the breath; one quick convulsive clutch of the little hands that rested on her husband's arm; a fearful shudder through every nerve in her frame; a change in the delicate pale features—deadly significant, though not one was distorted; a dropping, not a drooping, of the long black eyelashes——and Ida Luttrell had done with all shame and sorrow and pain on this side of Eternity.

Infinite Mercy did allow to that misguided spirit one moment of contrition, bitter and sincere, before its flitting; but the lips through which the outbreak of guilty passion gushed so freely, were sealed with the first whisper of penitence.

It was known that Ida's father had died of heart-disease; but no one had suspected its existence in her; nor had any dangerous symptoms shown themselves, up to the day when she was stricken down.

For some seconds, not one of the three men realized the truth. It broke first on Geoffrey Luttrell: he closed his eyes like one blinded by a lightning-flash, and sank slowly on one knee—his arm still coiled round the slender waist —staring stupidly down into the quiet white face.

'Don't—don't—you see she's fainted?' he said in a broken grating whisper.

The piteous pleading of his upturned glance belied his words: they saw at once what horrible fear possessed him, and could not contradict it; but tried to render what aid they could in sorrowful silence.

All the three had looked on death before, in more shapes than one; they could not long keep up the semblance of doubt. Geoffrey had begun to shake and totter under his light burden, before Chetwynde drew it gently out of his arms, and laid it down on the grass, a little aside.

Then ensued, perhaps the most terrible spectacle that can meet us on this earth of ours—the sight of a strong man's agony.

Paul and Maurice had really had the best intentions from the first, and thought they had acted wisely if not well. Did they think so now—looking on the dead woman's lovely face, where the death-smile was just beginning to dawn; while Geoffrey grovelled at their feet, tearing up the grass by handfuls, and crying on God to save him from the madness of despair?

Look to the End. A sound maxim surely: pity it is so hard to practise. For how far into the Future may we hope to pierce with this dim sight of ours? As we walk onward, around us and before us it is cloudy all: if we stray ever so little from the path that led our forefathers aright, it is well, if over the End brood not the 'blackness of Darkness for ever.'

That awful paroxysm lasted not long: when Luttrell

raised his face it was almost calm, though traces of the late convulsions still were there. He drew himself over to where the corpse lay, and knelt by its side, signing to the other two to imitate his example. Not one word was spoken; the faces of all the three were buried in their hands, and the prayer of each was known only to his own conscience; but, during those few minutes, I think Paul Chetwynde's heart went up nearer to Heaven than it had done since his boyhood ended.

Geoffrey first uncovered his eyes; he stooped and pressed a long kiss on the cold forehead; and then rose steadily on his feet.

'Maurice Dering,' he said, in a deep hollow voice, 'we have been fast friends for years, and I would have doubted the Bible's promises, rather than your faith and honour. I do not doubt them now Yet—do you know what I have just been praying for, with all the strength that is left me? It is, that I may be enabled to forgive you, as a Christian should forgive. My heart may change—perhaps I am mad still—I cannot tell; but, if I feel hereafter as I feel now, our hands never meet again.'

Before Maurice could answer, Paul Chetwynde sprang to his feet.

'You *are* mad,' he said, sternly, 'and even that scarcely excuses you. Trust his faith? You might well do it; and so you will say when you hear all the truth—as you *shall* hear it, when you are fit to listen, whether you will or no. My lips are sealed in this presence,'—he pointed to the corpse—'but the living shall have justice sooner or later.'

Maurice Dering caught the speaker roughly by the wrist.

'How dare you speak so cruelly?' he said, his eyes
flashing angrily through the tears that had made them
very dim. 'Geoffrey, dear old Geoffrey! listen to me—
not to him. I may have been miserably misguided; but
towards you, and towards *her*, I am innocent; before God
—I am innocent. There never was word of mine that you
might not have listened to, and if I kept one secret back,
it was only for both your sakes. See—I can swear it: I
can swear it—thus.'

And, kneeling still, he laid his hand, firmly, on the dead
woman's heart.

If the spirit that had so lately departed could have returned, but for one brief second—if those pale lips could
have uttered but one brief syllable—would testimony to
Maurice's truth have been withheld? I trow not. But
the trial by Ordeal is long since obsolete; and, even while
that ancient superstition prevailed, though the corpse would
bleed afresh at the touch of the murderer, it was neutral
and obdurate when the innocent made appeal.

But Dering's words carried conviction even to Geoffrey
Luttrell's tortured heart and dizzy brain.

'I believe you,' he said, gloomily. 'And perhaps I
shall thank you, some day, when I see things clearer. I
can see nothing now, but—this.'

As he spoke, he knelt down again, and began to gather
up the body of his wife into his arms, so carefully and tenderly, that the hair was not dishevelled as it rested on his
shoulder, nor was a fold of the dress disarranged. The
others would have helped him; but Geoffrey motioned
them impatiently back, muttering—'No one shall touch
her, but me.' And so he trode slowly away, towards the
house; looking neither to the right nor to the left, nor

even into the pale face so close to his own; but always
straight forward.

Yet—once he did turn his head. Though he looked at
the two who were following, it was evident that he was
speaking to himself rather than to them.

'She said—"Darling," before she died.'

Those few words would have carried piteous significance,
to the merest stranger. They told, plainly enough, of long
waiting and watching for love that never came; of checks
and disappointments not the less keenly felt, because even
to itself the honest heart dissembled its own bitterness,
and never waxed weary, or sullen, or cold.   Only—at the
last, it drank in that one little drop of sympathetic tenderness with a terrible avidity, as castaways on tropical seas
catch at stray drops of rain.

Not another word was spoken till they reached the house;
entering it by a side-door, whence a staircase led straight
to the Luttrells' apartments: it so chanced that they met
no one by the way.   The distance was not long; and, in
life, it was a light burden that Geoffrey carried.   But there
is an awful weight in a soul-less body, that only those
who have supported one can comprehend.   When Chetwynde got in advance to open that side-door, he was not
surprised to see the big drops standing like beads on his
friend's forehead, while the veins stood out like strained
cordage.

But Luttrell moved on, still steadily, without halting,
till he had laid Ida gently down on her own couch;
smoothing the pillows and her dress with the same careful
tenderness, that he had shown when he lifted her from the
grass.

Then he straightened himself up, and gazed steadfastly

into the corpse's face. It seemed as if some magnetic attraction there had influence over his own vitality; for, in a few seconds, Geoffrey Luttrell's cheek grew ashen-white; and without an effort to save himself, he fell forward across his dead wife's feet, in a lengthened swoon.

Only Paul Chetwynde was then standing by. Maurice Dering had said nothing of his intentions to the others; but when they entered the house, he drew back, and strode gloomily away, passing out of the demesne unobserved. He returned to town that same evening, and it was many a day before his feet trod again the wood-paths of Marston Lisle.

CHAPTER XXVI.

DE PROFUNDIS.

On Philip Gascoigne's distress and Georgie's more demonstrative grief, it is not necessary to dwell. It is enough to say, that for Ida Luttrell was made more and bitterer moan than is allotted to many who go stainless, if not sinless, to their graves. For, of a truth, the influence of these model-matrons seems sometimes to terminate with a strange abruptness; the world that did them such reverence while living, honours their obsequies with little beyond decorous regret.

Geoffrey determined at once that his wife should be buried at Minstercombe, and that the funeral should be as private as possible. Chetwynde hesitated long before he asked to be allowed to attend it; but afterwards he was

glad he had done so; for Luttrell consented, gratefully.
He never seemed to connect Paul in any way with the
train of circumstances that had, in all human probability,
hastened his unhappy wife's death. Yet he had himself
insisted on full explanations, as soon as he was physically
able to listen, and all the miserable truth was before him
now. He bore it with wonderful fortitude: men of his
calibre, especially when natural power of character is
backed by strong principle and faith, are often never more
reliable than immediately after the one utter break-down
that only happens—not twice in a life-time.

That Geoffrey did not dissemble, or even attempt to
palliate to himself, the extent of his wife's meditated guilt,
is most certain; but, when his idol lay shattered, he would
neither himself trample on the fragments, nor allow others
to insult them. When Chetwynde—whose treatment of
moral maladies was always rather excisive—hinted that
Ida's sudden death was not deeply to be regretted, inasmuch as bitter misery to herself and others had so been
spared, Luttrell checked him so sternly, that Paul felt
quite contrite and humble for the moment, as if he had
ventured on unknown ground, where he had no concern;
which, indeed, was very much the state of the case.

The night before the funeral procession left Marston,
Geoffrey sent to beg Mrs Gascoigne to visit him in his
own rooms, where he had secluded himself since Ida's
death, seeing no one but Philip and Chetwynde.

Georgie was dreadfully shocked at the change in his
appearance. His face was haggard and drawn; yet it
was very grave and calm. Suffering had refined the
features, once so bluff and jovial, into a sort of solemn
dignity. She partly guessed the purpose for which she

had been summoned; for she had not yet been allowed to see her dead cousin. So, indeed, it turned out.

Geoffrey wrung her hand hard when she entered, and without quitting it, or uttering one word, led her into the inner room, where the corpse lay in its open coffin.

A great awe and fear came over Georgie Gascoigne—looking, then, for the first time on death—as she gazed down on the delicately-chiselled face—white as the soft lace around it—not much more still and composed than it had often been seen in life; only—what had been listless indifference, was now eternal peace.

Then, in that changed voice of his, Geoffrey spoke.

'You loved her, very dearly?'

He was answered by a deep sob, and by a pressure from the fingers that he held.

'And you thought that she loved *you*? I know you did, or you would never have trusted her so far——'

A flush swept over her pale tear-stained face, and he felt her tremble; but he went on, never heeding.

'Listen,—this is a secret to be kept even from your husband,—she never *did* love you: more than this, she hated you bitterly, and would have helped to do you deadly wrong. Never ask me, why: I could not tell you if I would; I have only strength enough to tell you this; and that strength was only given me after long, long prayer. Now—knowing all this—can you say, after me—"I forgive her, and I trust that God has forgiven her, with all my heart and soul?"'

Amongst Georgie's many faults bearing of malice certainly was not one. Besides, she really had loved her cousin well, after her own light-minded fashion, though she had begun somewhat to fear her of late: if the meditated wrong had been wrought out to tho uttermost, she could never have cherished rancour against the poor senseless clay. It was not doubt, but grief and surprise that kept her silent. But Geoffrey misinterpreted her hesitation.

' Remember—you were children together, and—she died so very young.'

His voice, hoarse and deep till now, softened strangely in its pleading.

Georgie Gascoigne wrested her fingers out of Luttrell's grasp, with a passionate energy.

' Do you think I am made of stone or steel ? ' she said, through her sobs. ' God knows how I loved her; and, if she hated me, she could not have been in her right mind. Ida—darling Ida—what had I ever done to deserve it ? I don't want to know what wrong you speak of. If I did know, I would still say—what I say now.' She repeated Luttrell's very words, low and reverently, as she would have repeated any other prayer; and then laid her lips, without shrinking from the cold, on the brow of the corpse.

A wintry gleam of satisfaction lighted up Geoffrey's worn face : he drew a long deep breath of relief, as he said—

' I pray that, in this world and in the next, you may have your reward for the comfort you have given me this night. Now, come. What I have further to say, shall not be said *here.*'

He closed the door carefully behind them, before he spoke again.

' I will be very brief, and deal with you as gently as I may. But, remember ; I speak now, not only as an old friend of your husband's, and a true friend of yours, but as

God's minister. I know my duties, if hitherto I have been
slack in discharging them. I know, that it behoves me
to let no means of salvation slip, though I find them in the
depth of my own desolation. This past year has laid upon
us all heavy burdens; upon some, almost more than we
can bear. I believe, that in the background of the darkest
sorrows some sin or shame is to be found. Do *you* not
think so? Let your conscience answer me. I need no
confession in words.'

Before he had finished speaking, Georgie had sunk to
her knees, her face buried in her clasped fingers; Geoffrey
could hardly catch the broken whisper—

'Ah, spare—spare me. I have repented—indeed I have;
and I have tried so hard to be better.'

He laid his hand on her bowed head, with a solemn tenderness.

'Do not fear,' he said. 'What am I that I should judge
or condemn you?—I, who every hour have to appeal to
Heaven's mercy; for repining is a sin like the rest. Yes,
I do believe that you have repented, and that you are
striving to make atonement. I absolve you of the past, so
far as I may. It is for the future I would warn. You have
opportunities of doing good, such as are given to few: you
will be held accountable for neglecting no less than for
misusing them. You have it in your power still to make
Philip very happy; and this you ought to do at any self-
sacrifice. I say nothing of Cecil, for you need no prompting to your duties there. Above all things, remember this.
Other women, born coquettes like yourself—forgive me, I
must needs speak plainly—may indulge their vanity without serious guilt; but when temptation to such folly besets
you, you will be worse than reckless, if you forget that,

once, only God's great mercy saved you from falling into a pit, at the bottom of which lay dishonour and death. Now, my first and last sermon to you is done ; and I have only to say " Farewell." I took you *in there* first; because I would not frighten you into saying those words, for which I shall bless you while I live.'

Again their hands met—this time in earnest kindness ; for, on both sides, there was gratitude ; and if they parted with heavy hearts, surely the burden of either was lighter than when they met.

The funeral procession reached Minstercombe late one night; and early the next morning the burial-rites were read, by her own husband, over Ida Luttrell. None of the tenantry received any intimation of the ceremony, and only a few old servants of the family, besides Chetwynde, were present. The latter had tried to dissuade his friend from performing the last duties himself; but Geoffrey was firm. He went through the service with wonderful composure ; but Paul remarked that he read it throughout in one even monotone, quite unlike his usual voice, as if he were afraid of lingering, or hesitating over particular passages.

When all was over, and the two friends were left alone in the church, they both stood silent for awhile, gazing earnestly on the broad marble slab that had just fallen into its place again above the last of the dead Luttrells. At last, Geoffrey spoke, in a voice hushed and low, as befitted the place and time.

' Paul—I am not mad, now. I believe I do justice to every one—to Maurice Dering above all. In what has passed, I *can* see, now, the hand of God—not of any man. But I want you to promise one thing, here, for him as well as for yourself. I have asked it of Philip already—it is,

that neither you nor he will ever speak of *her* to each
other, or to me.'

Paul gave the promise as simply as it was asked : then
he moved quietly away, leaving Luttrell quite alone. Geoffrey followed soon after ; but he shut himself up in his own
room, and Chetwynde saw him no more that day. Indeed,
the latter guessed that utter solitude was what his friend
most desired just then : so the next evening, without attempting pretexts or excuses, he departed. If he had
feared of the other's misunderstanding him, the long cordial pressure of Luttrell's hand would have reassured him.
They parted, perhaps faster friends than ever.

The manner of the interment caused no small talk in the
country-side : to say nothing of the haste, which many
considered indecorous, it was thought strange that the
widower should himself have performed the burial-rites :
vague rumours were floating about for some time afterwards, and, had it not been for Geoffrey's personal po-
pularity, it might have gone hard with the fair fame of
the dead. But all liked the parson of Minstercombe, even
if they revered him not ; so the rustic marvel-mongers had
mercy on him in his bereavement, and forbore from tam-
pering with his young wife's memory. Even that ancient
dame, whose dignity poor Ida once so mortally offended,
betrayed no exultation at seeing her prophecies of evil so
speedily fulfilled.

It may seem to many absurdly unnatural that a woman
holding Ida Luttrell's position in the social scale, should
have indulged in such deliberate malice, with so much certain risk, so little probable gain. She must have known
how infinitely faint was her chance of ever tempting Maurice to sin ; and—were it otherwise—how unlikely it was

that Georgie would in anywise interfere with her designs. But the self-deception of some of those wilful, passionate natures, even when joined to a keen, cool intellect, is one of the most marvellous of moral phenomena. Ida was possessed with the fixed idea, that her cousin had once stood betwixt herself and her heart's desire, and might do so again; so, exaggerating the chances of the past, no less than those of the future—she resolved to remove her rival from her path once and for ever.

Of a truth, destructiveness, without any apparent object, is somewhat hard to realize or comprehend. Yet, I have heard of an eminently respectable matron, against whom scandal never dared to whisper, who—finding by chance a poisoned shaft in her quiver—forbore not to send it straight to its mark, though the enemy whom she wished to dishonour could never harm any creature more; and, indeed, was even then waiting for death, that came within the week.

CHAPTER XXVII.

DARKEST OF ALL.

Has any one of us forgotten the evil Spring, when there swept over this country of ours a blast from the East—fatal to many households as the wind from the wilderness that smote the banqueting-hall in Uz—chilling to many hearts as the deadly Sarsar? Have we forgotten how, with each successive mail, the wrath and the horror grew wilder; till the sluggish Anglo-Saxon nature became, as it were, possessed by a devil, and through the length and breadth of the land—from Shetland to Scilly, from Cape Clear to the Nore—there went up one awful cry for vengeance ? I speak of the Spring, when the news of the Great Mutiny came home.

Chetwynde chanced to be at his club on the evening of the day when the first definite or credible tidings arrived. He and others were talking over what they had just heard, —still hardly realizing the possibility of such things being true,—when there came in a friend of Paul's, a high Government official, who, of all men, was likely to be possessed of the last and most accurate information.

Harry Thurlowe's jovial round face was graver and gloomier than any one there had ever seen it : he shook his head ominously, while he 'hoped that the reports were much exaggerated;' but seemed very loth to enter upon the subject, and evaded inquiries with more than diplomatic reserve. When he extricated himself at last from the anxious group, he took Chetwynde's arm, and drew him away; never speaking till they were in one of the card-rooms, which at that hour was quite deserted. Then said Thurlowe, clearing his throat, huskily——

'By G—d, Paul, it's all true ; and there's worse to come yet, I fear. What we do know is bad enough. This is why I wanted to speak to you, especially. You would do much for Maurice Dering, wouldn't you ?'

'I would do *anything*, only too readily,' Chetwynde answered : his tone was measured and calm as usual, but a sick, cold apprehension began to rise within him.

'Then you must break to him the heaviest news—if I have guessed rightly—that man can bring to man,' the other said. 'I heard all about his adventure with the

bear, and how he was nursed at Drummond's hunting-
bungalow. I heard, too, a vague rumour of his being
engaged to Alice Leslie. It's more than likely. I saw a
good deal of her while she was in England—she was always
with my nieces—I can't fancy anything more loveable.
Well, one of the places from which we have *certain* news,
is—Darrah. The mutineers made about their earliest on-
slaught there : the next morning not an European was left
alive in the cantonment : what devilries were done before
the massacre was complete, the Fiend only knows.'

There was a terrible pause for several seconds; then
Chetwynde—whose face was whiter than it had been when
he waited for Annesleigh's fire—hissed through his clenched teeth—

' You ask me to tell Maurice Dering *this?* '

' I do,' the other answered firmly. ' Because, in a case
like this, if one single pang can be lightened, or one ounce
taken off from the weight of the first shock, a man's best
friend ought not to shrink from his duty. You *can* do it,
too; I don't think I could. I'm not braver than my
neighbours ; yet, I believe, I'd sooner face a battery.'

Paul Chetwynde gathered himself together, with one of
those physical efforts that only faintly typify the exertion
of will going on within.

' You are thoroughly right, Thurlowe. I'd do it, if it
killed me. But we never know how weak we are till our
manhood is really tried. The time is fearfully short.
Maurice comes to town to-night. I'll go straight to his
rooms, and wait for him. I won't give my cowardice a
chance. Once there, I must speak.'

And Chetwynde did straightway as he said.

Few men in their lifetime are destined to pass such a

miserable hour, as that which elapsed before Dering's return. Paul was temperate, as a rule, beyond his fellows; he drank more brandy during those sixty minutes than he had ever done in the same number of hours. He drank, not to give unnatural strength to his nerve, but simply to drive back the feeling of bodily weakness that seemed to chill and sicken him. His heart throbbed, like a frightened girl's, as Maurice's quick, firm step, sounded on the stairs.

One glance at Chetwynde's face was enough for Dering. You remember he was quick at guessing its expression.

'In God's name, what has happened?' he said.

Paul came forward and laid his two hands on the other's shoulders, as if he himself stood in need of support: then —without a syllable of preparation—in a dull mechanical voice, like that of one answering a mesmerist's questions, he repeated Thurlowe's news, almost word for word; only, not hinting at the possibility of other outrage than death. Now this was as different from the fashion in which he had intended to discharge his wretched embassage as it is possible to conceive. In no way could the news have been broken more abruptly; yet, perhaps, it was best so. 'If our hope and happiness are to perish,' say most of us, 'let them die without long preamble before, or elaborate consolation after the blow.' True and natural were the words of the bereaved bride in that pitiful romance of 'Sir Peter Harpedon's Ending,' when the page faltered in his sorrowful message :—

> I pray you tell your tale;
> And go on speaking fast, and heed me not
> Whether I scream or fall.

Many years ago, when in Tyrolese forests it was war to

the knife between the keepers and marauders of the game
—when men, on either side, were slaughtered without a
word of warning—one of the former, going his rounds, saw
the torso of a notorious poacher rise slowly up, on the
opposite side of a broad ravine, till the whole figure stood
upright against the sky-line. The forester hesitated
awhile, simply because the distance was very long; then
he drew a steady bead on the centre of his enemy's chest.
The poacher never sprang at the shot; but opened his vest
slowly, and gazed, for a full minute, into his own bosom,
with a vacant wonder; then he fell down stone-dead.

After that same fashion did Maurice Dering bear himself, when those tidings struck him to the heart. He with-
drew his shoulder—not abruptly—from the pressure of
Chetwynde's hand, and, retreating backward a pace or
two, sate quietly down, gazing into the other's face with a
surprise too stupified for horror. That gaze lasted longer
than Paul could bear it; for the first time in his life, he
felt his nerve utterly failing him. He laid his hand again
on Dering's shoulder, and shook it almost roughly.

'Maurice—Maurice—don't stare so horribly; and—say
something; or I shall think we are both going mad.'

The other passed his tongue twice or thrice over his
lips, that seemed to have grown suddenly parched and
black.

'Did—did they kill the women—*first?*'—he said, in a
hoarse whisper.

Paul shivered, as he answered—

'I trust in God, it was so; but, no one knows.'

(And no one ever did know. They heard in after days
how hard old Patrick Drummond had died; like one of his
own wild-boars, fighting and goring to the last: but round

T 2

the agony of sweet Alice Leslie and her mother—perhaps in mercy—was drawn a cloud of uncertainty, never lifted in this world.)

'Because,' Maurice went on, still in the same unnatural whisper, 'that dying woman, in her curse, spoke of dishonour as well as death. She's satisfied now, or she's hard to please.' He broke into a sort of ghastly laugh, worse to hear than any groan.

'For God's sake don't think of such things at this moment,' the other interrupted. 'I cannot comfort you, or even tell you not to despair; but keep your senses if you can: there's work—and bitter hard work—before you yet.'

Dering's eyes were fixed no longer in that vacant glazed stare; yet he hardly seemed to catch the meaning of Chetwynde's words, and began muttering to himself like one in a reverie.

'Her dream—yes, now I understand her dream: the pit, and the devils below, and the devil above who thrust her down. No wonder she was frightened: and I left her to her fate—such a fate—to come back and flatter that old man for his money. Ah, my darling! my darling!—if I had only been there to save you, or slay you with my own hand, and follow you quickly We should have felt no pain—then. And now—what does it matter if my brain should turn? Is there anything left to live for?'

'Nothing left to live for?' a deep voice said in his ear. 'Then you do not care for vengeance? If I had your sword-arm to strike with, I would have a life for every hair in that sweet innocent's head; though, I swear, I believe she died stainless. The God that she worshipped would never have looked on such horrors as you fear, and held

His hand. I don't speak canonically, because I speak as I feel; but even Geoffrey would hardly preach forgiveness of injuries here.'

Now if Chetwynde had been thrice as good a Christian as he was ever likely to be, it is probable he would have spoken in much the same strain, though more guardedly. His first object was to rouse Maurice from his stupor, at any cost ; and he knew that certain diseases, of mind and body, can only be touched by small doses of dangerous poisons. The dose worked, now at all events, effectually. When Dering rose to his feet, that vague, vacant look had left his face; it was possessed by an expression—that became its habitual one in the after-time,—an expression, neither savage nor moody, nor even melancholy, but darkly determined, as of a man who, through all the changes and chances of life, keeps a single purpose before him, unswervingly.

'You are right,' he said ; 'we shall have time enough to make our moan when our work is done. Forgiveness of injuries ? Why, if all the angels of Heaven—save one— stood in my way and warned, I would walk on straight to my revenge. Look here, Paul,—I'm not a natural philosopher, and I can't explain these things. I only know that I'm as much changed within the last few minutes as if I had been born over again. I've always tried to do my best, for others not less than myself ; I never hurt a living creature wilfully, till I shot that poor devil, who liked me after all. You know how that came off. Perhaps I deserved to be punished for it; but—not like this. I'll go my own way, now, and fight for my own hand. Do you think I am raving, still ? Feel my pulse, it's as steady as your own, I dare swear.'

As steady?   Ay, steadier far than was Chetwynde's
that night, or many a night after; for, indeed, all these repeated calamities, falling upon those very dear to him, told
heavily upon Paul's organization.   The very fact of his
being bound to look on as a passive spectator, was inexpressibly trying.   Instead of the cold composure that had
been its habitual expression, people began to remark a
restless dissatisfaction and anxiety on his face: there were
many comments thereon, and his friends or acquaintances
shook their heads ominously, hinting that 'Chetwynde
had certainly been speculating, and had got into difficulties.'   So, in truth, he had; but the speculations and
the difficulties were not such as the world ever gave him
credit for.

Paul himself never could remember what were the last
words that passed that night between himself and Dering.
He had a vague recollection of their having spoken with
tolerable calmness of Maurice's immediate departure.   But,
as he walked homewards, a certain relief mingled with intense depression: it was very much the feeling of a man
who has lost a ruinous stake, and paid it on the spot.   For,
as has been aforesaid, Paul's cynicism would not stand
wear and tear; it was apt to break down just at those critical seasons when it would have been useful, if not creditable, to its possessor.

Dering did not lose an hour in making the necessary arrangements for departure.   These were easily concluded;
for the War Office is not unaccommodating when a man
wishes to rejoin his regiment, in the most peaceful times.
Except when forced to go out on business, he never left
his rooms till after nightfall, when he would walk for an
hour or so with Chetwynde.   Even to Paul he would not

speak again about the past: their talk was all of the immediate future : no other of Maurice's friends saw him face to face.

That was a time rife with terrible reports and rumours ; some of them utterly groundless, all more or less vague. Somehow or another it began to be whispered about— though no one could give his authority—that Dering was among the chief of those who had awful wrongs to avenge. Amidst all the bustle of their own preparations, when the starting of the reinforcements was a question of hours, some of his old comrades found time to compassionate Maurice, and to speculate as to how he would bear himself in the coming struggle.

' You mark me, now,' one man said, who knew him well. ' We're none of us going out in an amiable frame of mind ; but, when Maurice gets well among 'em, I'll back him to do more damage than any other three. Pluck has got nothing to do with it. I've watched his eye often enough ; if there's not a wicked devil under all that *bonhommie* of his, I'm very much mistaken. It's not for nothing he's shut himself up ever since the news came in. Before many months are over, you'll see if in Pandy-killing he don't beat all he has done among the big game.'

And this—more elegantly expressed—was also the opinion of the chiefest club-oracles at The Bellona.

Three days before he started, Maurice Dering went down to Marston Lisle. Though he had been there on one fatal evening, you will remember that he had not seen the Gascoignes since the night before the duel. This time he only stayed a few hours ; but they were very painful ones. All pretext for reticence was, unhappily, over now ; so Philip told his wife of the terrible woe that had stricken

Dering, as soon as he himself heard of it. It would be difficult to say, which of the two was the most grieved and horrified. Yet, like Chetwynde, they were wise enough to abstain from set forms of consolation. Indeed, had either been so tempted, the first glance into Maurice's face would have checked the meditated condolence. It wore the same dark, determined look of which I have already spoken; the lips, once so mobile in mirth, rarely now unbraced themselves; the eyes, that used to flash and glitter so readily, were fixed in a strange earnestness, as if they were gazing intently on some object in the far distance.

The farewells were very trying. Both Philip and Georgie were aware that Maurice was going into the front of the battle, where he would be the last to spare himself. Dering did not seem to reckon on the possibility of his life being cut short before he had finished what was appointed for him to do; but he did not dissemble from his friends, that it would probably be long before they saw his face again.

During the few minutes that he spent alone with Gascoigne, Maurice made no allusion to his loss; neither had Philip courage to do so. Had it been a bereavement such as is common to man, it is probable that neither would have so avoided the subject; about this one there was a black, indefinite horror which set it beyond the pale of ordinary human sorrows. They spoke rather of their old friendship, which—though not by free-will of either— seemed to both very near an ending. For the health of the one was so precarious—though no change for the worse had been perceptible of late—the risks that the other was about to incur so heavy, that the chances against their meeting again in this life were more than even.

' It ought to have brought us better luck,' Philip said at last, pensively. 'I don't suppose four men have often lived so much and so long together, as you and I and Paul and Geoffrey, without a sullen look or sharp word passing among them. We did have some pleasant times, too, before these dark days came upon us. Is it not strange that, a year ago, three of us could not have seen one little white cloud in the sky; and now, over us all, it is bitter black and stormy? Yes, over all; for, I believe Paul's skeleton is as ghastly as any of ours, and of far more ancient date. He never told you of it? No: I thought not: he never would have told me, if he had not wished to make me use his help unscrupulously whenever I needed it. I said then, that he was more to be pitied than myself: I say now, that my burden is the lightest of all.'

' All are heavy enough, it seems to me,' the other answered, ' only you carry yours more easily. Yes—our boat was fairly manned, as you say, and we pulled well together; but I'm fatalist enough, *now*, to be certain that she never could have escaped wreck. I wonder who was the Jonah? Myself, I do believe; for of late there's a curse or a blight on all my good intentions; they crop up as different as possible from the seed I meant to sow. Whenever I try to keep any one out of a pit, I only fall headlong in myself. I'm nearly weary of it all.'

It was Maurice Dering who was speaking; outwardly— the same Maurice who, a few months ago, came back from the East, with so much cordial cheeriness about him, that, in his presence, neither Philip nor Philip's familiars could despond. The change was almost as terrible as that of which the old Norse legend tells, when the corpse of slain Asmundur rose up possessed by a fiend.

Philip Gascoigne's thin white fingers closed round the other's wrist, in remonstrance and pleading.

'Ah, Maurice, our last words must needs be dreary; but don't let them be desperate or unjust. For you *are* unjust, not to yourself only, but to me and mine. Have you forgotten what we owe you? Don't you know that my little Cecil has been taught to pray for you, ever since he could say " Our Father " plainly? Would he ever have been born, but for you? Surely that life saved, may stand against the life taken in your rashness. I don't attempt to excuse you about poor Annesleigh; simply because I can't at all comprehend it. I think you must have been out of your senses at the time; and I know you have since repented bitterly.'

Philip spoke in utter simplicity, without the faintest glimmering of the truth, and without an idea of entrapping Dering into an avowal. Very differently would he have spoken, had he guessed that the debt, since he set it down, had been more than doubled—that Maurice had risked less to save Georgie's life, than he risked to save her honour.

Many men would have been tempted to confess all, if it were only to leave no false impressions on an old friend's mind when they were parting, most likely for ever. But Maurice felt no such impulse; he held it better to leave everything as it then stood : it seemed to him that, here in England, he had no further concern with the affairs of friend or foe. Only there was a quaint, conscious look on his face as he answered, that did not quite escape Philip.

'Don't let us talk about debts, or gratitude, or I shall begin to think that I have never been half thankful enough for the hundreds of pleasant hours that I have spent at

Marston. The truth is, that betwoen *us*, thanks are absurd formalities. If anything could make me feel less dreary, it would be the certainty that never a word has passed between us that had better have been left unsaid; and that neither you nor I have once had a thought of the other, that we need repent of, now. There—I hear your wife's step: she is to go with me while I say "good-bye" to The Moor. Then I shall just have time, to say it to you all; and—you must let me go.'

A thick fall of black lace shaded all the upper part of Mrs Gascoigne's face, but the traces of weeping were very plain to discern; and as she walked to the stables by Dering's side, the heavy drops still kept brimming over. Neither spoke till they came to the loose-box where The Moor was standing. Maurice had hunted him all through the winter, and the horse had gone in his usual brilliant form; but directly the season was over, he returned to his quarters at Marston; and there he stood, just the same picture of a weight-carrier as ever—not a hair the worse for four months' hard work, and not looking a day older than when he beat Lady Agatha for the Gold Cup at Walmington. Georgie had only spoken the truth when she wrote—'He likes me much the best, now;' for though the good horse came to Maurice when he was called, his broad, bright eye turned first to the fairer face, and his nostrils sought the caress of the softer hand.

Maurice smiled, more sadly than bitterly.

'So you really have changed service, old man?' he said. 'That's just as it should be; for I was going to transfer it. Georgie' (he had addressed her thus more than once since his return, but always in Philip's presence), 'it's rather late in the day to ask you to take The Moor

for your own.   But you won't mind that.   He's as steady
as a church, and I hope will carry you pleasantly and
safely for many, many years; though he looks too much
for you.   Will you have him?'

Even in that dreary moment, the horse-language came
naturally to Dering's lips; but it did not sound absurd or
inconsistent to his hearer.   Georgie never was farther
from mirth than when she murmured her half-intelligible
thanks.

Dering had passed his arm round the big brown neck
that was curved over his shoulder, and was leaning his
cheek against it, apparently musing.   Indeed, a train of
thought, strangely connected, though infinitely rapid, possessed him then.

He saw Georgie, as he saw her for the very first time,
when, as she swept down The Row at a slinging canter,
his eyes, among many others, followed, admiringly, the
lithe, graceful figure, and the bright hair glinting back the
sun-rays like burnished metal.   He saw her as she had
ridden by his side—slowly, so slowly—through the green
lanes leading to the gate-tower of Harlestone, when the
net of her witcheries so nearly trapped him; he saw her,
white and distraught with terror, as she was when The
Moor's last effort brought him alongside, not a second too
soon : he saw her, as she had looked up at him through
her tears, just after he had clasped the marriage-gift upon
her arm, when all real peril was over, and a fast friendship
was signed and sealed.

He thought of her in all these phases, without the quickening of a pulse or the thrilling of a nerve, just as a man
in the extremity of old age may look upon the loves and
wars of his hot youth.   Nevertheless, the lines of Dering's

face did surely soften; though Georgie could only catch a partial glimpse of it, she guessed intuitively at the change in his mood. It emboldened her to draw nearer, and lay a little trembling hand on his shoulder.

'If you would only let me pity you!' she whispered. 'I would have loved her so dearly!'

Then one of those strange revulsions of feeling, that puzzle acutest physiologists, came over Dering. Though there never had been a shadow of rivalry between those two, perhaps, at any other time, Georgie Gascoigne was the last person alive that Maurice would have allowed to allude to Alice Leslie. But now those sweet, plaintive tones went straight to his heart—soothing while they saddened inexpressibly : it seemed as if no lips were worthier than *hers*, to make moan over his dead darling. One sob after another shook his stalwart frame from neck to heel; and, as he turned his head yet more aside, Georgie saw the big drops stealing through his locked fingers. She felt almost frightened at what she had done—indeed, the tears of manhood, seen for the first time, are to womanhood very terrible—and drew back into the outer stable. There she sat down on a low bench, and herself gave way to the weeping that she had hitherto partially controlled.

In a little while, a hand was laid softly on her shoulder : she looked up into a face once more hard and stern. I would I could say, that that brief yielding to natural emotion had wrought in Dering's heart for lasting good. It was not so : neither to man nor woman was it given, ever again to see his eyes grow moist, in tenderness, or compassion, or sorrow. Ah me! As with the winter without, so it is with the winter within : the second frost always lasts the longest. Maurice spoke quite calmly

'I am not in the least ashamed that you have seen my weakness—if it be a weakness. Only I cannot speak of *her*, even to you, who are so good and kind. But I am not the less grateful: you will remember that, whenever you think of me? We shall none of us quite forget, I know. If I never come back, you'll show Cecil over our racing-ground in The Chase sometimes, and tell him I'd have taught him to ride, if everything had not gone wrong. I think Philip is getting stronger; and I do believe there are bright days in store for all three of you— to say nothing of dear Aunt Nellie. I would say—"God grant it." But—I dare not: my good wishes of late have been fearfully like witches' prayers. Now, let us go back: I fear I have overstayed my time.'

The last farewells were very brief, as all such should be. Yet, though there was little demonstrative grief, and no wailing aloud, few sadder groups could have been found than the one gathered that afternoon on the steps of Marston Lisle. Only one circumstance deserves to be recorded.

Dering had said very affectionate adieus to Aunt Nellie, who was quite as fond of him as if he had been her blood-relation; and came to where Mrs Gascoigne stood with her boy by her side. Maurice clasped both her hands, warmly: while he held them, she looked up at him, with the soft bright eyes, that had not meant coquettish mischief for many a day, and said—'Kiss me—once, before you go.'

He stooped, and his lips just brushed the smooth white forehead: never, I think, was caress asked for or bestowed in purer simplicity, since gorse began to bloom.

The heir of Marston Lisle, though a very important per-

sonage in his own family circle, has scarcely been alluded
to in these pages. He had inherited the beauty of both
his parents in about equal shares; it was no wonder they
were so proud of him. Cecil was not at all afraid of swine,
or kine, or turkeys, or sudden noises, or other terrors to
which infancy is liable; but he was decidedly shy, and
slow in overcoming his dread of strangers. Of his special
favourites he was curiously fond. Chief amongst these
stood Maurice Dering. The child had seen comparatively
little of him; but had taken to him from the very first, and
would sit on his knee for hours, listening to stories about
bears and tigers—the more delightful because scarcely half
comprehended: he would be quite contented, too, when
his friend was talking to others; finding, apparently, sufficient amusement in winding his tiny soft hands in and
out of the profuse chestnut beard against which his own
curls were resting.

Cecil had watched the leave-taking with a sorrowful
wonder in his great dark eyes: he could understand every
one being sorry at the departure of his favourite; but why
every one was more sorry *this* time, he could not understand. The caress bestowed upon his mother puzzled him
most of all. *That* was clearly out of the ordinary run of
adieus, and contrary to all precedents: possibly, across his
infantine mind, there shot some vague idea of indecorum.
At any rate he deemed it time to come to the front, and
claim his share of the good things that were going: he
pulled his mother's dress, and signified, in his baby-
language, rather an imperious desire to be embraced immediately.

Maurice caught up the child in his strong arms, and
gazed for a second or two earnestly into the face, almost

too refined already in its delicate beauty; then he drew Cecil slowly towards him. But, as the latter stretched out his slender arms to clasp his friend's neck, the others saw Dering shiver all over as if a sudden chill had struck him: he thrust the child back, before the little rosebud-mouth touched his own; and set him down almost abruptly, muttering—

'No—not as I am. It would be cruel—he would never thrive.'

As if he could not trust himself farther, Maurice wrung Gascoigne's hand once—hard—as he passed him, and, springing into the cart that was waiting, drove hastily away.

Poor Cecil stood for a minute transfixed with wonder and grief: then he broke out into lamentation loud and long. So Maurice Dering departed from Marston Lisle with the sound of wailing in his ears, though that wailing was but a child's; ay, and the first sweep of the road brought him full in sight of that shrubbery, where a few months agone the fair white corpse pressed down the autumn leaves.

Does any one *quite* disbelieve in omens?

In after days,—as they heard with a shudder of the terrible deeds of semi-judicial vengeance that made Dering's name a by-word even in that bloody time,—Cecil's parents guessed why he had forborne to set his lips on their child's innocent brow, and did the unhappy man justice in their hearts.

CHAPTER XXVIII.

NO QUARTER.

ALL that winter through, Geoffrey Luttrell had shut himself up at Minstercombe. Though no direct explanation had passed between them, Dering knew that his friend held him entirely blameless in the matter of Ida, and several letters had been exchanged in the old spirit of kindliness. So he was not surprised, on his return from Marston, at finding a note to say that Geoffrey was in town, and would c ll early on the following morning: indeed, Maurice would have been bitterly disappointed if he had gone away without one last sight of that honest face.

There was no shadow of distrust or reproach between them, now; nevertheless, the meeting of those men was somewhat strange. Death brought them together, as death had parted them; only, this time, the fair corpse lay—not at their feet, but a thousand leagues away.

As Geoffrey held Maurice's hand, and gazed wistfully into his eyes, he felt his own grief grow faint and dim in presence of a more awful sorrow : his voice shook and faltered as he said, below his breath——

' I guessed it had gone hard with you, but—not so hard as this.'

Any outward evidence of misery he was prepared to meet; it was the set dark look of the worn face that shocked Luttrell so painfully : he thought the wildness of agony would have been better than that. He felt it would be almost a mockery, to talk of resignation or submission

U

here. Yet he was brave in his vocation, as in all things
else : he did try to speak, as his conscience commanded ;
though the sentences were not very coherent or clear.

Dering did not interrupt, but listened absently and indifferently ; as a man will do whose mind is thoroughly
made up, and does not think it worth while to discuss the
question : it was evident that the words affected him very
much as if they had been uttered from the pulpit. The
poor parson's heart sank within him, as he felt that his
simple theology was nearly exhausted, without one foot of
ground gained.

'You are right, I am sure,' Dering said at last. 'Only
you might as well be talking in an unknown tongue, as far
as my comprehending you goes. I suppose it is a question
of intellect ; and mine is very dull of late.'

'It is *not* a question of intellect,' the other retorted,
eagerly. 'It is a question of faith. Cannot you see that
our only safeguard, in this world, against despairing infidelity is, to accept *all* Divine decrees without questioning
or shifting them ? If we cannot bring ourselves to believe
—bitterly hard as it may be—that all blows dealt by His
hand are dealt in mercy, we are not far from the state of
the lost.'

Dering rose up upon his feet, and confronted the other,
with an evil light in his eyes.

'Look here,' he said, hoarsely. 'If you want me to
listen to you, you had better drop that word " mercy."
You may go too far in your special pleading, though your
case be ever so good and strong. I'm not an infidel, and
I don't want to become a blasphemer : nor do I dispute
the Creator's right to work His will with His own crea-

tures. You may say the Great Plague was sent in "mercy" if you choose, and I won't contradict you ; but I will—if you say it was in "mercy" that my innocent darling was given up to those unchained devils.'

He gnashed his teeth as he spoke, and his moustache grew white and wet with foam. Geoffrey frowned, though there was no anger on his sad face.

' I cannot hear such words without rebuking them. I must seem to speak hardly and harshly, when, God knows, I mean far otherwise. Have you not heard that there are such things as chastisements and expiations on this side of the grave ? Can you say, that you have incurred none of these ?'

Maurice bent his head, half assentingly, half humbly.

' I have thought of that,' he answered—' thought of it many times, since I held up Annesleigh's head, while he was dying. But I reckoned that the punishment of the blood-shedder would have fallen upon me. What harm had *she* done ?'

That other voice came in—deep and slow and solemn, as a funeral-bell tolling.

' Only to the man after His own heart did God give the choice of atonement. What harm had those little children done, who were stoned to death in the Valley of Achan ?'

Though the dark hour was heavy on Maurice Dering, those words impressed him with awe, real, albeit momentary.

He felt that it was the Truth he heard, however hard to understand ; though fresh pangs shot through his rankling wound, he knew that the priest was bound to use cautery, where the friend would fain have poured in balm.

'Have it your own way,' he said, rather wearily; 'at least for the present. What is it you would have me do?'

Quick and stern was Luttrell's answer.

'I would have you bear yourself like a Christian man, who had lost all he held dearest; not like a wild beast that has lost its young. Strike, as starkly as you please, in the front of the battle; I don't ask you to give quarter there; for I am of the same flesh and blood as you. But I do ask you, not to make duty a mere cloak for private revenge; I ask you not to slay the innocent with the guilty; not to turn slaughter into massacre. Do I ask too much? The lesson you have had already might teach you not to forget, again, the old text, "Vengeance is mine!"'

Dering, still standing, laid his clenched hand upon the table before him, with no apparent violence; yet you might have seen the veins and sinews starting out, one by one.

The honest parson's heart sank within him; he read the deadly meaning of the desperate face aright, and knew that warning and pleading, now, would be equally vain.

'I quite understand you,' Maurice said, in a slow, suppressed voice. 'You think I ought to temper justice with mercy, and show discrimination in punishment, and be generous in victory, and—all the rest of it. My dear good Geoffrey! Don't you see you are speaking, after your own light, to a blinded man? Once more, I do not deny the Almighty's right to deal with His creatures after His pleasure—to save or to destroy. He may make me powerless at any instant to harm a worm. I know that. But I know something else, too. If one mutineer, who could have been within a hundred miles of Darrah, on that accursed day, when once fairly within my arm's length or in my power, takes his life away with him, why—your theology is all astray ; for the age of miracles is not past.

Luttrell rose in his turn; feeling more miserably despondent than he had done since the night of Ida's funeral.

'Don't say another word. You have said enough already to make me wish I had written "Farewell" instead of speaking it. Poor Maurice—for I do pity you with my whole heart—what you have suffered is bad enough, but what you will suffer is worse still. Where will you find help, like that which you are wilfully casting away? I can do no more. As you are now, I dare not even ask God to bless you; but I *can* ask Him to turn and save you, and to forgive you, too. You will never be forgotten, while I have strength to pray. You will be sorry, some day, when you remember how your last words grieved me; for I never vexed you knowingly in my life; and never spoke sharply—but once, when my senses were gone. Yet I think, we surely shall meet again : it seems to me that both you and I have much work to do before we die.'

The two strong hands were knit together for a full minute, in an honest grip, that was worth a dozen protestations or promises : and truer friends never parted on earth, though just now the horror of darkness brooded over one—if not both—of their souls.

It was from Luttrell that Chetwynde first heard of this interview, for Maurice scarcely alluded to it, beyond remarking, that 'it was very good of Geoff. to come all that way to say good-bye.' The parson did not go much into details; and he was the less disposed to do so, when he saw that Paul's sympathies were enlisted already—not on his side.

In that same week Maurice paid a parting visit to his

god-father above-mentioned, in obedience to a very press-
ing summons. The old man was arbitrary and capricious
both by nature and habit, but neither hard nor cold-
hearted: he was dreadfully shocked at hearing of the fearful termination of all the matrimonial schemes that he discussed with his *protégé*; and glanced up at his god-son
when the latter came in, nervously—almost timidly; as if
he feared, that he might in some way be held accountable
for what had happened.

But, changed as Maurice was, he had not yet become
unjust or ungrateful; he remembered that Mr Grimstone
had acted considerately enough throughout, and had not
exacted more deference than he could fairly claim: so the
first greetings, though melancholy of course, were not less
kindly than usual.

After awhile the old man began to press Maurice to defer, if only for a little, his return to India; pleading, as
before, his own failing health, and growing incapacity to
look after his affairs.

'Look here, Maurice,'—he said, at last—'here's my will:
I shall never alter it now. If you read it, you'll see you
really ought to stay and help me: I shan't trouble you
many months—or weeks—longer. You are only taking
care of your own: you are my sole heir.'

The words were probably meant rather in rough consolation, than as a bribe; for, though hardly a miser, Mr
Grimstone had all his life long been wont to consider golden
salve an infallible remedy for all ills of body or mind. But
the kindness, if so it were intended, was clumsily offered
—unhappily timed. Maurice frowned darkly.

'I sail on Tuesday next,' he said. 'If it were to settle
the fortunes of England instead of yours, I would not stay

another hour. As for your health—I sincerely hope it is
better than you fancy, and that you will enjoy your riches
for years to come yet. I pray you do not think of me in
disposing of them. I have enough already to last me for
my life ; and, somehow, I feel as if I could no more touch
your money than if there were blood on it. Yes—I know :
it wasn't your fault, any more than it was poor Patrick
Drummond's. But if *he* had not told me it was my duty
to come home and consult *you*, I should have been thousands of miles nearer to my darling's murderers, now, if I
had not been near enough to die with her. Please don't
say another word; my temper's not what it used to be ;
but I've not forgotten yet, that you were always kind to
my father and to me. Let us part in peace.'

The dark resolute expression of Maurice's face, and his
harsh, stern tones, fairly disconcerted, if they did not alarm,
Mr Grimstone, in whose austere presence very few had
permitted themselves to indulge in violence, or even emotion. He was rather relieved when, after a few more words
of ordinary leave-taking, the door closed behind his god-
son : yet he looked after him wistfully.

'Poor boy, poor boy !' he muttered. ' I'm afraid his
brain is rather turned. I don't wonder—though I never
was in love myself—if she was like her picture. I wish he
had left it with me : I daren't ask him for it now Well
—well ; I suppose I shall have to die alone. It's hard :
but I sha'n't alter my will, for all that.'

Nor did he.

Chetwynde accompanied Dering to Southampton, and
saw him on board. They had little opportunity for confidential talk on the journey down, for three of Maurice's
comrades were in the same carriage; neither, perhaps, did

they desire it. Paul, as you know, was always taciturn, and Maurice, of late, rarely spoke unnecessarily. The deck of a Peninsular and Oriental steamer on the point of starting is never a very exhilarating scene. Till I myself witnessed it, I did not believe that so much quiet weeping could be done, in the midst of such a scramble, and bustle and uproar. On the present occasion the sight was unusually melancholy; for all those who stayed behind knew right well, what dark perils beyond the sea awaited the outward-bound. They would have to meet fiercer enemies, now, than sunstrokes and jungle-fevers.

The 'Tigris' was on the point of getting under way, and the first warning-bell had rung, when Chetwynde and Dering drew a little aside out of the turmoil, to say the last words. You must be nearly weary of all these leave-takings; but this one was briefest of all: nor on either side was there a trace of emotion: that was all past and done.

'I wonder how many years it will be before you care to see England again?' Chetwynde remarked. 'I dare say I shall get tired of it before you dream of coming back. When those troubles are over, if Philip keeps well—he's stronger: don't you think so?—I've a great mind to come out and see you.'

'It would be worth your while,' Dering answered, just as calmly. 'Though, when these troubles are over, India will be a very different place from what it has been. I shall look forward to it, all the same. Remember—we've only a few minutes more. I shall write to no one but you; and that, very seldom. You may be as liberal as you like with your letters, on that understanding. I'm glad you're going to stay at home, to look after Philip. Paul—perhaps I may not have another chance of telling you—I do trust you, so thoroughly !'

A faint red spot rose on Chetwynde's pale cheek ; he bit his lip, half angrily.

'Trust me ? It's very good of you to say so, thus late in the day. I've got you into one or two bad scrapes, and never helped you out of one that I remember. And I'm always just out of the line of fire, myself. I swear, I've felt at times shamefully Mazzinian. I can't charge myself with deliberate shirking ; but it comes to much the same thing, now, as if I had been both selfish and cowardly. It don't bear thinking of, I can tell you ; and it won't be better when you're away.'

Maurice looked earnestly into the speaker's face ; and, for an instant, a flash of the old frank kindliness lighted up his own, and his eyes sparkled once more.

'Hark, now, Paul,' he said, 'you'll keep your own judgment, of course, as you always do ; but take mine before I go. I don't like you better, that I know of, than either Philip, or poor, good Geoff. But we've been thrown more together, somehow. Besides, I've always felt we could not be weighed in the same scale as those other two : it might go hard with us if we were. Well—as to all that we are liable for, jointly and severally, I say just this. Whether we acted rightly or wrongly, does not seem as clear to me now, as when my conscience used to speak out plainly : but I know, we meant honestly. I know something more : in the same strait, we'd do the same things over again.'

The second warning-bell cut short the rest of their adieus. Five minutes later, Chetwynde was straining his eyes to distinguish the familiar features among the crowd of reverted faces that lined the gangway. No wonder that he failed; for they were not there. Maurice Dering was standing quite aloof from his comrades; and, amongst all those who went forth to 'smite and spare not,' his eyes alone, at the very moment of departure, were bent *forward* with an eager, hungry gaze.

CHAPTER XXIX.

REQUIESCANT

In India once more.

This time, you look on a broad, sandy plain, seamed with dry water-courses; with patches of cultivation here and there—all neglected, now; for the tillers of the soil have fled far away from the wrath to come, or are busy elsewhere in bloodier work. Everywhere there are traces of battle or slaughter—rather of the last than the first; for there are not many British uniforms among the tawny corpses that lie strewn about, singly or in groups, beginning to blacken already under the pitiless sun. In truth, a desultory fight became a hot pursuit an hour ago; the quick, dropping musketry begins to be concentrated into something like file-firing in line, about half a league ahead; that is where the river runs, beyond which the Mutineers may find safety for to-day. No wonder they strive so madly to reach the farther shore; for every minute comes a broader flash and a rounder ring; and we know that, in spite of rough ground and ditches like small nullahs, the horse-gunners have thundered to the front, and that their grape is even now lashing up the water into crimson foam.

But with the main scene of slaughter we have nought to do. Turn aside to that clump of forest trees, a full mile to the right. In the centre of this is a tank, and one of those huge masses of nondescript masonry—half temple, half tomb—under which the Rajahs of old times loved to lay their bones. All round the clump is a *cordon* of cavalry—it is small and easily surrounded—too close for a single fugitive to slip through; the remainder of the squadron is dismounted, under the trees immediately round the building.

The lower part of it somewhat resembles a crypt above ground : there are the same low, solid arches and narrow apertures that admit more air than light. From within there comes a confused murmur, sometimes swelling into loud discordance, such as may be heard in any crowd agitated by wrath, or fear, or bewilderment.

Ten score or more of Sepoys and Sowars are penned up within that narrow place of refuge; and corpses, scattered far back on the track, show that many fled not fast enough to escape the sabres led on by Maurice Dering.

Not a shot has been exchanged since the last of the fugitives plunged through the low, dark arch of entrance : almost all had cast their firelocks away in the wild terror of their flight; and such as had still weapons and cartridges left, never dreamt of uselessly irritating their dreadful enemy.

For Dering's name was up already amongst the mutineers : not only did they impute to him supernatural activity in pursuit, and a blood-thirstiness exceeding their own ; but they also gave him credit for some charm that made him bullet-proof. The Rohillas had just the same superstition about the famous Brigadier, who for years was the terror of their frontier.

So, after a few minutes of vague uproar within, a soiled white turban-cloth, flecked here and there with dusky red stains, fluttered out of one of the narrow window slits; and then came forth a cry from many parched throats for 'Quarter' and 'Pardon.'

Maurice strode out alone from among his troopers, till he stood within a few paces of the walls of the tomb. He spoke Hindustani well enough to make himself understood; indeed his speech was very brief and simple : he refused to treat on any terms whatever : the rebels might come forth if they chose, ten at a time; or they might wait the storming where they were. As he spoke the last word, a sharp snap was heard within, followed by a slight scuffle and a smothered groan. One desperate fanatic, who chanced to have kept a loaded rifle, could not resist proving, for the last time, the invulnerability of his terrible enemy : the cap missed fire, and the man was instantly cut down by his comrades,—furious at seeing their faint chance of mercy imperilled.

Dering did not appear to notice the incident; but turned on his heel and walked slowly back to where his charger was held. After a few minutes of noisy deliberation, a hoarse voice from within cried, 'That they would come forth, trusting to the Great Sahib's mercy.' And they began to throw their weapons out of the door and windows, till the ground outside was thickly strewn.

A squad of dismounted troopers marched up to the entrance-arch, ranging themselves on either side of it, before the first ten mutineers came out—their faces blanched to lividness—their great eye-balls rolling wildly—their shining teeth gnashing, as if ferocity had not quite given place to fear. The men walked straight up to the spot where Dering was standing; and, bowing themselves in obeisance, waited his orders. Maurice never spoke, but pointed with his finger towards a certain part of the clump where the trees grew thickest. The prisoners moved off in that direction, without questioning : they were scarcely hidden from view of the tomb-door, when a smothered shriek was heard—drowned in a roll of fire-arms—then a dead silence. Those ten men had marched right into the faces of their appointed executioners.

The miserable wretches within the tomb guessed the fate of their comrades at once ; the measured rattle of the carbines was significant enough. A tumult of howls and shrieks arose ; when it partly subsided, many cried out, 'that no more would come forth, the Sahib might kill them, where they were.'

It is better to stop here.

Do you remember the 'murder grim and great' that avenged beautiful Hypatia ? *This* carnage was worse a thousand-fold : for it was wrought, not under the fresh clear night-sky, but in a close, darkened slaughter-house. Every now and then one of the executioners came staggering out into the open air—drunk and faint with the scent of blood. And Dering stood by—with that dark pitiless look on his face whereof we have before spoken— allowing no pause in the work till it was thoroughly performed.

Reader of mine—do you think all this wildly exaggerated ? Perchance you fancy that all the incidents of that awful time were set down in official reports, and recorded by special correspondents. I speak only from hearsay; but I believe there lives a man on the full-pay of our army who saw these things done—very much as I have here described them.

Nevertheless you will augur ill for Maurice Dering's future, when you know that you look on him, now, for the very last time.

The last sketch of the picture-gallery, in which you have been pleased to linger so long, shall not be so repellant or gloomy.

It is a warm summer evening; so still, that the leaves of the great beech-trees scarcely rustle in the soft west wind that has been dying away ever since noon. It is an evening made for invalids, no less than for others in stronger health; so, at least, thinks Philip Gascoigne, as he lounges on a pile of cushions, with his fair wife nestling by his side. At the further end of the lawn is Cecil with—it is unnecessary to say—Aunt Nellie in close attendance: he and his favourite playmate have had their last race and gambol for the night; and the child is walking soberly along; his slender arm wound round the huge deer-hound's brindled neck.

But the father and mother are not watching their pet just now. Can you guess why?

Georgie—from one of those sudden impulses that cannot be explained, but are generally safe to follow—has taken heart of grace this night, and made full confession to her husband of the old folly that came so near to guilt.

'Philip, dear '—she went on, when she had told him all, even to that perilous interview in the Géronstère—' I never loved him, as I love you now; nor, I do believe, as I loved you then. Sometimes I think, I did not love him at all. It was a foolish romance with me, at first; and at last I got helplessly frightened. But I was very wicked —so wicked that I don't deserve to be as happy as we are now; for we are happy, darling, in our quiet way. Ah,— say you are not angry with me: it was so long ago; and have I not been good since?'

In truth that appeal seemed not altogether needless; for Philip's brow was very grave and thoughtful. But he drew the pretty penitent closer to his side, and kissed her fondly before he answered—

'No, my own darling, I'm not angry; indeed, I have not one reproach ready. Stronger-minded women than my little Georgie have gone down before the fascination that that unhappy man seemed able to exercise—always for evil. To my life's end I shall not cease to thank God for having forbidden the accomplishment of your misery and mine. Yours would have lasted longest, darling: it would have killed me very soon. No; I was not thinking of blaming you, I was thinking, whether Maurice knew of all this when he went out with Annesleigh. Poor fellow! he was so different then from what he must be now—if half the tales are true—that I can't help fearing something of the sort. It's odd, I never suspected it before.'

'Oh, I hope—I hope not,' Georgie murmured; and her sweet face grew paler than it had been since she began her confession.

Philip could not see his pet distressed, even for a moment, without petting or consoling her.

'Don't fret, darling,' he whispered. 'It's only a stupid suspicion of mine, founded on no sort of warranty, that I might just as well have kept to myself. I'll ask Paul about it, the next time I see him.'

Gascoigne did question Chetwynde, but got little satisfaction from that saturnine sage, who, as has been aforesaid,
was rather prone to indulge in dark sayings and parables.

'Philip,' said he, upon this occasion, ' you quite surprise
me. I always rather envied your memory. Surely, it s
not failing you ? '

'What on earth do you mean?' the other inquired,
rather impatiently

'Why, I thought " Lenore " was your favourite ballad;
and you seem to have utterly forgotten the *refrain* that
I've heard you quote a hundred times—

Lass sie ruh'n, die Todten.

No other word could ever be extracted from Paul on that
subject; nor indeed did Gascoigne ever broach it again.

So—as we leave Marston Lisle—if the sky be not
radiantly blue above, there is at least promise of fair, calm
weather. Pleasant parties gather there not unfrequently;
though there are none of the brilliant festivals of the old
time. The Duchess of Devorgoil ought to be satisfied;
for fair Georgie Gascoigne is discreet—not dignified; that
she could never be—as the haughtiest *grande dame* of
them all; indeed certain coquettish matrons, undergoing
a *very* gradual process of reformation, point to her as an
illustration of what *they* will come to, if they are only let
alone.

Philip's health improves rather than otherwise, though
he still needs great care; but many indolent people would
think it no hardship, to be such an invalid—petted and
nursed so tenderly.

It is otherwise at Minstercombe: the curse of childlessness still abides over the heritage of the Luttrells; and will

—through this generation—abide. For, though Geoffrey is no longer a recluse, but mixes in quiet society much as he was wont to do, no maiden on her promotion has yet been found audacious enough to aspire to Ida's vacant place. He indulges in field-sports keenly as ever; but, even whilst pursuing these, is rather prone to solitude : and the old villagers, who have known him from a boy, shake their heads sometimes, ominously, as they point to the parson's skiff rocking, alone, on the verge of the bay— much too far from land, considering that black cloud-bank to seaward. Some, too, have noticed that there is always a change in his voice when it recites that one petition— 'Forgive us our trespasses, as we forgive them that trespass against us'—and the broad blue eyes turn, with a piteous meaning, towards that corner of the chancel under which the dead Luttrells sleep.

Yet, perchance, even to him there may come peace, at the last.

In Paul Chetwynde there appears little, if any, change : on such as he the battle of life leaves no scars ; and they can generally dissemble their wounds, unless stricken to the death. He talks of going to India next year. Maurice Dering's regiment must soon be ordered home ; but no one supposes he will accompany it. The pursuit of the big game—the more perilous the better—seems to be his one object, now ; and every hour of leave is spent as far up in the hills as hard riding, to and fro, will carry him. His absences are not much regretted by his regiment : 'he is no use, off parade,' the subalterns say : in truth, that hard, haggard face—not softened by the huge beard, now deeply grizzled, is very fatal to the simple convivialities of

x

his mess-room. His comrades might almost as well have the Egyptian skeleton there.

Of the few subordinate characters in this our drama, it is surely needless to speak : it is more than enough if the principals have carried your interest with them thus far. One word of poor Penrhyn Bligh. Some of his relatives, who had cast him off long ago, took compassion on his desolate destitution, and came to take charge of him ; they were just in time to add some comforts to his last brief illness ; and they gave him decent burial.

And now, the story of the Quadrilateral is told.

Against fair or open assault, the defenders of that miniature fortress might perchance have held their own. What wonder if the battle went hard against them at the last ? If a woman—wily or wicked—be once within the walls, never was ravelin or rampart that long could keep the besiegers at bay.

It was so, before the night that made Rahab the harlot famous among her kind : it will be so, when the Rock is dust that bears Tarpeia's name.

THE END.

JOHN CHILDS AND SON, PRINTERS.